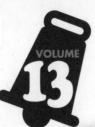

VOLUME 13

GOOD-BYE... KOGANE-TAN...
YOU'LL MAKE IT HARD TO EAT THEM!!
SO (PAT)
DON'T NAME THE POTATOES !!!

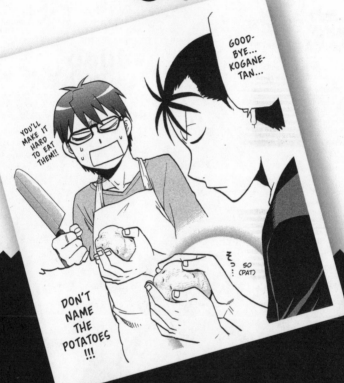

Silver Spoon

HIROMU ARAKAWA

STORY & CHARACTERS

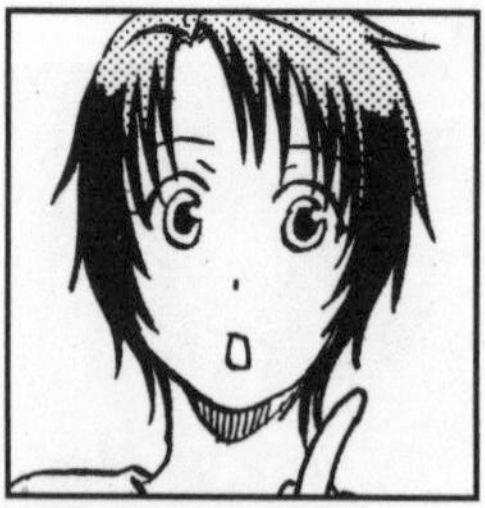

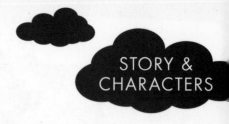

AKI MIKAGE

A second-year student at Ooezo Agricultural High School, enrolled in the Dairy Science Program. Her family has accepted that she means to work with horses rather than carry on the farm on the condition she goes to college.

YUUGO HACHIKEN

A second-year student at Ooezo Agricultural High School, enrolled in the Dairy Science Program. A city kid from Sapporo who got in through the general entrance exam. He's found a goal—starting a business—and founded his company with Ookawa-senpai, but....

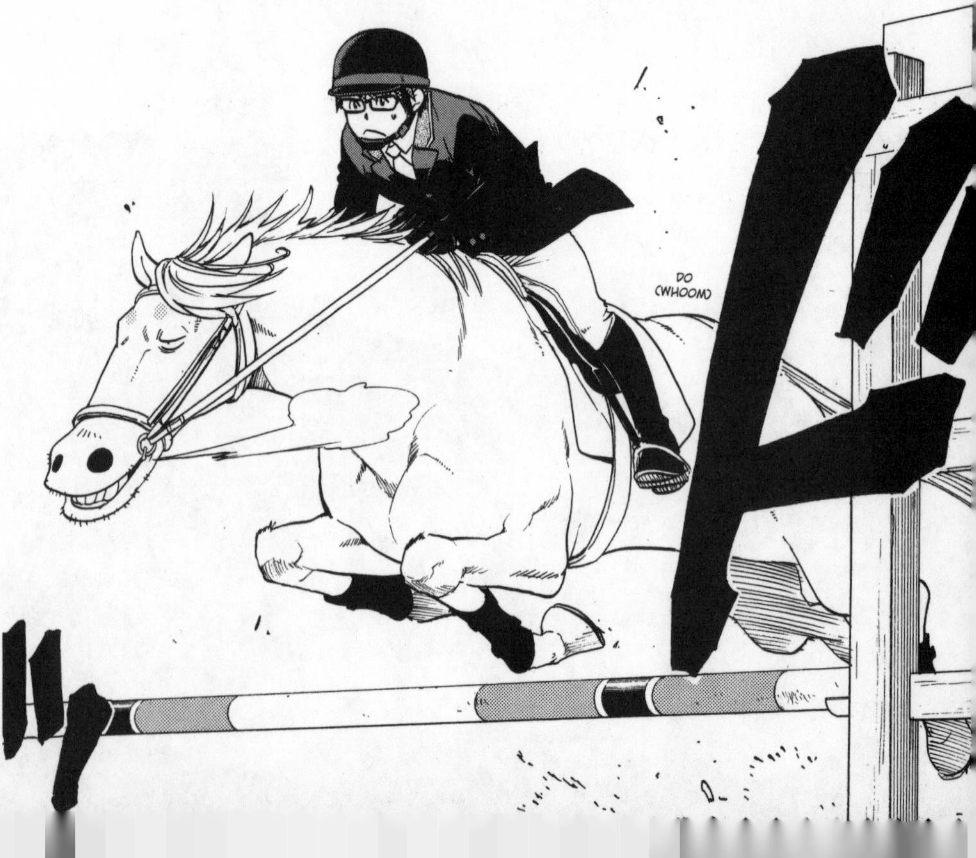
DO (WHOOM)

AYAME MINAMIKUJOU

Aki's childhood friend. Has resolved to get into college to compete with her. Hachiken's older brother Yuugo is now overseeing her college prep.

ICHIROU KOMABA

A former student at Ooezo Agricultural High School, enrolled in the Dairy Science Program. He had planned to take over the family farm after graduation before it went out of business. Still, he hasn't abandoned his dream of owning his own ranch, and it seems he's decided something...

SHINEI OOKAWA

A graduate of Ooezo Agricultural High School's Agricultural Engineering Program and former Equestrian Club president. He graduated without finding permanent employment, but has since started a company with Hachiken and became its president.

The Story Thus Far:

When Ookawa-senpai obtains a single black pig by chance, Hachiken and Ookawa-senpai move forward with a plan to breed pigs for meat. Remembering the pizza party that first built up his confidence back in his first year at Ezo Ag, Hachiken decides to use the pork to make and sell pizzas at the Ban'ei stadium and busies himself preparing for Silver Spoon's first business venture. Meanwhile, Komaba—who had no choice but to drop out of Ezo Ag when the family farm went bankrupt—gets a push from his mother and little sisters that seems to have encouraged him to set out toward his own dream...

CONTENTS

Silver Spoon

Chapter 106: Tale of Four Seasons ⑨

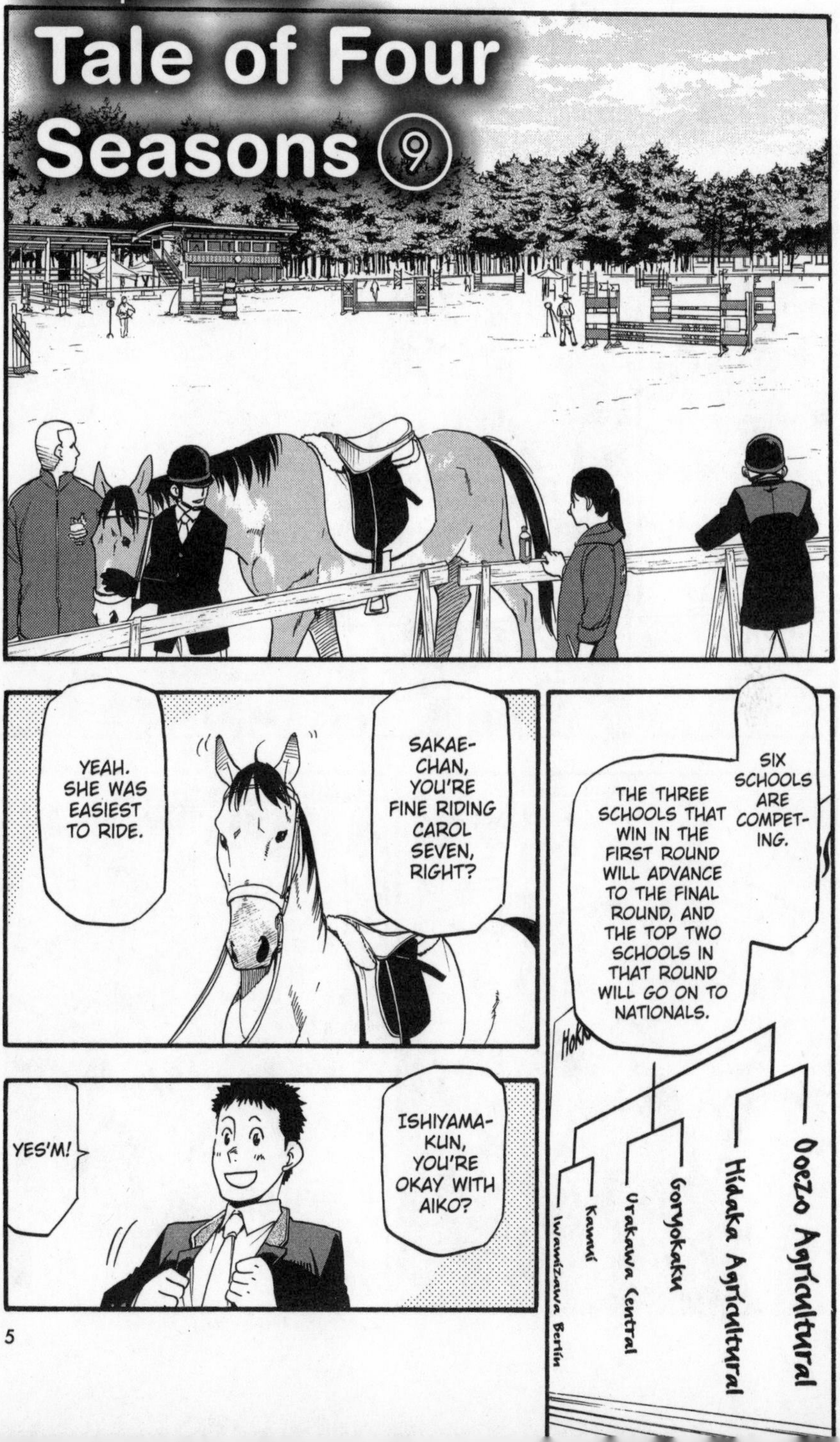
SIX SCHOOLS ARE COMPETING.
THE THREE SCHOOLS THAT WIN IN THE FIRST ROUND WILL ADVANCE TO THE FINAL ROUND, AND THE TOP TWO SCHOOLS IN THAT ROUND WILL GO ON TO NATIONALS.
Ooezo Agricultural
Hidaka Agricultural
Goryokaku
Urakawa Central
Kamui
Iwamizawa Berlin
SAKAE-CHAN, YOU'RE FINE RIDING CAROL SEVEN, RIGHT?
YEAH. SHE WAS EASIEST TO RIDE.
ISHIYAMA-KUN, YOU'RE OKAY WITH AIKO?
YES'M!

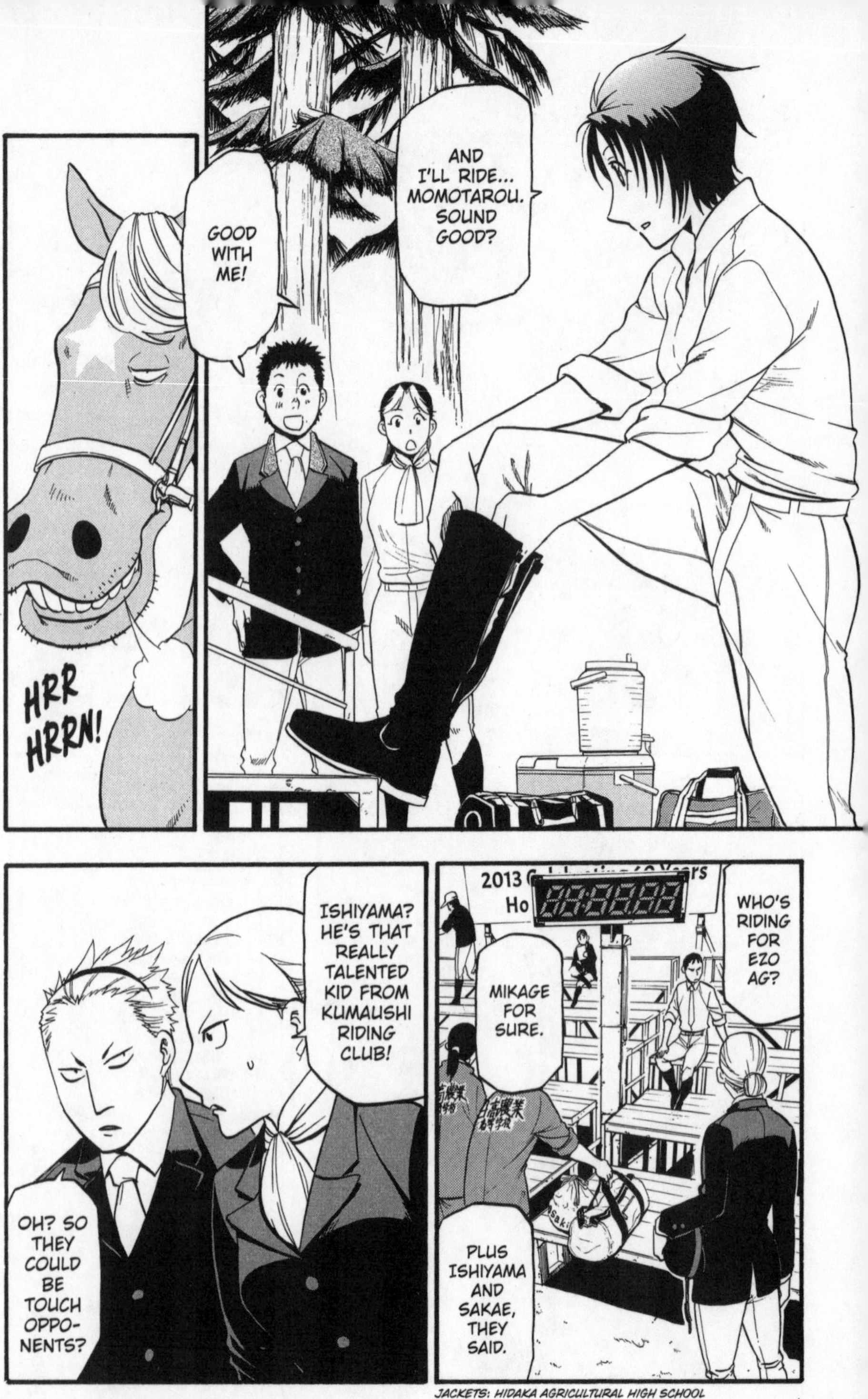
AND I'LL RIDE... MOMOTAROU. SOUND GOOD?
GOOD WITH ME!
HRR HRRN!
WHO'S RIDING FOR EZO AG?
MIKAGE FOR SURE.
PLUS ISHIYAMA AND SAKAE, THEY SAID.
ISHIYAMA? HE'S THAT REALLY TALENTED KID FROM KUMAUSHI RIDING CLUB!
OH? SO THEY COULD BE TOUCH OPPO-NENTS?

JACKETS: HIDAKA AGRICULTURAL HIGH SCHOOL

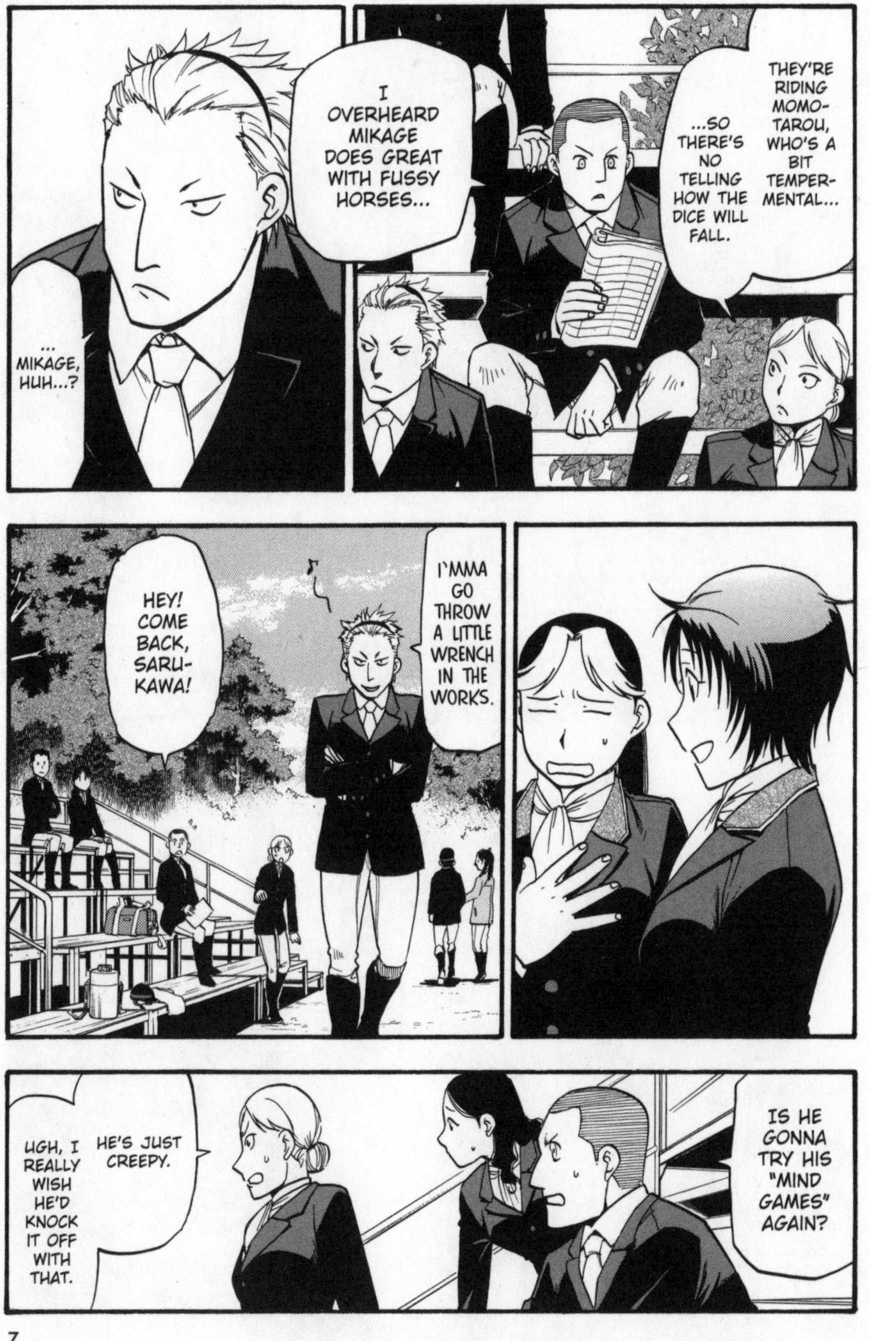
THEY'RE RIDING MOMOTAROU, WHO'S A BIT TEMPERMENTAL...
...SO THERE'S NO TELLING HOW THE DICE WILL FALL.
I OVERHEARD MIKAGE DOES GREAT WITH FUSSY HORSES...
...MIKAGE, HUH...?
I'MMA GO THROW A LITTLE WRENCH IN THE WORKS.
HEY! COME BACK, SARUKAWA!
IS HE GONNA TRY HIS "MIND GAMES" AGAIN?
HE'S JUST CREEPY.
UGH, I REALLY WISH HE'D KNOCK IT OFF WITH THAT.

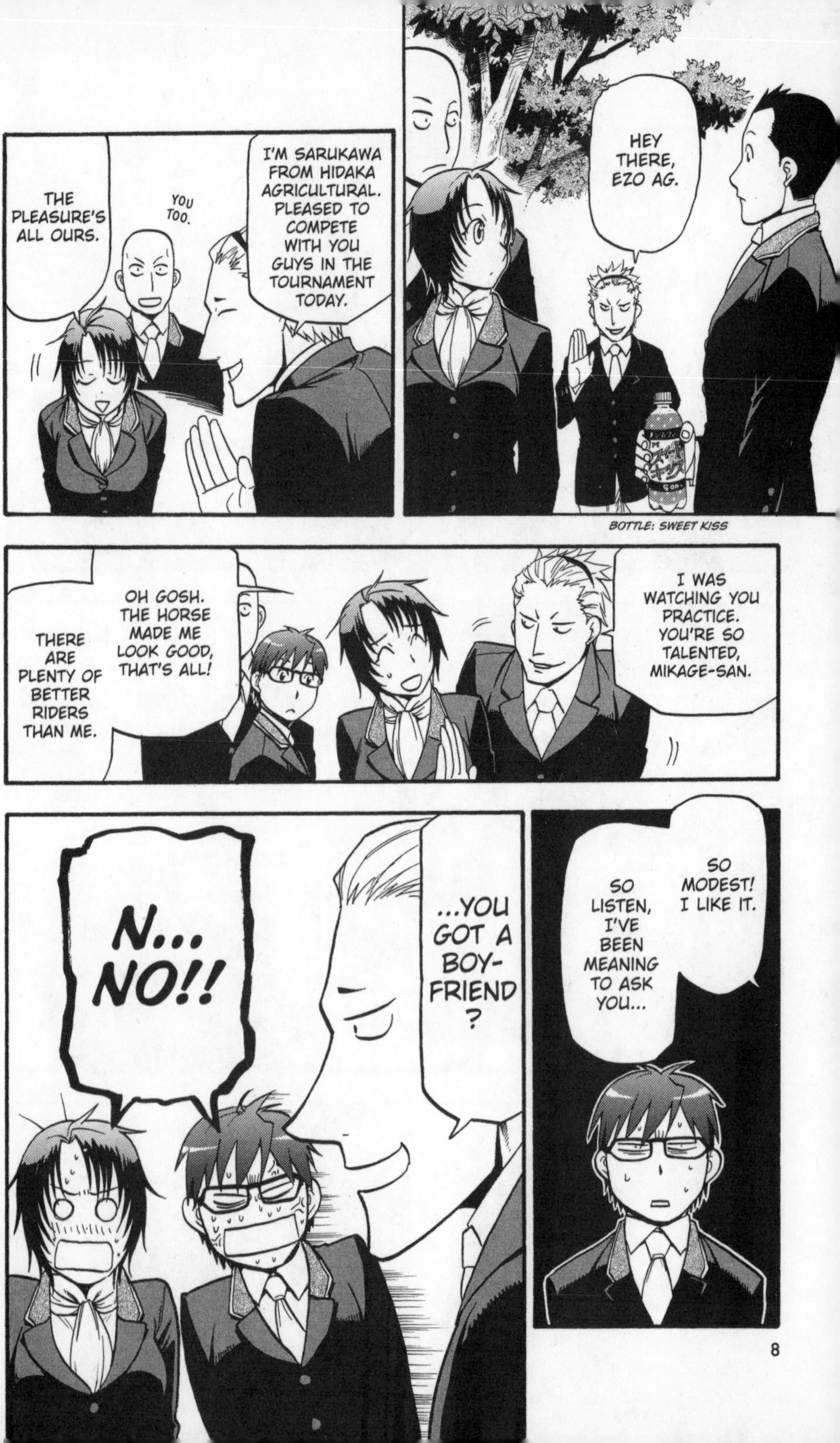

HEY THERE, EZO AG.
I'M SARUKAWA FROM HIDAKA AGRICULTURAL. PLEASED TO COMPETE WITH YOU GUYS IN THE TOURNAMENT TODAY.
YOU TOO.
THE PLEASURE'S ALL OURS.
BOTTLE: SWEET KISS
I WAS WATCHING YOU PRACTICE. YOU'RE SO TALENTED, MIKAGE-SAN.
OH GOSH. THE HORSE MADE ME LOOK GOOD, THAT'S ALL!
THERE ARE PLENTY OF BETTER RIDERS THAN ME.
SO MODEST! I LIKE IT.
SO LISTEN, I'VE BEEN MEANING TO ASK YOU...
...YOU GOT A BOY-FRIEND?
N... NO!!

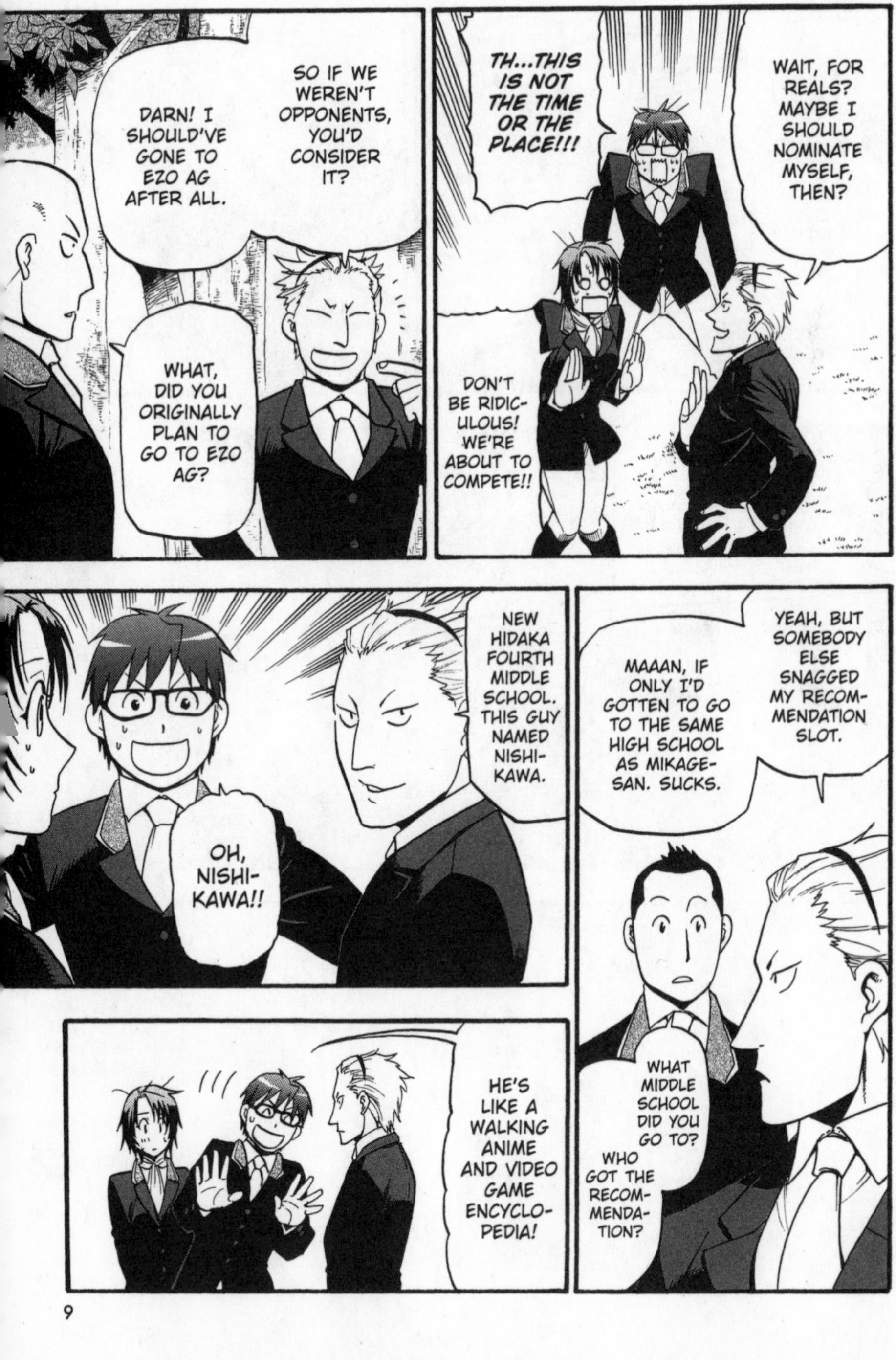
WAIT, FOR REALS? MAYBE I SHOULD NOMINATE MYSELF, THEN?
TH...THIS IS NOT THE TIME OR THE PLACE!!!
DON'T BE RIDICULOUS! WE'RE ABOUT TO COMPETE!!
SO IF WE WEREN'T OPPONENTS, YOU'D CONSIDER IT?
DARN! I SHOULD'VE GONE TO EZO AG AFTER ALL.
WHAT, DID YOU ORIGINALLY PLAN TO GO TO EZO AG?
YEAH, BUT SOMEBODY ELSE SNAGGED MY RECOMMENDATION SLOT.
MAAAN, IF ONLY I'D GOTTEN TO GO TO THE SAME HIGH SCHOOL AS MIKAGE-SAN. SUCKS.
WHAT MIDDLE SCHOOL DID YOU GO TO?
WHO GOT THE RECOMMENDATION?
NEW HIDAKA FOURTH MIDDLE SCHOOL. THIS GUY NAMED NISHIKAWA.
OH, NISHIKAWA!!
HE'S LIKE A WALKING ANIME AND VIDEO GAME ENCYCLOPEDIA!

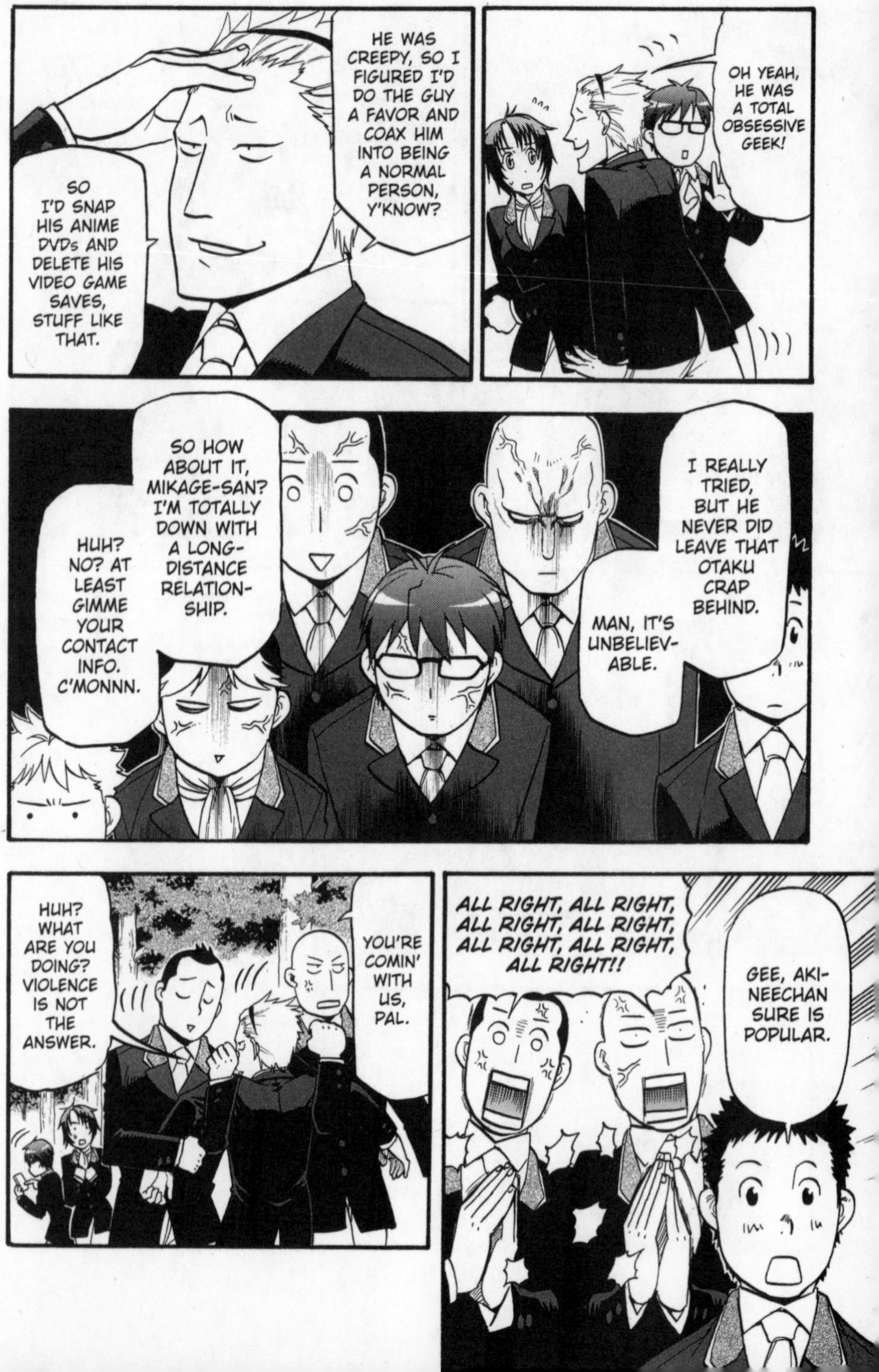
OH YEAH, HE WAS A TOTAL OBSESSIVE GEEK!
HE WAS CREEPY, SO I FIGURED I'D DO THE GUY A FAVOR AND COAX HIM INTO BEING A NORMAL PERSON, Y'KNOW?
SO I'D SNAP HIS ANIME DVDs AND DELETE HIS VIDEO GAME SAVES, STUFF LIKE THAT.
I REALLY TRIED, BUT HE NEVER DID LEAVE THAT OTAKU CRAP BEHIND.
MAN, IT'S UNBELIEVABLE.
SO HOW ABOUT IT, MIKAGE-SAN? I'M TOTALLY DOWN WITH A LONG-DISTANCE RELATIONSHIP.
HUH? NO? AT LEAST GIMME YOUR CONTACT INFO. C'MONNN.
GEE, AKI-NEECHAN SURE IS POPULAR.
ALL RIGHT, ALL RIGHT, ALL RIGHT, ALL RIGHT, ALL RIGHT, ALL RIGHT, ALL RIGHT!!
YOU'RE COMIN' WITH US, PAL.
HUH? WHAT ARE YOU DOING? VIOLENCE IS NOT THE ANSWER.

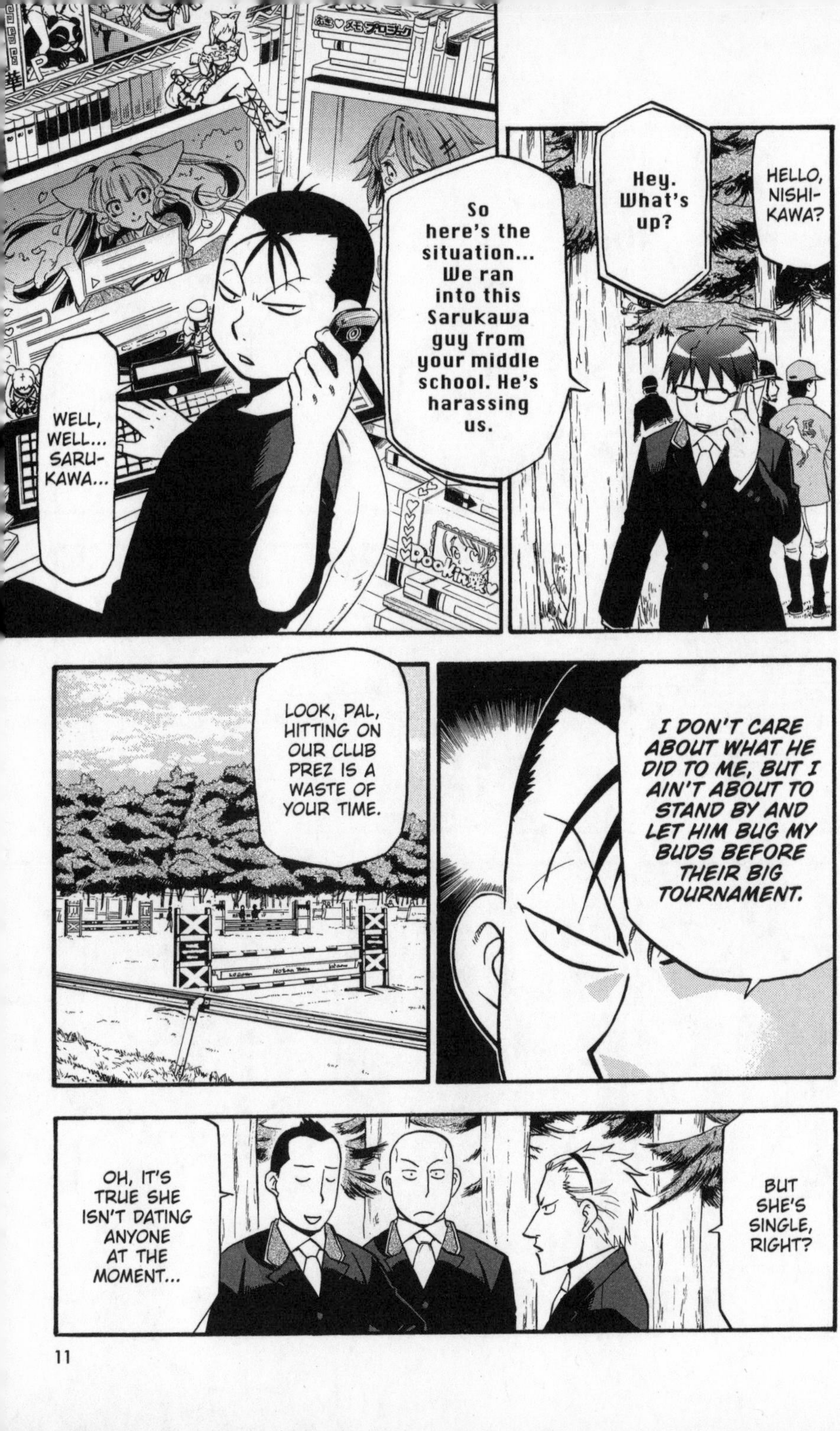
HELLO, NISHIKAWA?
Hey. What's up?
So here's the situation... We ran into this Sarukawa guy from your middle school. He's harassing us.
WELL, WELL... SARUKAWA...
I DON'T CARE ABOUT WHAT HE DID TO ME, BUT I AIN'T ABOUT TO STAND BY AND LET HIM BUG MY BUDS BEFORE THEIR BIG TOURNAMENT.
LOOK, PAL, HITTING ON OUR CLUB PREZ IS A WASTE OF YOUR TIME.
BUT SHE'S SINGLE, RIGHT?
OH, IT'S TRUE SHE ISN'T DATING ANYONE AT THE MOMENT...

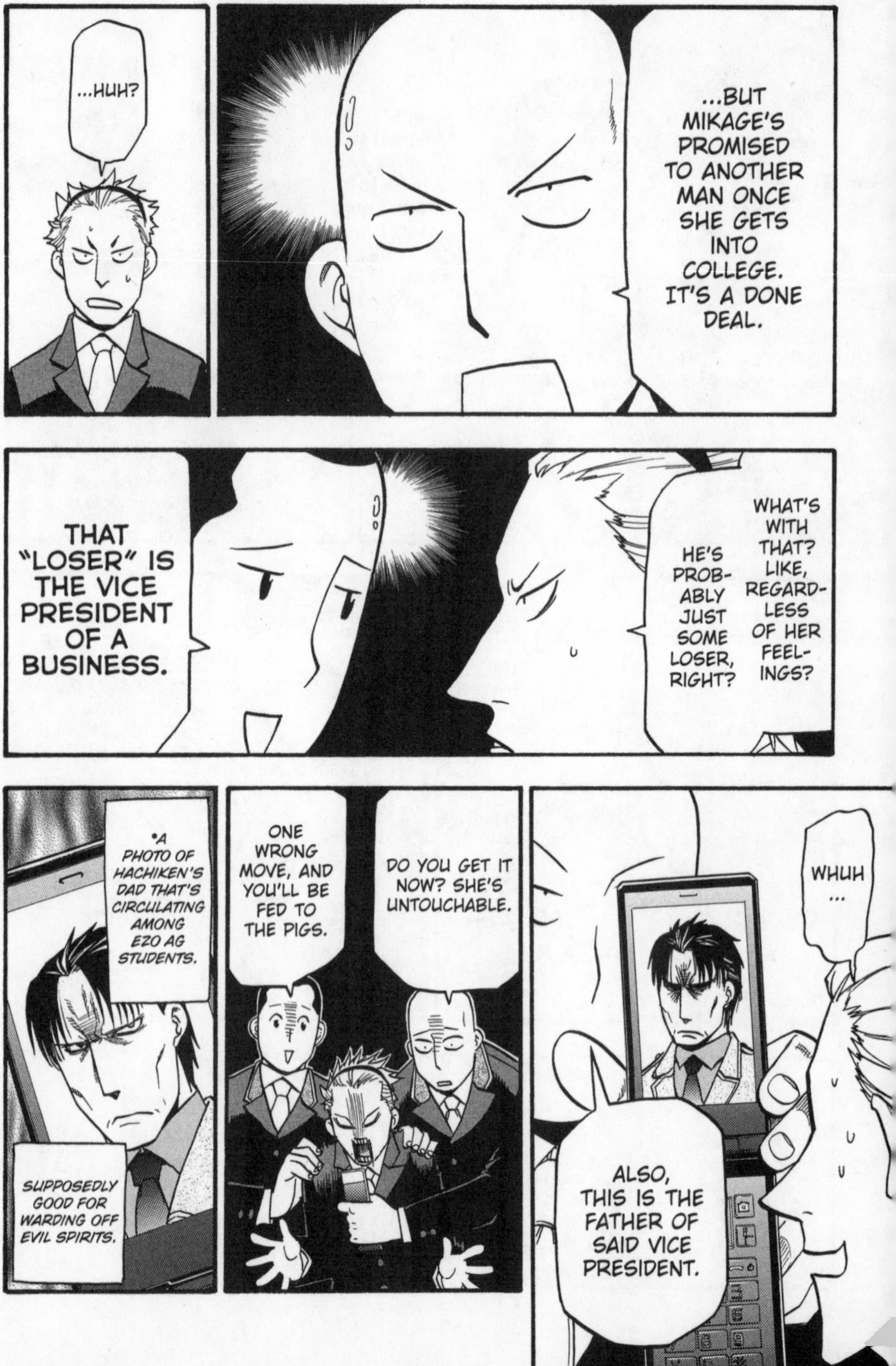
...BUT MIKAGE'S PROMISED TO ANOTHER MAN ONCE SHE GETS INTO COLLEGE. IT'S A DONE DEAL.
...HUH?
WHAT'S WITH THAT? LIKE, REGARDLESS OF HER FEELINGS?
HE'S PROBABLY JUST SOME LOSER, RIGHT?
THAT "LOSER" IS THE VICE PRESIDENT OF A BUSINESS.
WHUH ...
ALSO, THIS IS THE FATHER OF SAID VICE PRESIDENT.
DO YOU GET IT NOW? SHE'S UNTOUCHABLE.
ONE WRONG MOVE, AND YOU'LL BE FED TO THE PIGS.
*A PHOTO OF HACHIKEN'S DAD THAT'S CIRCULATING AMONG EZO AG STUDENTS.
SUPPOSEDLY GOOD FOR WARDING OFF EVIL SPIRITS.

HEY, SARU-KAWA-KUN. C'MERE.

HE'S TOTALLY YAKUZA... YAKUZA...

I'M TOLD YOU WERE ~~IN~~ MIDDLE SCHOOL?

WAAAAAH!!!

DOGARA (CLATTER) GOON (CLONG)

WAAH!!?

YOU ~~A~~ GIRL, AND NOW YOU PRETEND IT NEVER HAPPENED...

OH, AND ALSO, YOUR ~~IS~~, RIGHT?

WAAAH!!!

WHAT HAP-PENED!?

SARU-KAWA IS A TOTAL MESS!!

KUI (PUSH)

DOGARAN

HE WHO CONTROLS INFORMATION CONTROLS THE WORLD!!

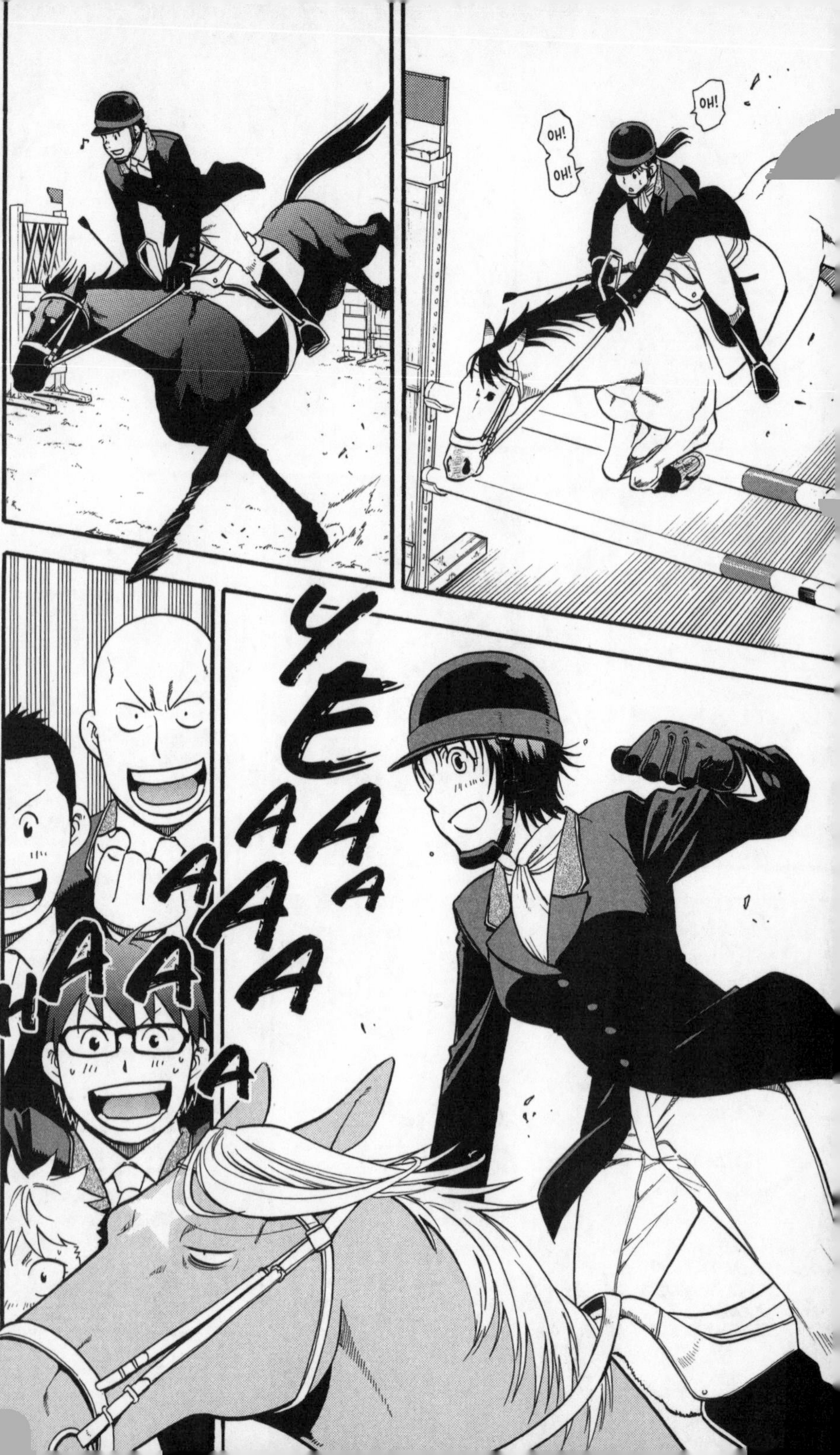
OH!
OH!
OH!
YEAAAAAAAAAAAAAH!!

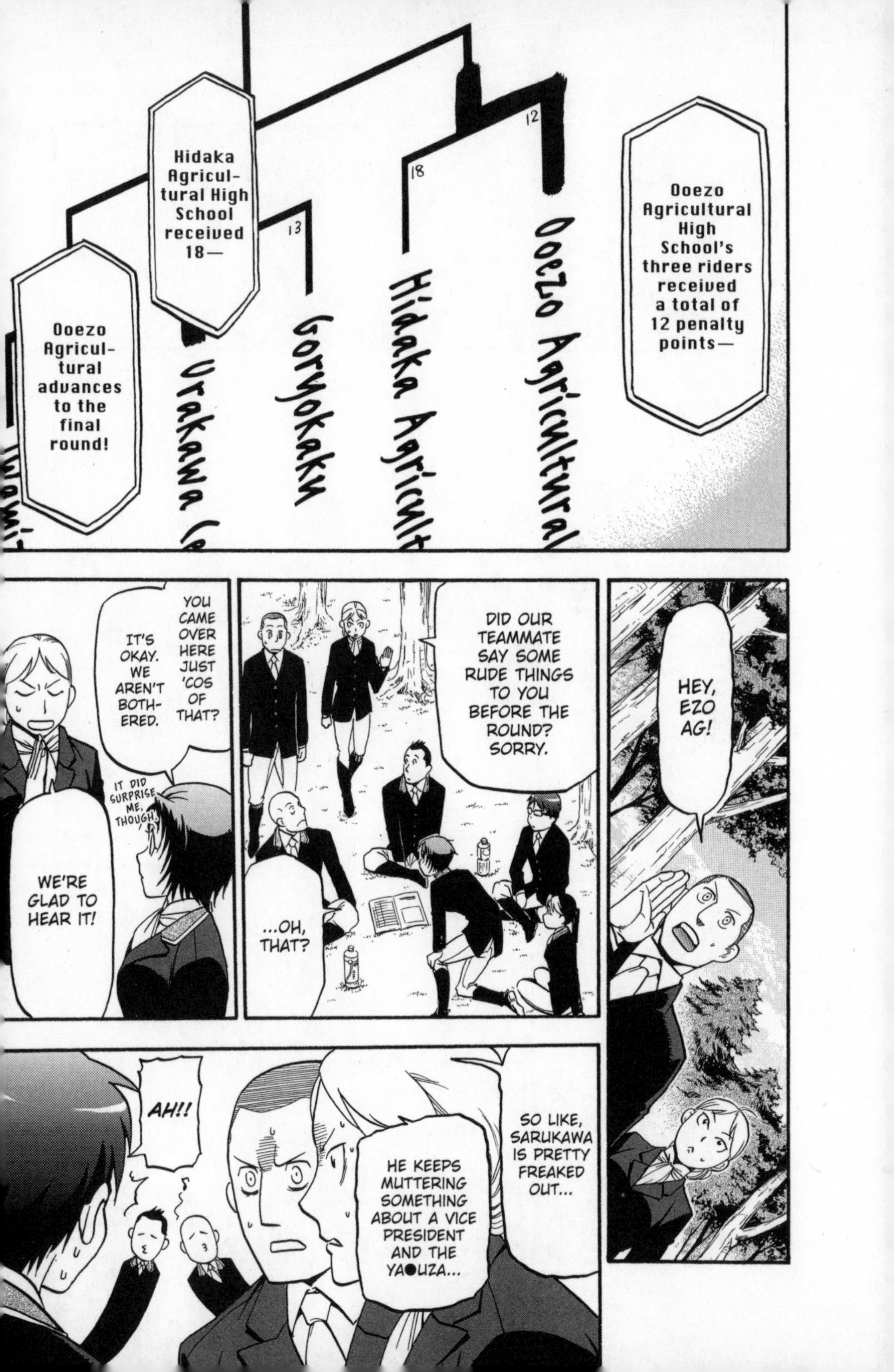
Ooezo Agricultural High School's three riders received a total of 12 penalty points—
12
Ooezo Agricultural
18
Hidaka Agricult
13
Goryokaku
Urakawa
Hidaka Agricultural High School received 18—
Ooezo Agricultural advances to the final round!
HEY, EZO AG!
DID OUR TEAMMATE SAY SOME RUDE THINGS TO YOU BEFORE THE ROUND? SORRY.
...OH, THAT?
YOU CAME OVER HERE JUST 'COS OF THAT?
IT'S OKAY. WE AREN'T BOTHERED.
IT DID SURPRISE ME, THOUGH.
WE'RE GLAD TO HEAR IT!
SO LIKE, SARUKAWA IS PRETTY FREAKED OUT...
HE KEEPS MUTTERING SOMETHING ABOUT A VICE PRESIDENT AND THE YA●UZA...
AH!!

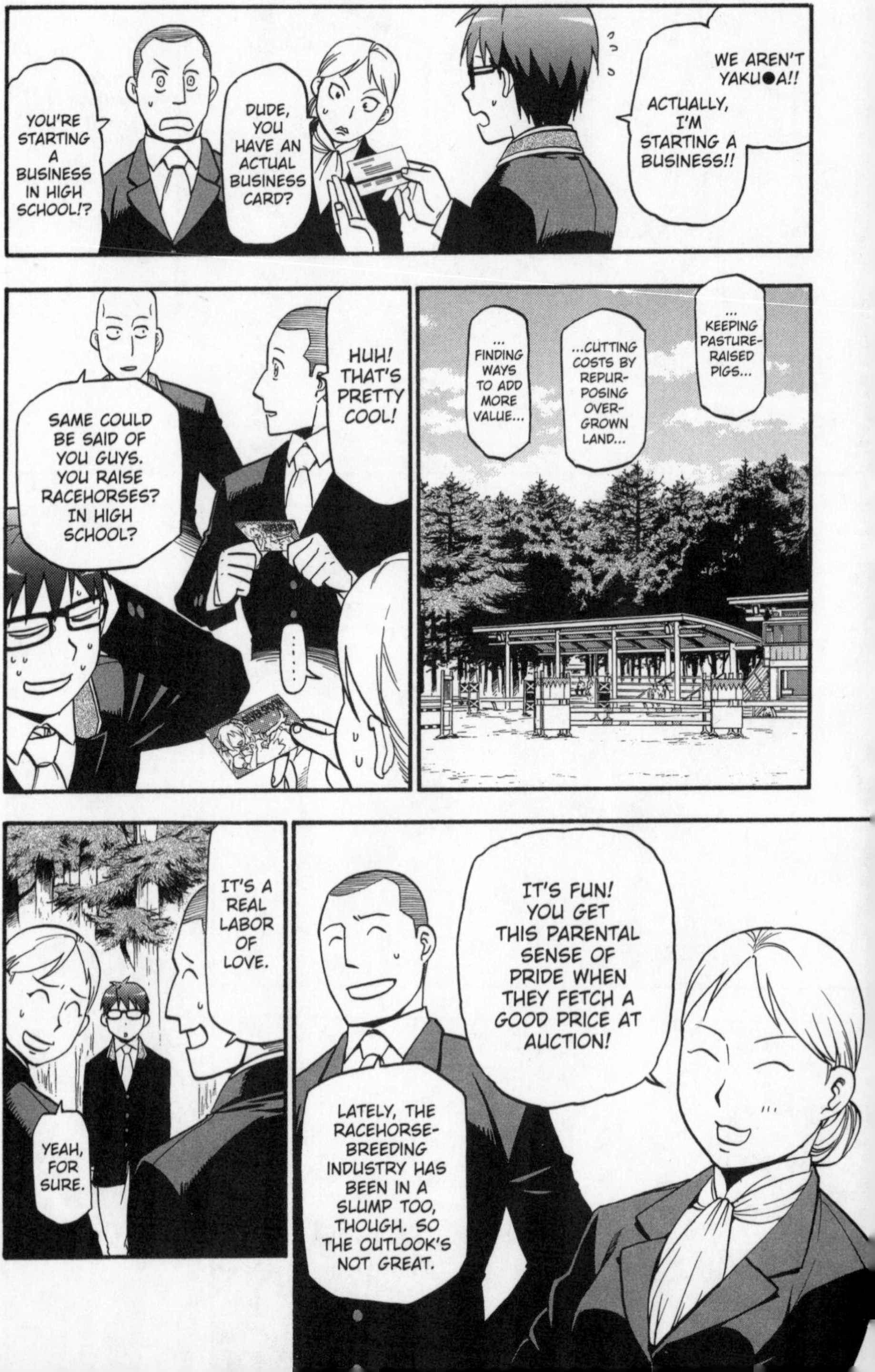
WE AREN'T YAKU●A!! ACTUALLY, I'M STARTING A BUSINESS!!
DUDE, YOU HAVE AN ACTUAL BUSINESS CARD?
YOU'RE STARTING A BUSINESS IN HIGH SCHOOL!?
...KEEPING PASTURE-RAISED PIGS...
...CUTTING COSTS BY REPURPOSING OVERGROWN LAND...
...FINDING WAYS TO ADD MORE VALUE...
HUH! THAT'S PRETTY COOL!
SAME COULD BE SAID OF YOU GUYS. YOU RAISE RACEHORSES? IN HIGH SCHOOL?
......
IT'S FUN! YOU GET THIS PARENTAL SENSE OF PRIDE WHEN THEY FETCH A GOOD PRICE AT AUCTION!
LATELY, THE RACEHORSE-BREEDING INDUSTRY HAS BEEN IN A SLUMP TOO, THOUGH. SO THE OUTLOOK'S NOT GREAT.
IT'S A REAL LABOR OF LOVE.
YEAH, FOR SURE.

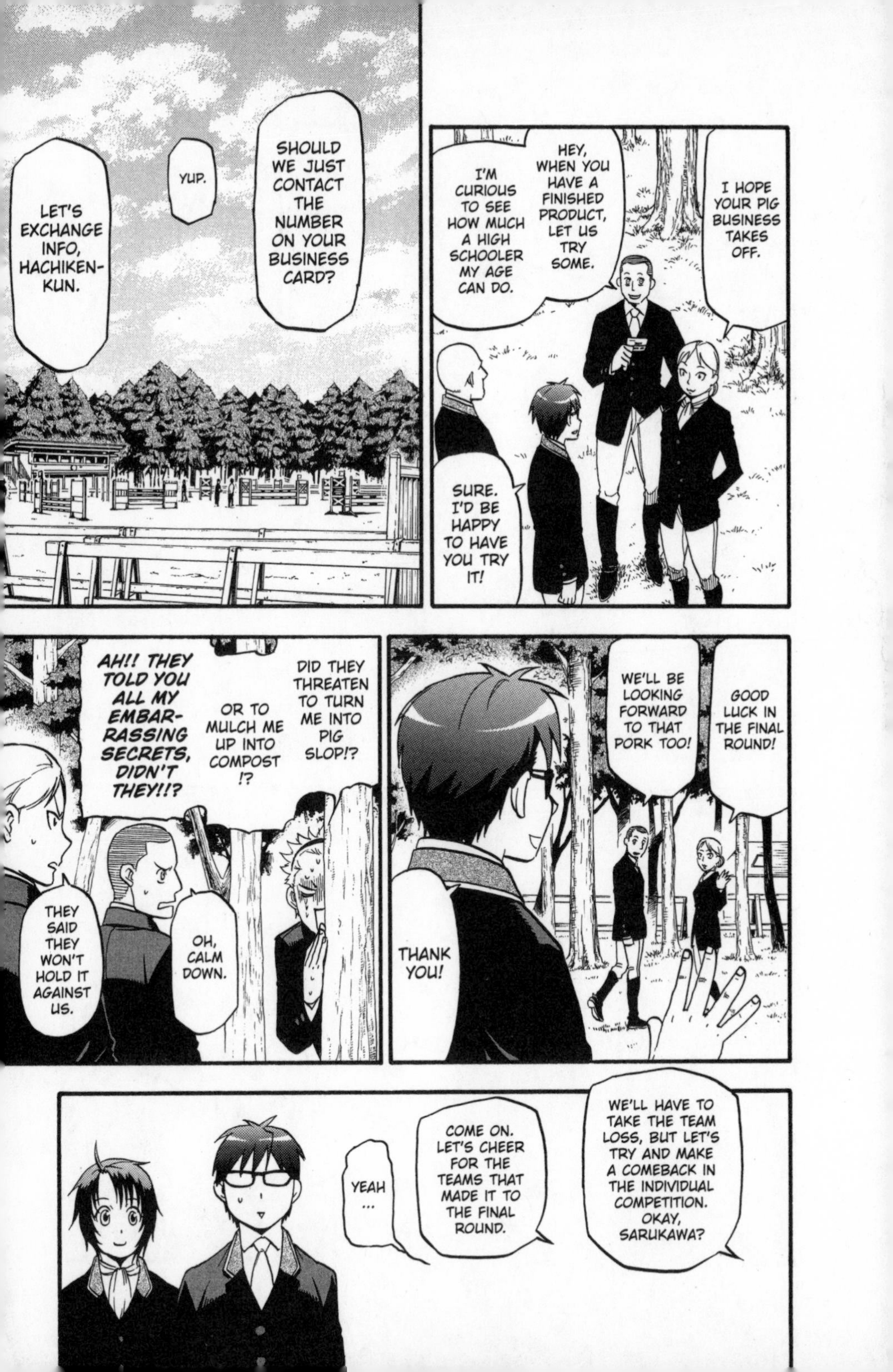
I HOPE YOUR PIG BUSINESS TAKES OFF.
HEY, WHEN YOU HAVE A FINISHED PRODUCT, LET US TRY SOME.
I'M CURIOUS TO SEE HOW MUCH A HIGH SCHOOLER MY AGE CAN DO.
SURE. I'D BE HAPPY TO HAVE YOU TRY IT!
SHOULD WE JUST CONTACT THE NUMBER ON YOUR BUSINESS CARD?
YUP.
LET'S EXCHANGE INFO, HACHIKEN-KUN.
GOOD LUCK IN THE FINAL ROUND!
WE'LL BE LOOKING FORWARD TO THAT PORK TOO!
THANK YOU!
DID THEY THREATEN TO TURN ME INTO PIG SLOP!?
OR TO MULCH ME UP INTO COMPOST !?
AH!! THEY TOLD YOU ALL MY EMBAR-RASSING SECRETS, DIDN'T THEY!!?
OH, CALM DOWN.
THEY SAID THEY WON'T HOLD IT AGAINST US.
WE'LL HAVE TO TAKE THE TEAM LOSS, BUT LET'S TRY AND MAKE A COMEBACK IN THE INDIVIDUAL COMPETITION. OKAY, SARUKAWA?
COME ON. LET'S CHEER FOR THE TEAMS THAT MADE IT TO THE FINAL ROUND.
YEAH ...

THE HORSES FOR THE FINAL TEAM ROUND ARE AGNES, KINTOKI, AND FINE ACE.

Final Round

	A	B	C

Kawai H.S.

Horse	#	Rider Name	Pts.	Place
Agnes	1			
Kintoki	5			
Fine Ace	6			
		Total Pts.		
		Total Pts.		

Ooizu Agricultural H.S.

	#	Rider Name	Pts.	Place
	4	Hachiken		
	2	Ishiyama		
	8	Hikage		
				Place

Urakawa Central H.S.

		Rider Name	Pts.	Place

HAAAH...

...THE FINAL ROUND. GAAH...

FUSSY HORSES...

SERIOUSLY, WHY ME...?

AH.

THIS IS A FUSSIER GROUP OF HORSES THAN IN THE PREVIOUS ROUND.

YOU'RE UP, HACHI-KEN-KUN.

GEH!!!

GOT ANY TIPS ON HOW TO MAKE RIDING HORSES LIKE THAT MORE ENJOYABLE?

IS IT JUST ABOUT GETTING BETTER SO YOU CAN GET IN THAT ZONE WITH THEM?

IT'S KIND OF LIKE...A PLUG AND OUTLET?

TIPS? HMMM...

18

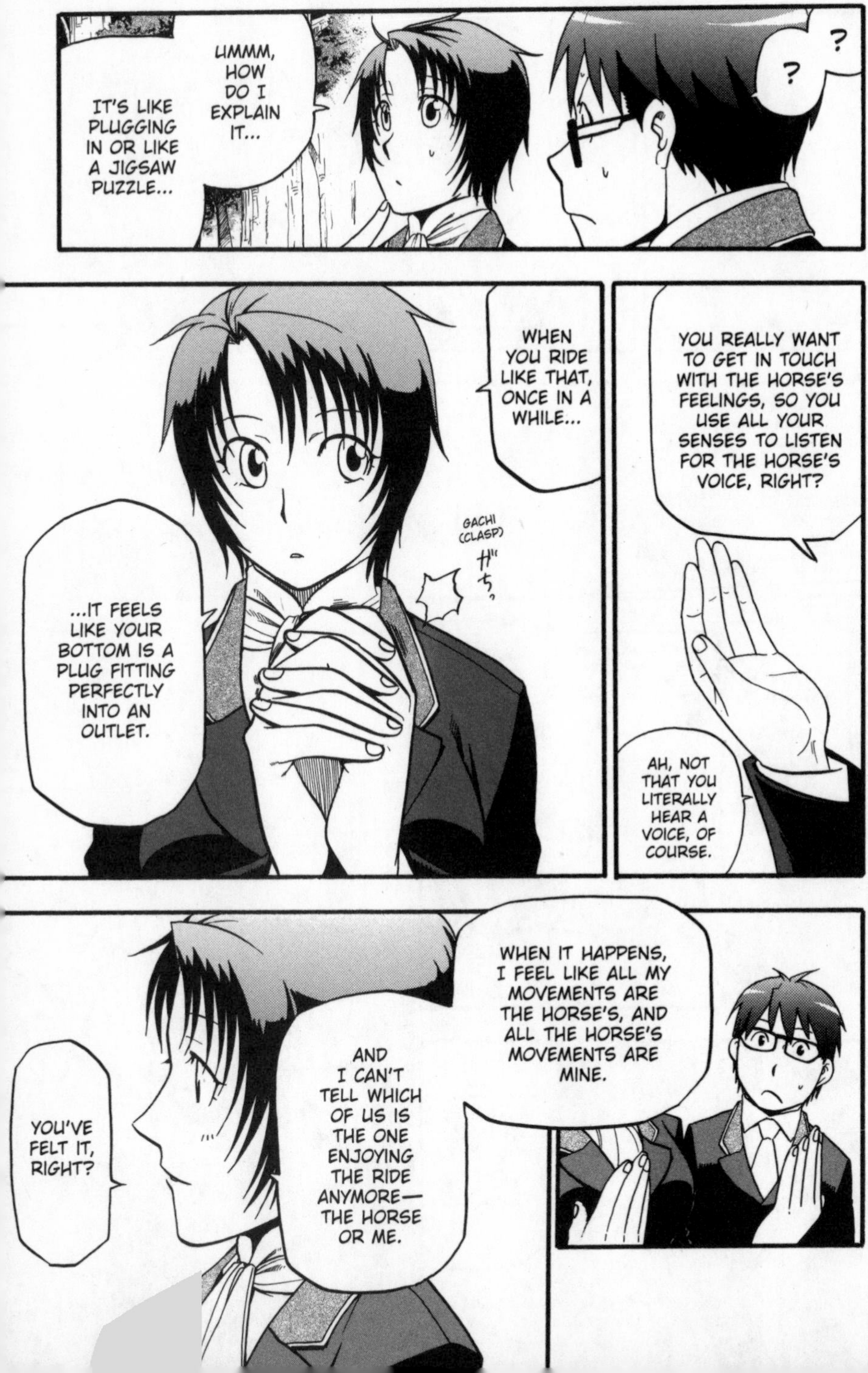
? ?
UMMM, HOW DO I EXPLAIN IT...
IT'S LIKE PLUGGING IN OR LIKE A JIGSAW PUZZLE...
YOU REALLY WANT TO GET IN TOUCH WITH THE HORSE'S FEELINGS, SO YOU USE ALL YOUR SENSES TO LISTEN FOR THE HORSE'S VOICE, RIGHT?
AH, NOT THAT YOU LITERALLY HEAR A VOICE, OF COURSE.
WHEN YOU RIDE LIKE THAT, ONCE IN A WHILE...
GACHI (CLASP)
...IT FEELS LIKE YOUR BOTTOM IS A PLUG FITTING PERFECTLY INTO AN OUTLET.
WHEN IT HAPPENS, I FEEL LIKE ALL MY MOVEMENTS ARE THE HORSE'S, AND ALL THE HORSE'S MOVEMENTS ARE MINE.
AND I CAN'T TELL WHICH OF US IS THE ONE ENJOYING THE RIDE ANYMORE—THE HORSE OR ME.
YOU'VE FELT IT, RIGHT?

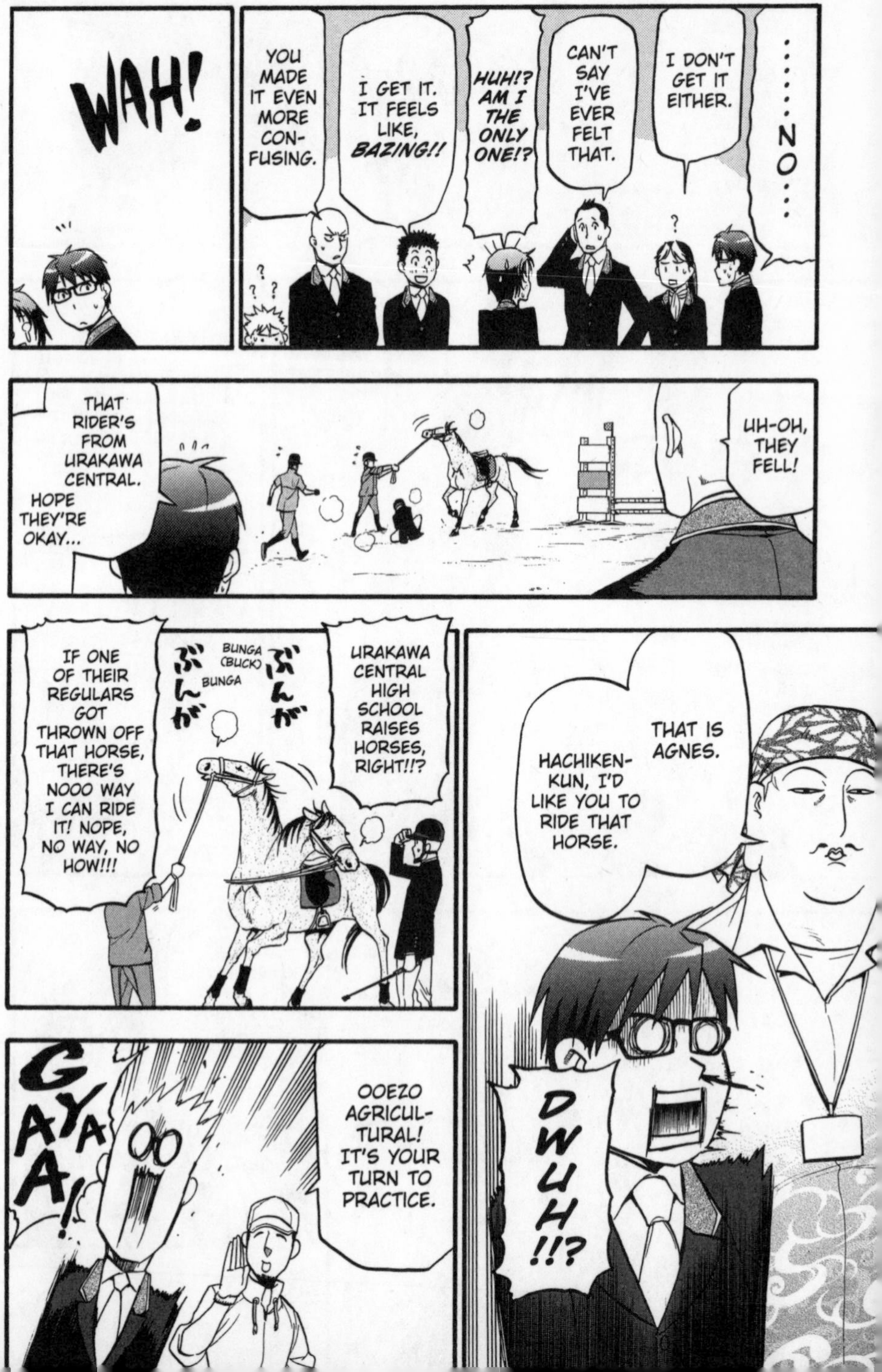
......NO......
I DON'T GET IT EITHER.
CAN'T SAY I'VE EVER FELT THAT.
HUH!? AM I THE ONLY ONE!?
I GET IT. IT FEELS LIKE, BAZING!!
YOU MADE IT EVEN MORE CON-FUSING.
WAH!
UH-OH, THEY FELL!
THAT RIDER'S FROM URAKAWA CENTRAL.
HOPE THEY'RE OKAY...
THAT IS AGNES.
HACHIKEN-KUN, I'D LIKE YOU TO RIDE THAT HORSE.
DWUH!!?
URAKAWA CENTRAL HIGH SCHOOL RAISES HORSES, RIGHT!!?
ぶんが BUNGA (BUCK)
ぶんが BUNGA
IF ONE OF THEIR REGULARS GOT THROWN OFF THAT HORSE, THERE'S NOOO WAY I CAN RIDE IT! NOPE, NO WAY, NO HOW!!!
OOEZO AGRICUL-TURAL! IT'S YOUR TURN TO PRACTICE.
GYAAA!

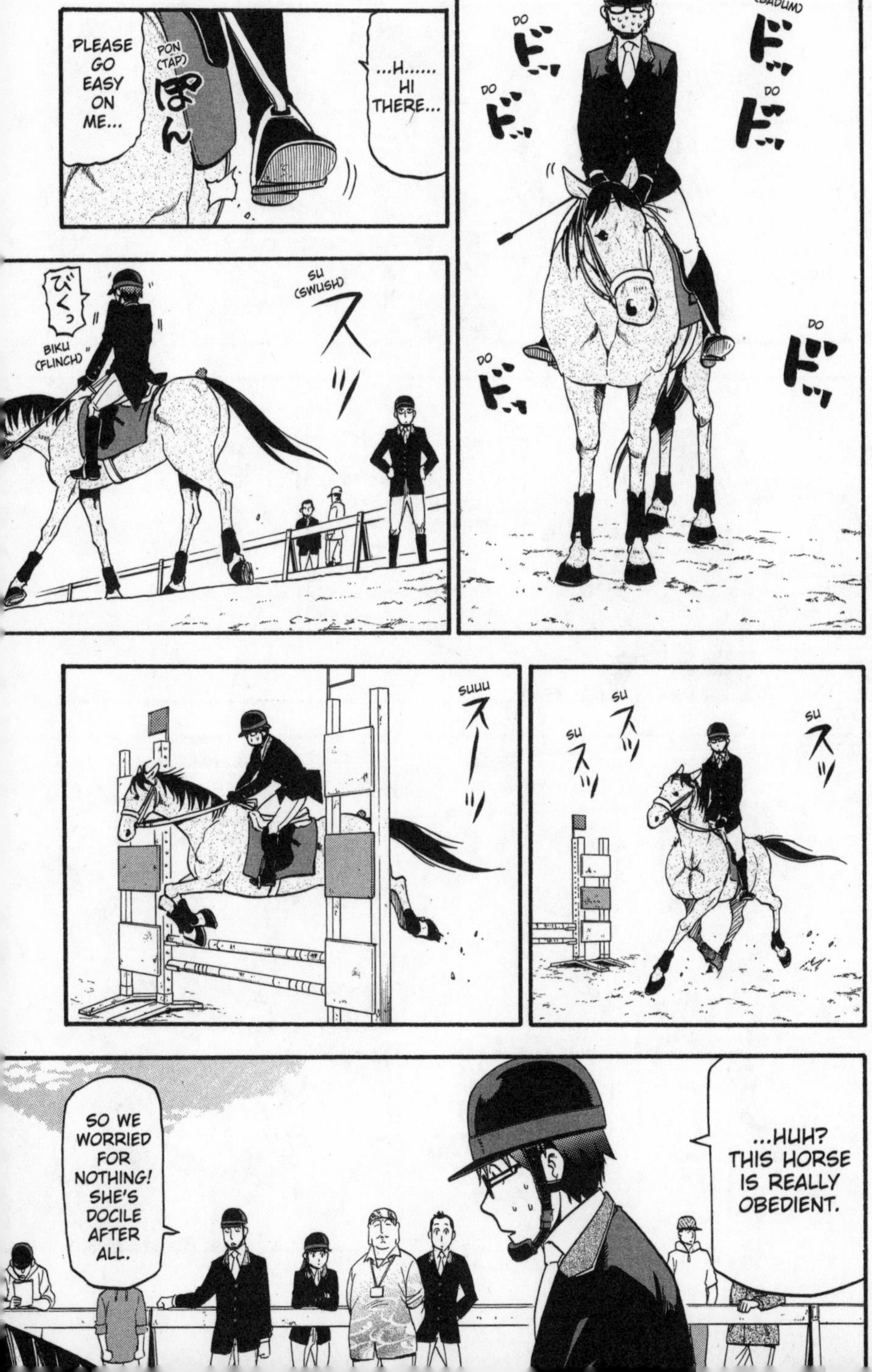
DO (BADUM)
ドッ
DO
ドッ
DO
ドッ
DO
ドッ
DO
ドッ
DO
ドッ
...H...... HI THERE...
PON (TAP)
ぽん
PLEASE GO EASY ON ME...
SU (SWUSH)
スッ
びくっ
BIKU (FLINCH)
SU
スッ
SU
スッ
SU
スッ
SUUU
スーッ
...HUH? THIS HORSE IS REALLY OBEDIENT.
SO WE WORRIED FOR NOTHING! SHE'S DOCILE AFTER ALL.

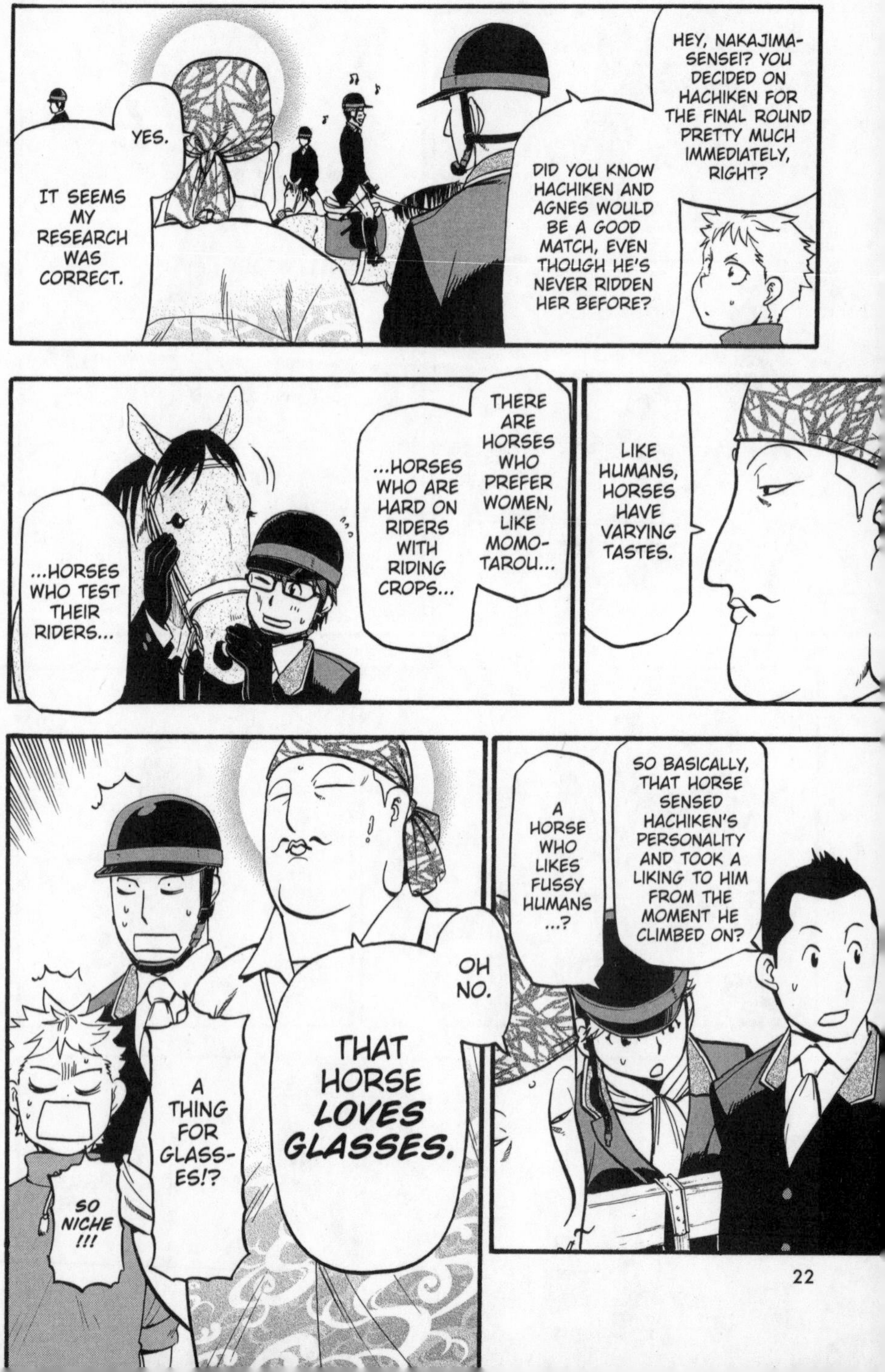
HEY, NAKAJIMA-SENSEI? YOU DECIDED ON HACHIKEN FOR THE FINAL ROUND PRETTY MUCH IMMEDIATELY, RIGHT?
DID YOU KNOW HACHIKEN AND AGNES WOULD BE A GOOD MATCH, EVEN THOUGH HE'S NEVER RIDDEN HER BEFORE?
YES.
IT SEEMS MY RESEARCH WAS CORRECT.
LIKE HUMANS, HORSES HAVE VARYING TASTES.
THERE ARE HORSES WHO PREFER WOMEN, LIKE MOMOTAROU...
...HORSES WHO ARE HARD ON RIDERS WITH RIDING CROPS...
...HORSES WHO TEST THEIR RIDERS...
SO BASICALLY, THAT HORSE SENSED HACHIKEN'S PERSONALITY AND TOOK A LIKING TO HIM FROM THE MOMENT HE CLIMBED ON?
A HORSE WHO LIKES FUSSY HUMANS ...?
OH NO.
THAT HORSE LOVES GLASSES.
A THING FOR GLASSES!?
SO NICHE!!!

Silver Spoon

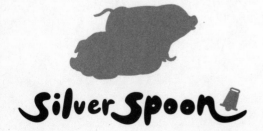

HIDAKA AGRICULTURAL
HIGH SCHOOL
EQUESTRIAN CLUB

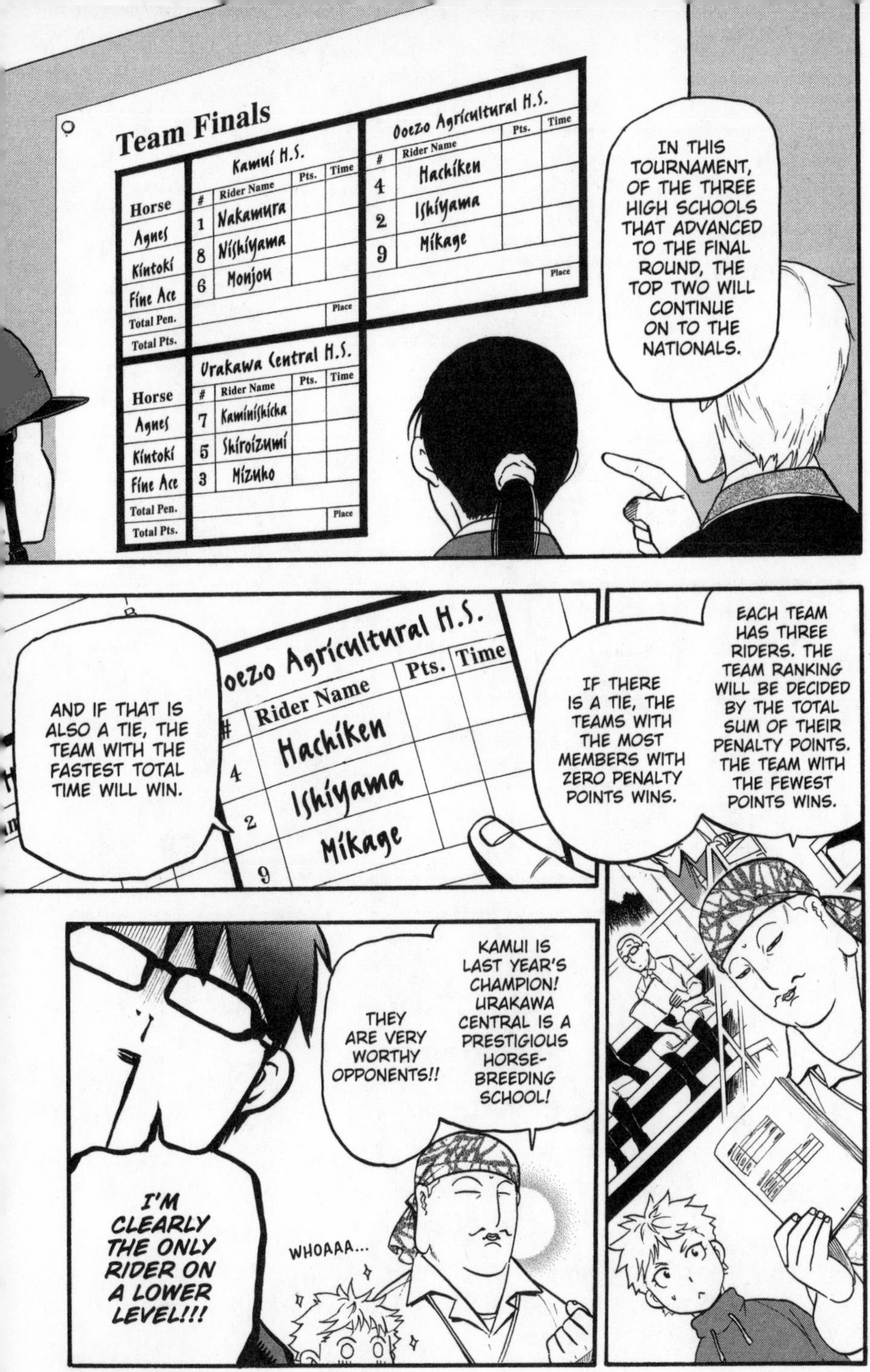
Team Finals
Kamui H.S.
Horse
Rider Name Pts. Time
Agnes 1 Nakamura
Kintoki 8 Nishiyama
Fine Ace 6 Monjou
Total Pen.
Total Pts.
Place
Ooezo Agricultural H.S.
Rider Name Pts. Time
4 Hachiken
2 Ishiyama
9 Mikage
Place
Urakawa Central H.S.
Horse
Rider Name Pts. Time
Agnes 7 Kaminishicha
Kintoki 5 Shiroizumi
Fine Ace 3 Mizuho
Total Pen.
Total Pts.
Place
IN THIS TOURNAMENT, OF THE THREE HIGH SCHOOLS THAT ADVANCED TO THE FINAL ROUND, THE TOP TWO WILL CONTINUE ON TO THE NATIONALS.
EACH TEAM HAS THREE RIDERS. THE TEAM RANKING WILL BE DECIDED BY THE TOTAL SUM OF THEIR PENALTY POINTS. THE TEAM WITH THE FEWEST POINTS WINS.
IF THERE IS A TIE, THE TEAMS WITH THE MOST MEMBERS WITH ZERO PENALTY POINTS WINS.
Ooezo Agricultural H.S.
Rider Name Pts. Time
4 Hachiken
2 Ishiyama
9 Mikage
AND IF THAT IS ALSO A TIE, THE TEAM WITH THE FASTEST TOTAL TIME WILL WIN.
KAMUI IS LAST YEAR'S CHAMPION! URAKAWA CENTRAL IS A PRESTIGIOUS HORSE-BREEDING SCHOOL!
THEY ARE VERY WORTHY OPPONENTS!!
WHOAAA...
I'M CLEARLY THE ONLY RIDER ON A LOWER LEVEL!!!

Chapter 107:
Tale of Four Seasons⑩

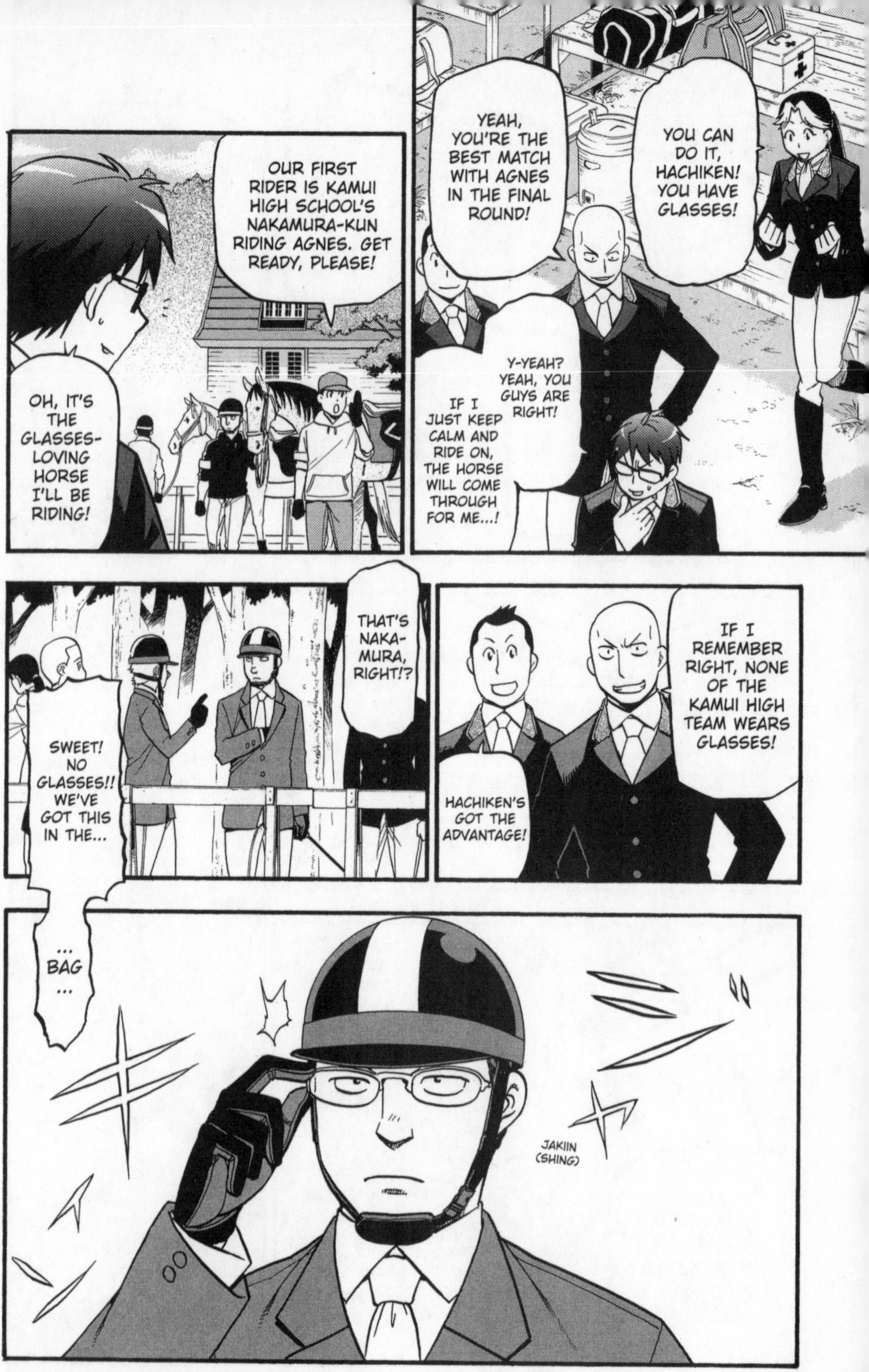
YOU CAN DO IT, HACHIKEN! YOU HAVE GLASSES!
YEAH, YOU'RE THE BEST MATCH WITH AGNES IN THE FINAL ROUND!
Y-YEAH? YEAH, YOU GUYS ARE RIGHT!
IF I JUST KEEP CALM AND RIDE ON, THE HORSE WILL COME THROUGH FOR ME...!
OUR FIRST RIDER IS KAMUI HIGH SCHOOL'S NAKAMURA-KUN RIDING AGNES. GET READY, PLEASE!
OH, IT'S THE GLASSES-LOVING HORSE I'LL BE RIDING!
IF I REMEMBER RIGHT, NONE OF THE KAMUI HIGH TEAM WEARS GLASSES!
HACHIKEN'S GOT THE ADVANTAGE!
THAT'S NAKAMURA, RIGHT!?
SWEET! NO GLASSES!! WE'VE GOT THIS IN THE...
...BAG...
JAKIIN (SHING)

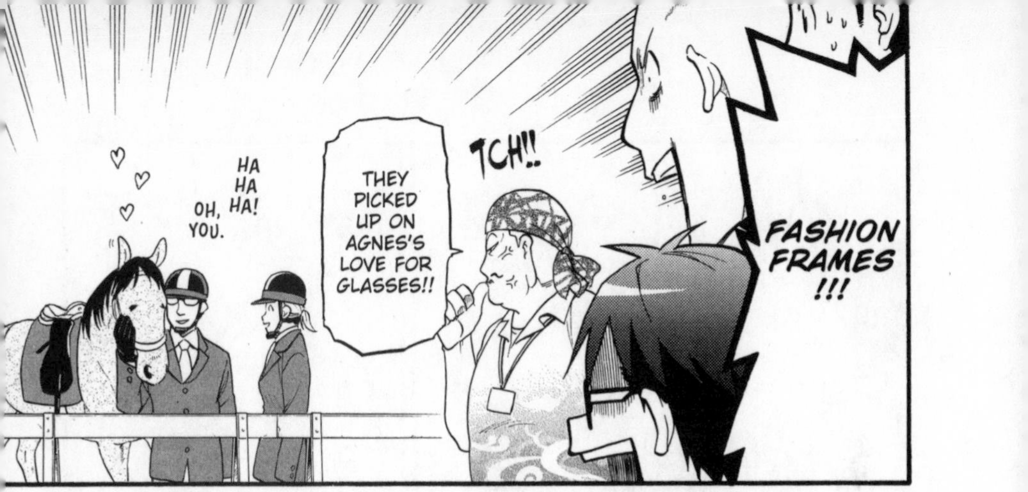
FASHION FRAMES!!!
TCH!!
THEY PICKED UP ON AGNES'S LOVE FOR GLASSES!!
HA HA HA!
OH, YOU.

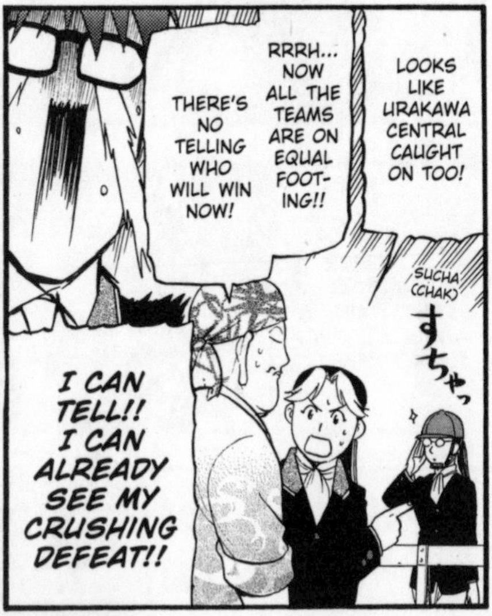
LOOKS LIKE URAKAWA CENTRAL CAUGHT ON TOO!
RRRH... NOW ALL THE TEAMS ARE ON EQUAL FOOTING!!
THERE'S NO TELLING WHO WILL WIN NOW!
SUCHA (CHAK)
すちゃっ
I CAN TELL!! I CAN ALREADY SEE MY CRUSHING DEFEAT!!

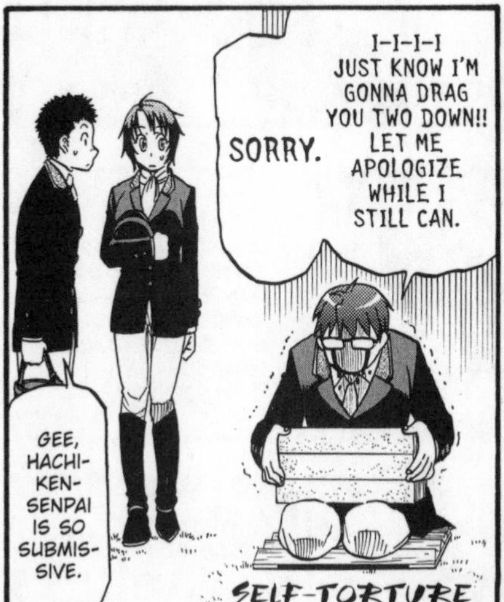
I-I-I-I JUST KNOW I'M GONNA DRAG YOU TWO DOWN!! LET ME APOLOGIZE WHILE I STILL CAN.
SORRY.
GEE, HACHIKEN-SENPAI IS SO SUBMISSIVE.
SELF-TORTURE

Chapter 107:

Tale of Four Seasons ⑩

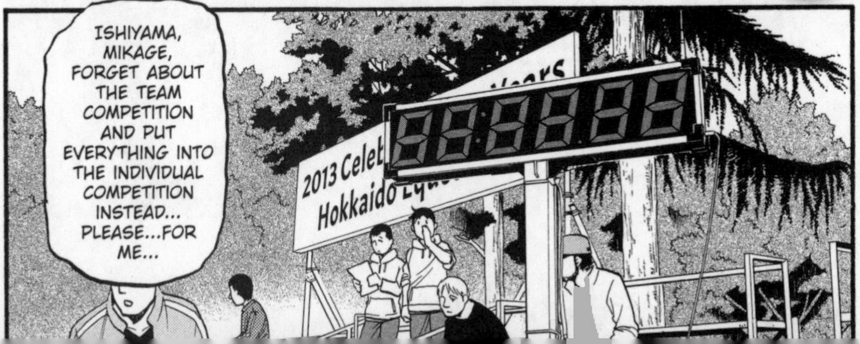
ISHIYAMA, MIKAGE, FORGET ABOUT THE TEAM COMPETITION AND PUT EVERYTHING INTO THE INDIVIDUAL COMPETITION INSTEAD... PLEASE...FOR ME...

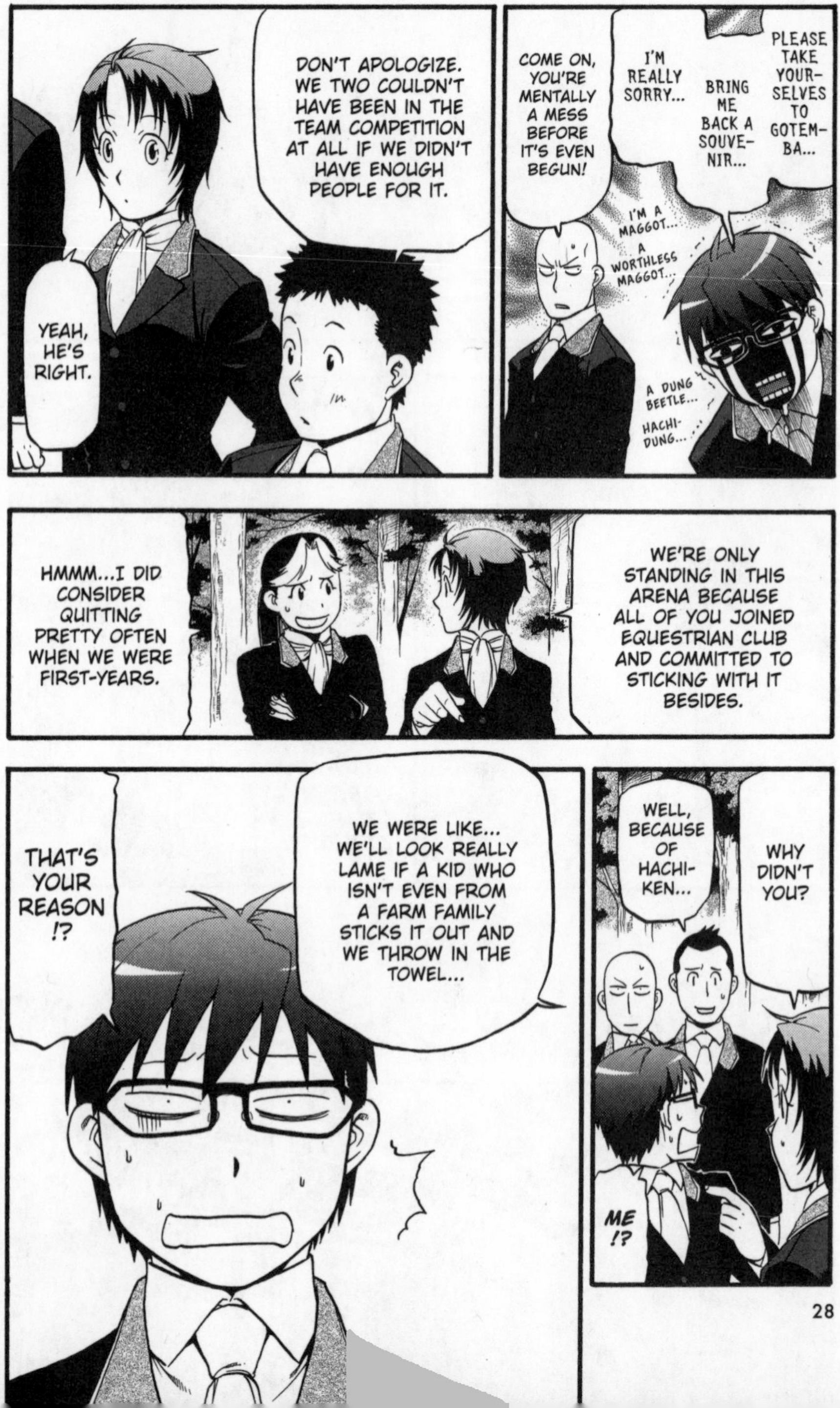
PLEASE TAKE YOURSELVES TO GOTEMBA...
BRING ME BACK A SOUVENIR...
I'M REALLY SORRY...
COME ON, YOU'RE MENTALLY A MESS BEFORE IT'S EVEN BEGUN!
I'M A MAGGOT... A WORTHLESS MAGGOT...
A DUNG BEETLE... HACHI-DUNG...
DON'T APOLOGIZE. WE TWO COULDN'T HAVE BEEN IN THE TEAM COMPETITION AT ALL IF WE DIDN'T HAVE ENOUGH PEOPLE FOR IT.
YEAH, HE'S RIGHT.
WE'RE ONLY STANDING IN THIS ARENA BECAUSE ALL OF YOU JOINED EQUESTRIAN CLUB AND COMMITTED TO STICKING WITH IT BESIDES.
HMMM...I DID CONSIDER QUITTING PRETTY OFTEN WHEN WE WERE FIRST-YEARS.
WHY DIDN'T YOU?
WELL, BECAUSE OF HACHI-KEN...
ME!?
WE WERE LIKE... WE'LL LOOK REALLY LAME IF A KID WHO ISN'T EVEN FROM A FARM FAMILY STICKS IT OUT AND WE THROW IN THE TOWEL...
THAT'S YOUR REASON!?

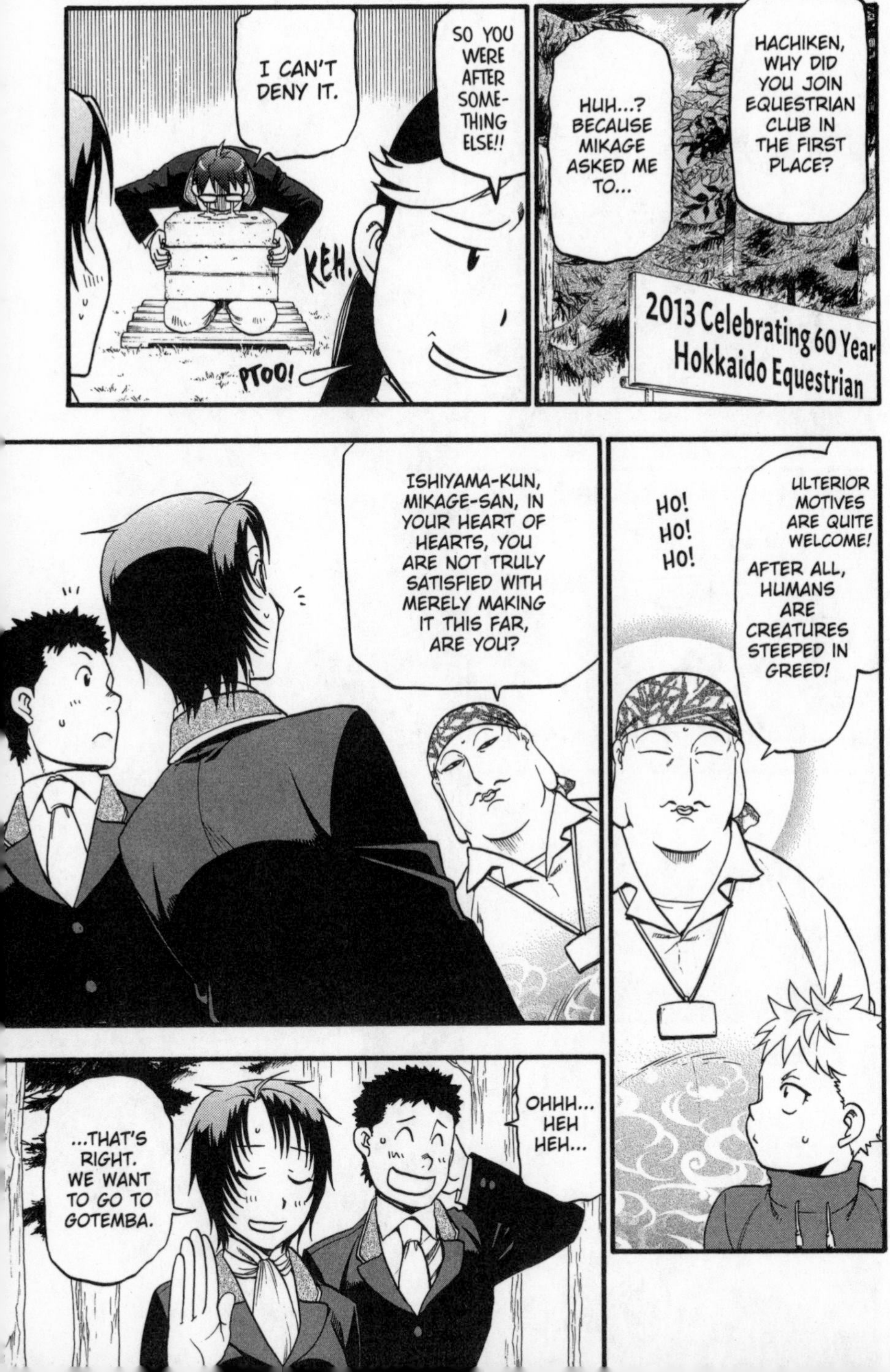
HACHIKEN, WHY DID YOU JOIN EQUESTRIAN CLUB IN THE FIRST PLACE?
HUH...? BECAUSE MIKAGE ASKED ME TO...
2013 Celebrating 60 Year
Hokkaido Equestrian
SO YOU WERE AFTER SOME-THING ELSE!!
I CAN'T DENY IT.
KEH.
PTOO!
ULTERIOR MOTIVES ARE QUITE WELCOME!
AFTER ALL, HUMANS ARE CREATURES STEEPED IN GREED!
HO! HO! HO!
ISHIYAMA-KUN, MIKAGE-SAN, IN YOUR HEART OF HEARTS, YOU ARE NOT TRULY SATISFIED WITH MERELY MAKING IT THIS FAR, ARE YOU?
OHHH... HEH HEH...
...THAT'S RIGHT. WE WANT TO GO TO GOTEMBA.

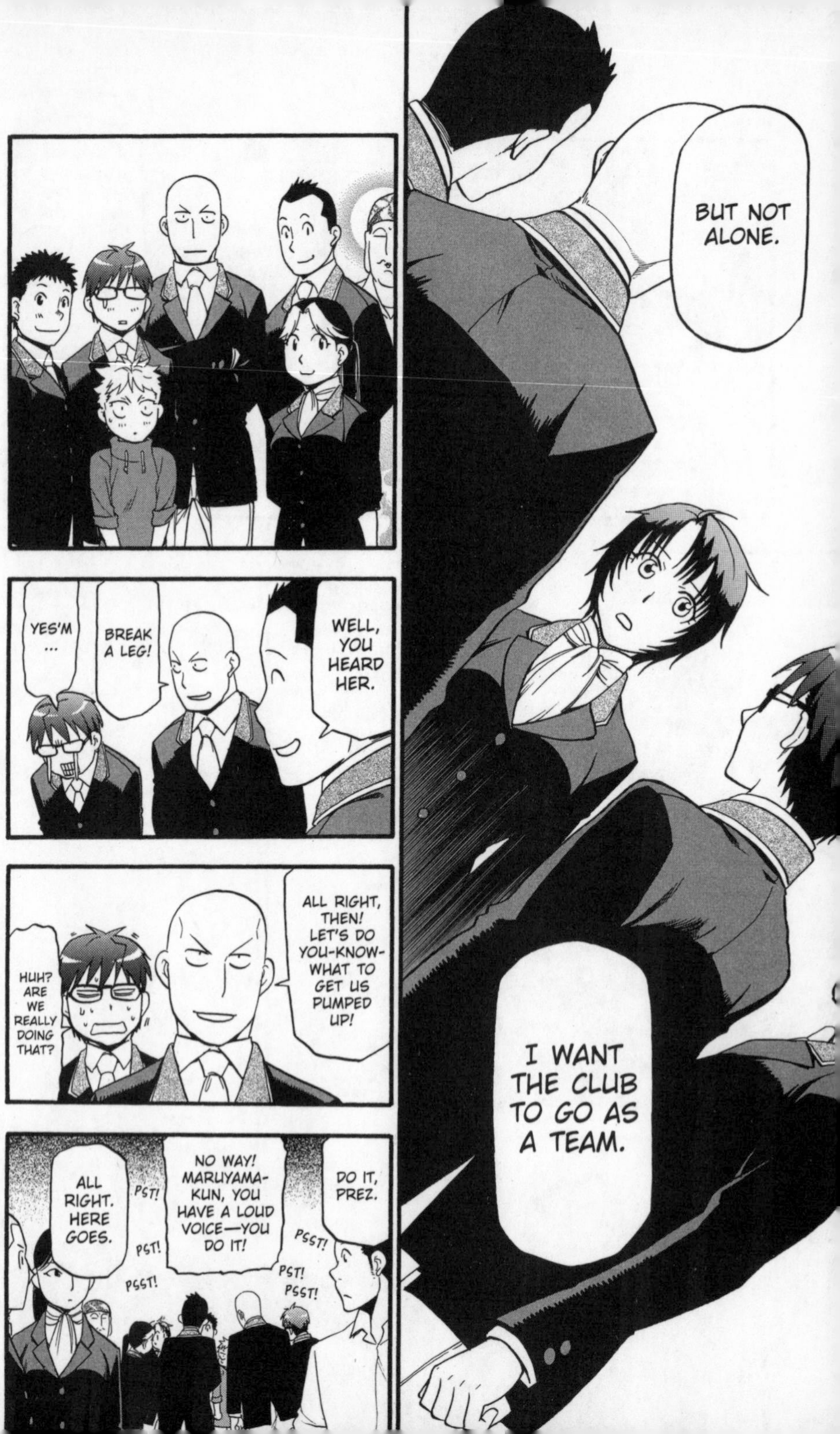
BUT NOT ALONE.
I WANT THE CLUB TO GO AS A TEAM.
WELL, YOU HEARD HER.
BREAK A LEG!
YES'M ...
ALL RIGHT, THEN! LET'S DO YOU-KNOW-WHAT TO GET US PUMPED UP!
HUH? ARE WE REALLY DOING THAT?
DO IT, PREZ.
NO WAY! MARUYAMA-KUN, YOU HAVE A LOUD VOICE—YOU DO IT!
ALL RIGHT. HERE GOES.
PSST!
PST!
PSST!
PST!
PST!
PSST!
PST!

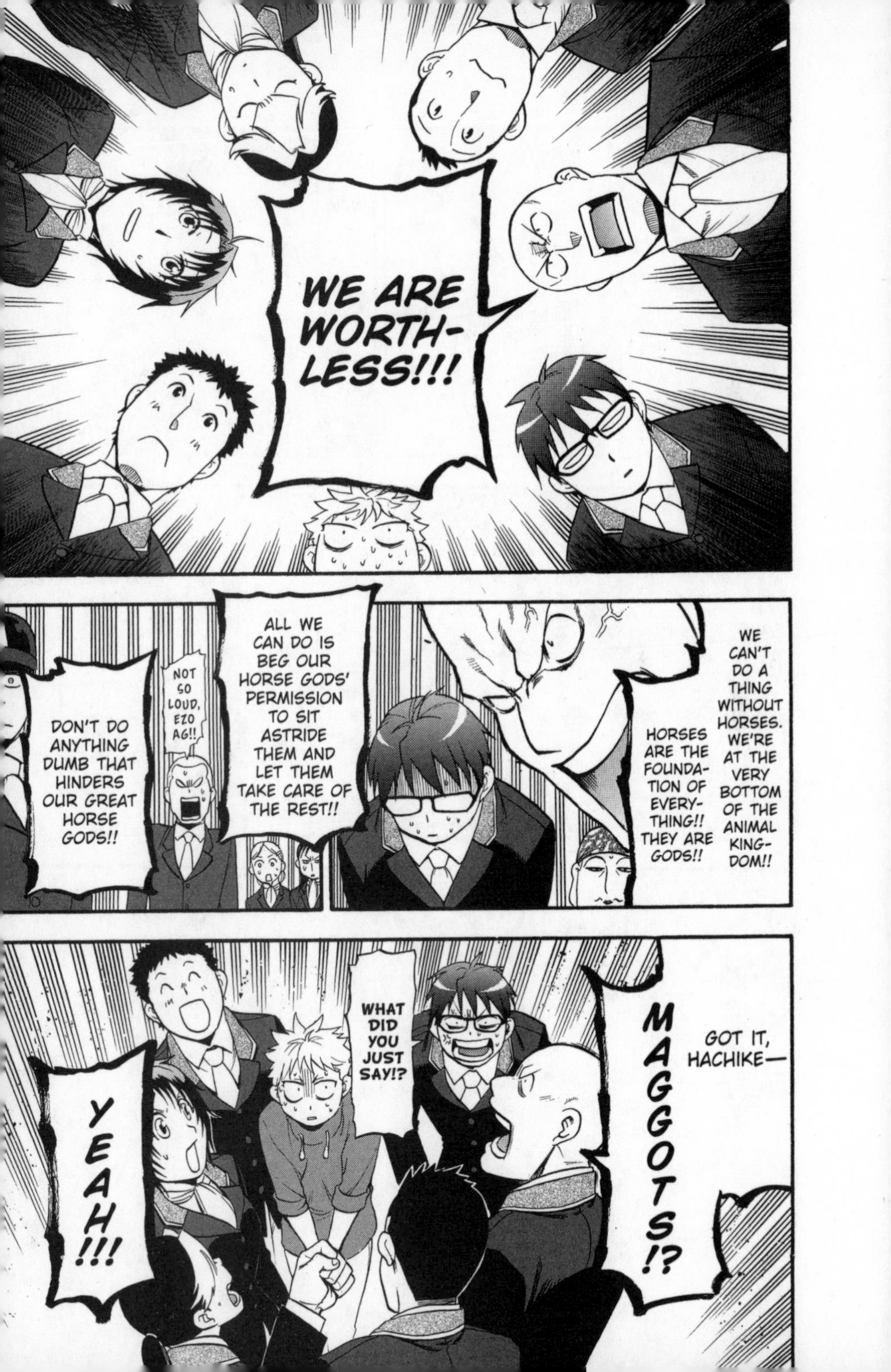
WE ARE WORTH-LESS!!!
WE CAN'T DO A THING WITHOUT HORSES. WE'RE AT THE VERY BOTTOM OF THE ANIMAL KINGDOM!!
HORSES ARE THE FOUNDATION OF EVERYTHING!! THEY ARE GODS!!
ALL WE CAN DO IS BEG OUR HORSE GODS' PERMISSION TO SIT ASTRIDE THEM AND LET THEM TAKE CARE OF THE REST!!
NOT SO LOUD, EZO AG!!
DON'T DO ANYTHING DUMB THAT HINDERS OUR GREAT HORSE GODS!!
GOT IT, HACHIKE—
MAGGOTS!?
WHAT DID YOU JUST SAY!?
YEAH!!!

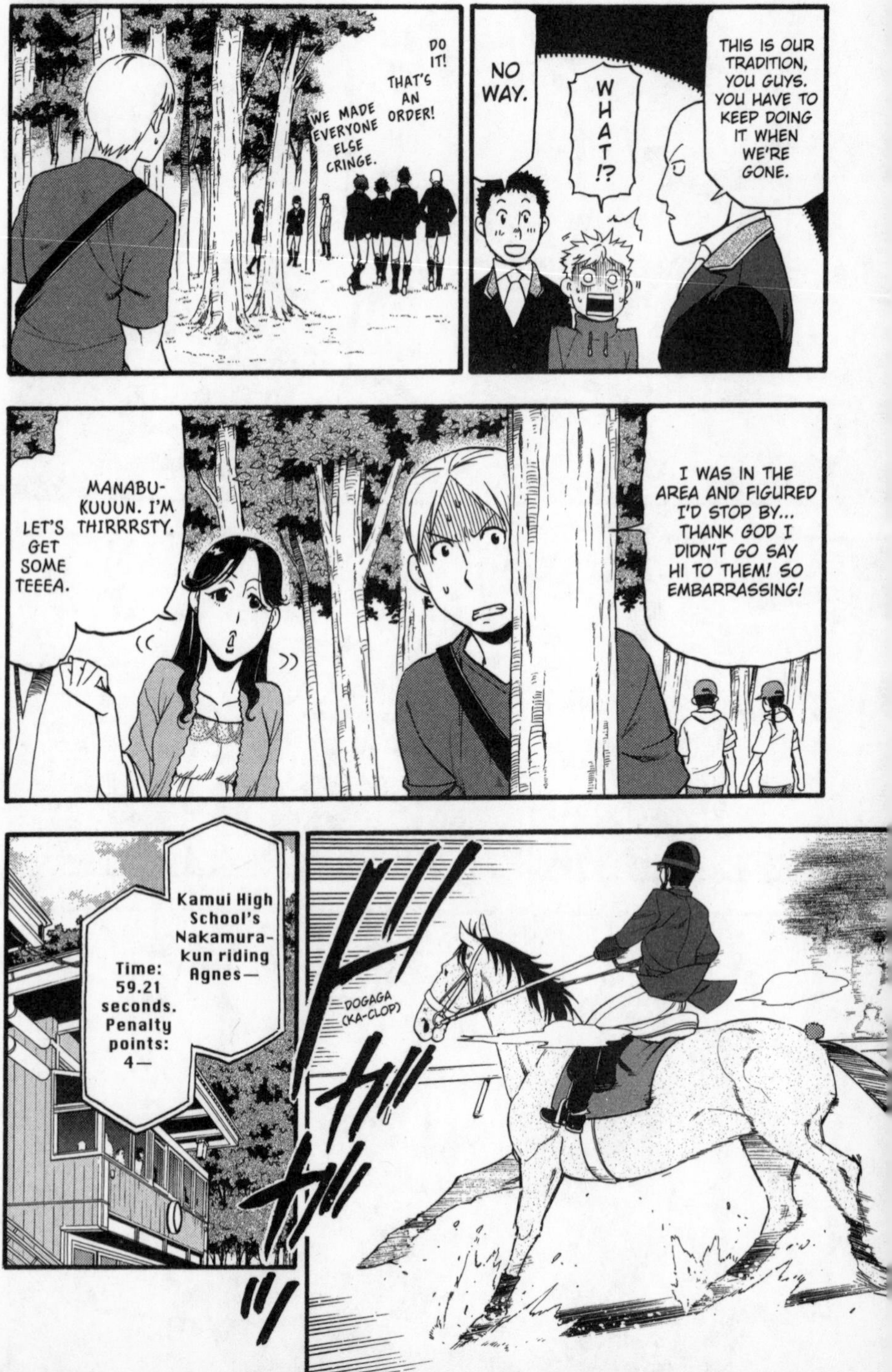
THIS IS OUR TRADITION, YOU GUYS. YOU HAVE TO KEEP DOING IT WHEN WE'RE GONE.
WHAT!?
NO WAY.
DO IT!
THAT'S AN ORDER!
WE MADE EVERYONE ELSE CRINGE.
I WAS IN THE AREA AND FIGURED I'D STOP BY... THANK GOD I DIDN'T GO SAY HI TO THEM! SO EMBARRASSING!
MANABU-KUUUN. I'M THIRRRSTY.
LET'S GET SOME TEEEA.
DOGAGA (KA-CLOP)
Kamui High School's Nakamura-kun riding Agnes—
Time: 59.21 seconds. Penalty points: 4—

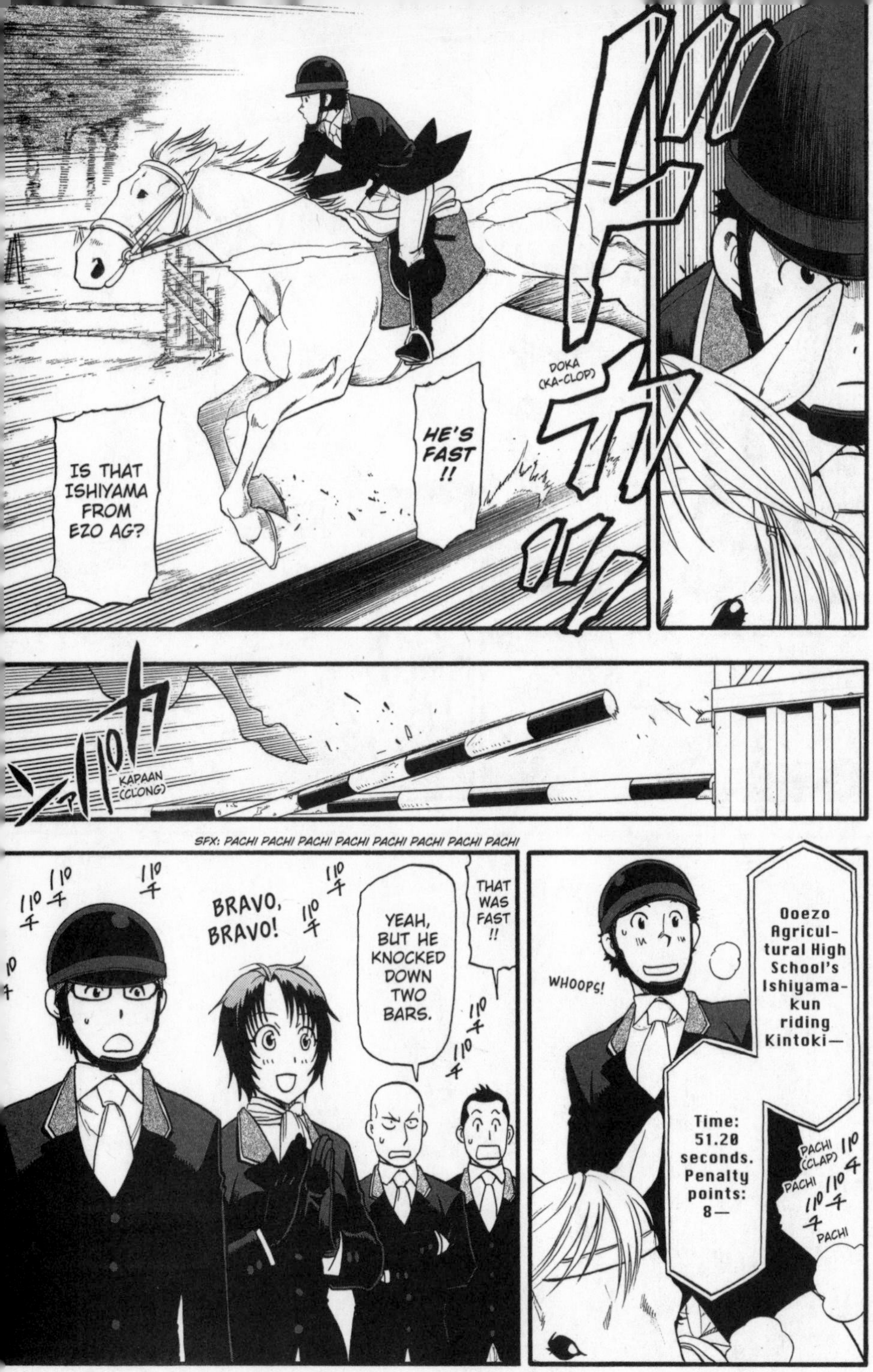
DOKA (KA-CLOP)
HE'S FAST!!
IS THAT ISHIYAMA FROM EZO AG?
KAPAAN (CLONG)
SFX: PACHI PACHI PACHI PACHI PACHI PACHI PACHI PACHI
Ooezo Agricultural High School's Ishiyama-kun riding Kintoki—
WHOOPS!
Time: 51.20 seconds. Penalty points: 8—
PACHI (CLAP) PACHI PACHI
THAT WAS FAST!!
YEAH, BUT HE KNOCKED DOWN TWO BARS.
BRAVO, BRAVO!

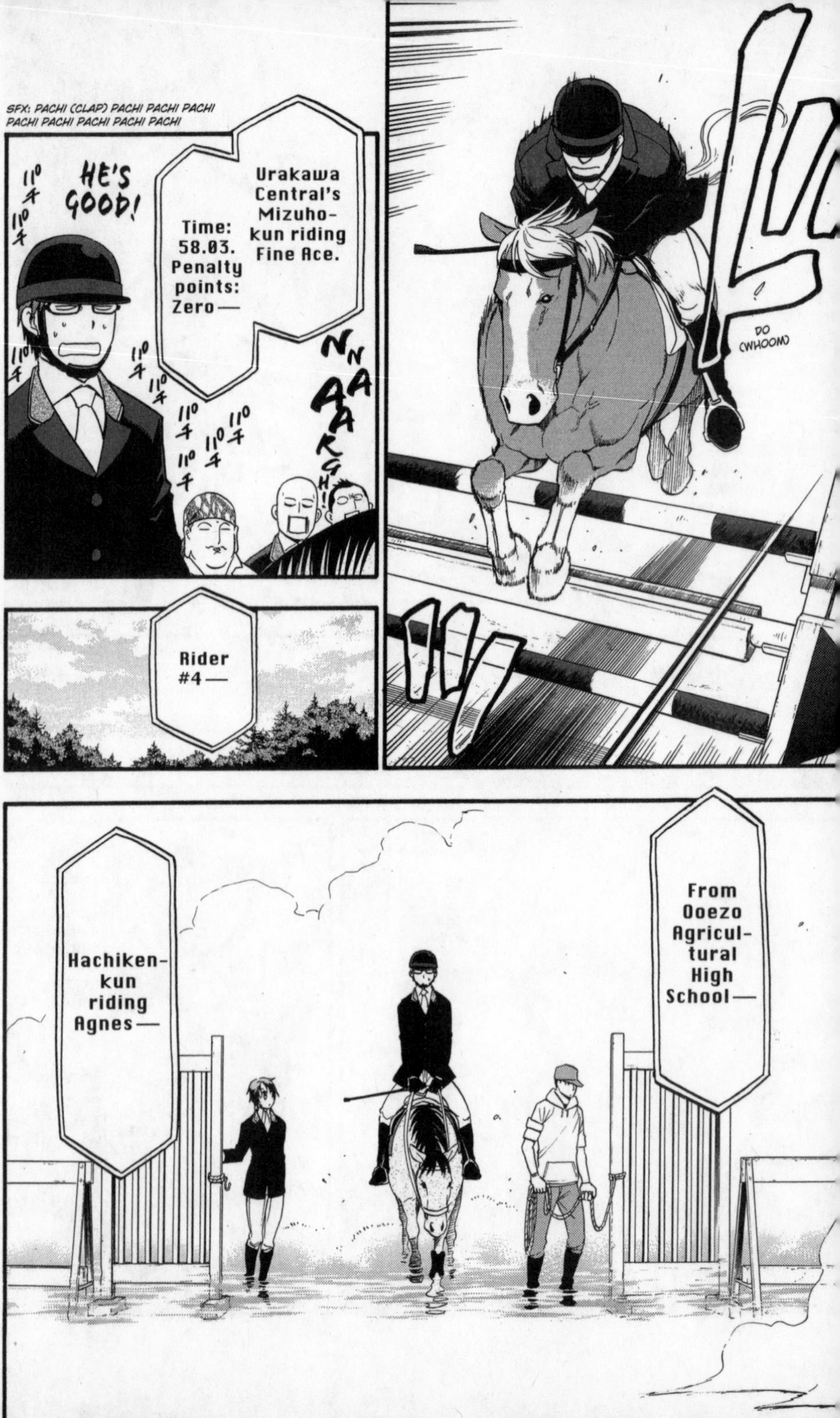
DO (WHOOM)
SFX: PACHI (CLAP) PACHI PACHI PACHI PACHI PACHI PACHI PACHI PACHI
Urakawa Central's Mizuho-kun riding Fine Ace.
Time: 58.03. Penalty points: Zero—
HE'S GOOD!
NNAAARGH!
Rider #4—
From Ooezo Agricultural High School—
Hachiken-kun riding Agnes—

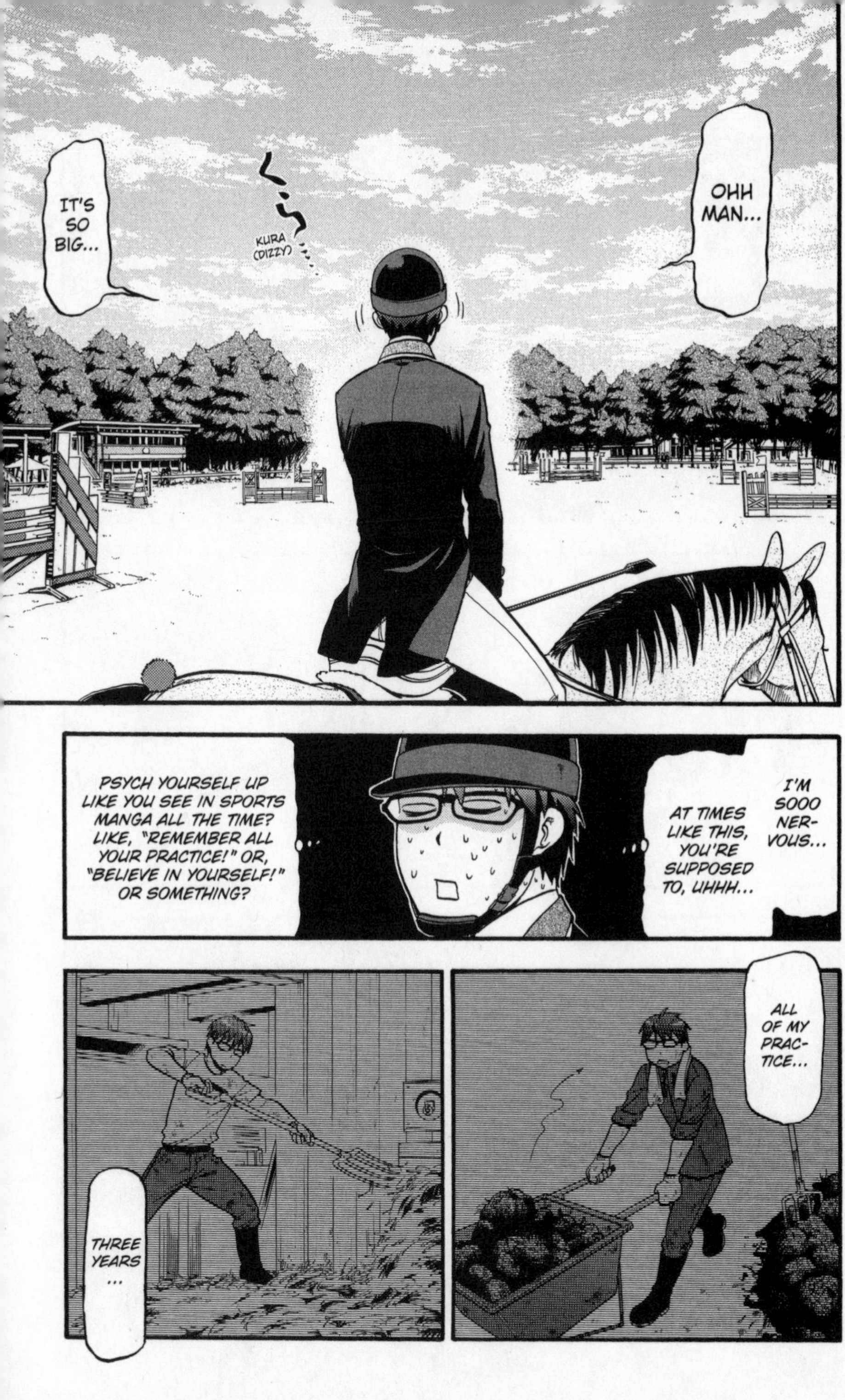

OHH MAN...
くら
KURA (DIZZY)
IT'S SO BIG...
I'M SOOO NER-VOUS...
AT TIMES LIKE THIS, YOU'RE SUPPOSED TO, UHHH...
PSYCH YOURSELF UP LIKE YOU SEE IN SPORTS MANGA ALL THE TIME? LIKE, "REMEMBER ALL YOUR PRACTICE!" OR, "BELIEVE IN YOURSELF!" OR SOMETHING?
ALL OF MY PRAC-TICE...
THREE YEARS ...

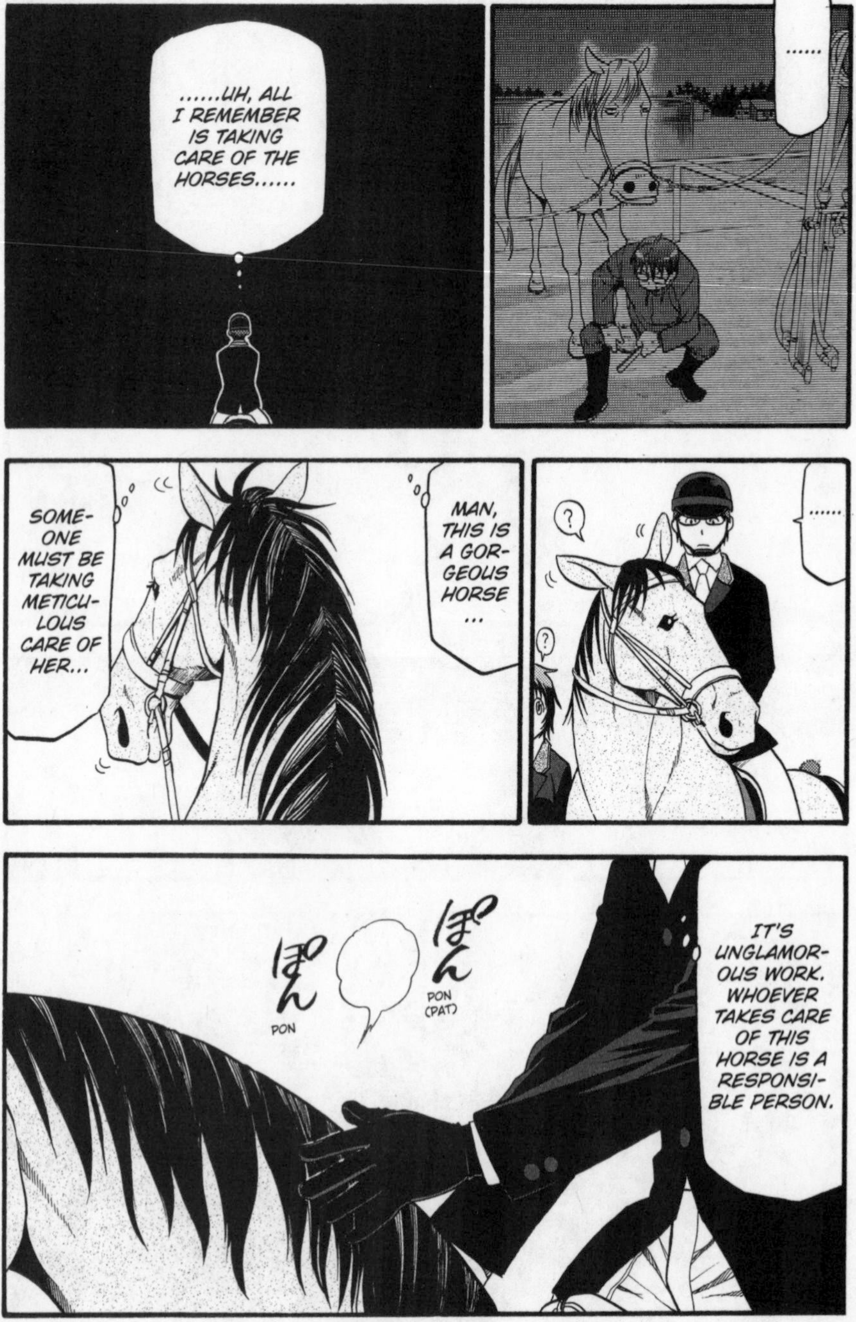
......
......UH, ALL I REMEMBER IS TAKING CARE OF THE HORSES......
?
?
......
MAN, THIS IS A GORGEOUS HORSE ...
SOME-ONE MUST BE TAKING METICULOUS CARE OF HER...
IT'S UNGLAMOROUS WORK. WHOEVER TAKES CARE OF THIS HORSE IS A RESPONSIBLE PERSON.
ぽん
PON (PAT)
ぽん
PON

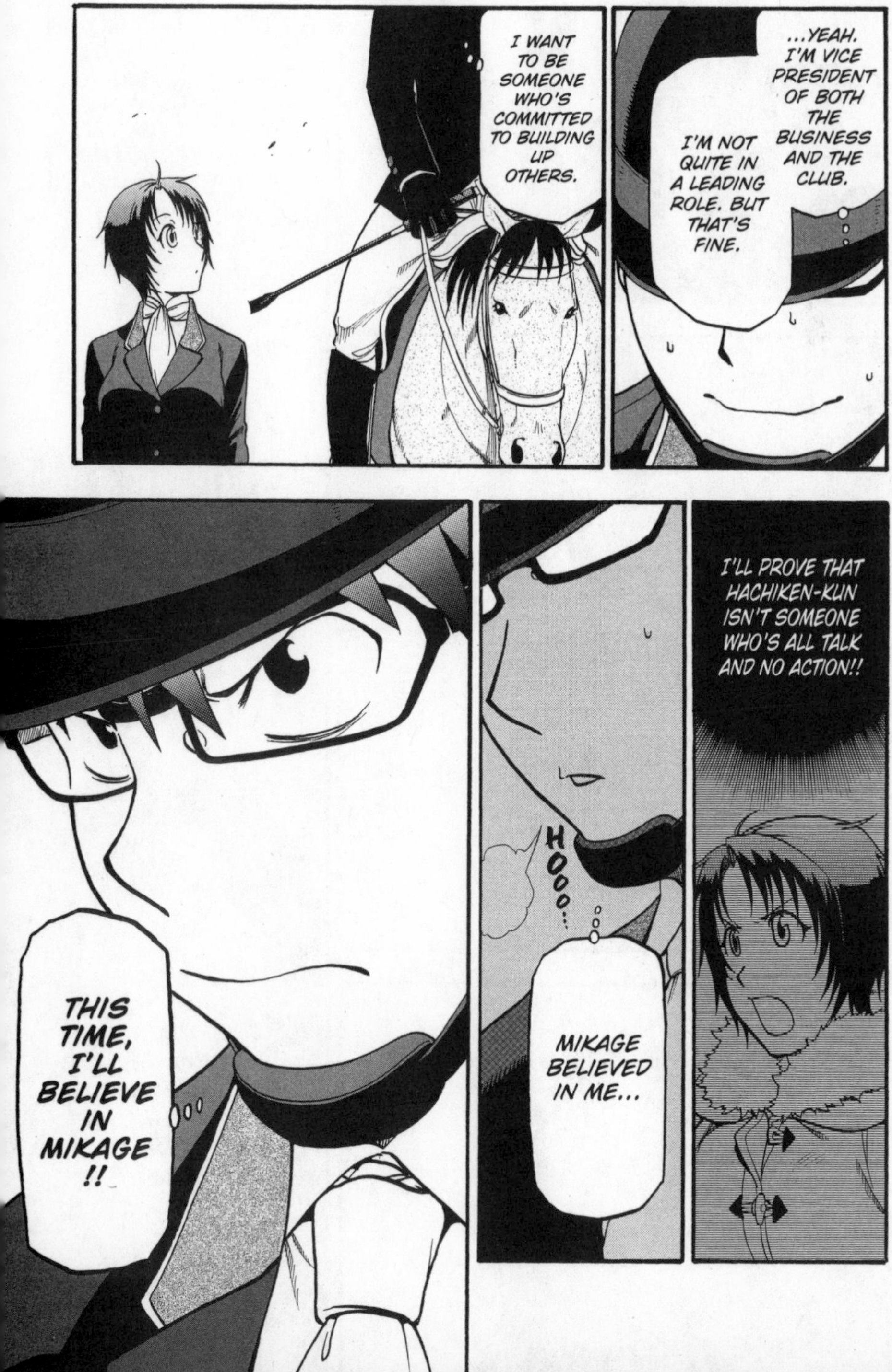
...YEAH. I'M VICE PRESIDENT OF BOTH THE BUSINESS AND THE CLUB.
I'M NOT QUITE IN A LEADING ROLE. BUT THAT'S FINE.
I WANT TO BE SOMEONE WHO'S COMMITTED TO BUILDING UP OTHERS.
I'LL PROVE THAT HACHIKEN-KUN ISN'T SOMEONE WHO'S ALL TALK AND NO ACTION!!
HOOO...
MIKAGE BELIEVED IN ME...
THIS TIME, I'LL BELIEVE IN MIKAGE!!

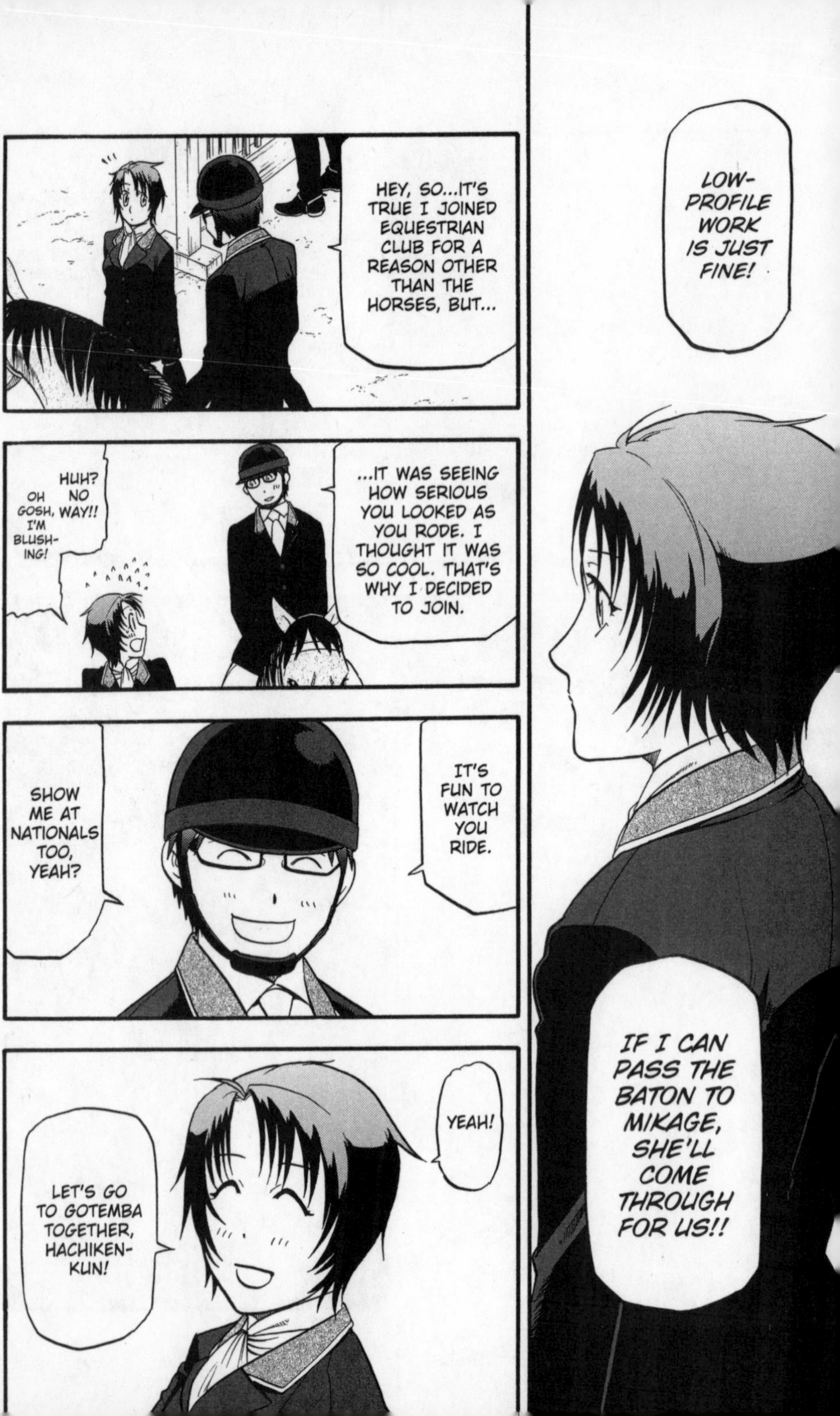
LOW-PROFILE WORK IS JUST FINE!
IF I CAN PASS THE BATON TO MIKAGE, SHE'LL COME THROUGH FOR US!!
HEY, SO...IT'S TRUE I JOINED EQUESTRIAN CLUB FOR A REASON OTHER THAN THE HORSES, BUT...
...IT WAS SEEING HOW SERIOUS YOU LOOKED AS YOU RODE. I THOUGHT IT WAS SO COOL. THAT'S WHY I DECIDED TO JOIN.
HUH? NO WAY!!
OH GOSH, I'M BLUSHING!
IT'S FUN TO WATCH YOU RIDE.
SHOW ME AT NATIONALS TOO, YEAH?
YEAH!
LET'S GO TO GOTEMBA TOGETHER, HACHIKEN-KUN!

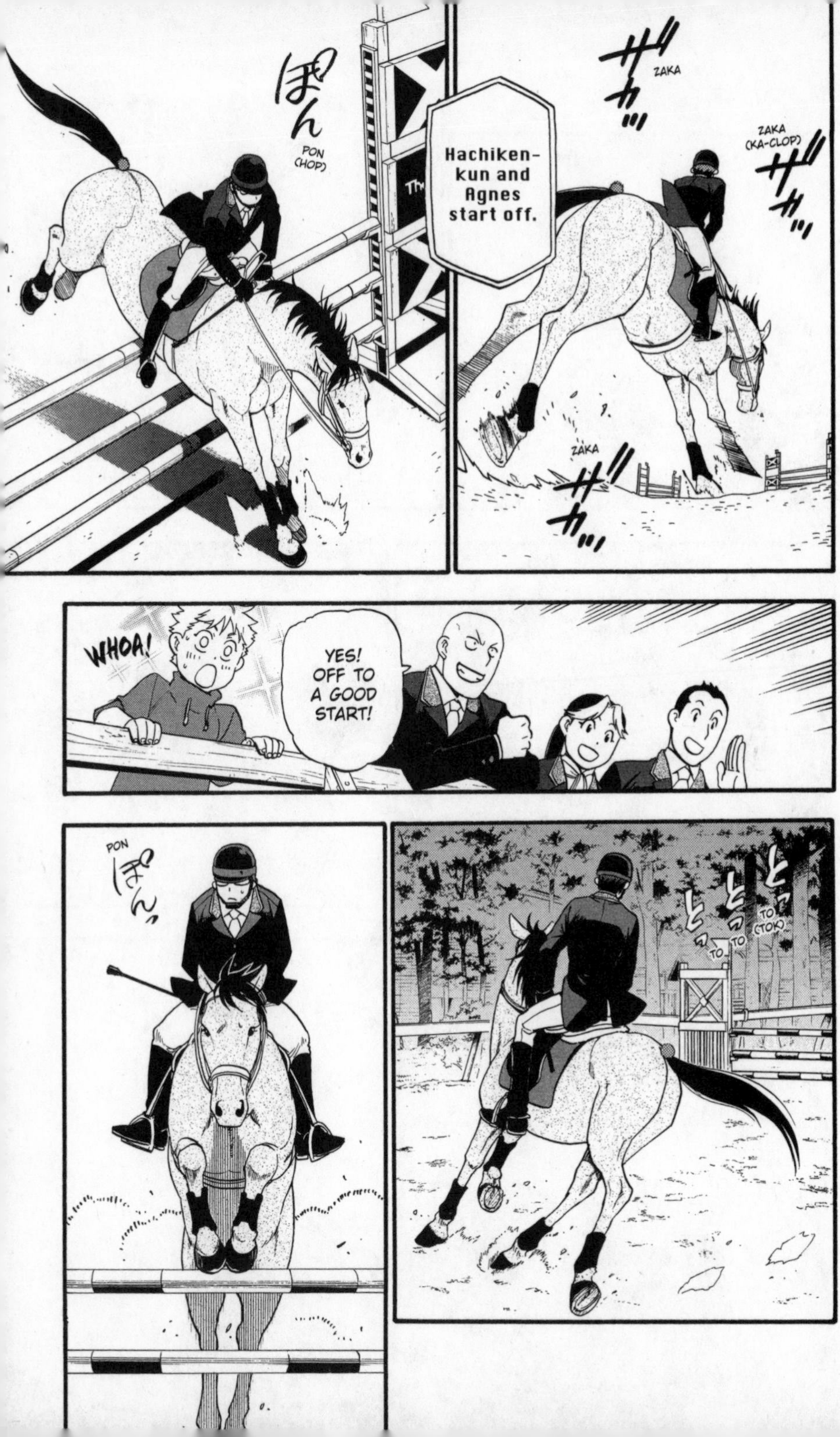
ザカ
ZAKA
ZAKA (KA-CLOP)
ザカ
ZAKA
ザカ
Hachiken-kun and Agnes start off.
ぽん
PON (HOP)
YES! OFF TO A GOOD START!
WHOA!
とっ
TO (TOK)
とっ
TO
とっ
TO
PON
ぽん

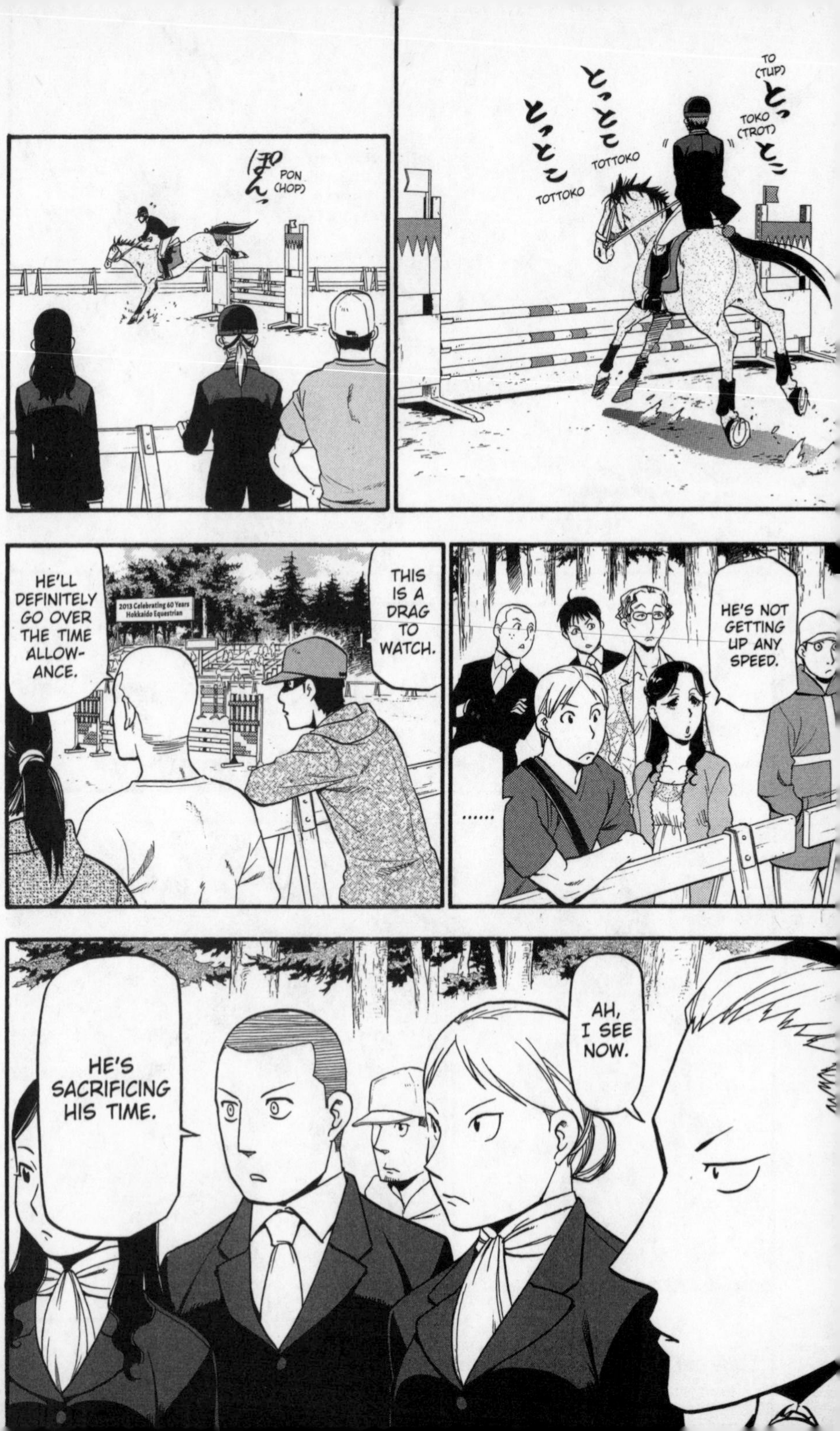

とっ TO (TUP)
とこっ TOKO (TROT)
とっとこ TOTTOKO
とっとこ TOTTOKO
ぽんっ PON (HOP)
HE'S NOT GETTING UP ANY SPEED.
......
THIS IS A DRAG TO WATCH.
2013 Celebrating 60 Years Hokkaido Equestrian
HE'LL DEFINITELY GO OVER THE TIME ALLOWANCE.
AH, I SEE NOW.
HE'S SACRIFICING HIS TIME.

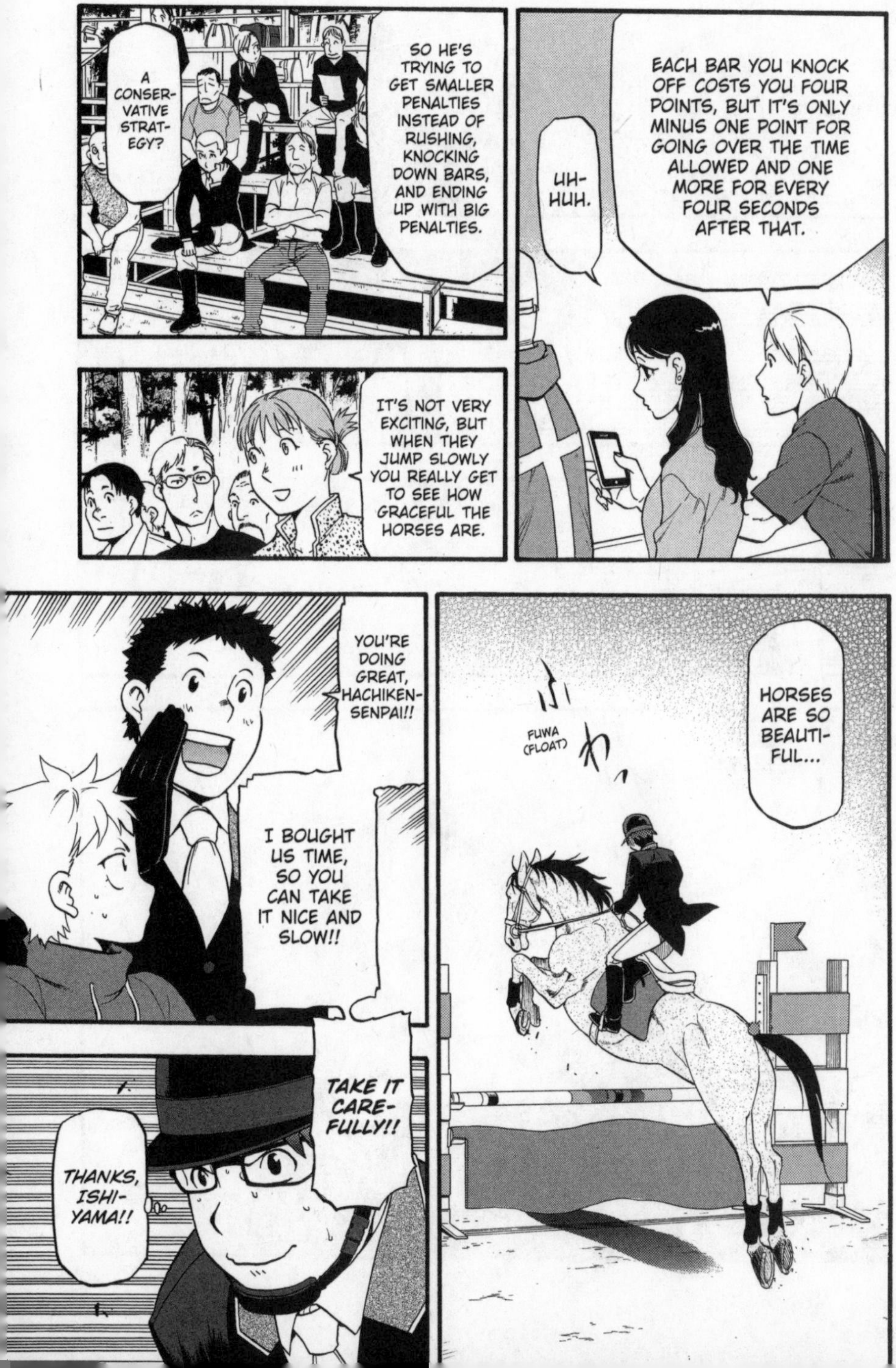
EACH BAR YOU KNOCK OFF COSTS YOU FOUR POINTS, BUT IT'S ONLY MINUS ONE POINT FOR GOING OVER THE TIME ALLOWED AND ONE MORE FOR EVERY FOUR SECONDS AFTER THAT.
UH-HUH.
SO HE'S TRYING TO GET SMALLER PENALTIES INSTEAD OF RUSHING, KNOCKING DOWN BARS, AND ENDING UP WITH BIG PENALTIES.
A CONSERVATIVE STRATEGY?
IT'S NOT VERY EXCITING, BUT WHEN THEY JUMP SLOWLY YOU REALLY GET TO SEE HOW GRACEFUL THE HORSES ARE.
HORSES ARE SO BEAUTIFUL...
FUWA (FLOAT)
YOU'RE DOING GREAT, HACHIKEN-SENPAI!!
I BOUGHT US TIME, SO YOU CAN TAKE IT NICE AND SLOW!!
TAKE IT CAREFULLY!!
THANKS, ISHIYAMA!!

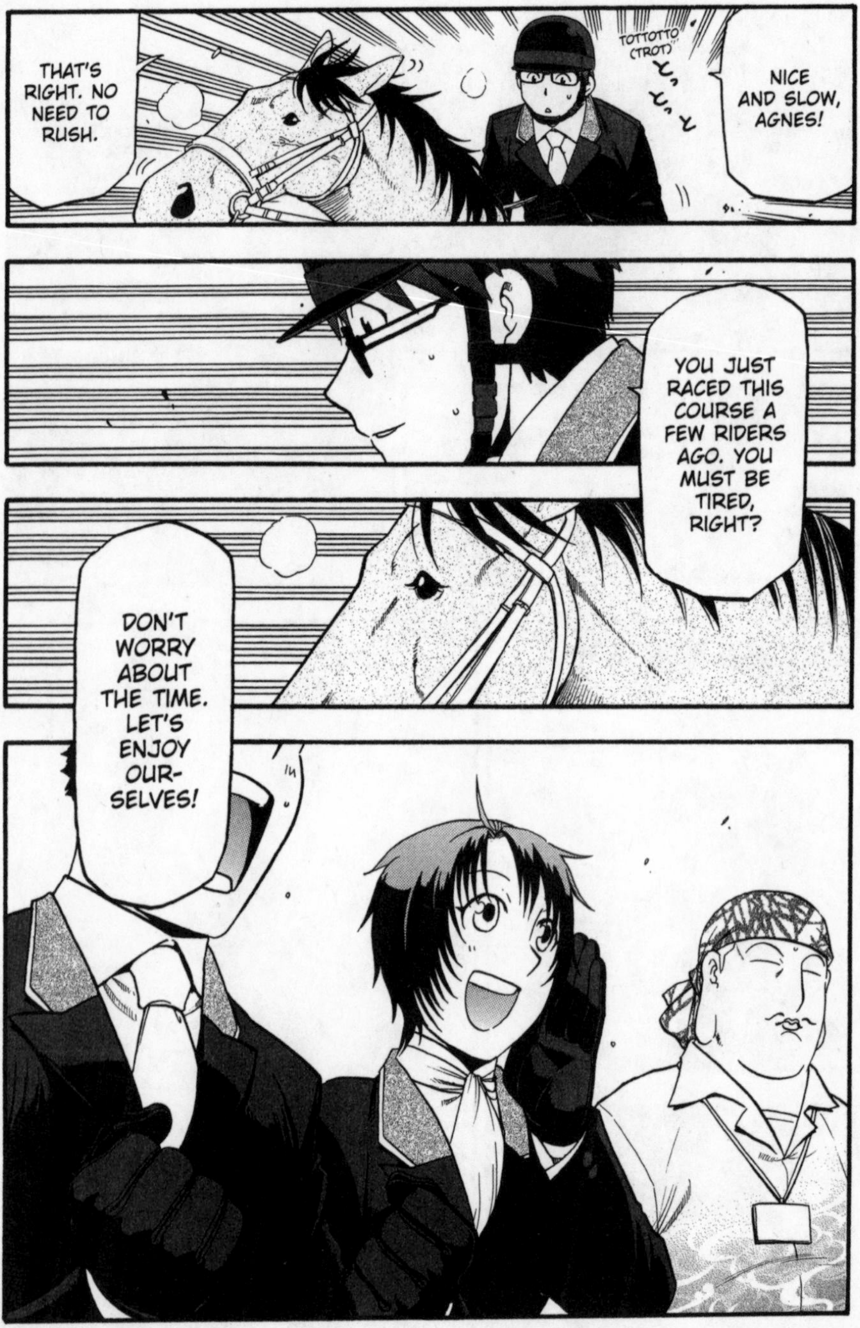
NICE AND SLOW, AGNES!
TOTTOTTO (TROT)
THAT'S RIGHT. NO NEED TO RUSH.
YOU JUST RACED THIS COURSE A FEW RIDERS AGO. YOU MUST BE TIRED, RIGHT?
DON'T WORRY ABOUT THE TIME. LET'S ENJOY OUR-SELVES!

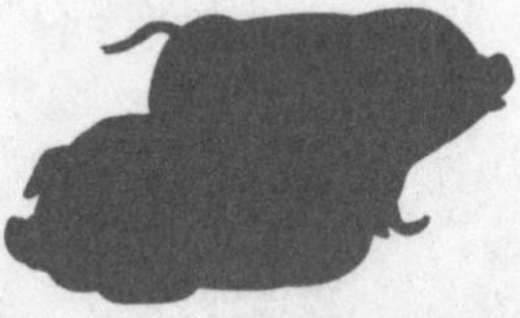

Silver Spoon

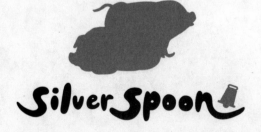

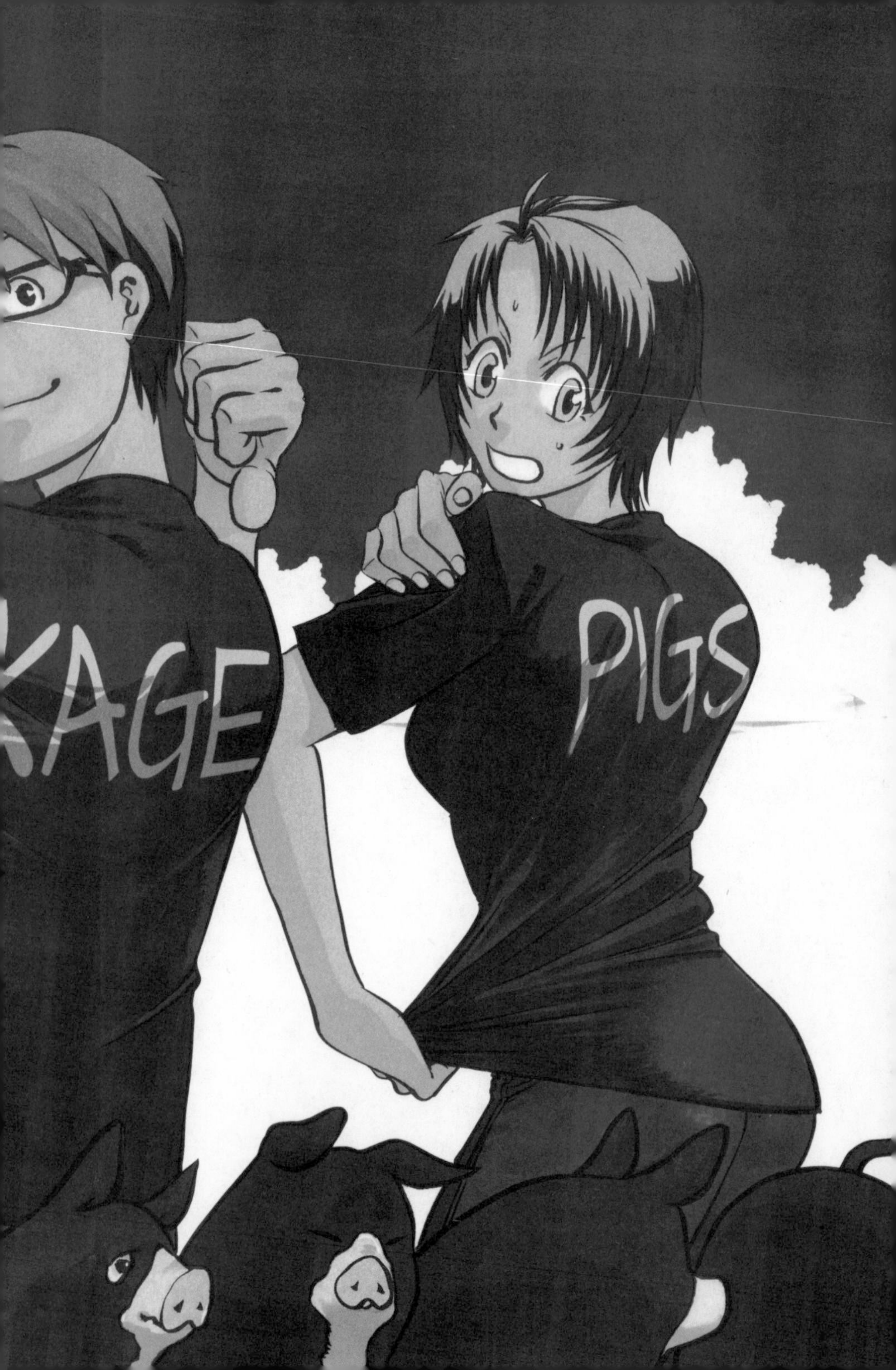
KAGE
PIGS

Chapter 108: Tale of Four Seasons ⑪

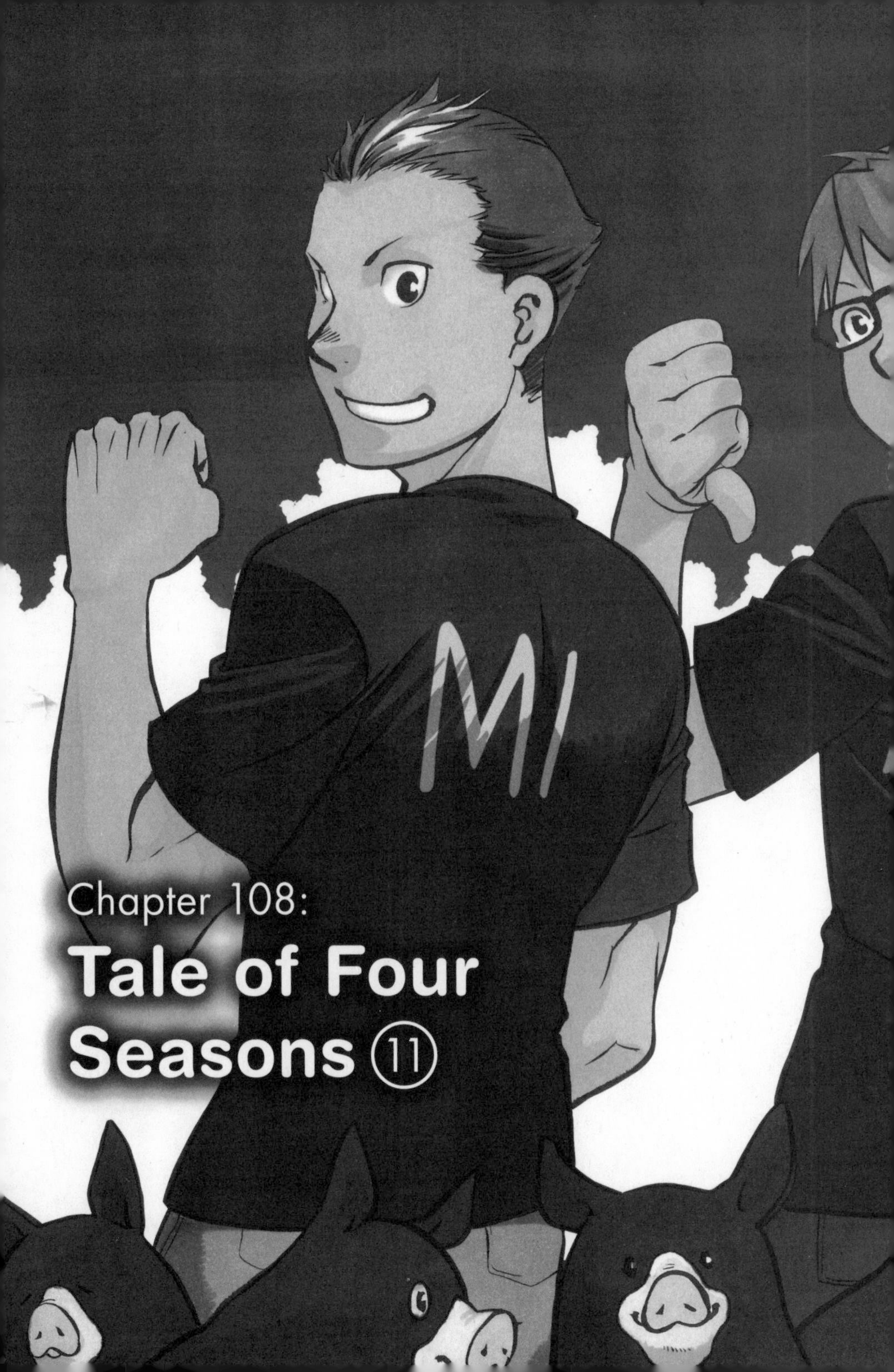
MI

BROTHERS?

MOMOTAROU
THOROUGHBRED

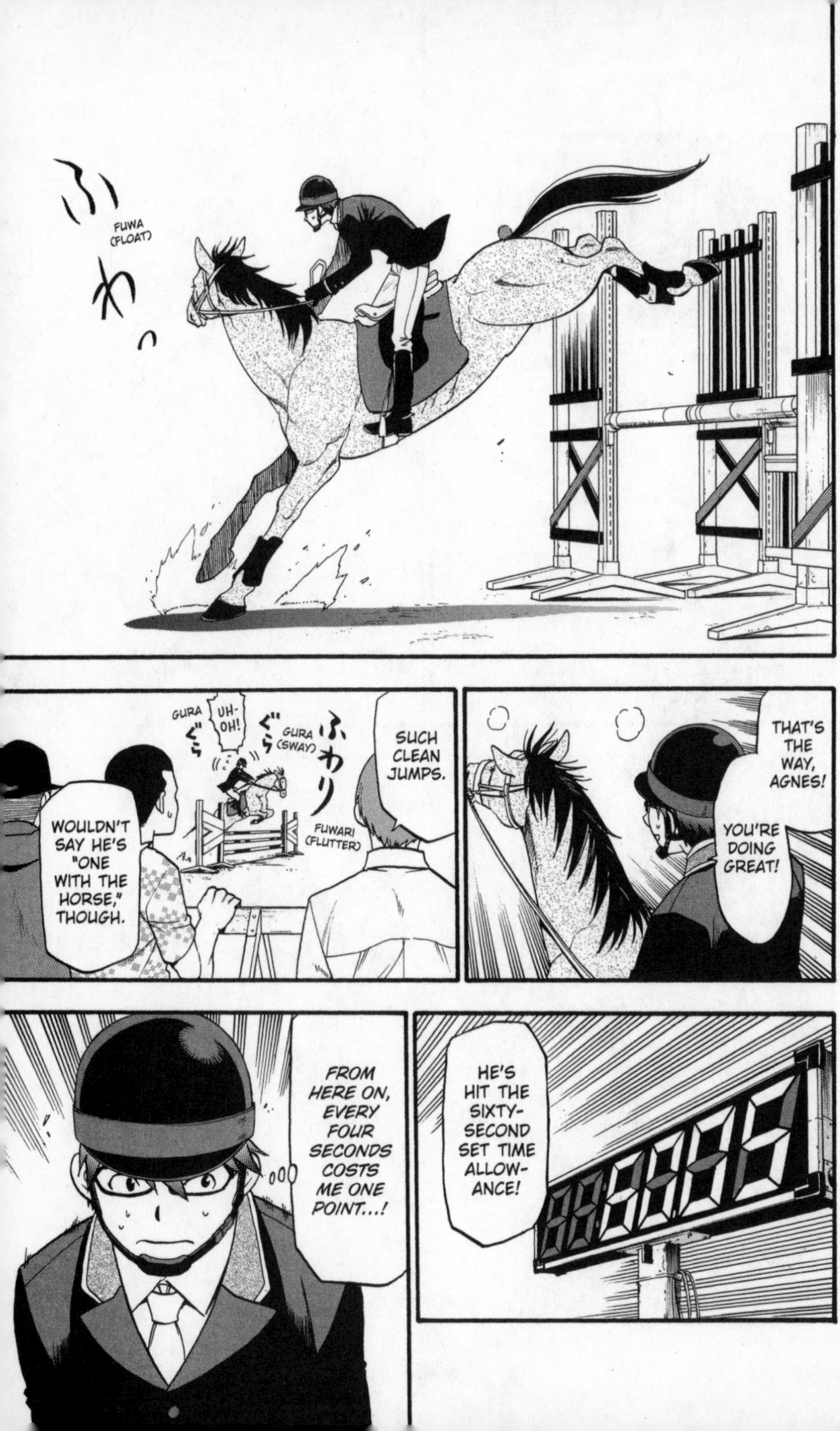
ふわっ
FUWA (FLOAT)
THAT'S THE WAY, AGNES!
YOU'RE DOING GREAT!
SUCH CLEAN JUMPS.
ふわり
FUWARI (FLUTTER)
ぐら
GURA (SWAY)
UH-OH!
ぐら
GURA
WOULDN'T SAY HE'S "ONE WITH THE HORSE," THOUGH.
HE'S HIT THE SIXTY-SECOND SET TIME ALLOWANCE!
FROM HERE ON, EVERY FOUR SECONDS COSTS ME ONE POINT...!

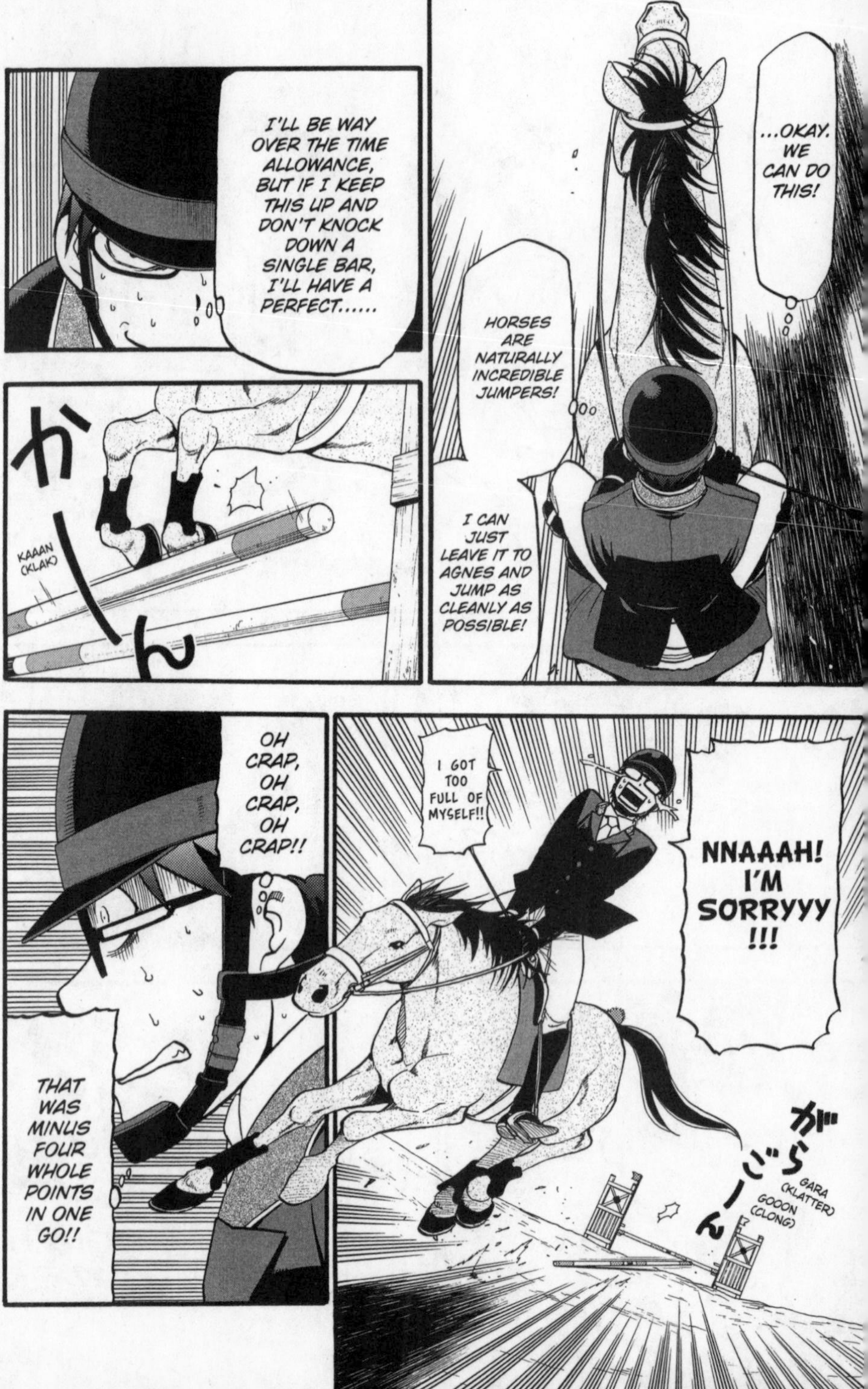
...OKAY. WE CAN DO THIS!
HORSES ARE NATURALLY INCREDIBLE JUMPERS!
I CAN JUST LEAVE IT TO AGNES AND JUMP AS CLEANLY AS POSSIBLE!
I'LL BE WAY OVER THE TIME ALLOWANCE, BUT IF I KEEP THIS UP AND DON'T KNOCK DOWN A SINGLE BAR, I'LL HAVE A PERFECT......
かーん
KAAAN (KLAK)
NNAAAH! I'M SORRYYY!!!
I GOT TOO FULL OF MYSELF!!
がらごーん
GARA (KLATTER) GOOON (CLONG)
OH CRAP, OH CRAP, OH CRAP!!
THAT WAS MINUS FOUR WHOLE POINTS IN ONE GO!!

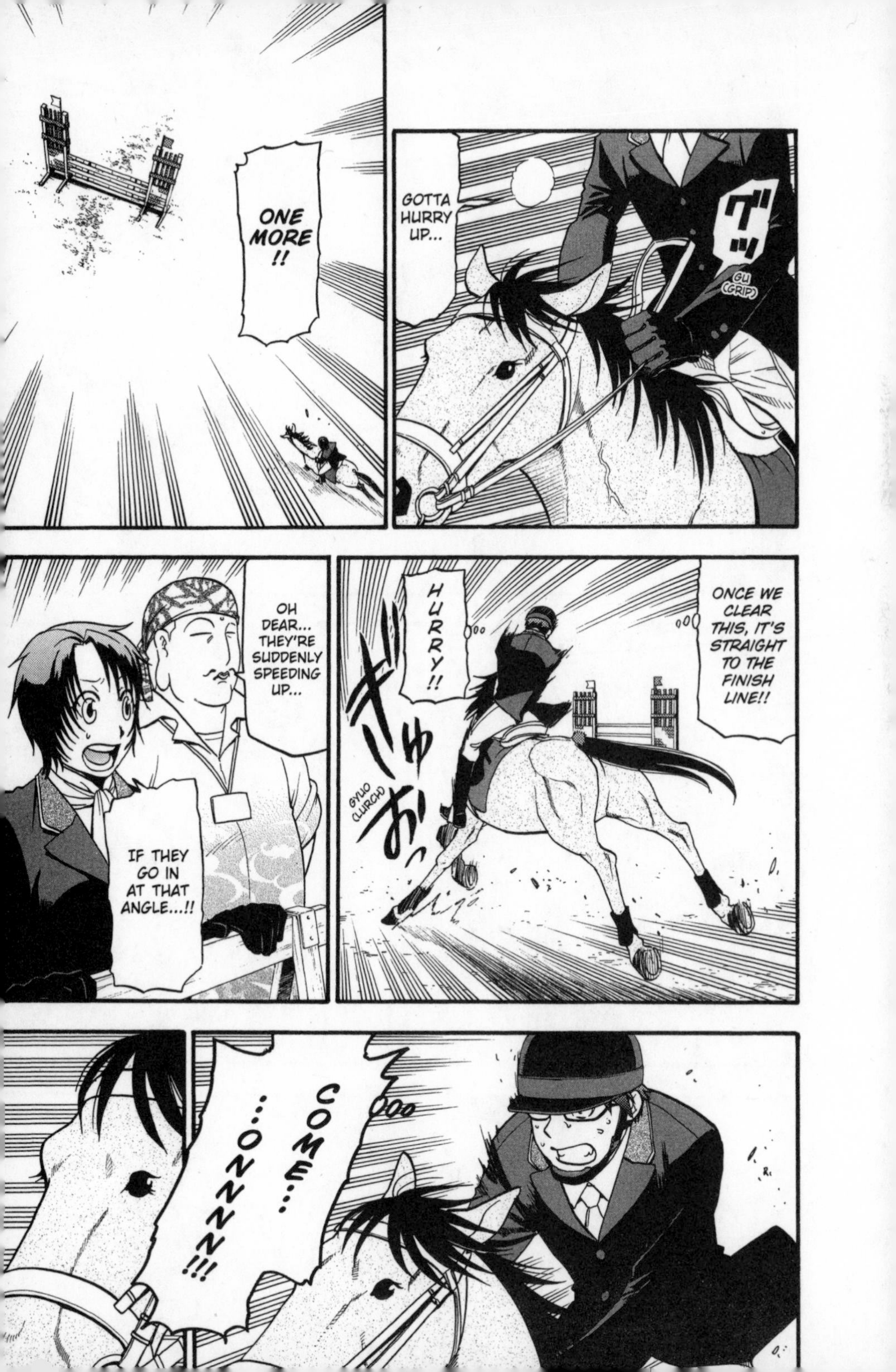
GOTTA HURRY UP...
グッ
GU (GRIP)
ONE MORE !!
ONCE WE CLEAR THIS, IT'S STRAIGHT TO THE FINISH LINE!!
HURRY!!
ぎゅおっ
GYUO (LURCH)
OH DEAR... THEY'RE SUDDENLY SPEEDING UP...
IF THEY GO IN AT THAT ANGLE...!!
COME... ...ONNNN!!!

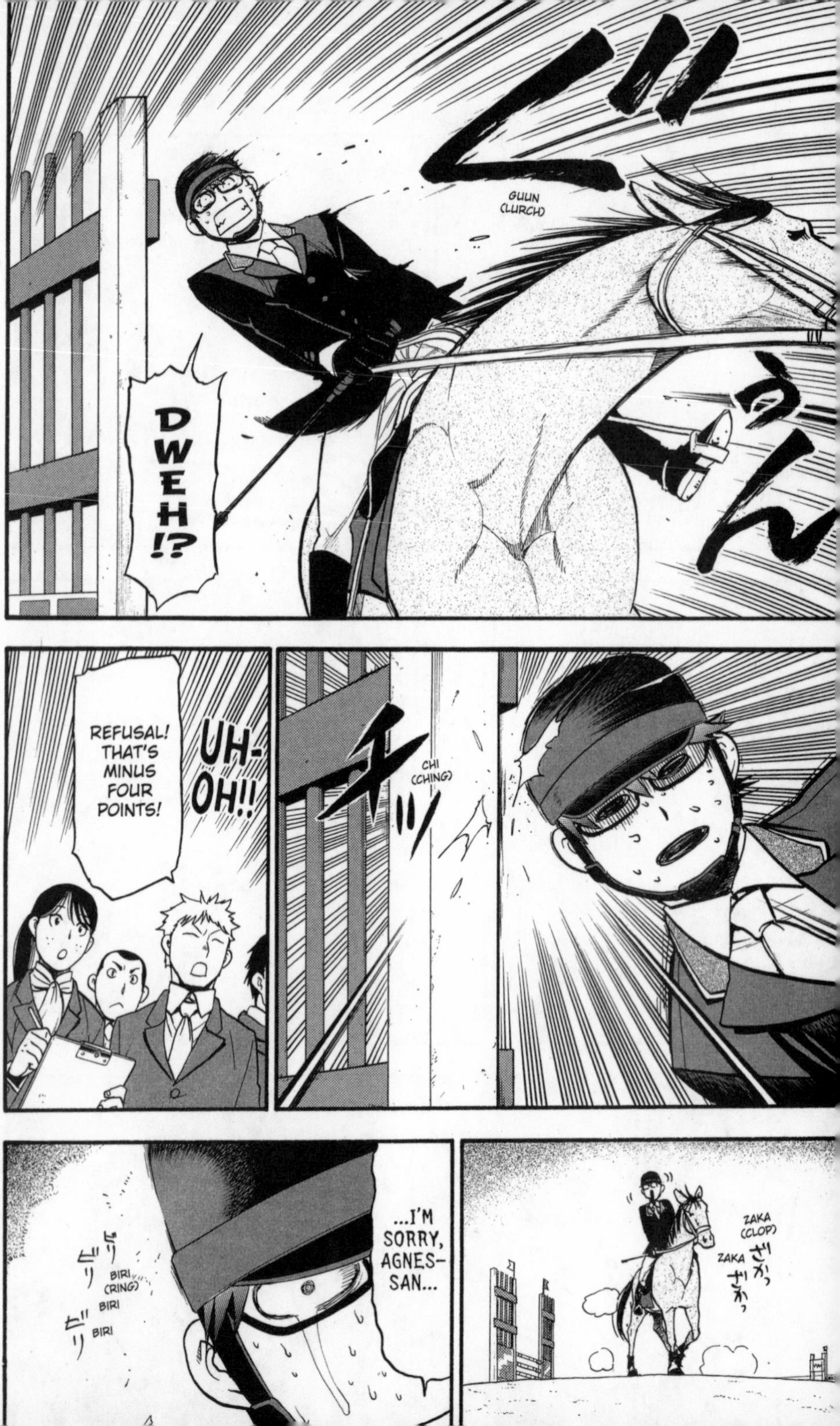

GUUN (LURCH)
DWEH!?
CHI (CHING)
チッ
UH-OH!!
REFUSAL! THAT'S MINUS FOUR POINTS!
ZAKA (CLOP) ZAKA
ざかっ ざかっ
...I'M SORRY, AGNES-SAN...
ビリ ビリ
BIRI (RING) BIRI BIRI

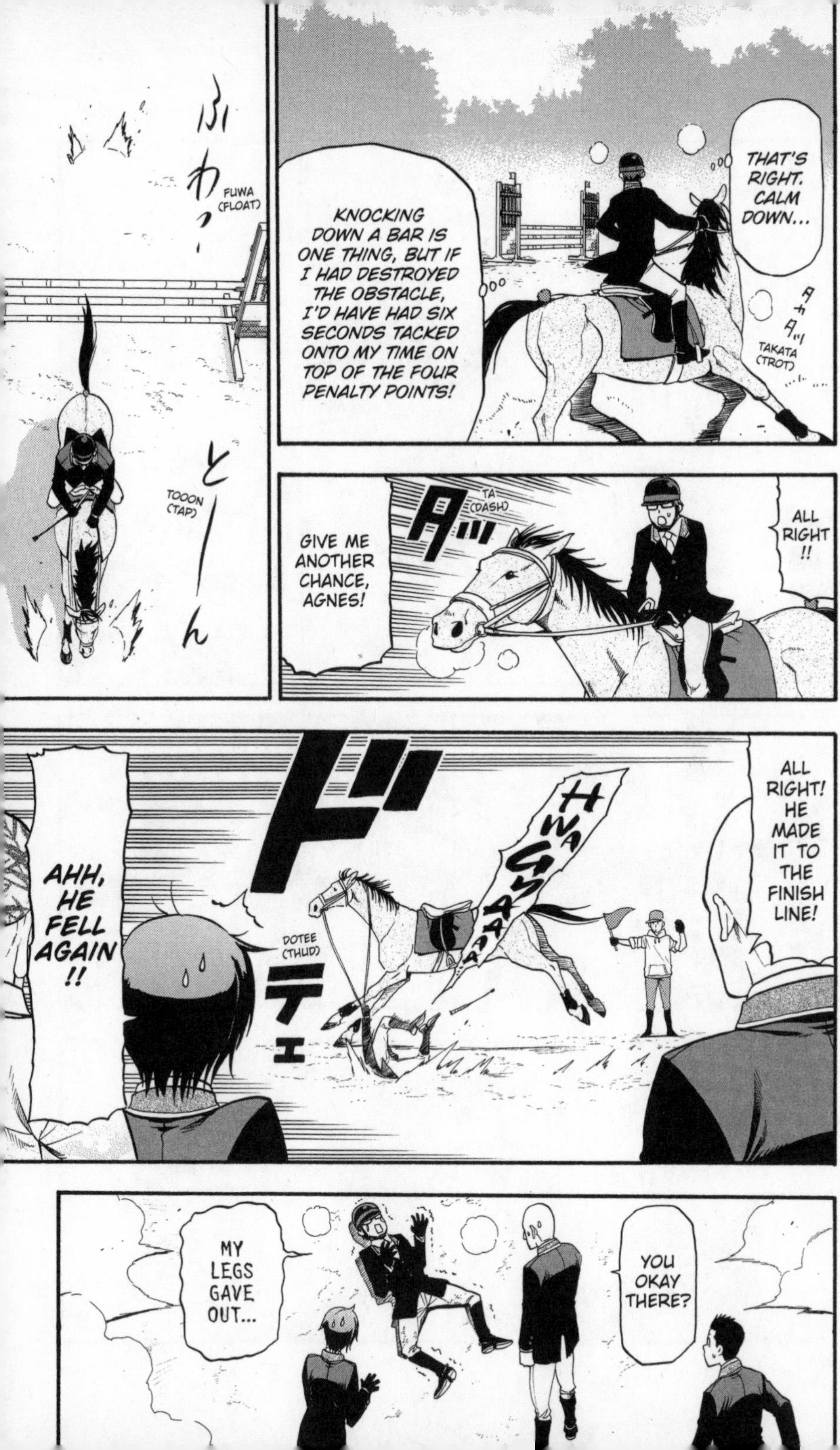
THAT'S RIGHT. CALM DOWN...
KNOCKING DOWN A BAR IS ONE THING, BUT IF I HAD DESTROYED THE OBSTACLE, I'D HAVE HAD SIX SECONDS TACKED ONTO MY TIME ON TOP OF THE FOUR PENALTY POINTS!
TAKATA (TROT)
ALL RIGHT!!
GIVE ME ANOTHER CHANCE, AGNES!
TA (DASH)
FUWA (FLOAT)
TOOON (TAP)
ALL RIGHT! HE MADE IT TO THE FINISH LINE!
HWAGYAAAA
DOTEE (THUD)
AHH, HE FELL AGAIN!!
YOU OKAY THERE?
MY LEGS GAVE OUT...

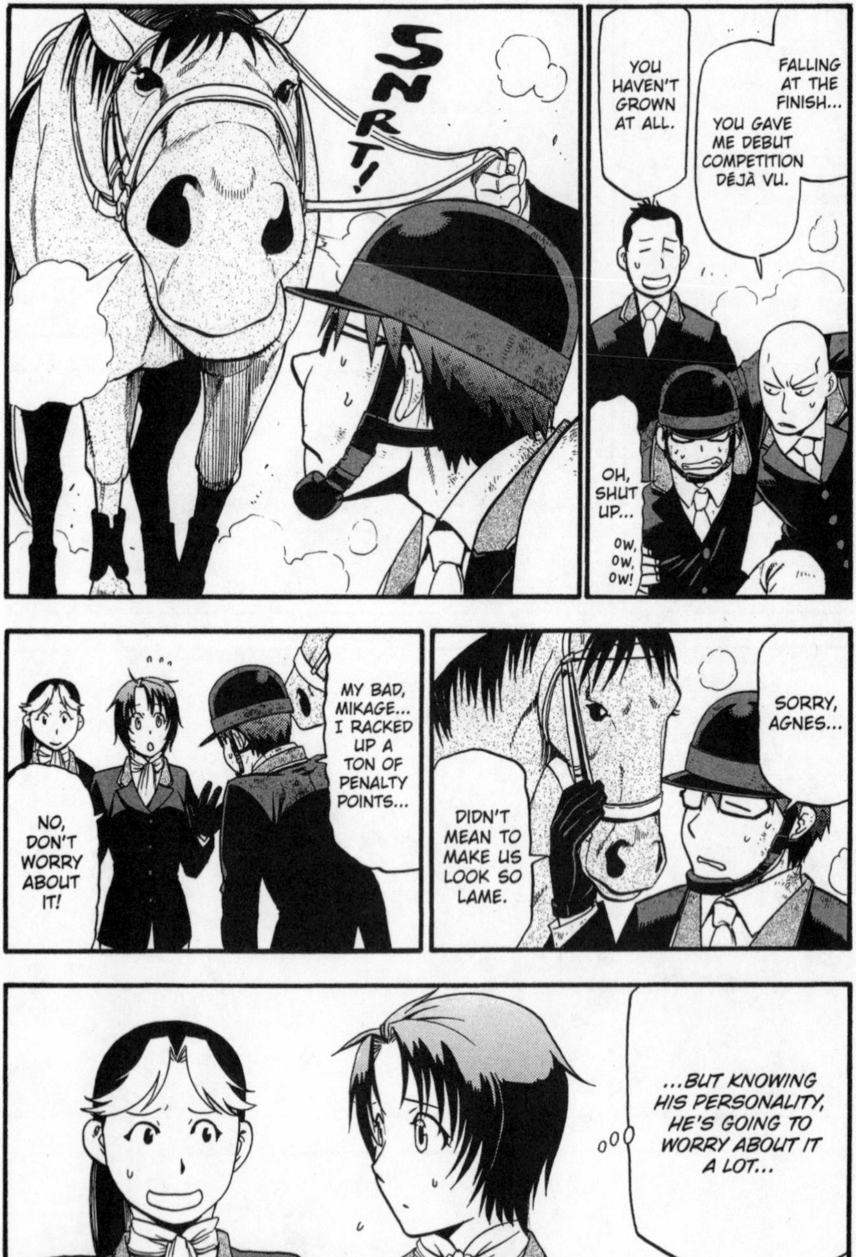
FALLING AT THE FINISH... YOU GAVE ME DEBUT COMPETITION DÉJÀ VU.
YOU HAVEN'T GROWN AT ALL.
OH, SHUT UP...
OW, OW, OW!
SNRT!
SORRY, AGNES...
DIDN'T MEAN TO MAKE US LOOK SO LAME.
MY BAD, MIKAGE... I RACKED UP A TON OF PENALTY POINTS...
NO, DON'T WORRY ABOUT IT!
...BUT KNOWING HIS PERSONALITY, HE'S GOING TO WORRY ABOUT IT A LOT...

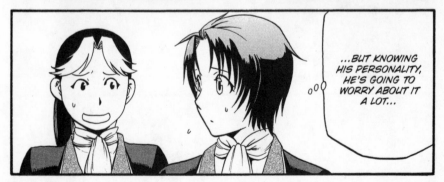

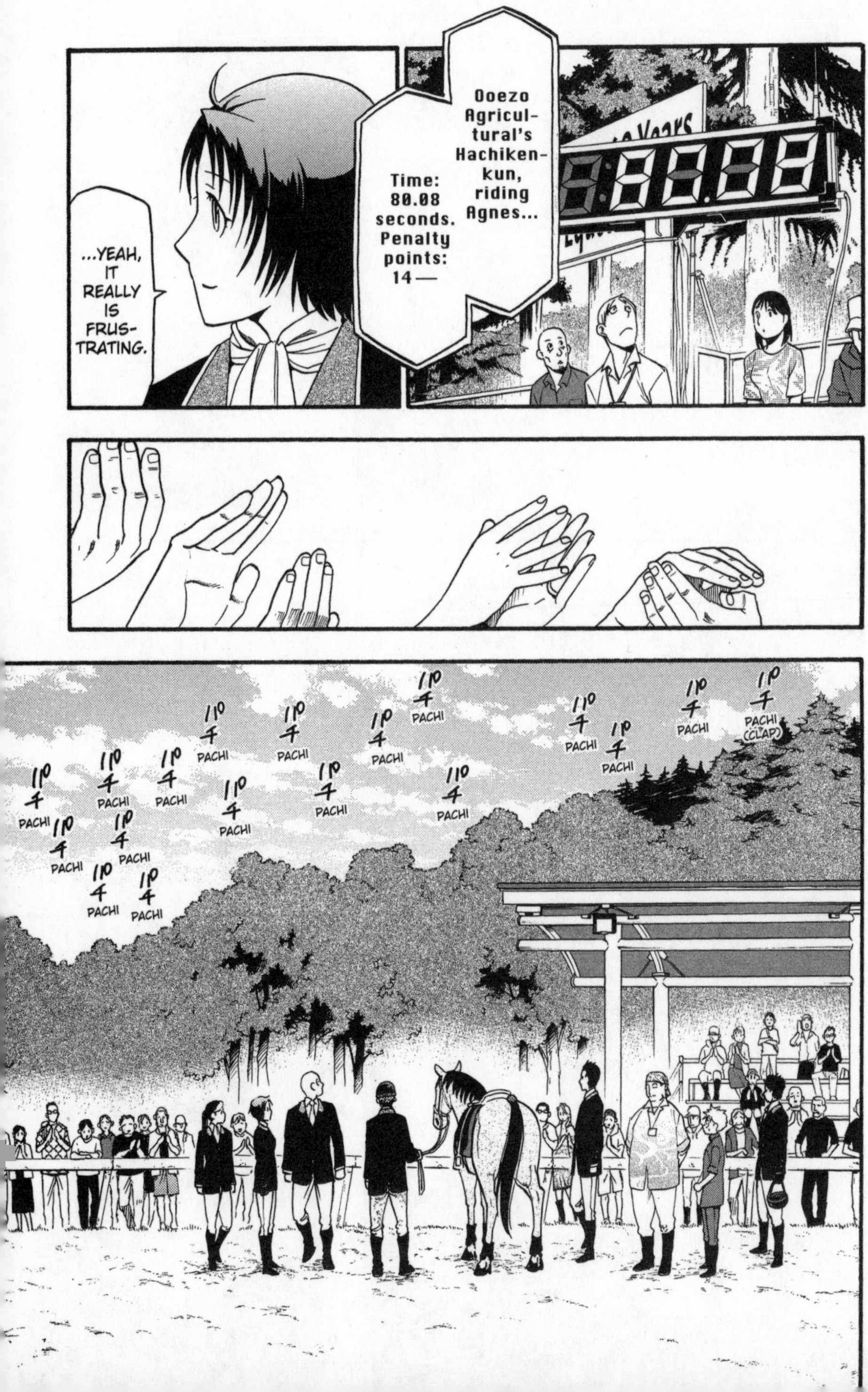
Ooezo Agricultural's Hachiken-kun, riding Agnes...
Time: 80.08 seconds. Penalty points: 14—
...YEAH, IT REALLY IS FRUSTRATING.
PACHI (CLAP)
PACHI
PACHI
PACHI
PACHI
PACHI
PACHI
PACHI
PACHI
PACHI
PACHI
PACHI
PACHI
PACHI
PACHI
PACHI
PACHI
PACHI
PACHI

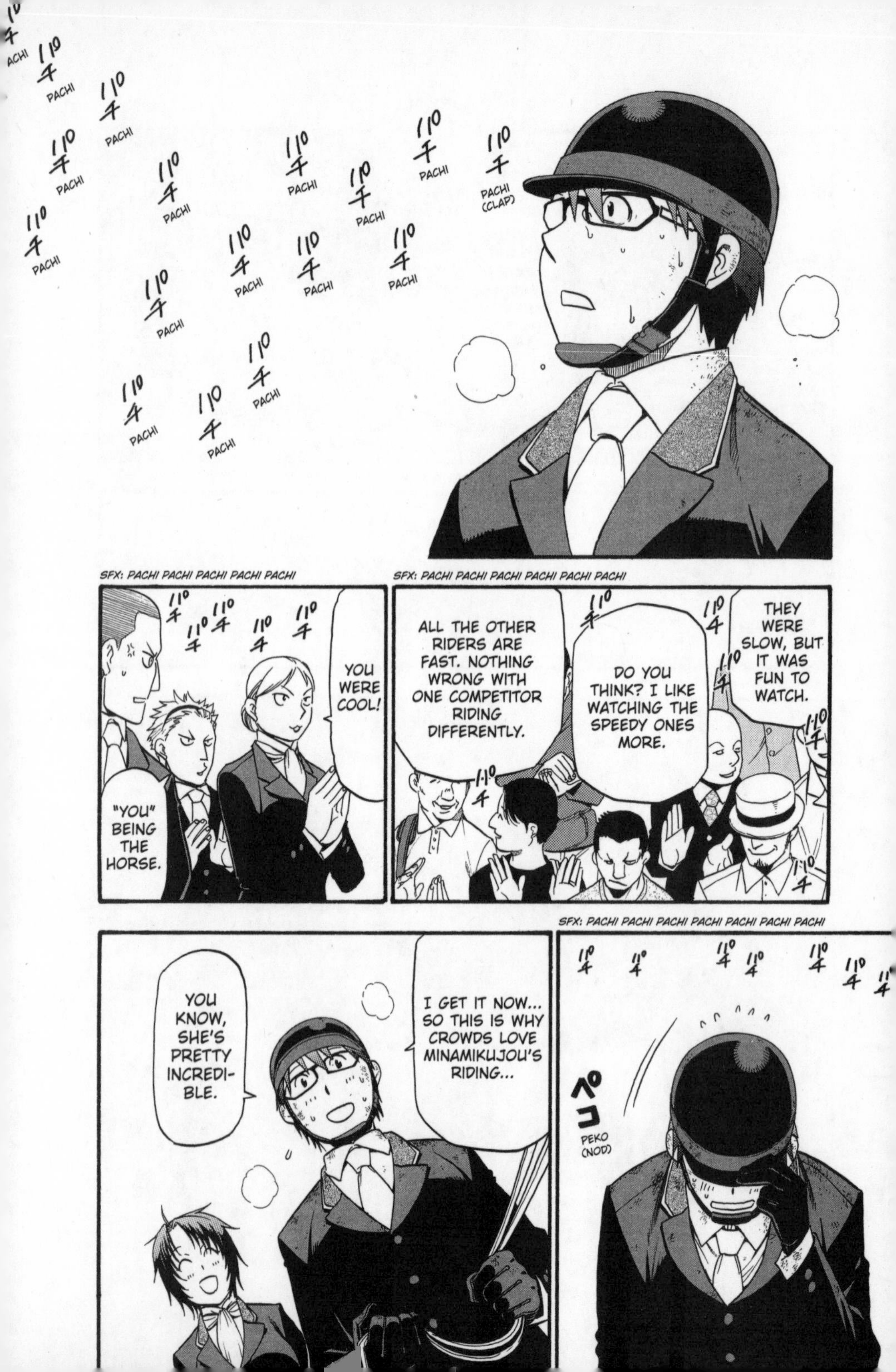
PACHI
PACHI (CLAP)
SFX: PACHI PACHI PACHI PACHI PACHI PACHI
THEY WERE SLOW, BUT IT WAS FUN TO WATCH.
DO YOU THINK? I LIKE WATCHING THE SPEEDY ONES MORE.
ALL THE OTHER RIDERS ARE FAST. NOTHING WRONG WITH ONE COMPETITOR RIDING DIFFERENTLY.
SFX: PACHI PACHI PACHI PACHI PACHI
YOU WERE COOL!
"YOU" BEING THE HORSE.
SFX: PACHI PACHI PACHI PACHI PACHI PACHI PACHI
PEKO (NOD)
I GET IT NOW... SO THIS IS WHY CROWDS LOVE MINAMIKUJOU'S RIDING...
YOU KNOW, SHE'S PRETTY INCREDIBLE.

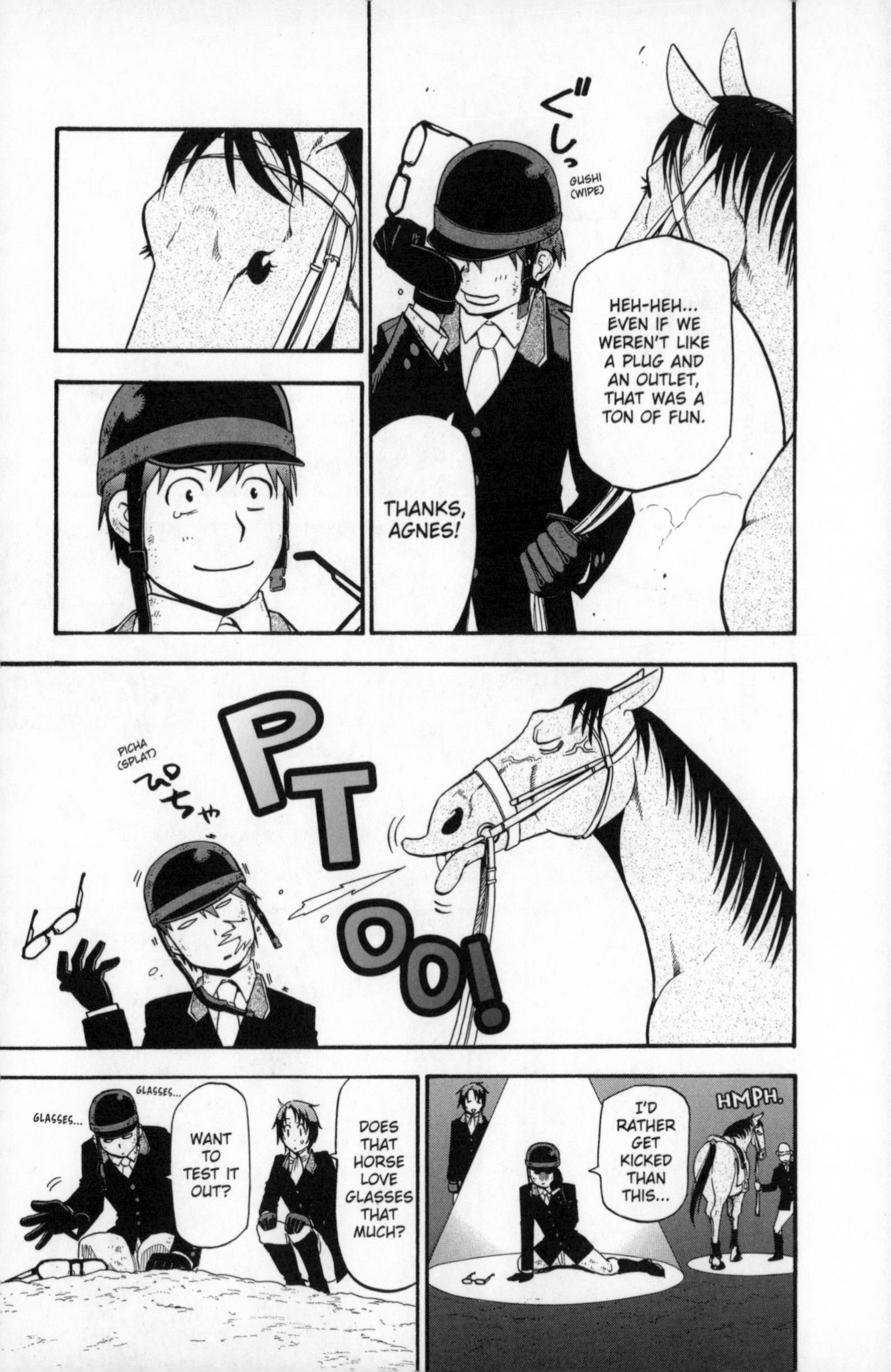
ぐしっ
GUSHI (WIPE)
HEH-HEH... EVEN IF WE WEREN'T LIKE A PLUG AND AN OUTLET, THAT WAS A TON OF FUN.
THANKS, AGNES!
PICHA (SPLAT)
ぴちゃ
PTOO!
HMPH.
I'D RATHER GET KICKED THAN THIS...
DOES THAT HORSE LOVE GLASSES THAT MUCH?
GLASSES...
WANT TO TEST IT OUT?
GLASSES...

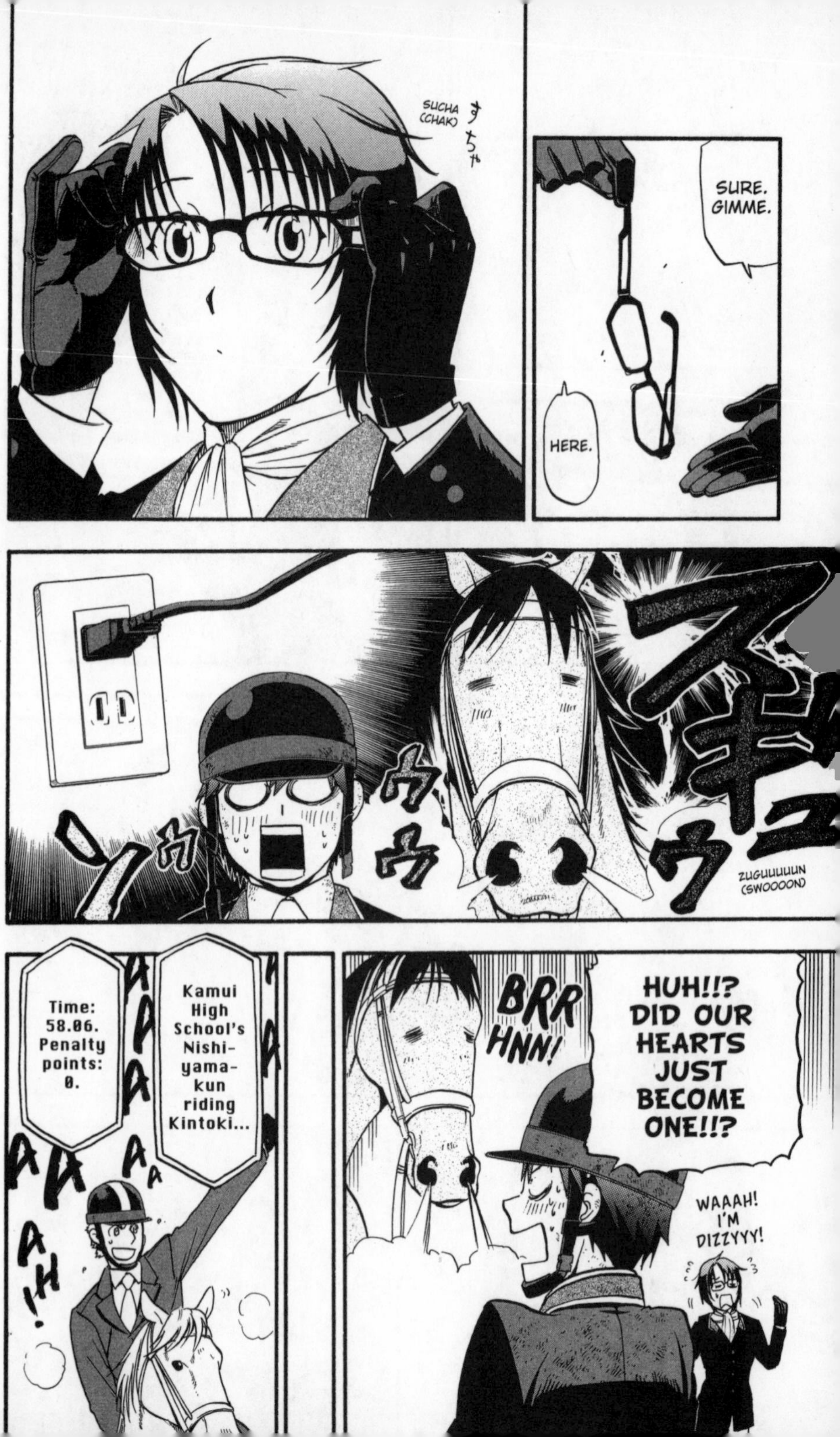
SURE. GIMME.
HERE.
SUCHA (CHAK)
すちゃ
ZUGUUUUUN (SWOOOON)
HUH!!? DID OUR HEARTS JUST BECOME ONE!!?
BRR HNN!
WAAAH! I'M DIZZYYY!
Kamui High School's Nishi-yama-kun riding Kintoki...
Time: 58.06. Penalty points: 0.
AAAAAAAH!

TSK!
TSK!
TSK!

WE AND KAMUI ARE TIED AT 22 PENALTY POINTS RIGHT NOW...

...SO IF AKI GETS DOCKED EVEN ONE POINT, WE LOSE!

UHHH, URAKAWA CENTRAL CLINCHED FIRST PLACE!

HOW ARE THE STANDINGS!?

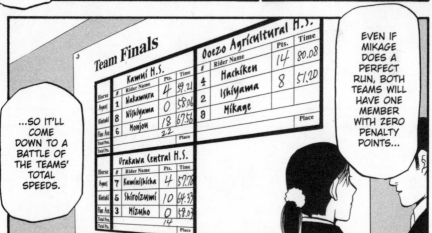

...SO IT'LL COME DOWN TO A BATTLE OF THE TEAMS' TOTAL SPEEDS.

EVEN IF MIKAGE DOES A PERFECT RUN, BOTH TEAMS WILL HAVE ONE MEMBER WITH ZERO PENALTY POINTS...

Team Finals

Kamui H.S.

Horse	#	Rider Name	Pts.	Time
Agnes	1	Nakamura	4	59.24
Kintoki	8	Nishiyama	0	58.06
Fine An	6	Monjou	18	67.56
Total Pos.			22	
Total Pts.				Place

Oozzo Agricultural H.S.

Horse	#	Rider Name	Pts.	Time
	4	Hachiken	14	80.08
	2	Ishiyama	8	51.20
	9	Mikage		
				Place

Urakawa Central H.S.

Horse	#	Rider Name	Pts.	Time
Agnes	7	Kaminishikka	4	57.78
Kintoki	5	Shiroizumi	10	64.33
Fine An	3	Mizuho	0	58.09
Total Pos.			14	
Total Pts.				Place

IT'LL BE TIGHT...

FOR EZO AG TO WIN, SHE'LL HAVE TO FINISH WITHIN 53.54 SECONDS.

ADDING THEM UP...

FOR REAL?

KACHI CLICK KACHI

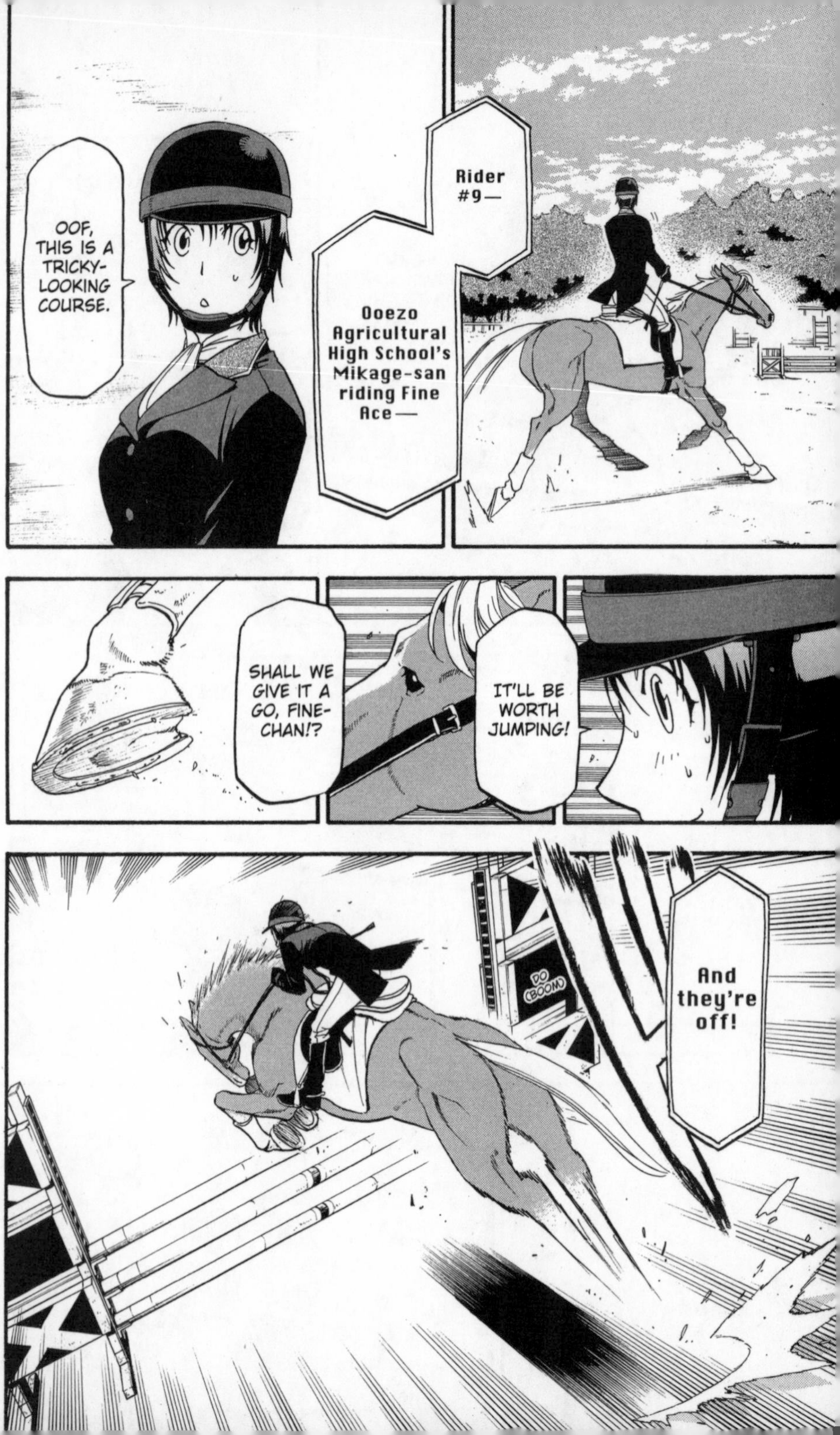
Rider #9—
Ooezo Agricultural High School's Mikage-san riding Fine Ace—
OOF, THIS IS A TRICKY-LOOKING COURSE.
IT'LL BE WORTH JUMPING!
SHALL WE GIVE IT A GO, FINE-CHAN!?
And they're off!
DO (BOOM)

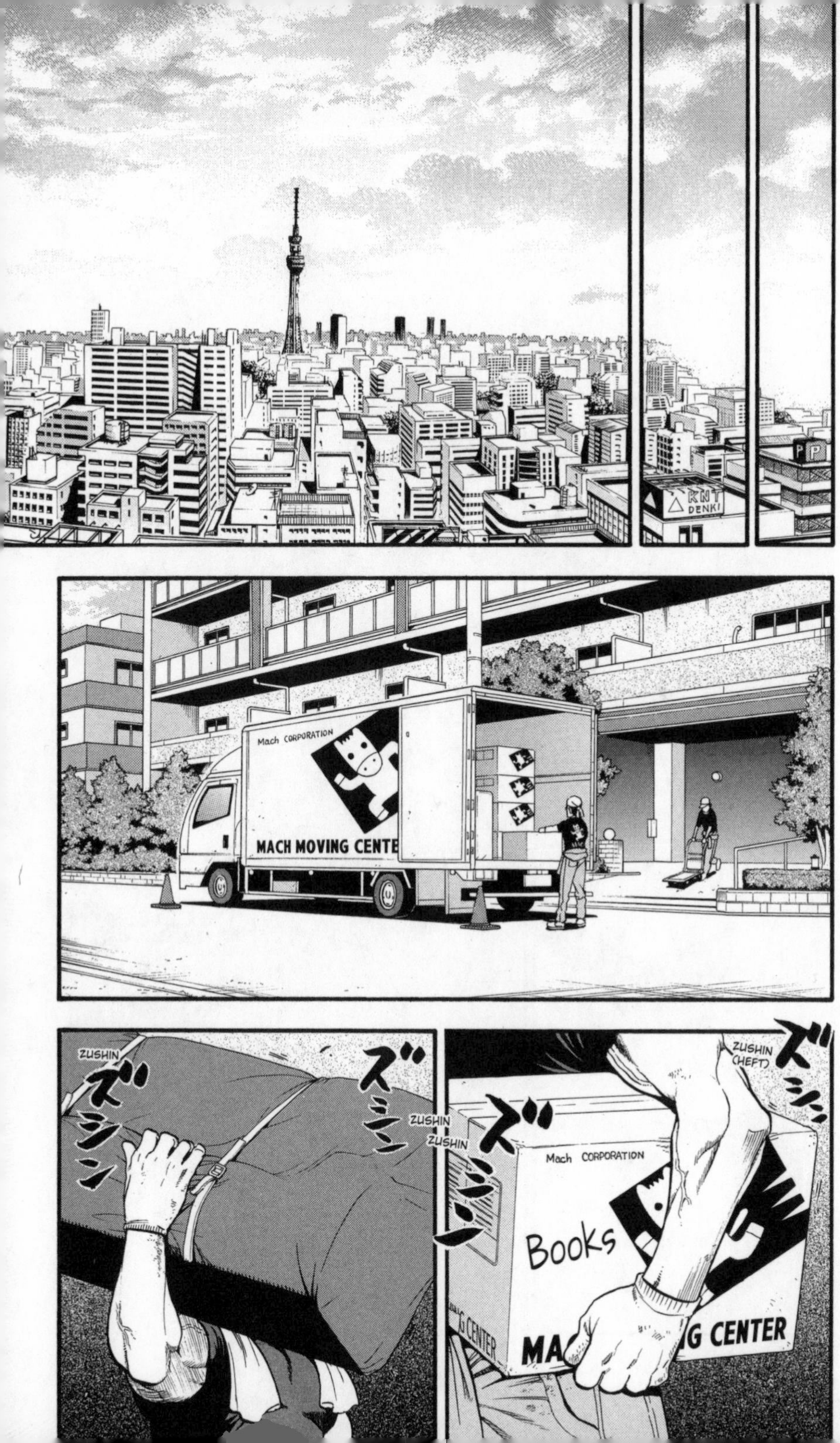

KNT
DENKI
Mach CORPORATION
MACH MOVING CENTE
ZUSHIN (HEFT)
ズシン
ZUSHIN
ZUSHIN
ズシン
Mach CORPORATION
Books
G CENTER
MAC G CENTER
ZUSHIN
ズシン
ズシン

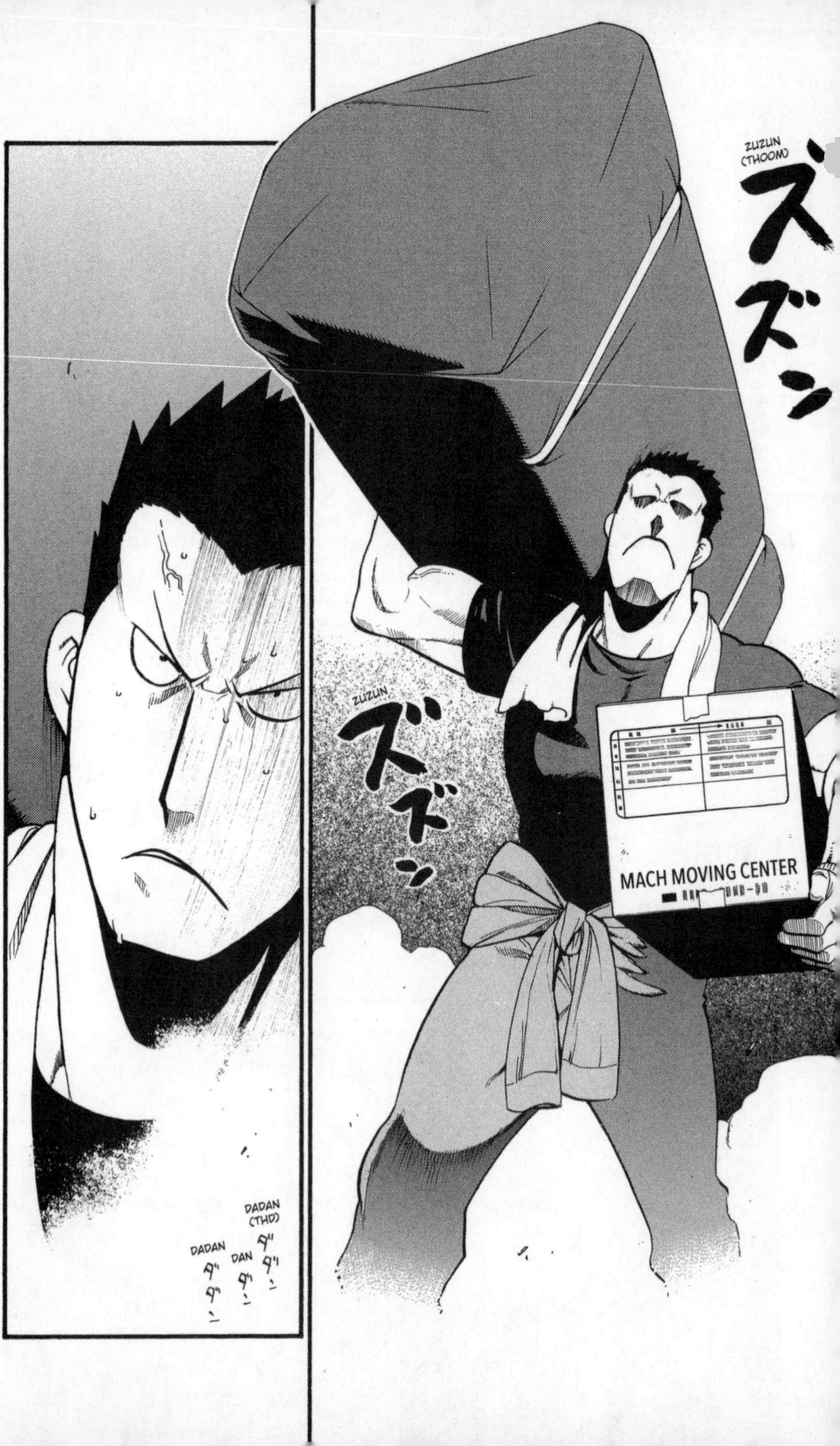
ZUZUN (THOOM)
ズズン
ZUZUN
ズズン
MACH MOVING CENTER
DADAN (THD)
ダダン
DAN
ダン
DADAN
ダダン

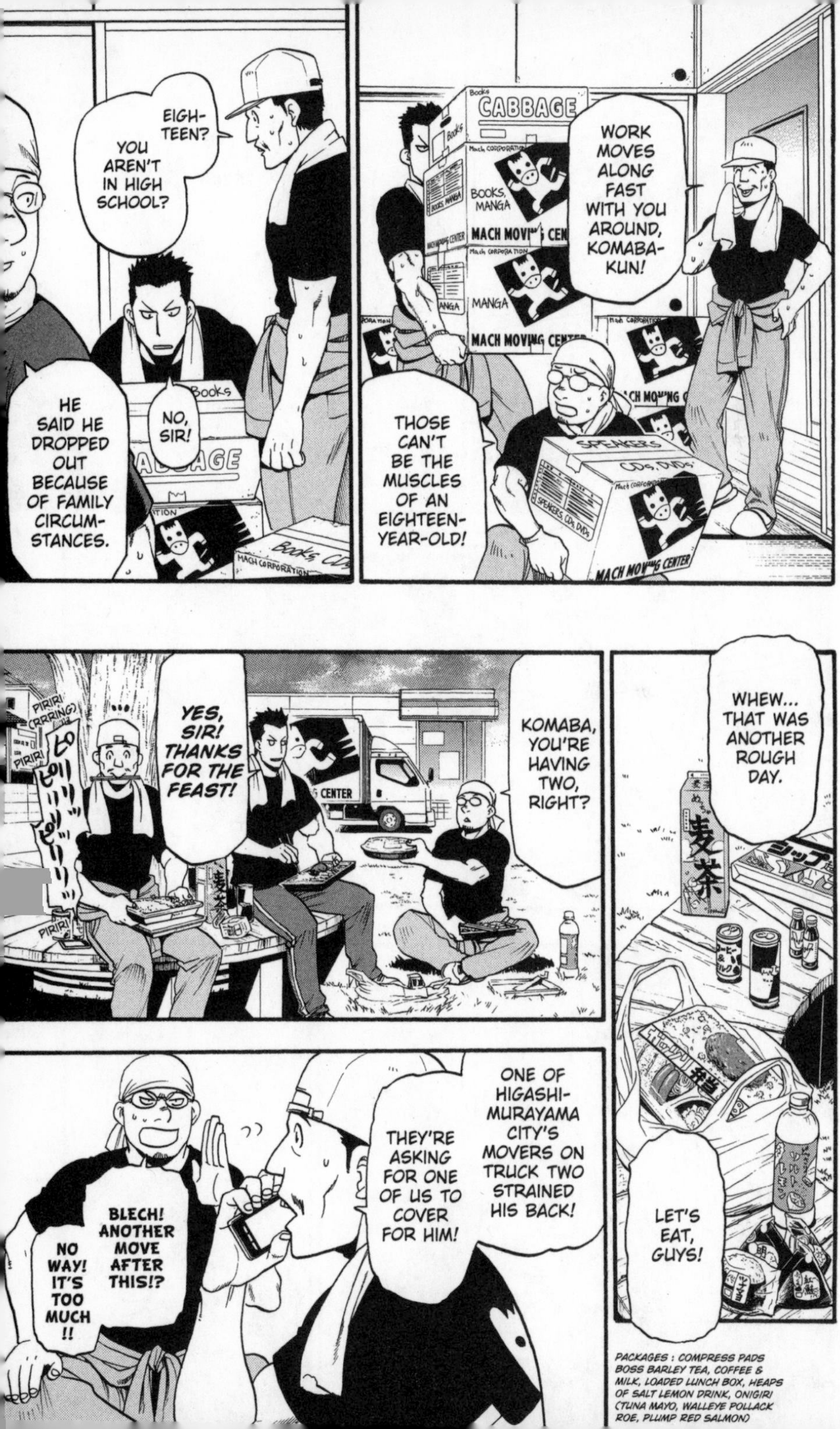
WORK MOVES ALONG FAST WITH YOU AROUND, KOMABA-KUN!
THOSE CAN'T BE THE MUSCLES OF AN EIGHTEEN-YEAR-OLD!
EIGH-TEEN?
YOU AREN'T IN HIGH SCHOOL?
NO, SIR!
HE SAID HE DROPPED OUT BECAUSE OF FAMILY CIRCUM-STANCES.
WHEW... THAT WAS ANOTHER ROUGH DAY.
LET'S EAT, GUYS!
PACKAGES : COMPRESS PADS BOSS BARLEY TEA, COFFEE & MILK, LOADED LUNCH BOX, HEAPS OF SALT LEMON DRINK, ONIGIRI (TUNA MAYO, WALLEYE POLLACK ROE, PLUMP RED SALMON)
KOMABA, YOU'RE HAVING TWO, RIGHT?
YES, SIR! THANKS FOR THE FEAST!
PIRIRI (CRRRING)
PIRIRI
PIRIRI
ONE OF HIGASHI-MURAYAMA CITY'S MOVERS ON TRUCK TWO STRAINED HIS BACK!
THEY'RE ASKING FOR ONE OF US TO COVER FOR HIM!
BLECH! ANOTHER MOVE AFTER THIS!?
NO WAY! IT'S TOO MUCH!!

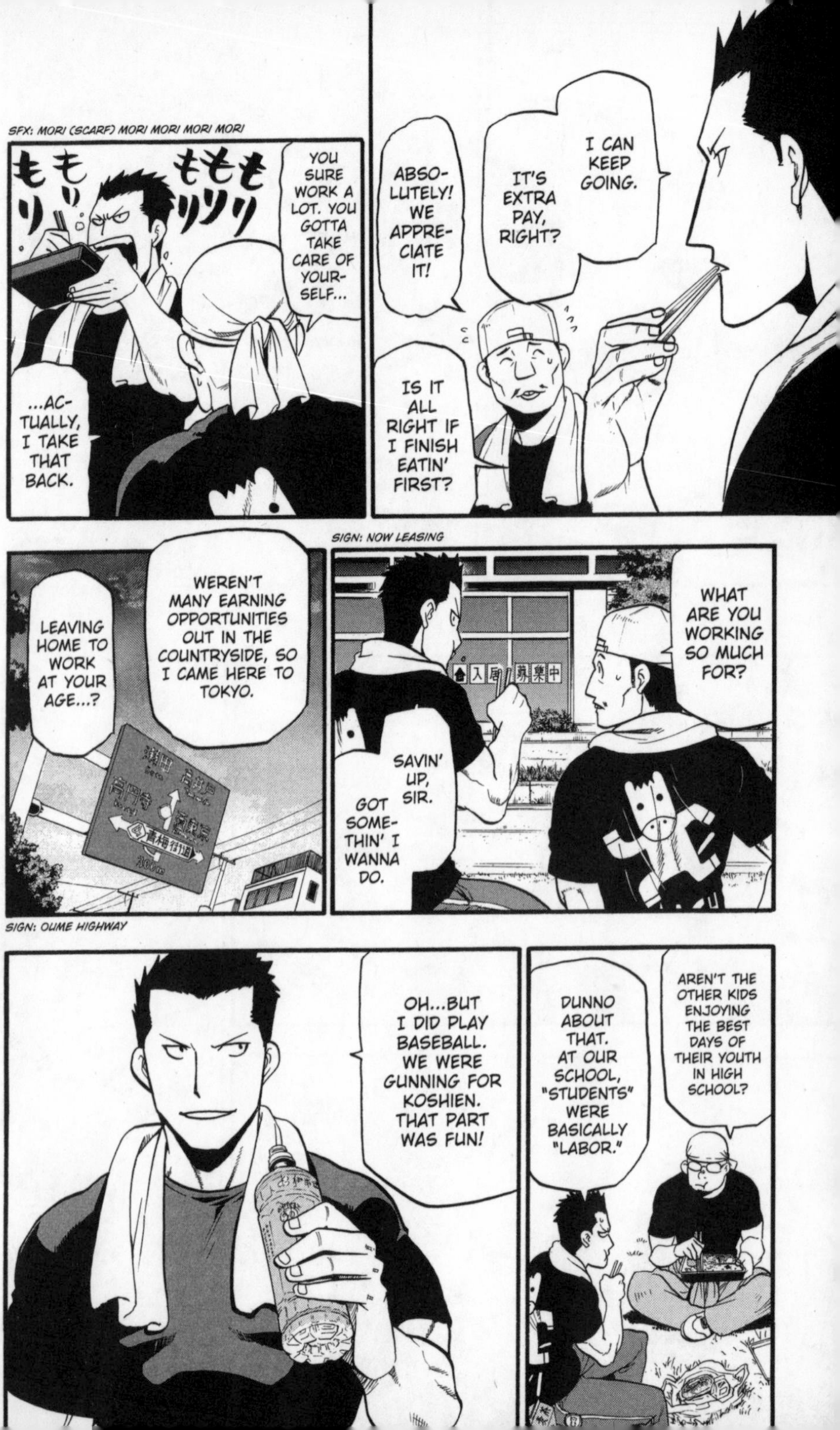
I CAN KEEP GOING.
IT'S EXTRA PAY, RIGHT?
ABSOLUTELY! WE APPRECIATE IT!
IS IT ALL RIGHT IF I FINISH EATIN' FIRST?
SFX: MORI (SCARF) MORI MORI MORI MORI
もりもももリツツリ
YOU SURE WORK A LOT. YOU GOTTA TAKE CARE OF YOURSELF...
...ACTUALLY, I TAKE THAT BACK.
SIGN: NOW LEASING
WHAT ARE YOU WORKING SO MUCH FOR?
入居募集中
SAVIN' UP, SIR.
GOT SOMETHIN' I WANNA DO.
WEREN'T MANY EARNING OPPORTUNITIES OUT IN THE COUNTRYSIDE, SO I CAME HERE TO TOKYO.
LEAVING HOME TO WORK AT YOUR AGE...?
SIGN: OUME HIGHWAY
AREN'T THE OTHER KIDS ENJOYING THE BEST DAYS OF THEIR YOUTH IN HIGH SCHOOL?
DUNNO ABOUT THAT. AT OUR SCHOOL, "STUDENTS" WERE BASICALLY "LABOR."
OH...BUT I DID PLAY BASEBALL. WE WERE GUNNING FOR KOSHIEN. THAT PART WAS FUN!

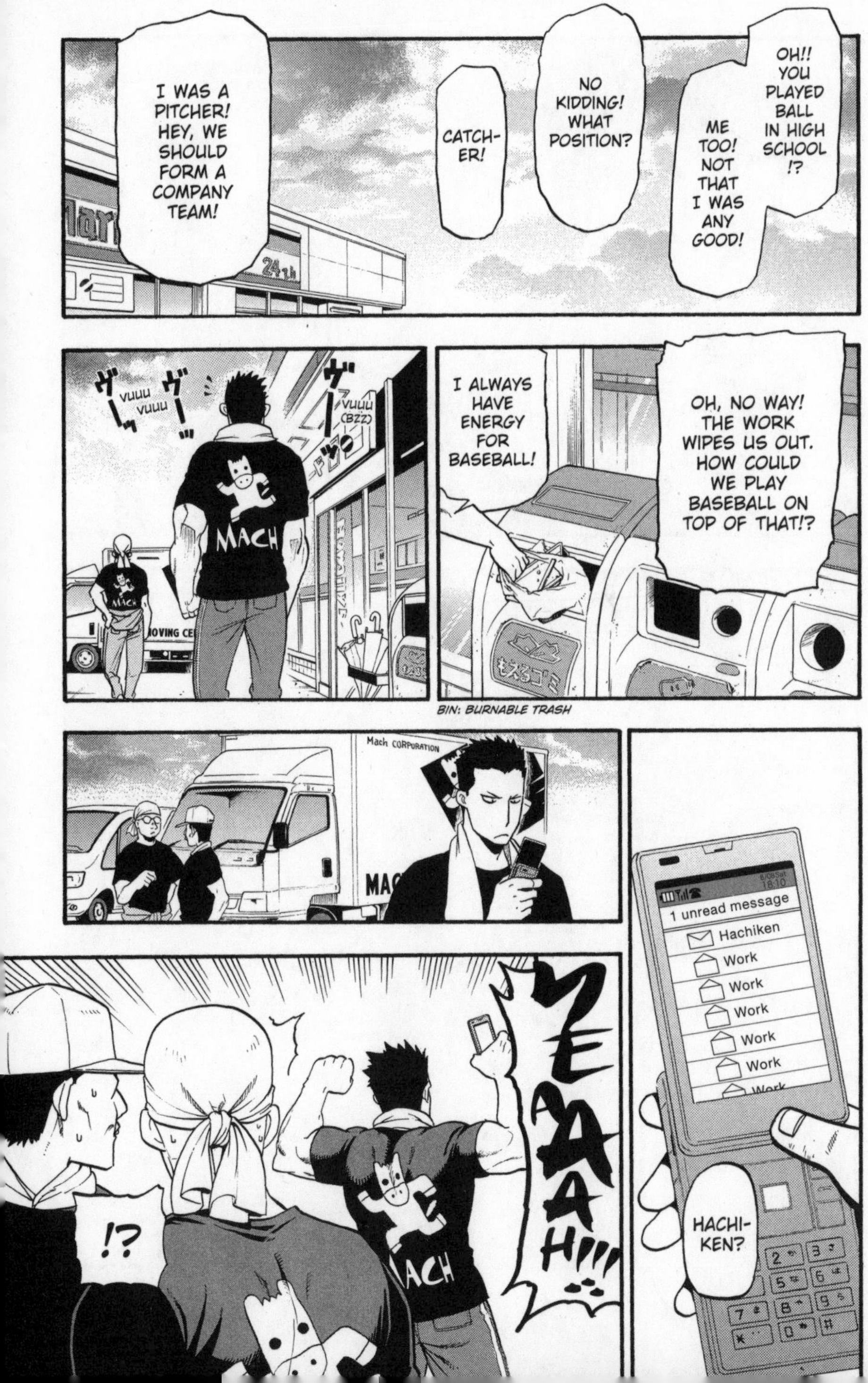
OH!! YOU PLAYED BALL IN HIGH SCHOOL!?
ME TOO! NOT THAT I WAS ANY GOOD!
NO KIDDING! WHAT POSITION?
CATCHER!
I WAS A PITCHER! HEY, WE SHOULD FORM A COMPANY TEAM!
24
OH, NO WAY! THE WORK WIPES US OUT. HOW COULD WE PLAY BASEBALL ON TOP OF THAT!?
I ALWAYS HAVE ENERGY FOR BASEBALL!
VUUU (BZZ)
VUUU VUUU
MACH
BIN: BURNABLE TRASH
1 unread message
Hachiken
Work
Work
Work
Work
Work
HACHI-KEN?
Mach CORPORATION
MEAAAH!!!
!?

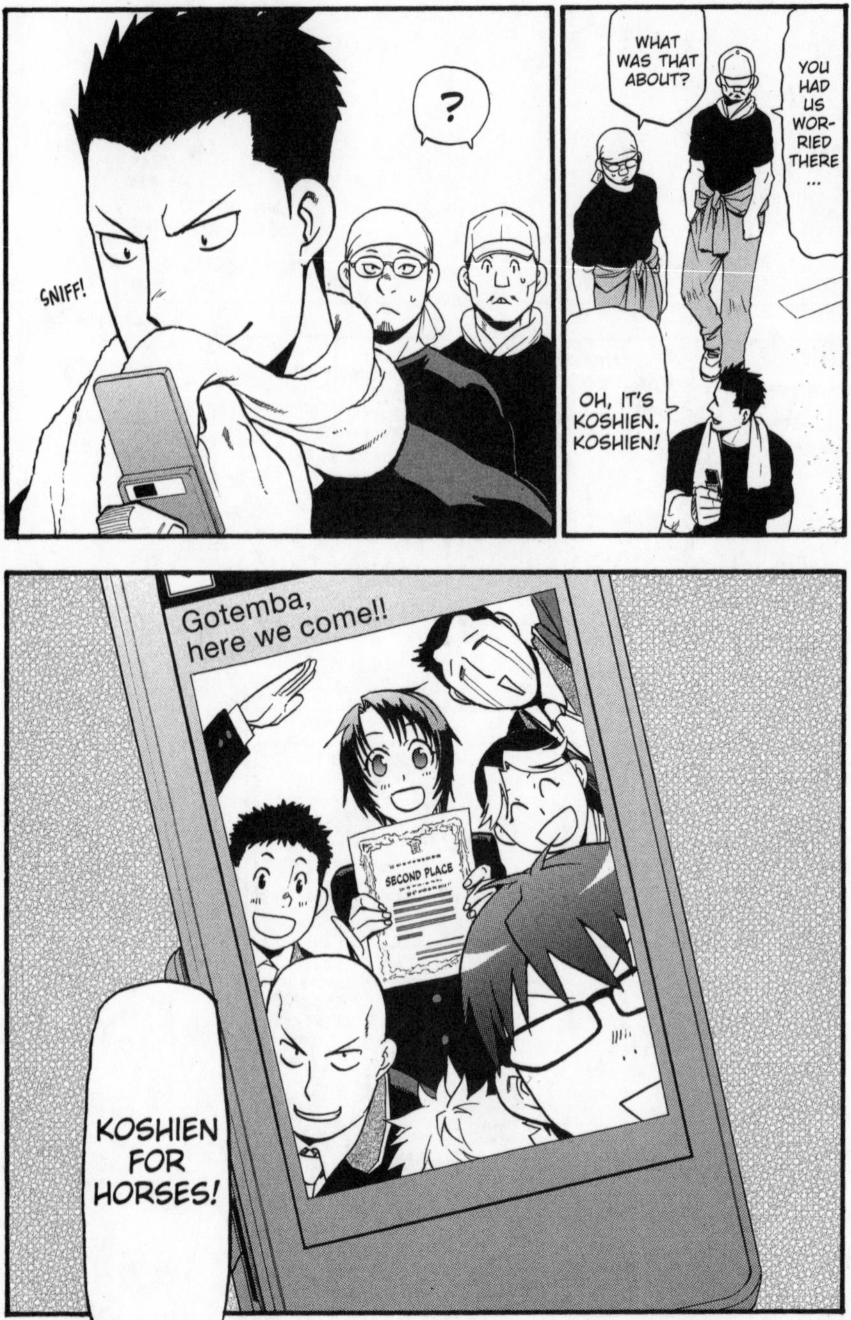
YOU HAD US WORRIED THERE...
WHAT WAS THAT ABOUT?
OH, IT'S KOSHIEN. KOSHIEN!
?
SNIFF!
Gotemba, here we come!!
SECOND PLACE
KOSHIEN FOR HORSES!

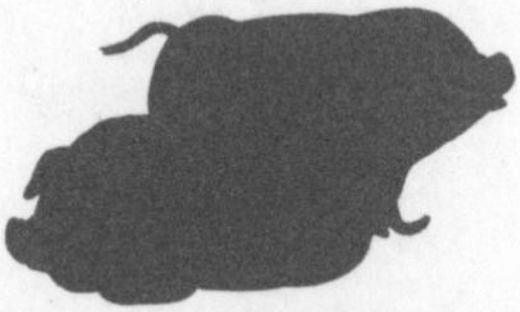

Silver Spoon

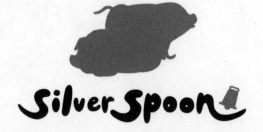

SWOOOOOOOON!♥
THE TARSIER: BIG EYES LIKE GLASSES.
AGNES

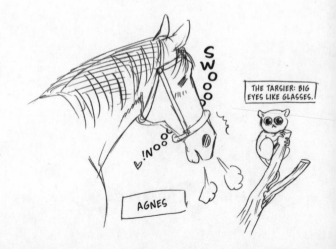

Chapter 109: Tale of Four Seasons ⑫

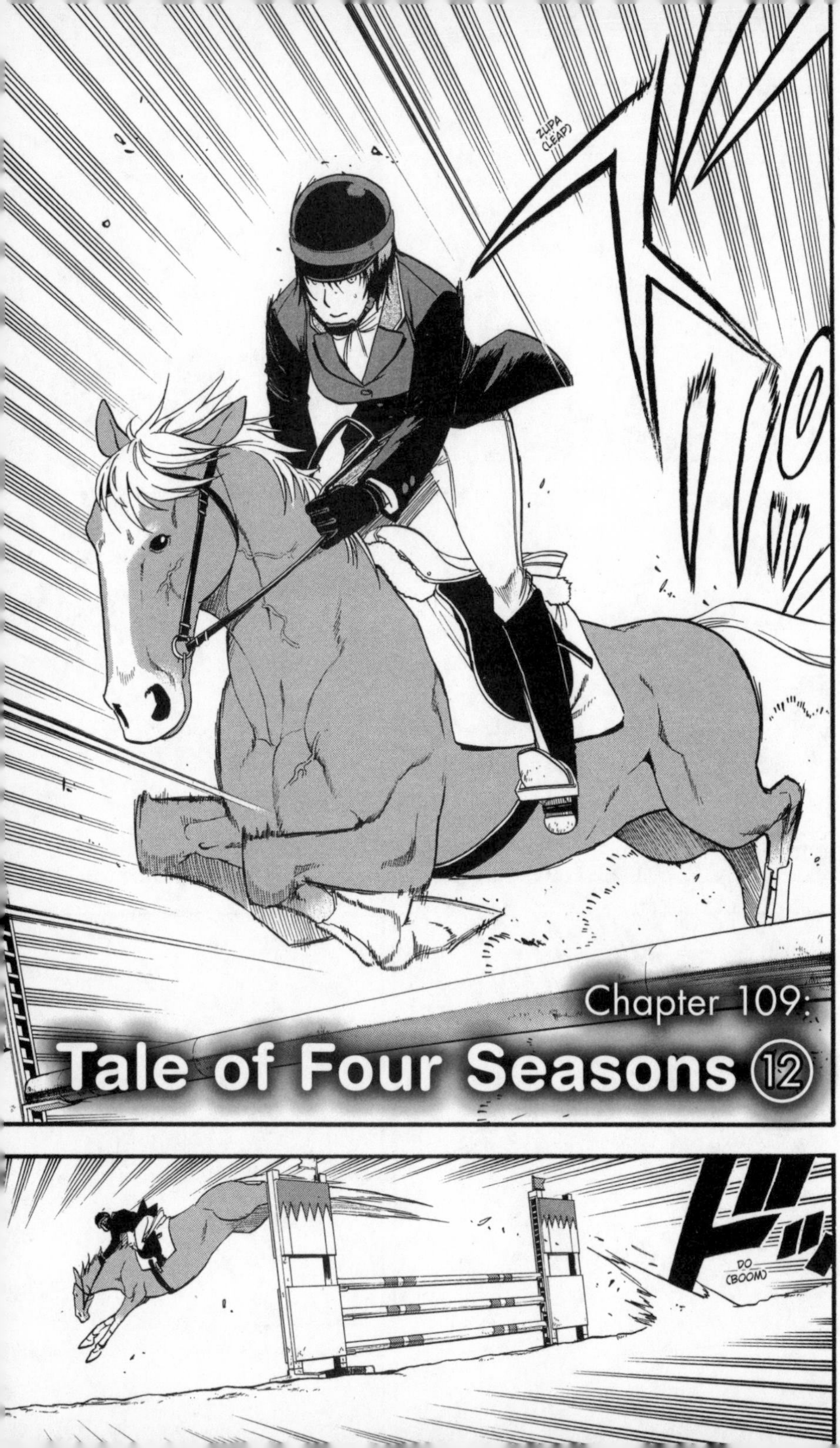
ZUPA
(LEAP)
DO
(BOOM)

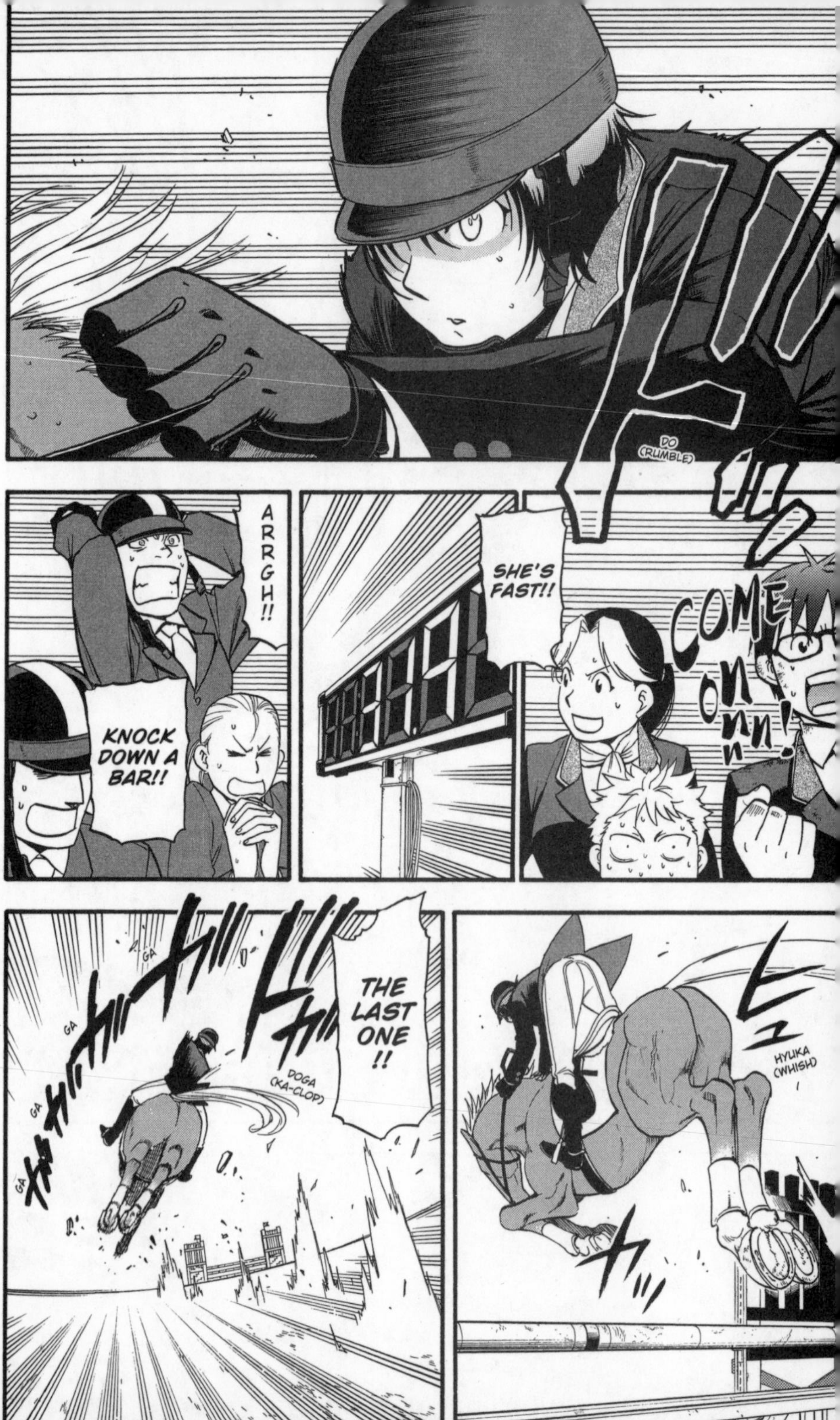
DO (RUMBLE)
COME ON NNN!
SHE'S FAST!!
ARRGH!!
KNOCK DOWN A BAR!!
HYUKA (WHISH)
THE LAST ONE!!
DOGA (KA-CLOP)
GA
GA
GA
GA

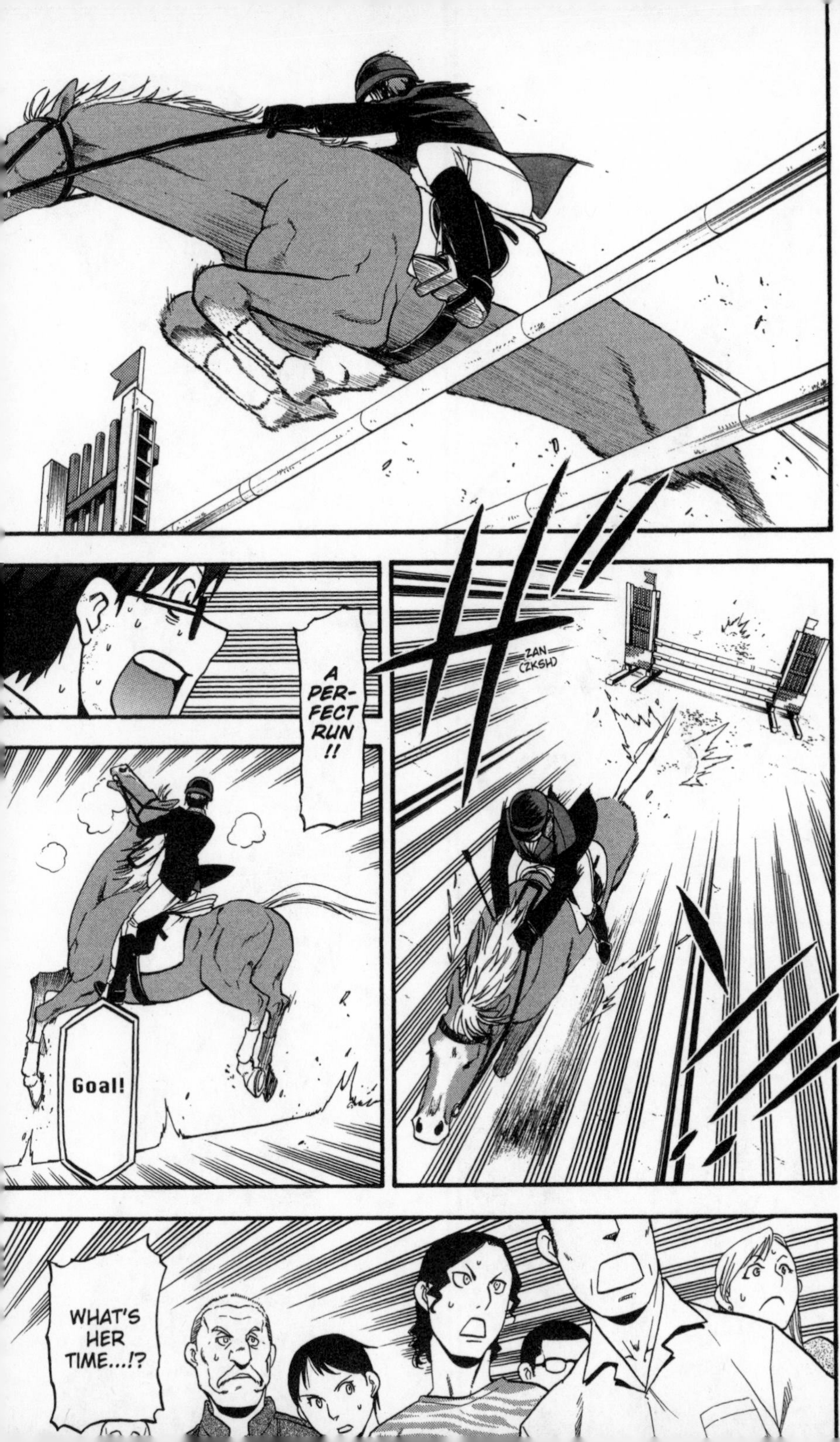

ZAN (ZKSH)
A PERFECT RUN!!
Goal!
WHAT'S HER TIME...!?

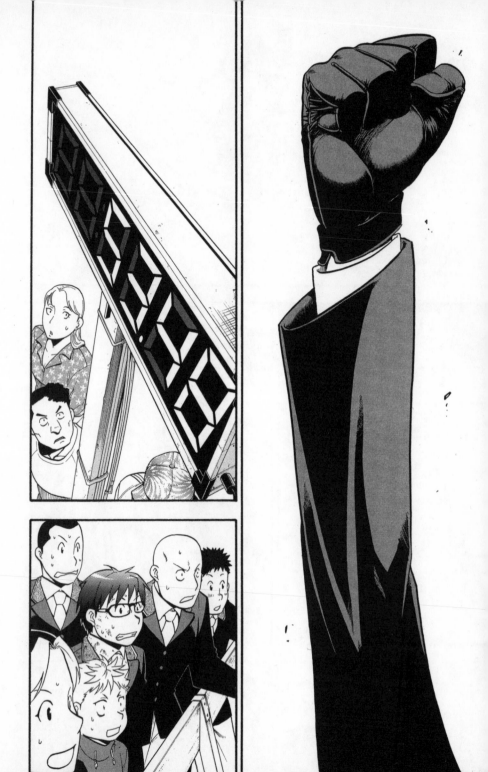

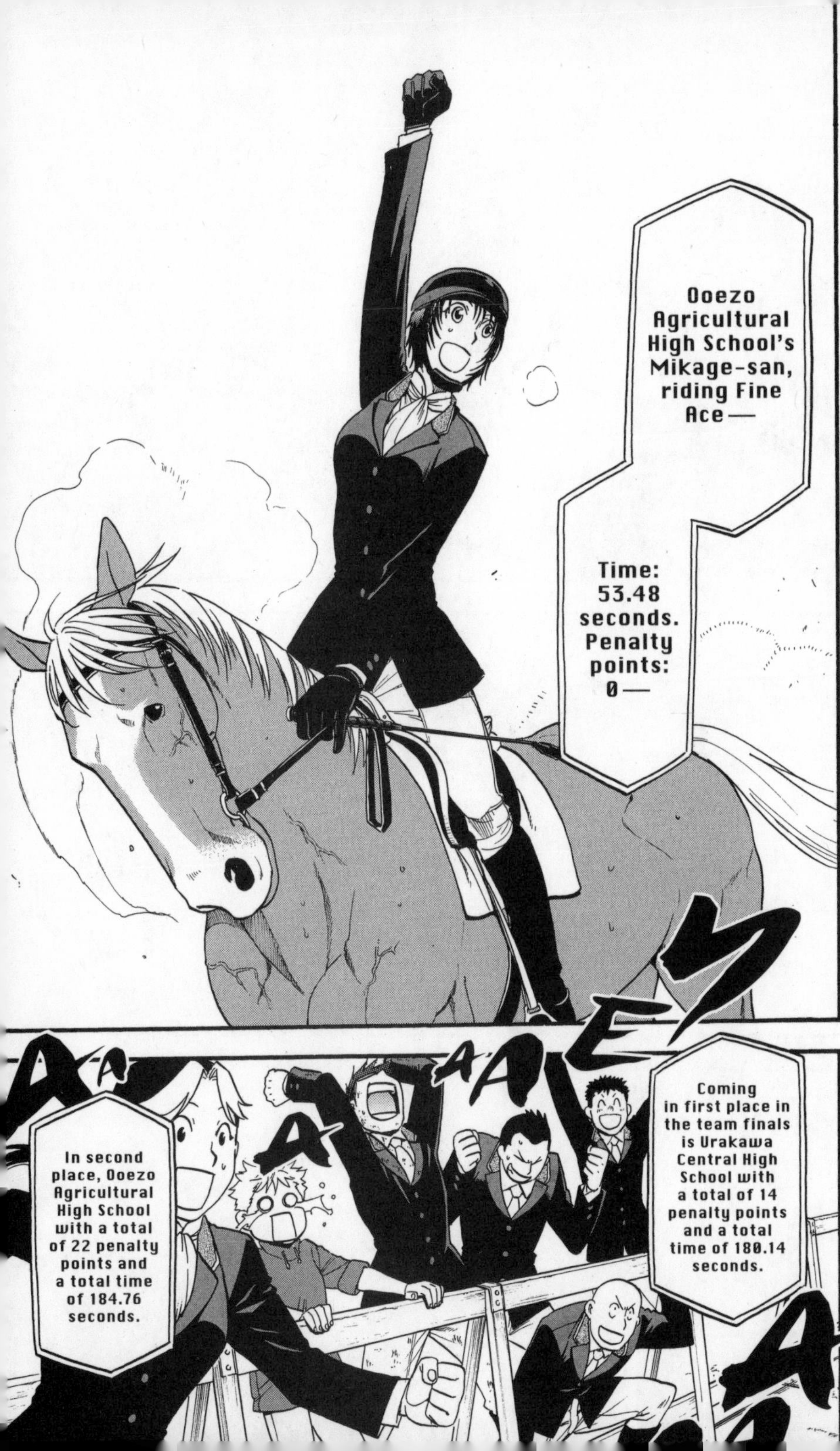
Ooezo Agricultural High School's Mikage-san, riding Fine Ace—
Time: 53.48 seconds. Penalty points: 0—
MAAAAE!
Coming in first place in the team finals is Urakawa Central High School with a total of 14 penalty points and a total time of 180.14 seconds.
In second place, Ooezo Agricultural High School with a total of 22 penalty points and a total time of 184.76 seconds.

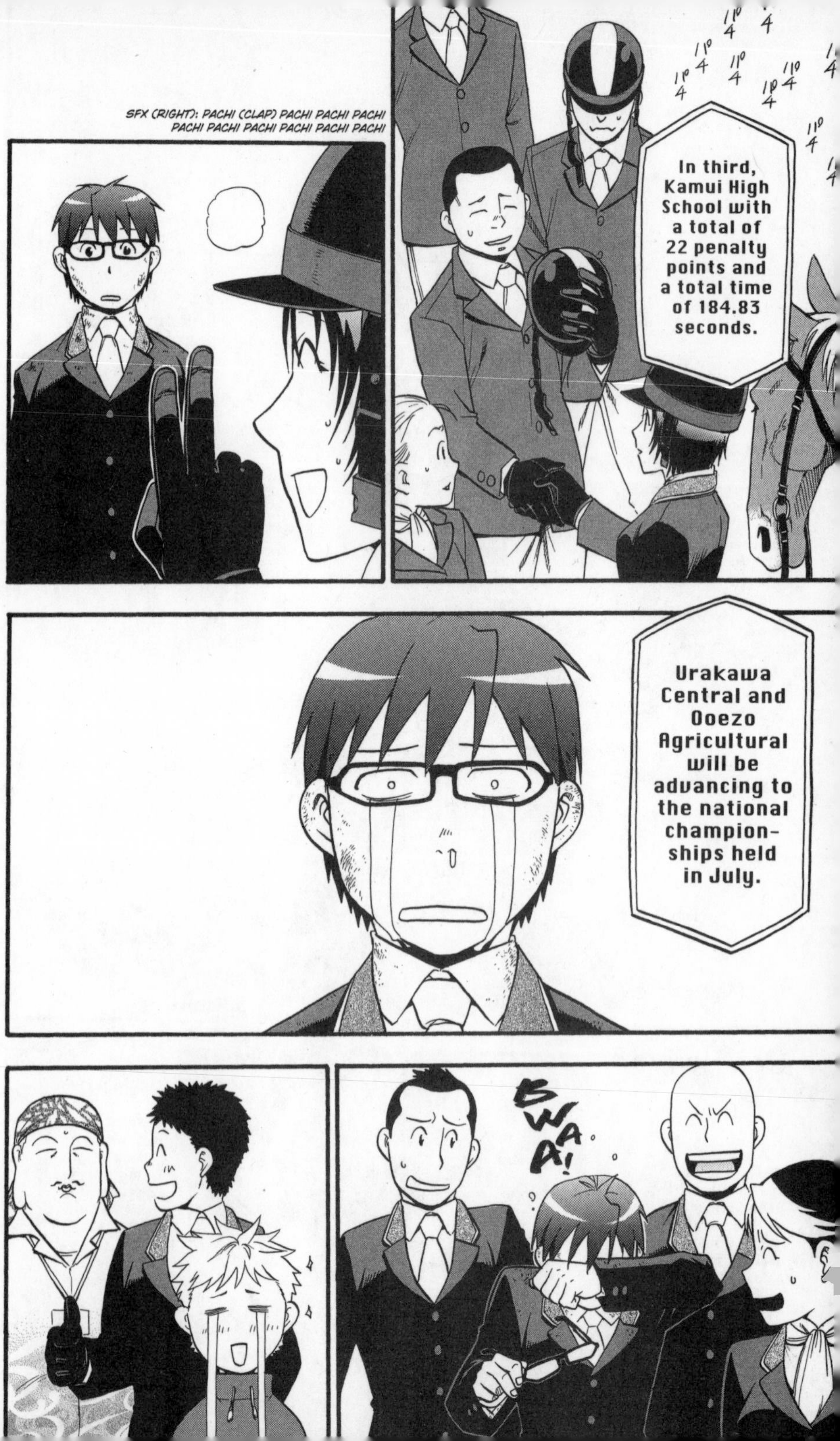
In third, Kamui High School with a total of 22 penalty points and a total time of 184.83 seconds.
SFX (RIGHT): PACHI (CLAP) PACHI PACHI PACHI PACHI PACHI PACHI PACHI PACHI PACHI
Urakawa Central and Ooezo Agricultural will be advancing to the national champion-ships held in July.
BWAA!

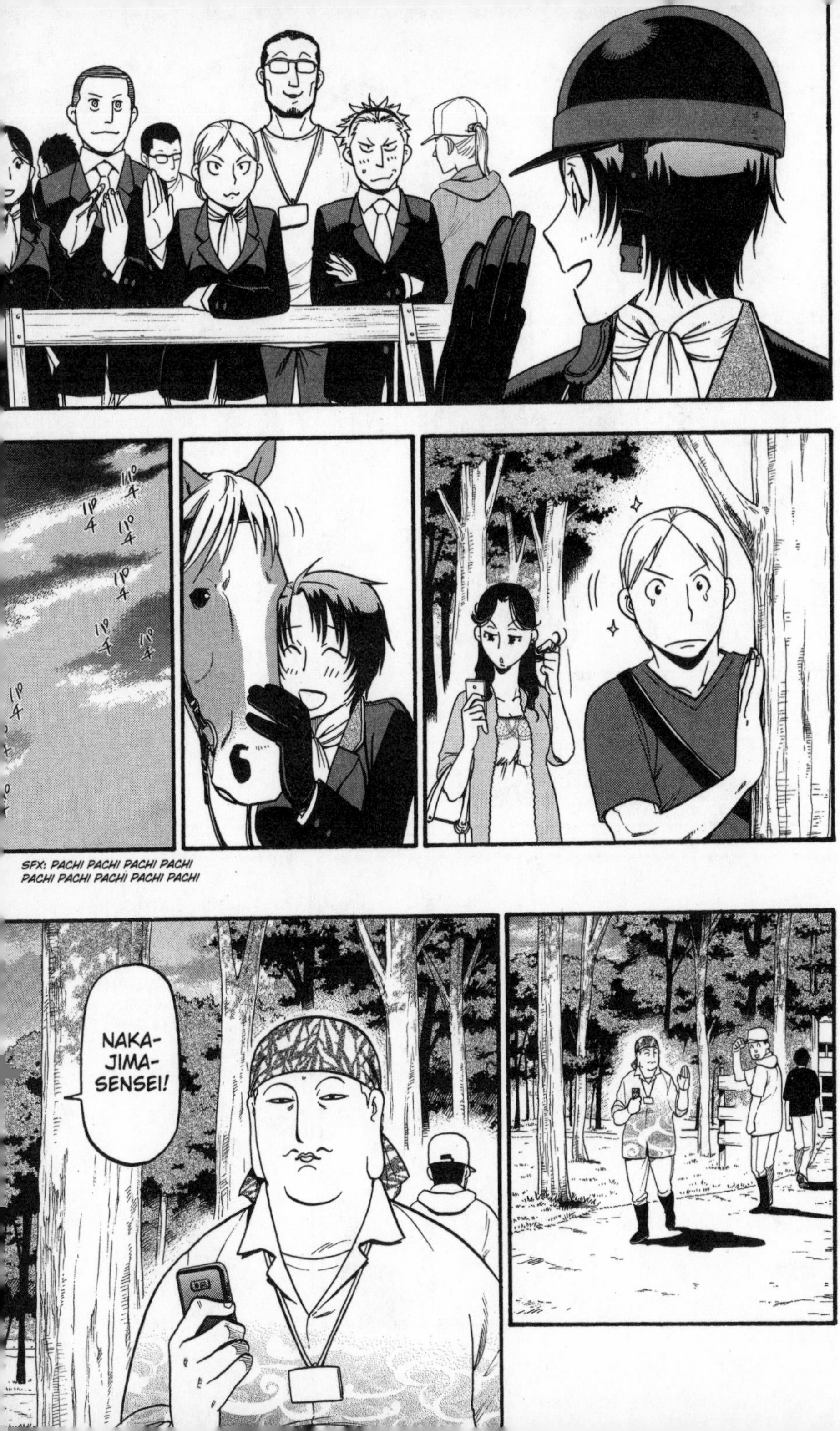
パチ
パチ
パチ
パチ
パチ
パチ
パチ
SFX: PACHI PACHI PACHI PACHI
PACHI PACHI PACHI PACHI PACHI
NAKA-JIMA-SENSEI!

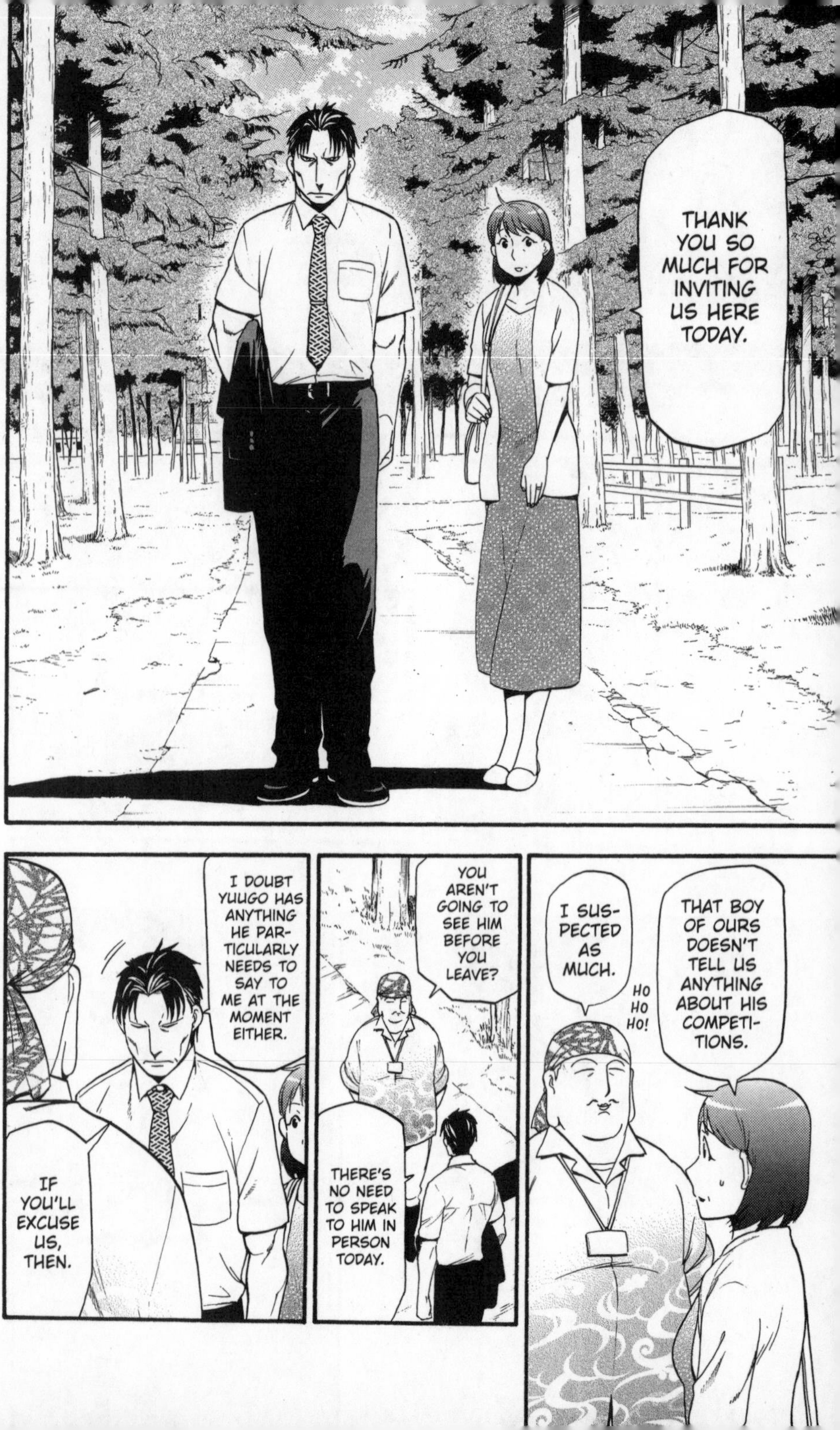
THANK YOU SO MUCH FOR INVITING US HERE TODAY.
THAT BOY OF OURS DOESN'T TELL US ANYTHING ABOUT HIS COMPETITIONS.
HO HO HO!
I SUSPECTED AS MUCH.
YOU AREN'T GOING TO SEE HIM BEFORE YOU LEAVE?
THERE'S NO NEED TO SPEAK TO HIM IN PERSON TODAY.
I DOUBT YUUGO HAS ANYTHING HE PARTICULARLY NEEDS TO SAY TO ME AT THE MOMENT EITHER.
IF YOU'LL EXCUSE US, THEN.

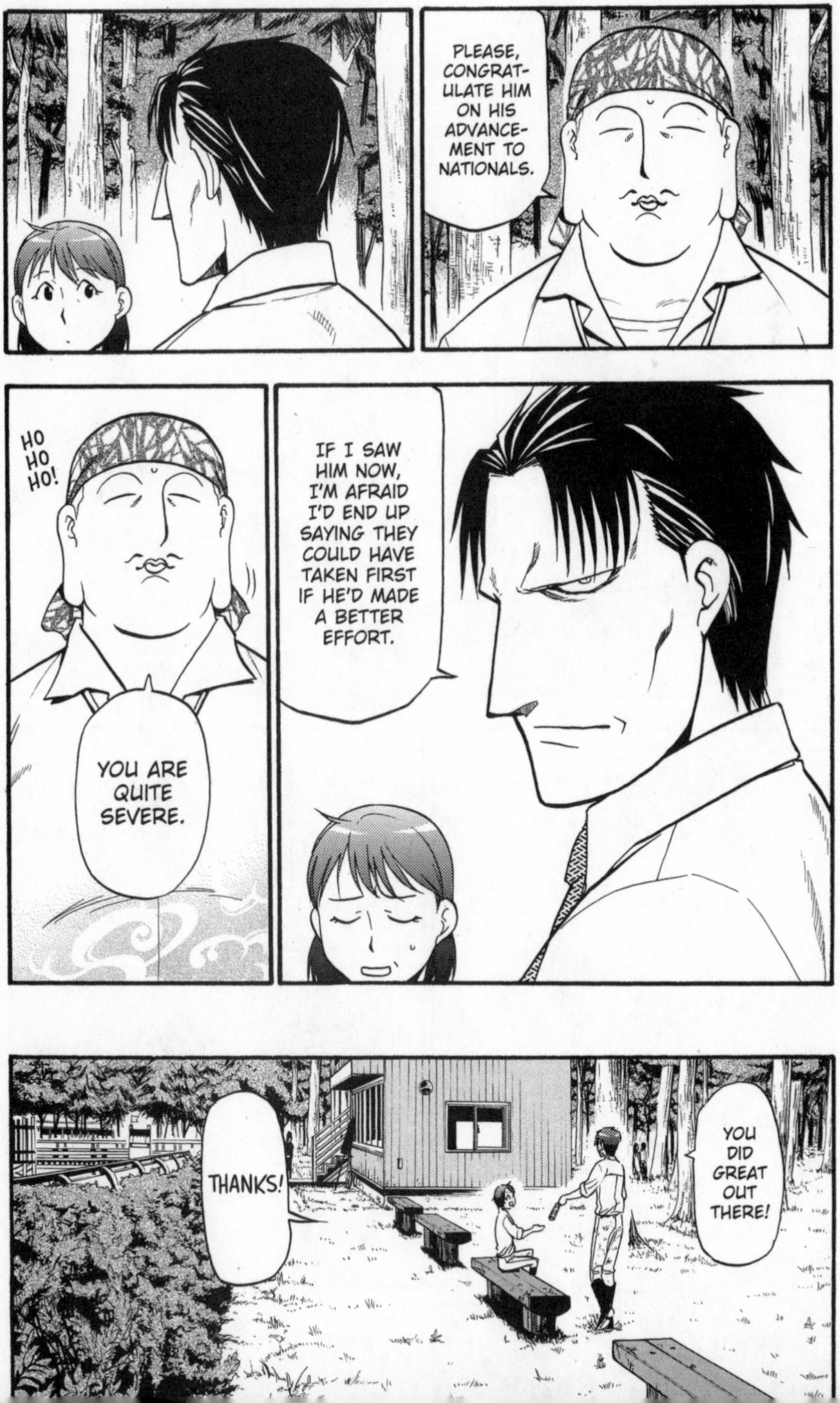
PLEASE, CONGRAT-ULATE HIM ON HIS ADVANCE-MENT TO NATIONALS.
IF I SAW HIM NOW, I'M AFRAID I'D END UP SAYING THEY COULD HAVE TAKEN FIRST IF HE'D MADE A BETTER EFFORT.
HO HO HO!
YOU ARE QUITE SEVERE.
YOU DID GREAT OUT THERE!
THANKS!

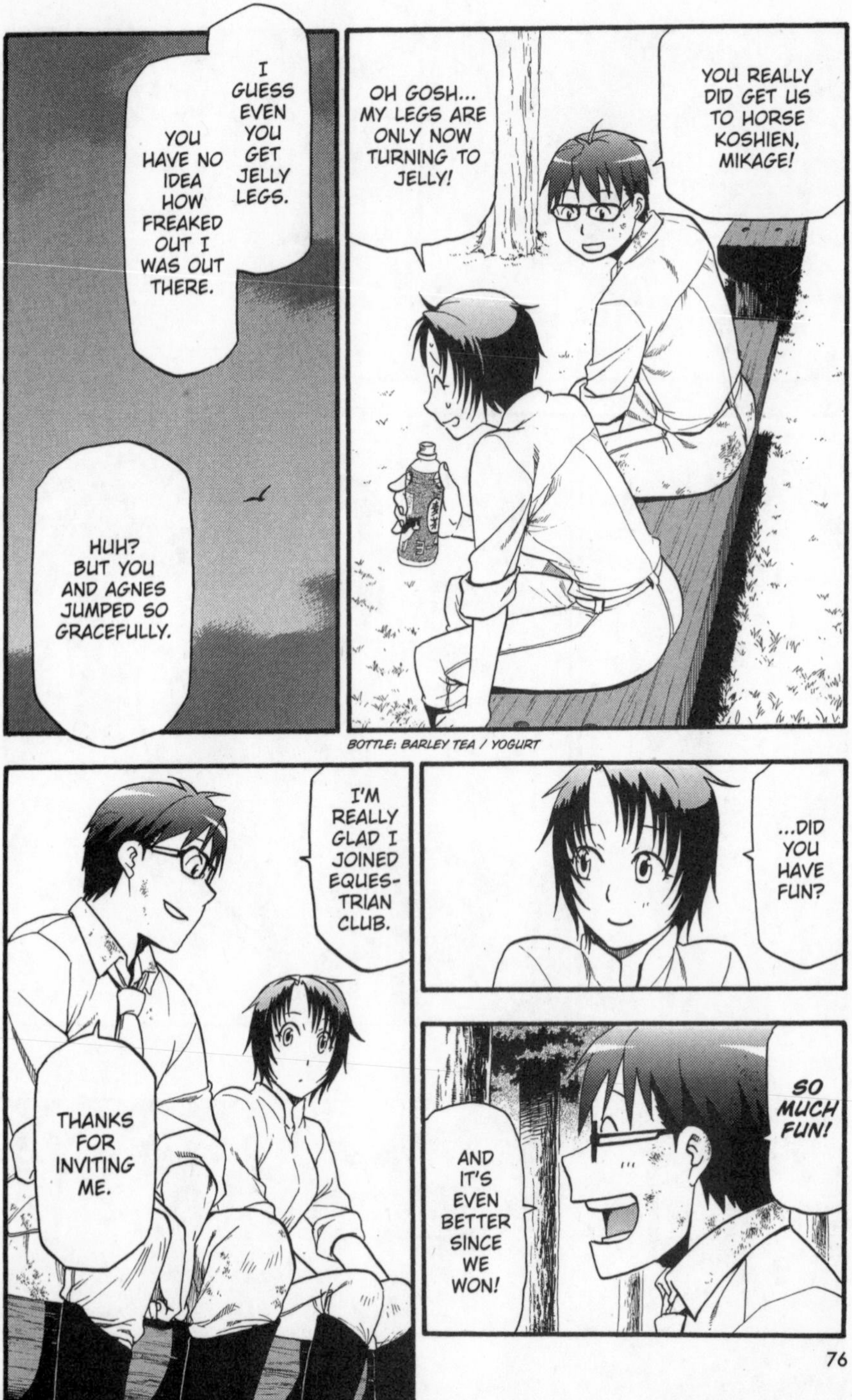
YOU REALLY DID GET US TO HORSE KOSHIEN, MIKAGE!
OH GOSH... MY LEGS ARE ONLY NOW TURNING TO JELLY!
BOTTLE: BARLEY TEA / YOGURT
I GUESS EVEN YOU GET JELLY LEGS.
YOU HAVE NO IDEA HOW FREAKED OUT I WAS OUT THERE.
HUH? BUT YOU AND AGNES JUMPED SO GRACEFULLY.
...DID YOU HAVE FUN?
SO MUCH FUN!
AND IT'S EVEN BETTER SINCE WE WON!
I'M REALLY GLAD I JOINED EQUES-TRIAN CLUB.
THANKS FOR INVITING ME.

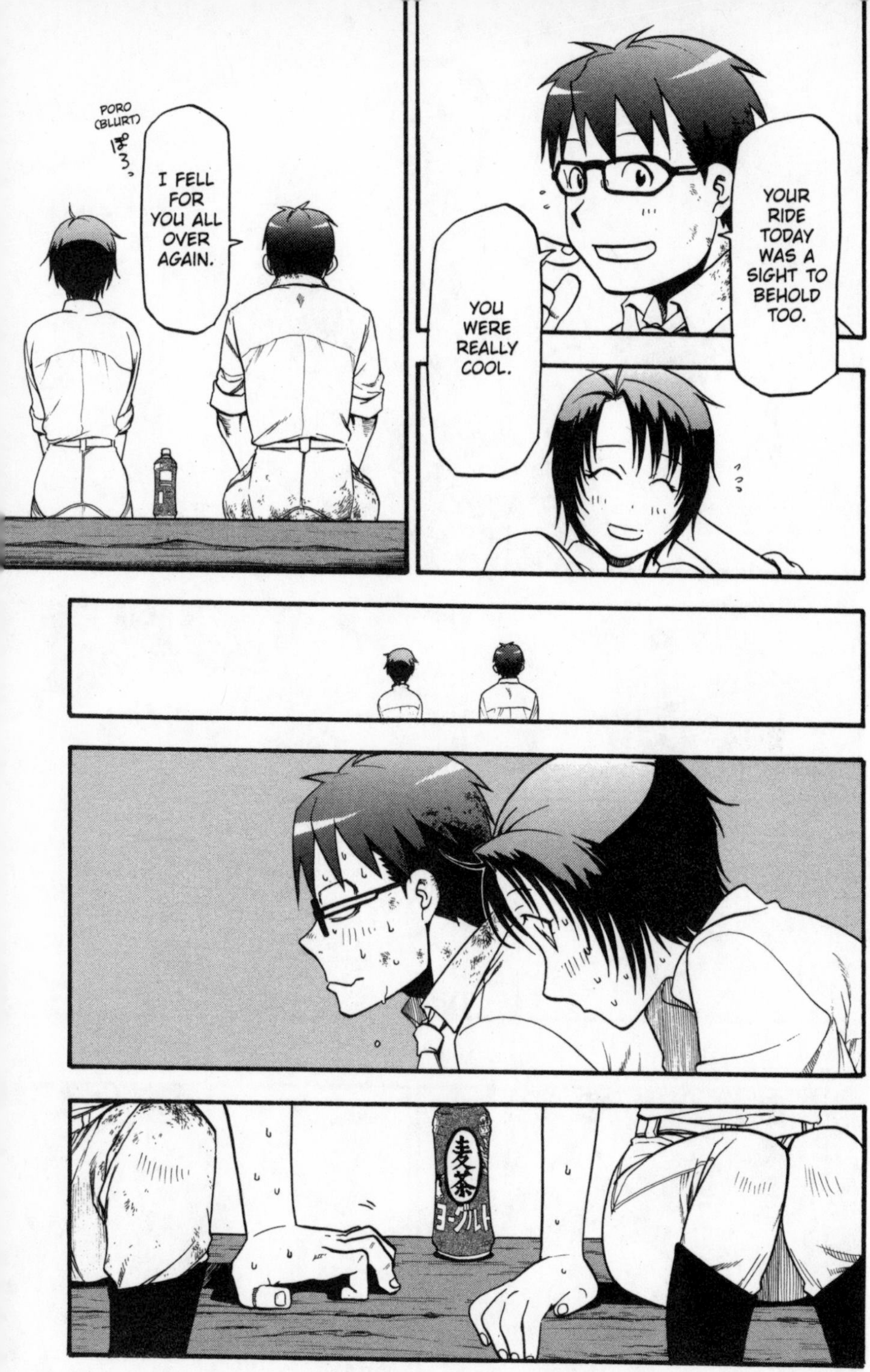
YOUR RIDE TODAY WAS A SIGHT TO BEHOLD TOO.
YOU WERE REALLY COOL.
I FELL FOR YOU ALL OVER AGAIN.
PORO (BLURT)
ぽろっ
麦茶
ヨーグルト

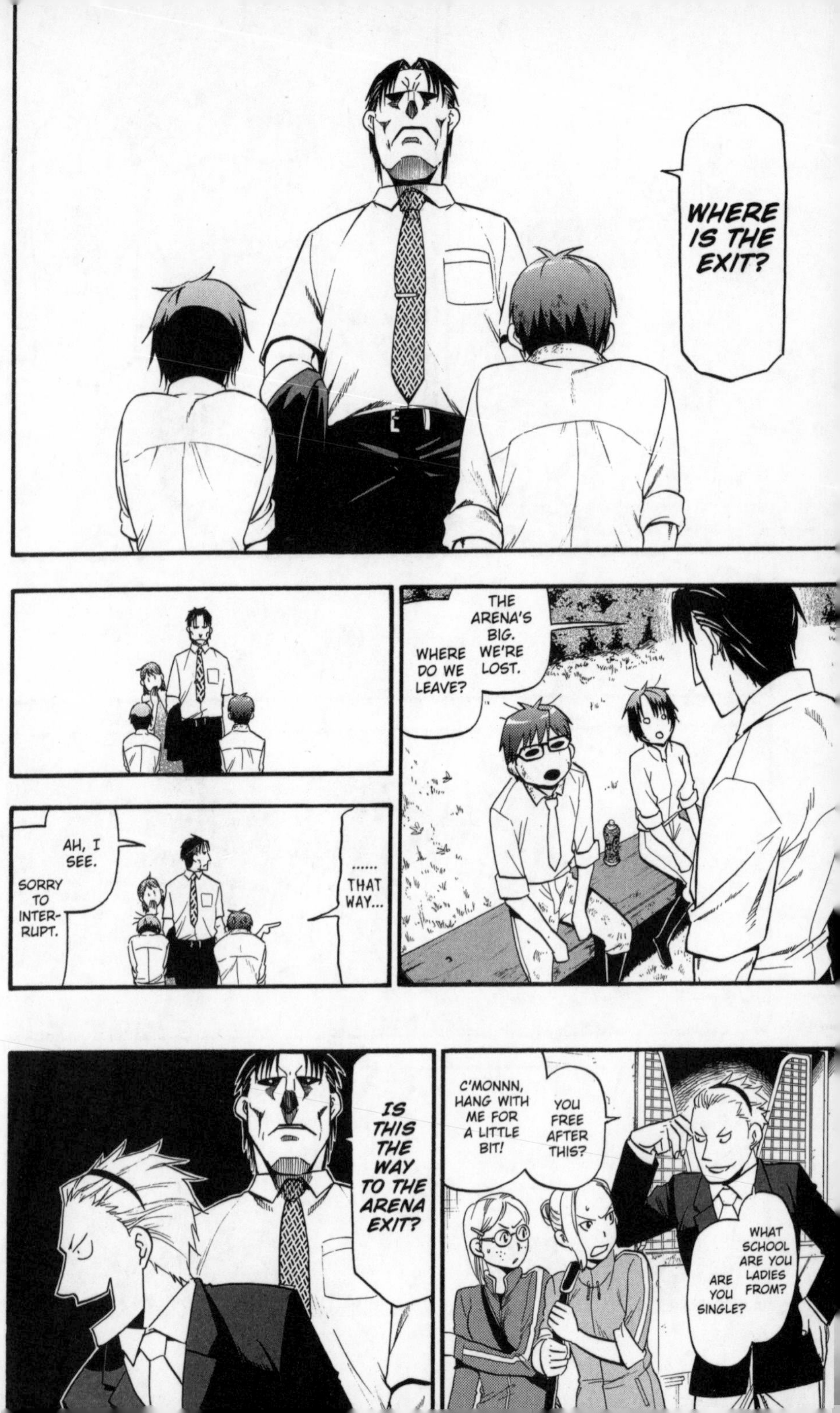
WHERE IS THE EXIT?
THE ARENA'S BIG. WE'RE LOST.
WHERE DO WE LEAVE?
...... THAT WAY...
AH, I SEE.
SORRY TO INTERRUPT.
YOU FREE AFTER THIS?
C'MONNN, HANG WITH ME FOR A LITTLE BIT!
WHAT SCHOOL ARE YOU LADIES FROM?
ARE YOU SINGLE?
IS THIS THE WAY TO THE ARENA EXIT?

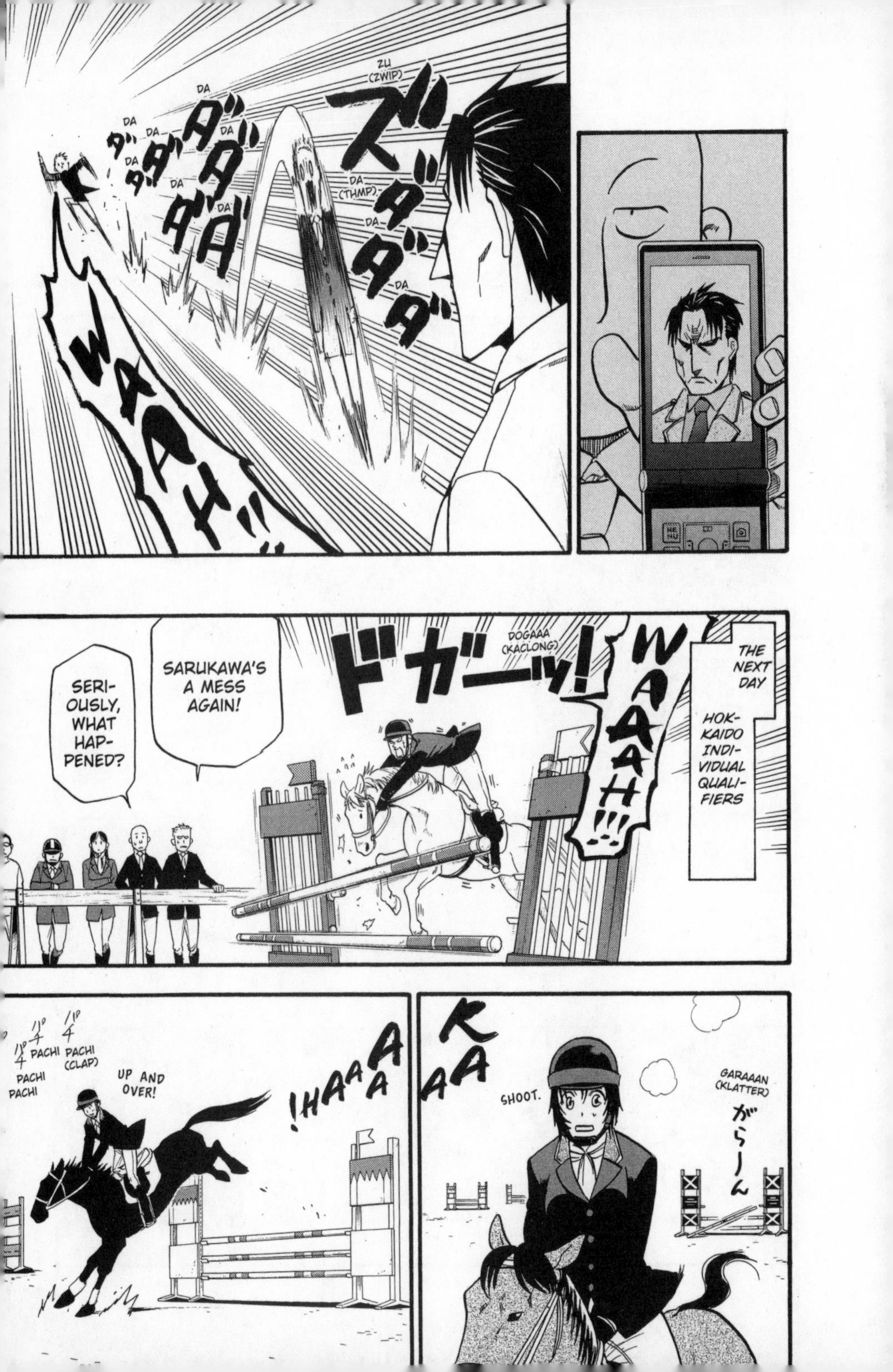
ZU (ZWIP)
ズ
DA (THMP) DA DA DA
ダダダダ
DA DA DA DA DA DA DA
ダダダダダダ
WAAAH
THE NEXT DAY
HOKKAIDO INDIVIDUAL QUALIFIERS
WAAAH!!!
DOGAAA (KACLONG)
ドガーッ!
SARUKAWA'S A MESS AGAIN!
SERIOUSLY, WHAT HAPPENED?
GARAAAN (KLATTER)
がら～ん
SHOOT.
KRAAA
AAAAH!
UP AND OVER!
PACHI PACHI PACHI PACHI (CLAP)
パチパチ

ARGH! SO CLOSE!

National High School Equestrian Qualifiers

	Individual Rankings
Winner	Hidaka Ag: Fukuma
Runner-up	Urakawa C: Mizuho
Third-place	Ooezo Ag: Ishiyan

2013 Celebrating 60 Years
Hokkaido Equestrian

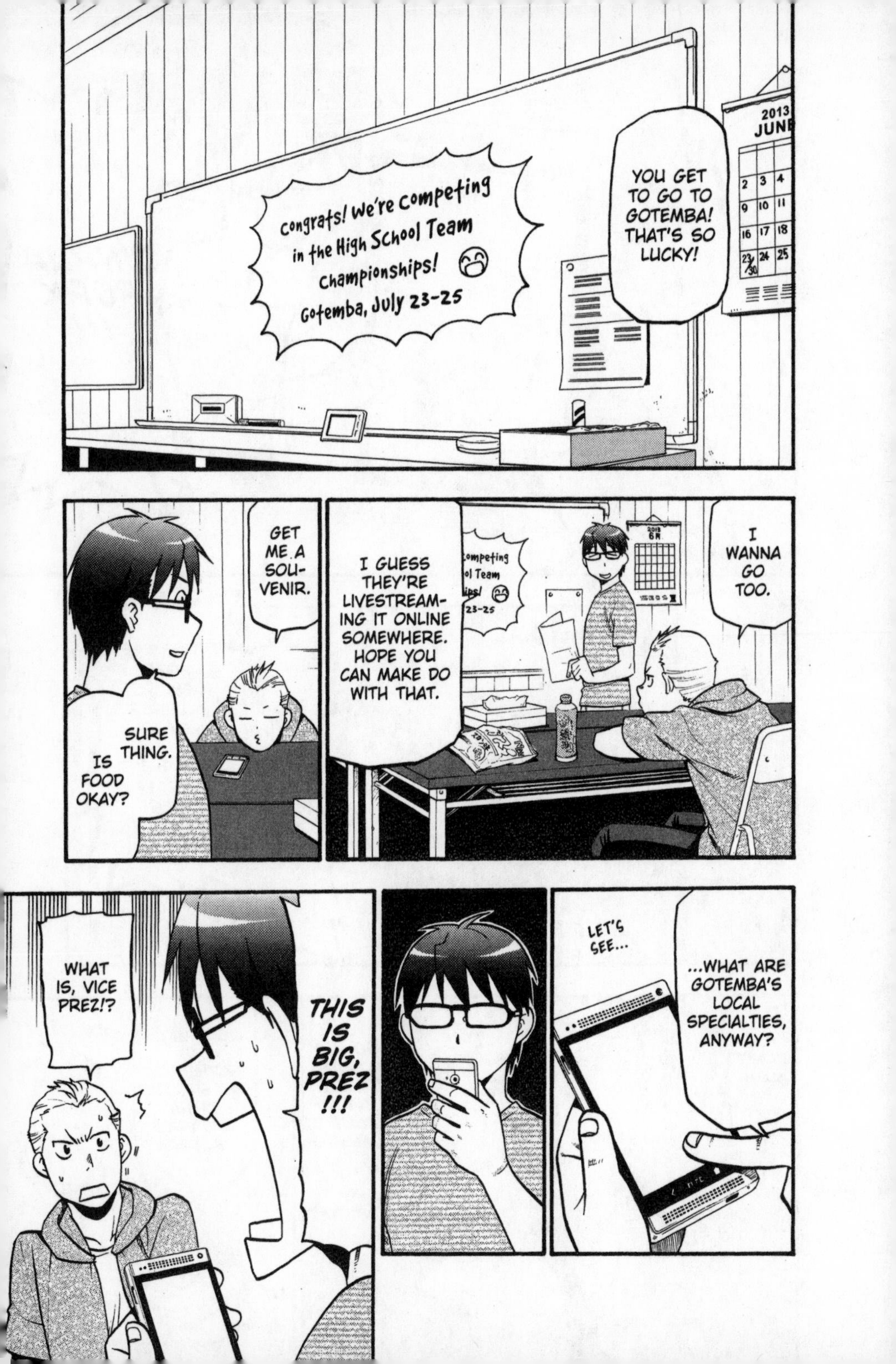
YOU GET TO GO TO GOTEMBA! THAT'S SO LUCKY!
Congrats! We're competing in the High School Team Championships!
Gotemba, July 23-25
I WANNA GO TOO.
I GUESS THEY'RE LIVESTREAMING IT ONLINE SOMEWHERE. HOPE YOU CAN MAKE DO WITH THAT.
GET ME A SOUVENIR.
SURE THING. IS FOOD OKAY?
LET'S SEE...
...WHAT ARE GOTEMBA'S LOCAL SPECIALTIES, ANYWAY?
THIS IS BIG, PREZ!!!
WHAT IS, VICE PREZ!?

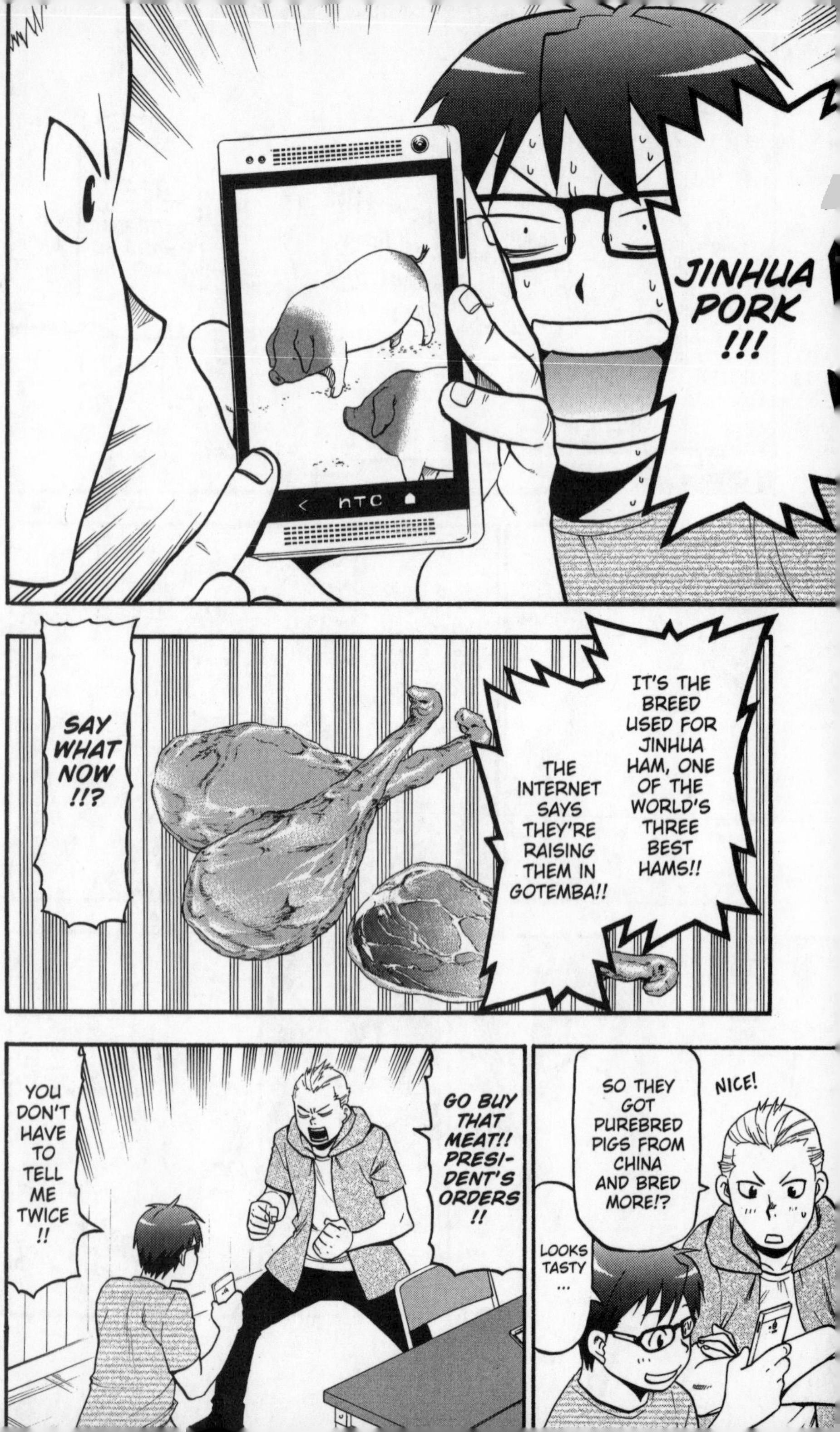
JINHUA PORK !!!
IT'S THE BREED USED FOR JINHUA HAM, ONE OF THE WORLD'S THREE BEST HAMS!!
THE INTERNET SAYS THEY'RE RAISING THEM IN GOTEMBA!!
SAY WHAT NOW !!?
NICE!
SO THEY GOT PUREBRED PIGS FROM CHINA AND BRED MORE!?
LOOKS TASTY ...
GO BUY THAT MEAT!! PRESI-DENT'S ORDERS !!
YOU DON'T HAVE TO TELL ME TWICE !!

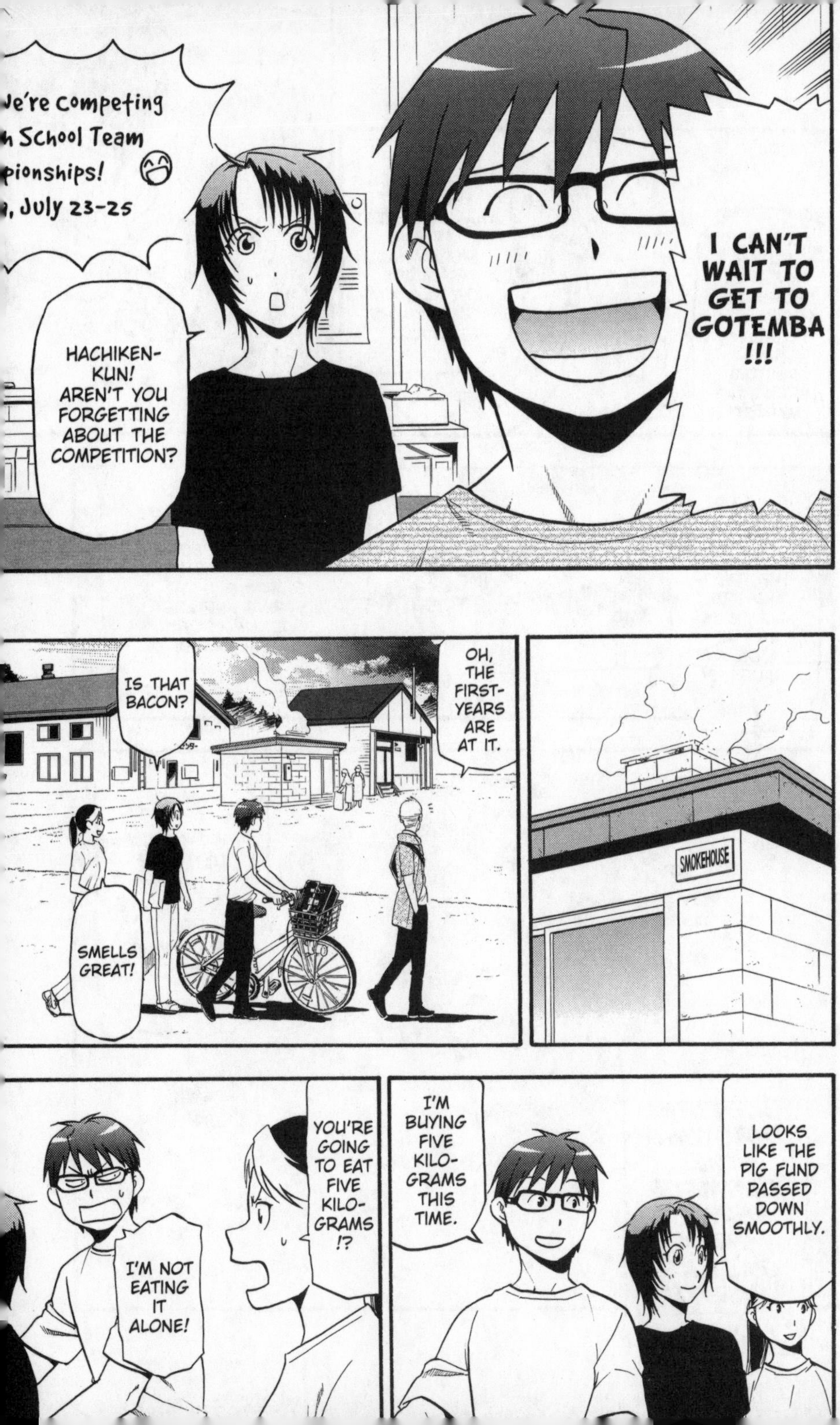
I CAN'T WAIT TO GET TO GOTEMBA!!!
HACHIKEN-KUN! AREN'T YOU FORGETTING ABOUT THE COMPETITION?
e're competing
School Team
pionships!
, July 23-25
SMOKEHOUSE
OH, THE FIRST-YEARS ARE AT IT.
IS THAT BACON?
SMELLS GREAT!
LOOKS LIKE THE PIG FUND PASSED DOWN SMOOTHLY.
I'M BUYING FIVE KILOGRAMS THIS TIME.
YOU'RE GOING TO EAT FIVE KILOGRAMS!?
I'M NOT EATING IT ALONE!

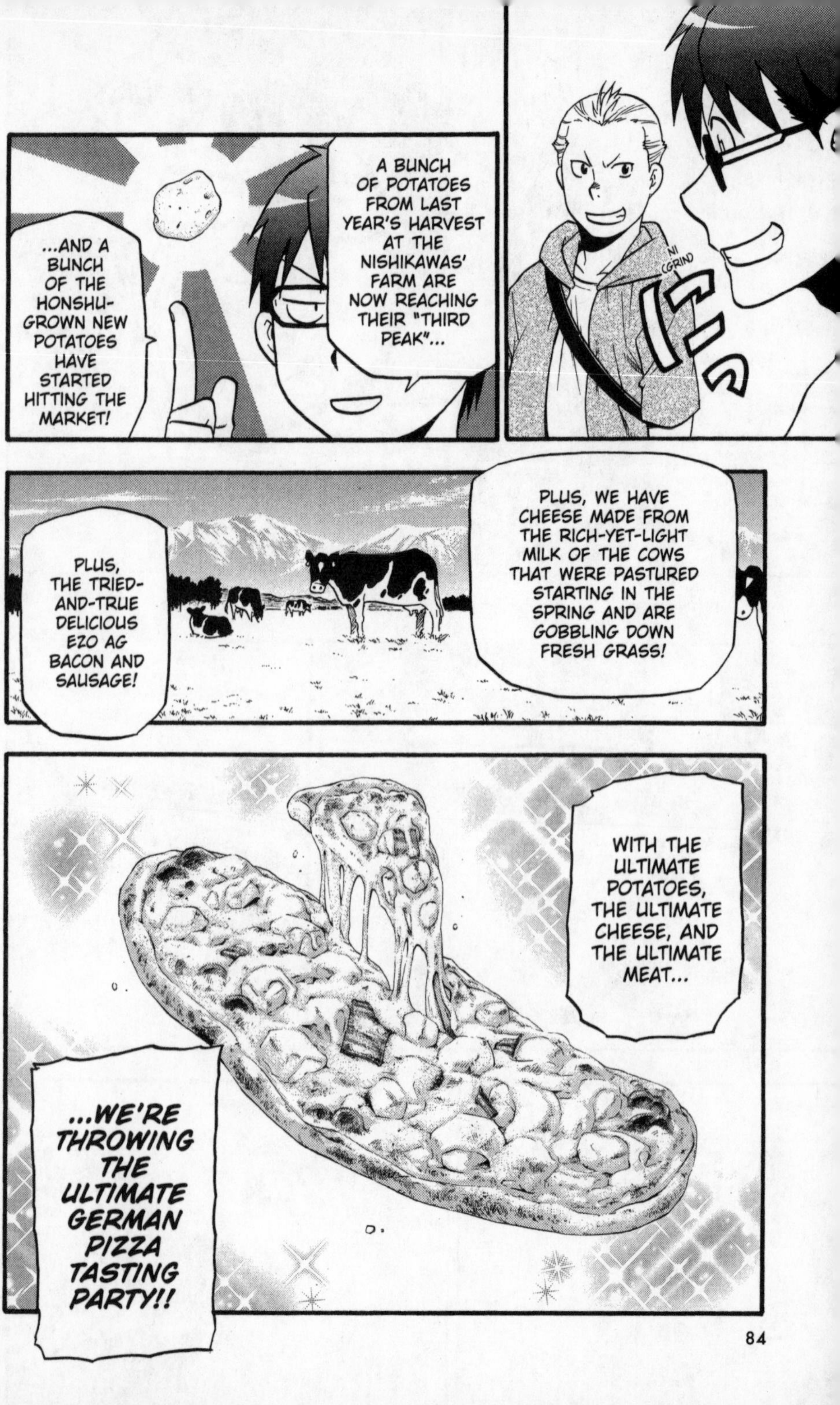
NI GRIND
A BUNCH OF POTATOES FROM LAST YEAR'S HARVEST AT THE NISHIKAWAS' FARM ARE NOW REACHING THEIR "THIRD PEAK"...
...AND A BUNCH OF THE HONSHU-GROWN NEW POTATOES HAVE STARTED HITTING THE MARKET!
PLUS, WE HAVE CHEESE MADE FROM THE RICH-YET-LIGHT MILK OF THE COWS THAT WERE PASTURED STARTING IN THE SPRING AND ARE GOBBLING DOWN FRESH GRASS!
PLUS, THE TRIED-AND-TRUE DELICIOUS EZO AG BACON AND SAUSAGE!
WITH THE ULTIMATE POTATOES, THE ULTIMATE CHEESE, AND THE ULTIMATE MEAT...
...WE'RE THROWING THE ULTIMATE GERMAN PIZZA TASTING PARTY!!

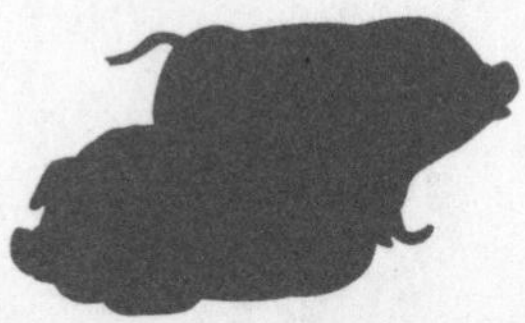

Silver Spoon

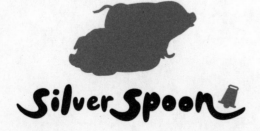

THE AGRICULTURE ROCK BAND THAT PERFORMED AT EZO AG FEST: "NO DAYS OFF"

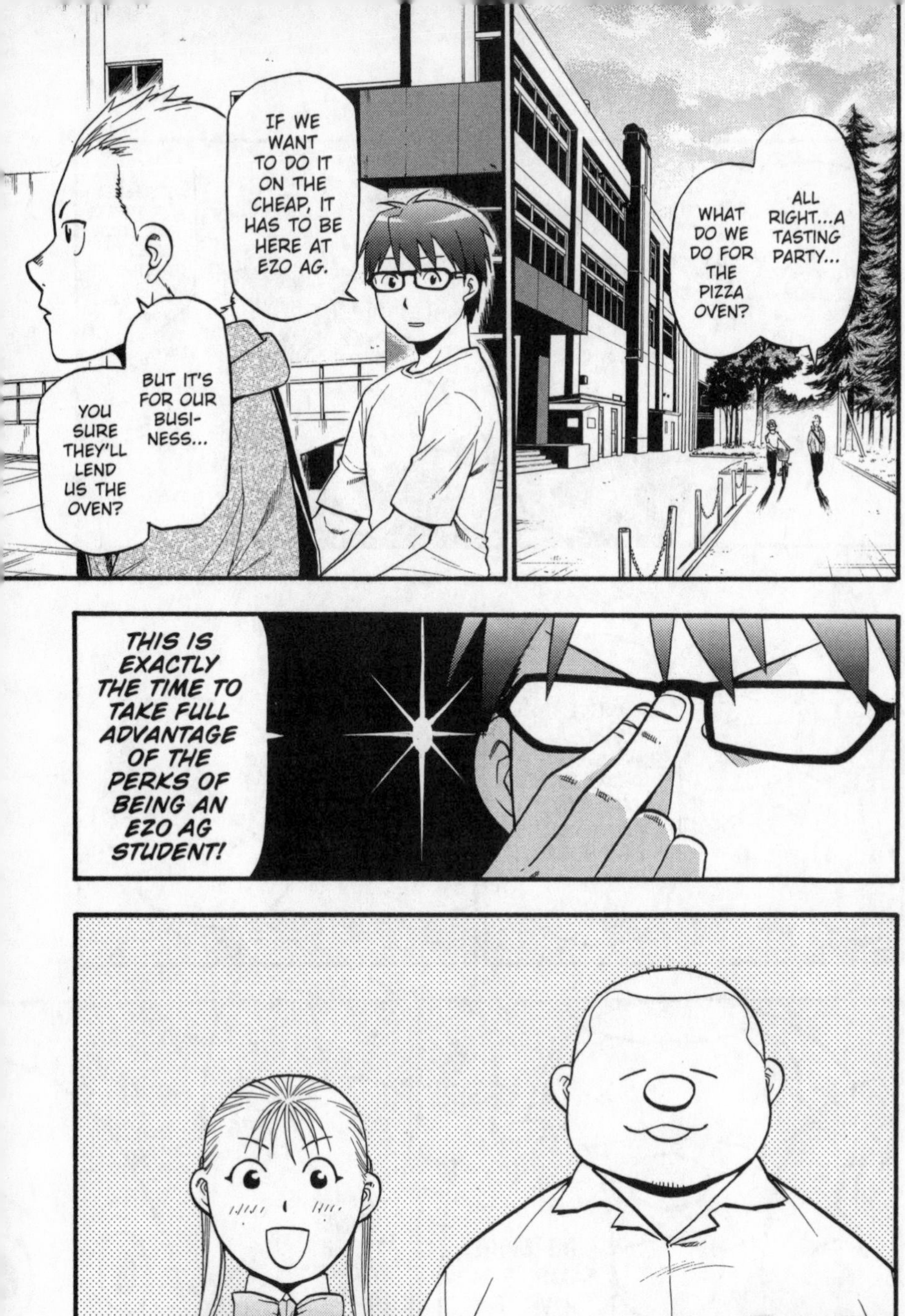
ALL RIGHT...A TASTING PARTY...
WHAT DO WE DO FOR THE PIZZA OVEN?
IF WE WANT TO DO IT ON THE CHEAP, IT HAS TO BE HERE AT EZO AG.
BUT IT'S FOR OUR BUSINESS...
YOU SURE THEY'LL LEND US THE OVEN?
THIS IS EXACTLY THE TIME TO TAKE FULL ADVANTAGE OF THE PERKS OF BEING AN EZO AG STUDENT!
Chapter 110:
Tale of Four Seasons ⑬

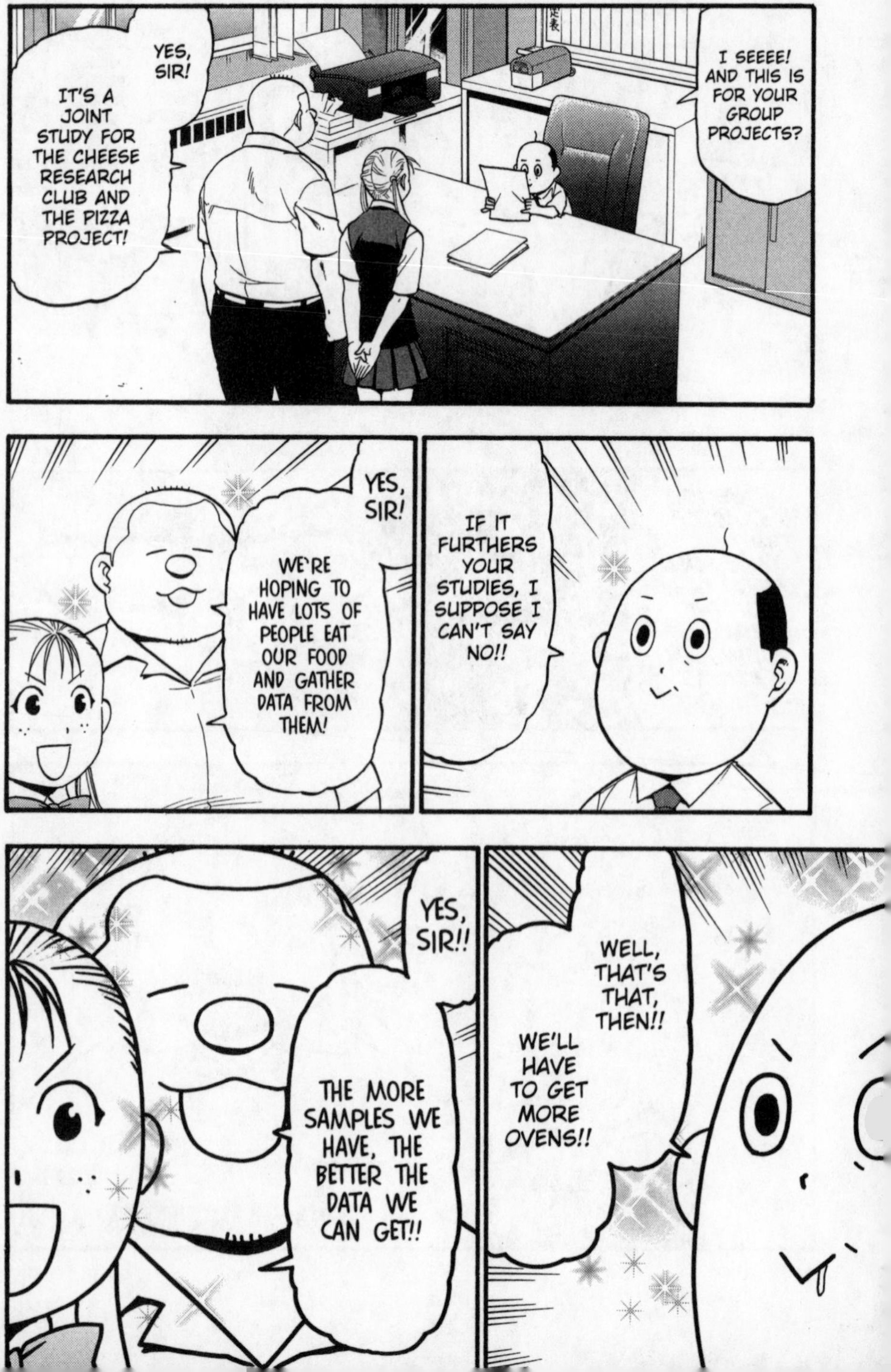
I SEEEE! AND THIS IS FOR YOUR GROUP PROJECTS?
YES, SIR!
IT'S A JOINT STUDY FOR THE CHEESE RESEARCH CLUB AND THE PIZZA PROJECT!
IF IT FURTHERS YOUR STUDIES, I SUPPOSE I CAN'T SAY NO!!
YES, SIR!
WE'RE HOPING TO HAVE LOTS OF PEOPLE EAT OUR FOOD AND GATHER DATA FROM THEM!
WELL, THAT'S THAT, THEN!!
WE'LL HAVE TO GET MORE OVENS!!
YES, SIR!!
THE MORE SAMPLES WE HAVE, THE BETTER THE DATA WE CAN GET!!

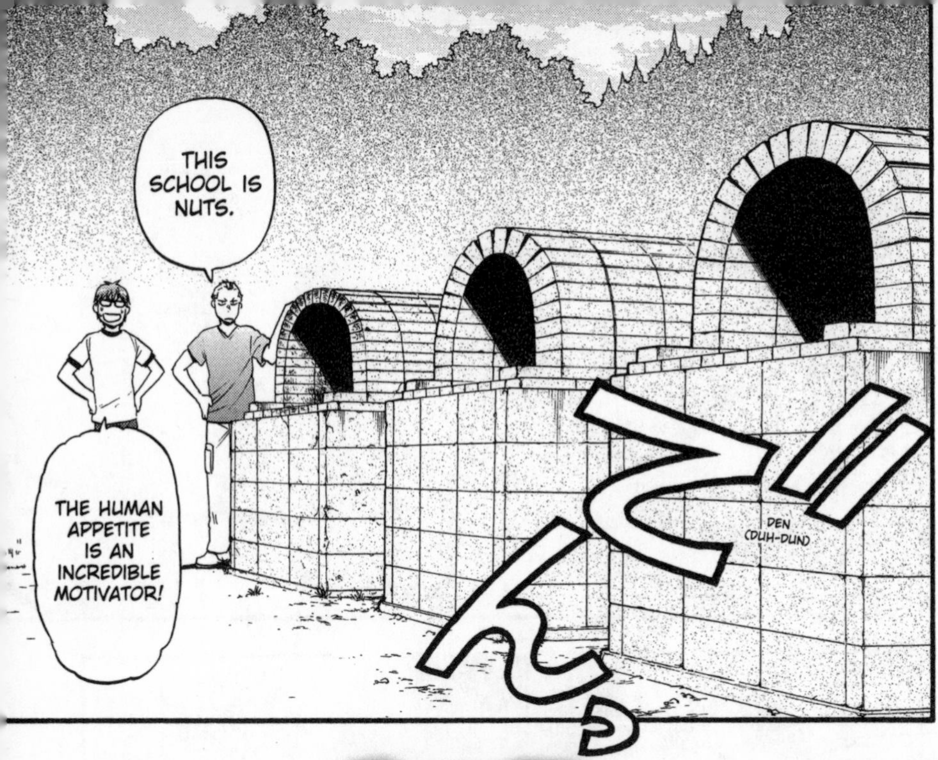
THIS SCHOOL IS NUTS.
THE HUMAN APPETITE IS AN INCREDIBLE MOTIVATOR!
DEN (DUH-DUND)

Chapter 110:
Tale of Four Seasons ⑬

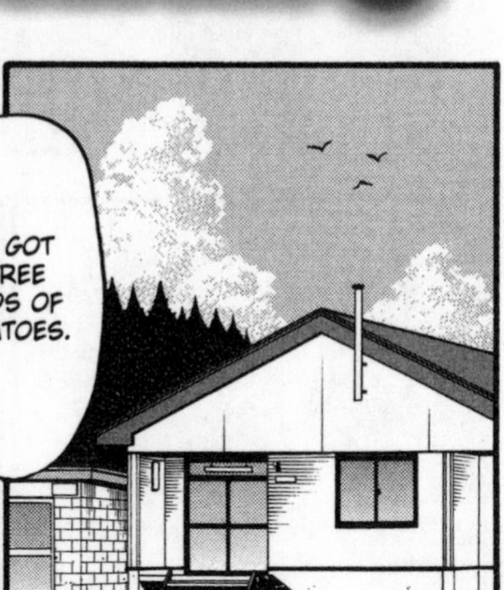

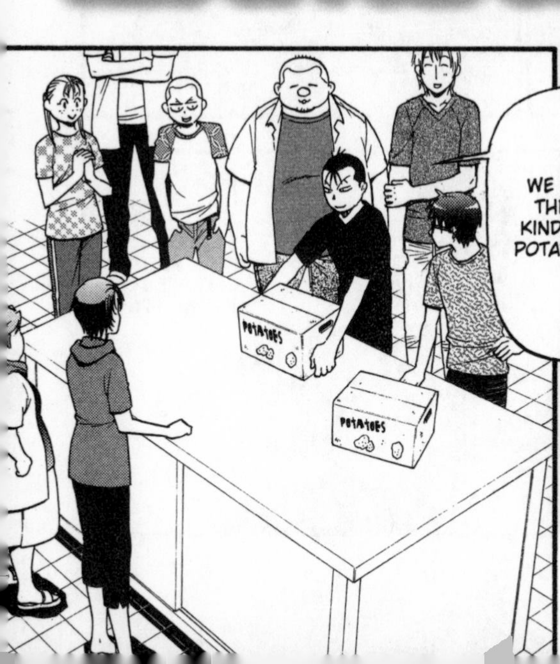
WE GOT THREE KINDS OF POTATOES.
POTATOES
POTATOES

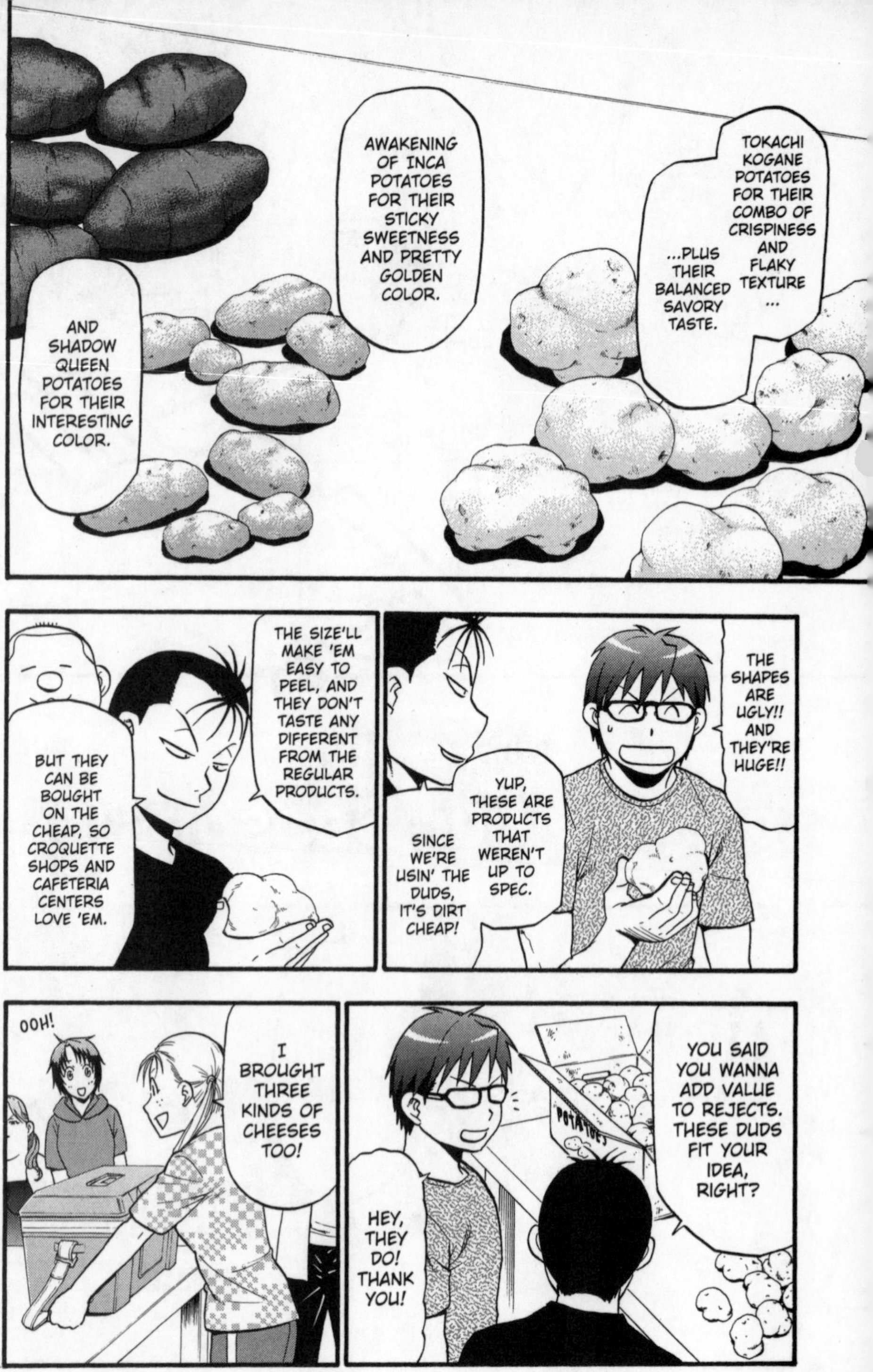
TOKACHI KOGANE POTATOES FOR THEIR COMBO OF CRISPINESS AND FLAKY TEXTURE ...
...PLUS THEIR BALANCED SAVORY TASTE.
AWAKENING OF INCA POTATOES FOR THEIR STICKY SWEETNESS AND PRETTY GOLDEN COLOR.
AND SHADOW QUEEN POTATOES FOR THEIR INTERESTING COLOR.
THE SHAPES ARE UGLY!! AND THEY'RE HUGE!!
YUP, THESE ARE PRODUCTS THAT WEREN'T UP TO SPEC.
SINCE WE'RE USIN' THE DUDS, IT'S DIRT CHEAP!
THE SIZE'LL MAKE 'EM EASY TO PEEL, AND THEY DON'T TASTE ANY DIFFERENT FROM THE REGULAR PRODUCTS.
BUT THEY CAN BE BOUGHT ON THE CHEAP, SO CROQUETTE SHOPS AND CAFETERIA CENTERS LOVE 'EM.
YOU SAID YOU WANNA ADD VALUE TO REJECTS. THESE DUDS FIT YOUR IDEA, RIGHT?
POTATOES
HEY, THEY DO! THANK YOU!
I BROUGHT THREE KINDS OF CHEESES TOO!
OOH!

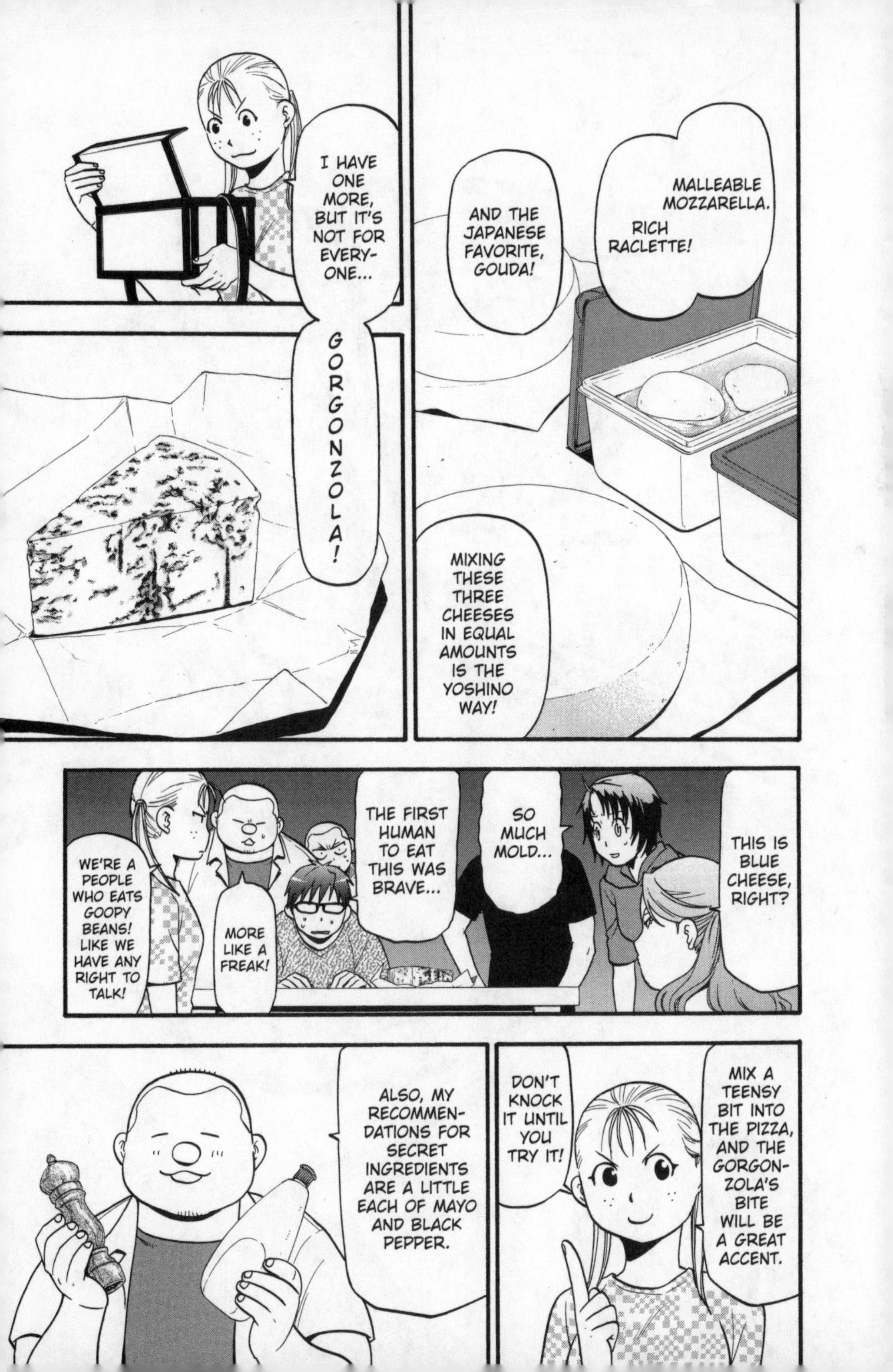
MALLEABLE MOZZARELLA.
RICH RACLETTE!
AND THE JAPANESE FAVORITE, GOUDA!
MIXING THESE THREE CHEESES IN EQUAL AMOUNTS IS THE YOSHINO WAY!
I HAVE ONE MORE, BUT IT'S NOT FOR EVERY-ONE...
GORGONZOLA!
THIS IS BLUE CHEESE, RIGHT?
SO MUCH MOLD...
THE FIRST HUMAN TO EAT THIS WAS BRAVE...
MORE LIKE A FREAK!
WE'RE A PEOPLE WHO EATS GOOPY BEANS! LIKE WE HAVE ANY RIGHT TO TALK!
MIX A TEENSY BIT INTO THE PIZZA, AND THE GORGON-ZOLA'S BITE WILL BE A GREAT ACCENT.
DON'T KNOCK IT UNTIL YOU TRY IT!
ALSO, MY RECOMMEN-DATIONS FOR SECRET INGREDIENTS ARE A LITTLE EACH OF MAYO AND BLACK PEPPER.

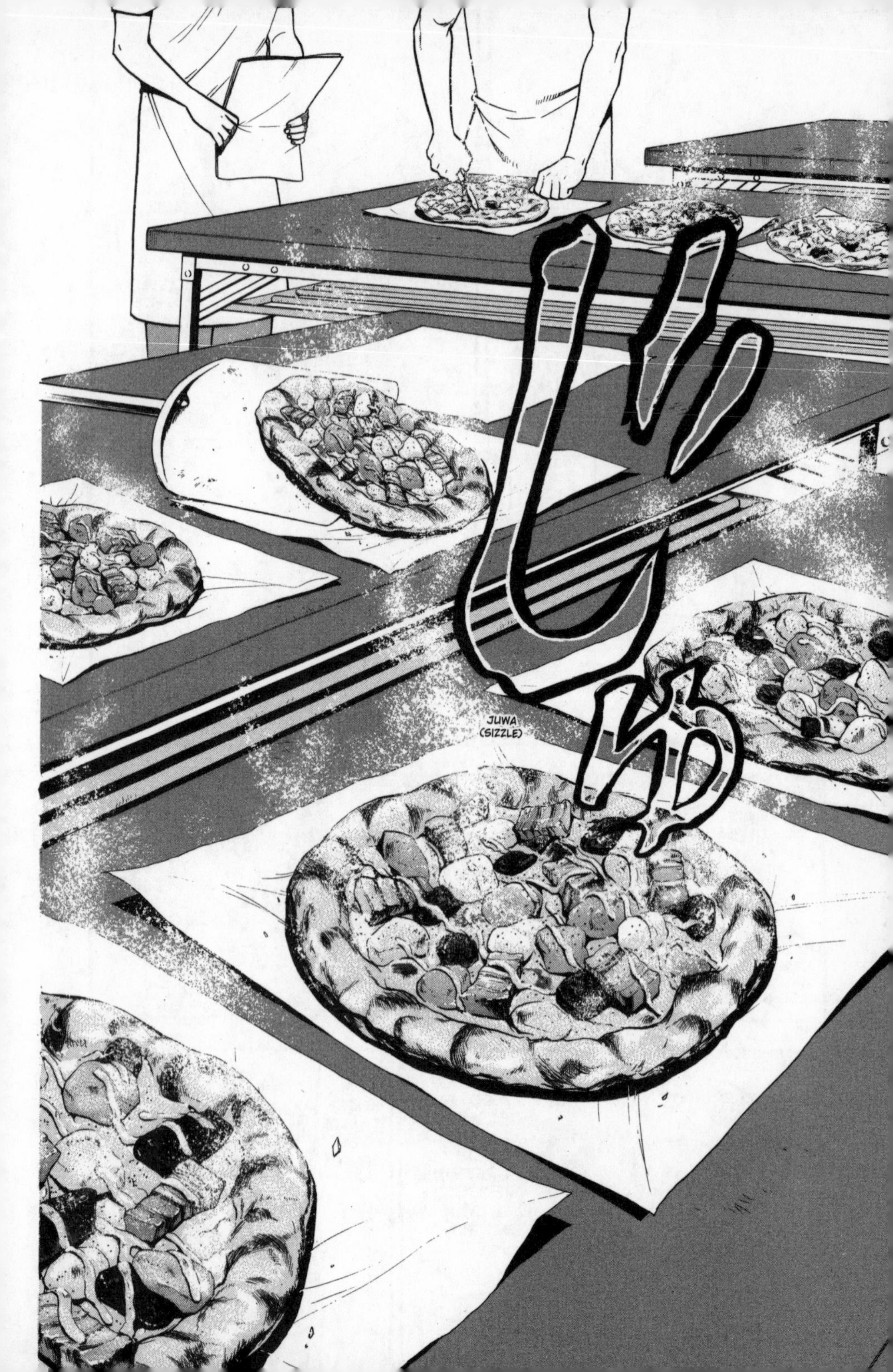
JUWA
(SIZZLE)

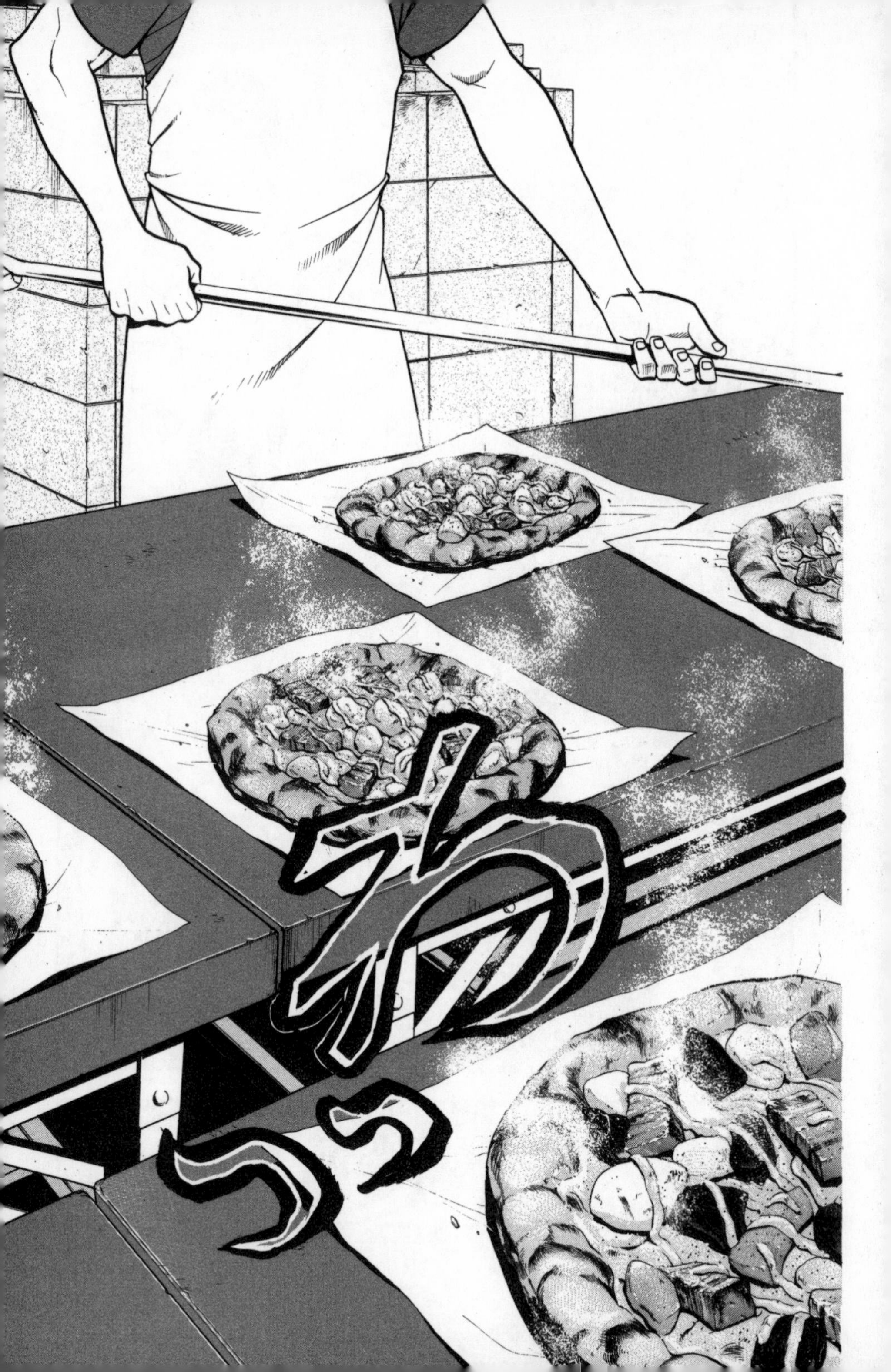
わっ

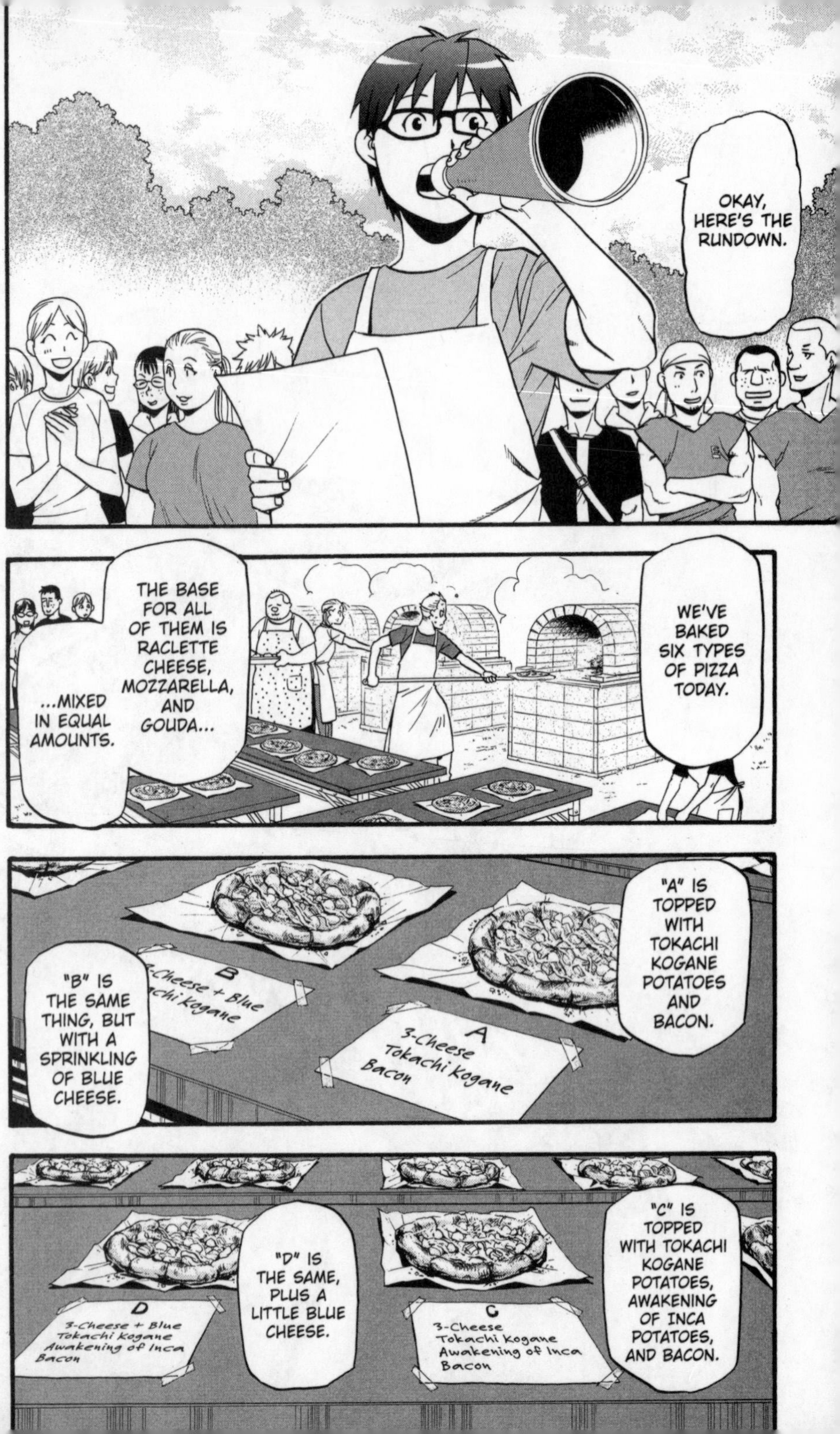
OKAY, HERE'S THE RUNDOWN.
WE'VE BAKED SIX TYPES OF PIZZA TODAY.
THE BASE FOR ALL OF THEM IS RACLETTE CHEESE, MOZZARELLA, AND GOUDA...
...MIXED IN EQUAL AMOUNTS.
"A" IS TOPPED WITH TOKACHI KOGANE POTATOES AND BACON.
A
3-Cheese
Tokachi Kogane
Bacon
"B" IS THE SAME THING, BUT WITH A SPRINKLING OF BLUE CHEESE.
B
"C" IS TOPPED WITH TOKACHI KOGANE POTATOES, AWAKENING OF INCA POTATOES, AND BACON.
C
3-Cheese
Tokachi Kogane
Awakening of Inca
Bacon
"D" IS THE SAME, PLUS A LITTLE BLUE CHEESE.
D
3-Cheese + Blue
Tokachi Kogane
Awakening of Inca
Bacon

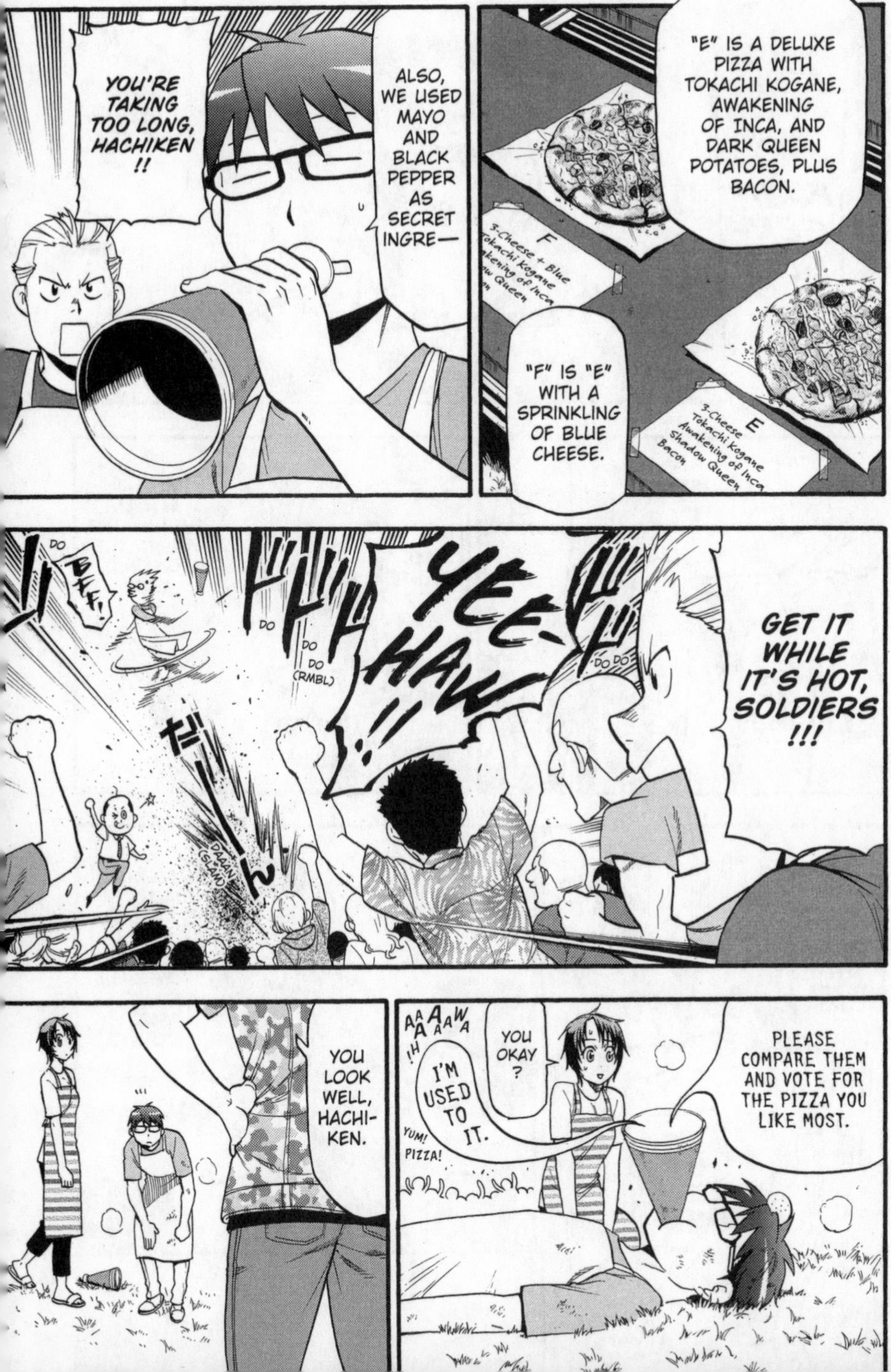
"E" IS A DELUXE PIZZA WITH TOKACHI KOGANE, AWAKENING OF INCA, AND DARK QUEEN POTATOES, PLUS BACON.
F
3-Cheese + Blue
Tokachi kogane
E
3-Cheese
Tokachi kogane
Awakening of Inca
Shadow Queen
Bacon
"F" IS "E" WITH A SPRINKLING OF BLUE CHEESE.
ALSO, WE USED MAYO AND BLACK PEPPER AS SECRET INGRE—
YOU'RE TAKING TOO LONG, HACHIKEN!!
GET IT WHILE IT'S HOT, SOLDIERS!!!
DO DO
YEE-HAW!!!
DO
DO
DO
(RMBL)
DO
BEF!
PAAAN (SLAM)
PLEASE COMPARE THEM AND VOTE FOR THE PIZZA YOU LIKE MOST.
YOU OKAY?
I'M USED TO IT.
AAAAAAWA
YUM! PIZZA!
YOU LOOK WELL, HACHI-KEN.

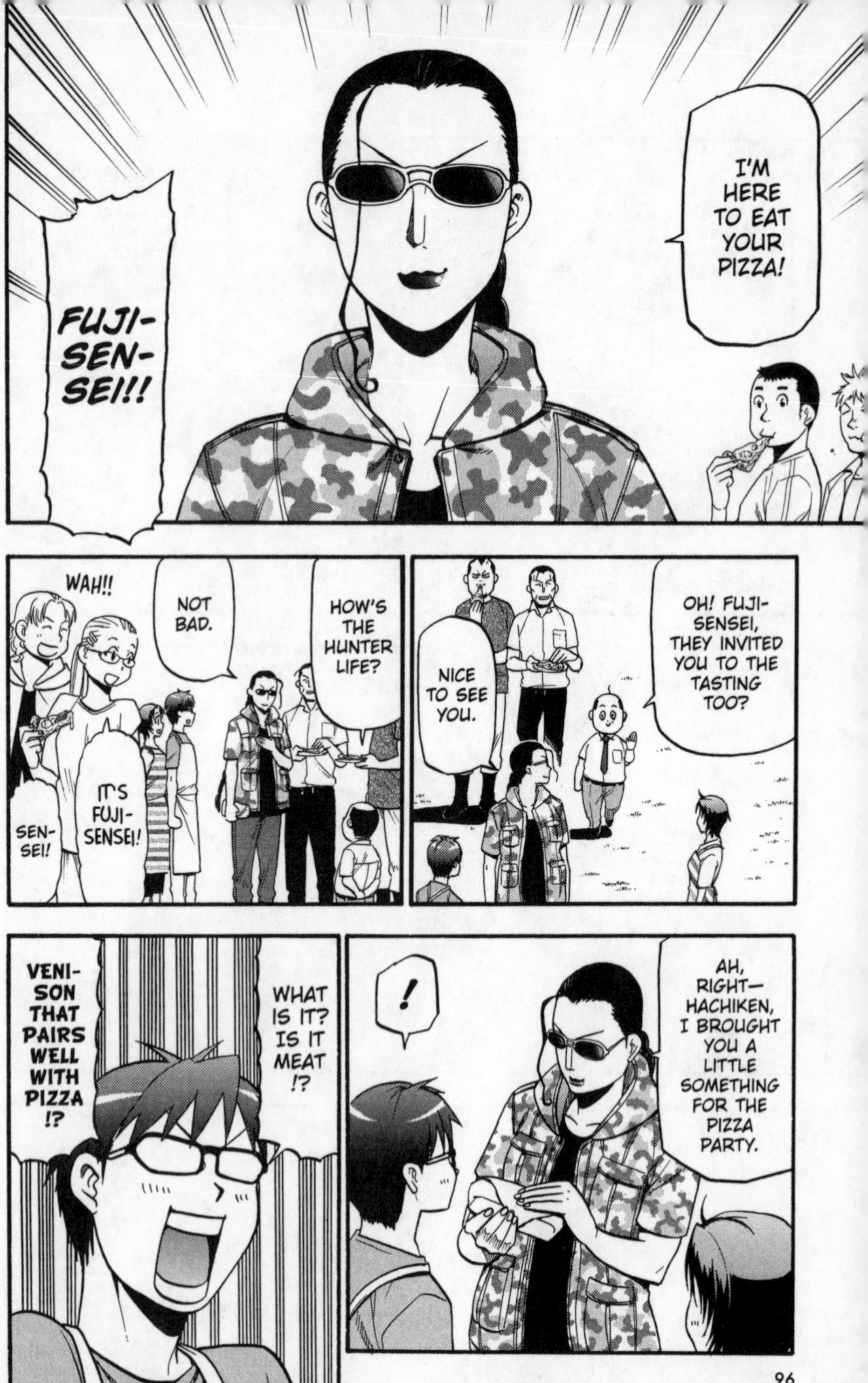
I'M HERE TO EAT YOUR PIZZA!
FUJI-SENSEI!!
OH! FUJI-SENSEI, THEY INVITED YOU TO THE TASTING TOO?
NICE TO SEE YOU.
HOW'S THE HUNTER LIFE?
NOT BAD.
WAH!!
IT'S FUJI-SENSEI!
SEN-SEI!
AH, RIGHT— HACHIKEN, I BROUGHT YOU A LITTLE SOMETHING FOR THE PIZZA PARTY.
!
WHAT IS IT? IS IT MEAT!?
VENISON THAT PAIRS WELL WITH PIZZA!?

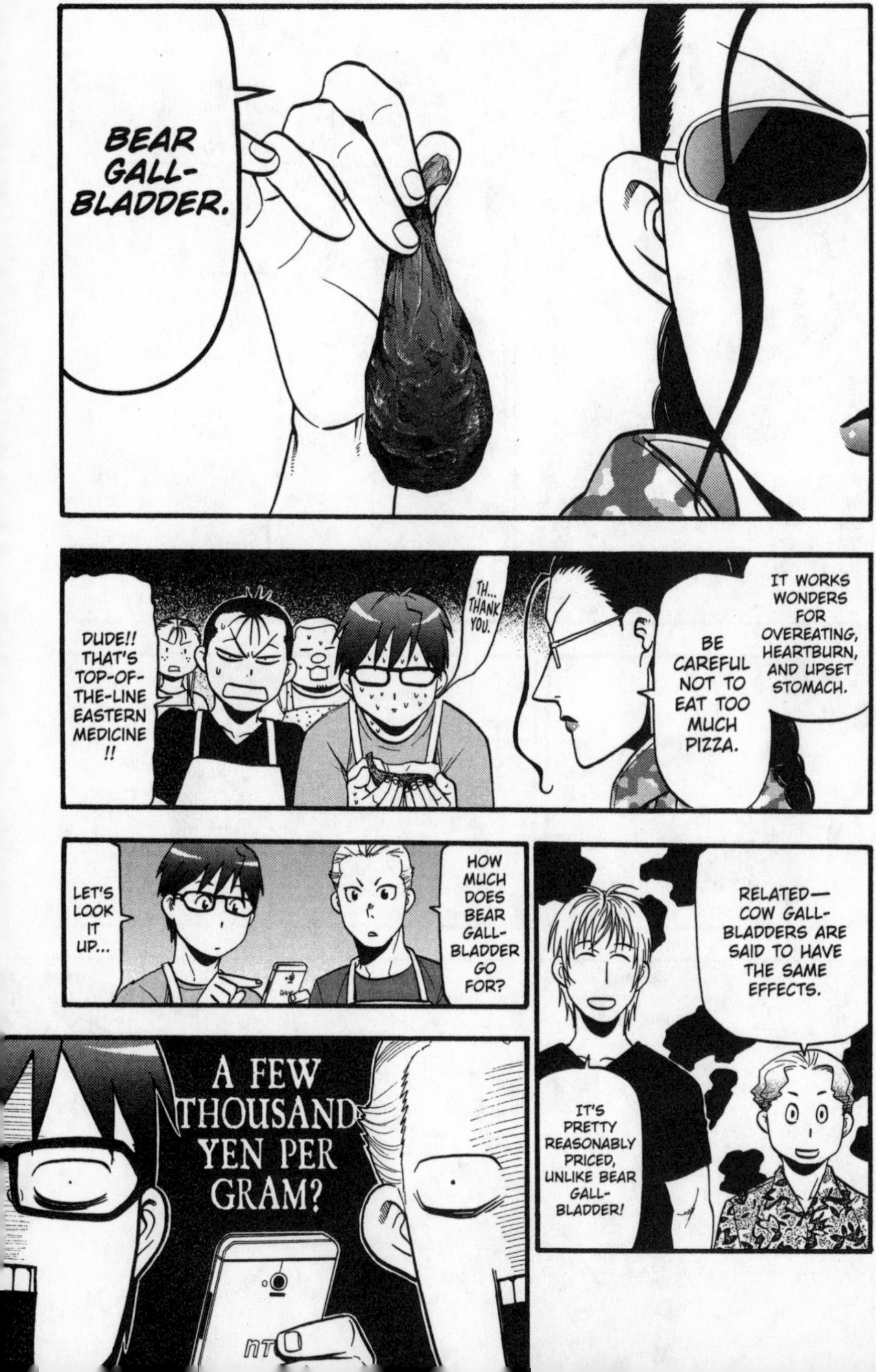
BEAR GALL-BLADDER.
IT WORKS WONDERS FOR OVEREATING, HEARTBURN, AND UPSET STOMACH.
BE CAREFUL NOT TO EAT TOO MUCH PIZZA.
TH... THANK YOU.
DUDE!! THAT'S TOP-OF-THE-LINE EASTERN MEDICINE!!
RELATED—COW GALL-BLADDERS ARE SAID TO HAVE THE SAME EFFECTS.
IT'S PRETTY REASONABLY PRICED, UNLIKE BEAR GALL-BLADDER!
HOW MUCH DOES BEAR GALL-BLADDER GO FOR?
LET'S LOOK IT UP...
A FEW THOUSAND YEN PER GRAM?

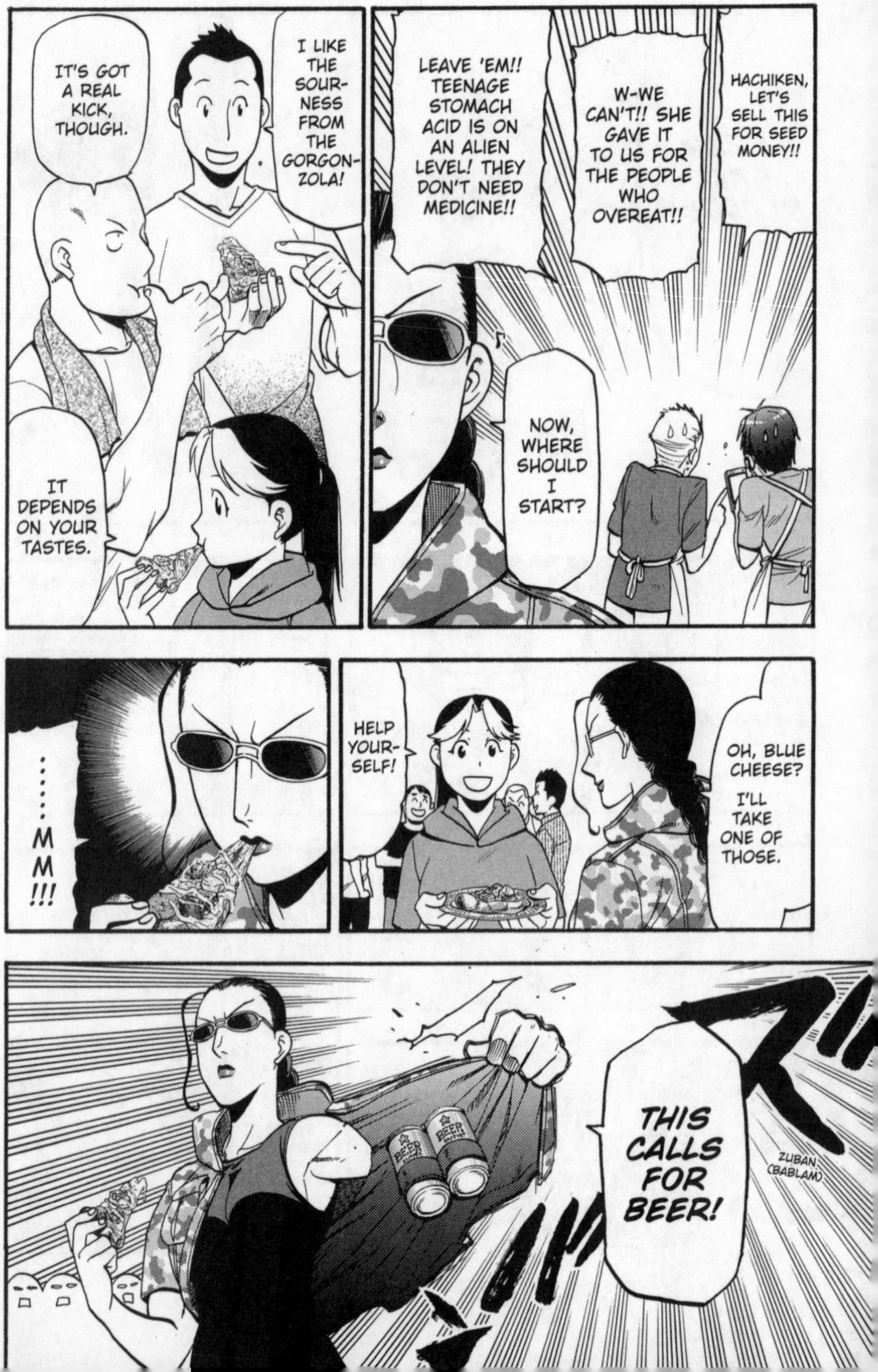
HACHIKEN, LET'S SELL THIS FOR SEED MONEY!!
W-WE CAN'T!! SHE GAVE IT TO US FOR THE PEOPLE WHO OVEREAT!!
LEAVE 'EM!! TEENAGE STOMACH ACID IS ON AN ALIEN LEVEL! THEY DON'T NEED MEDICINE!!
NOW, WHERE SHOULD I START?
I LIKE THE SOUR-NESS FROM THE GORGON-ZOLA!
IT'S GOT A REAL KICK, THOUGH.
IT DEPENDS ON YOUR TASTES.
OH, BLUE CHEESE?
I'LL TAKE ONE OF THOSE.
HELP YOUR-SELF!
......MM!!!
THIS CALLS FOR BEER!
ZUBAN (BABLAM)
BEER
BEER

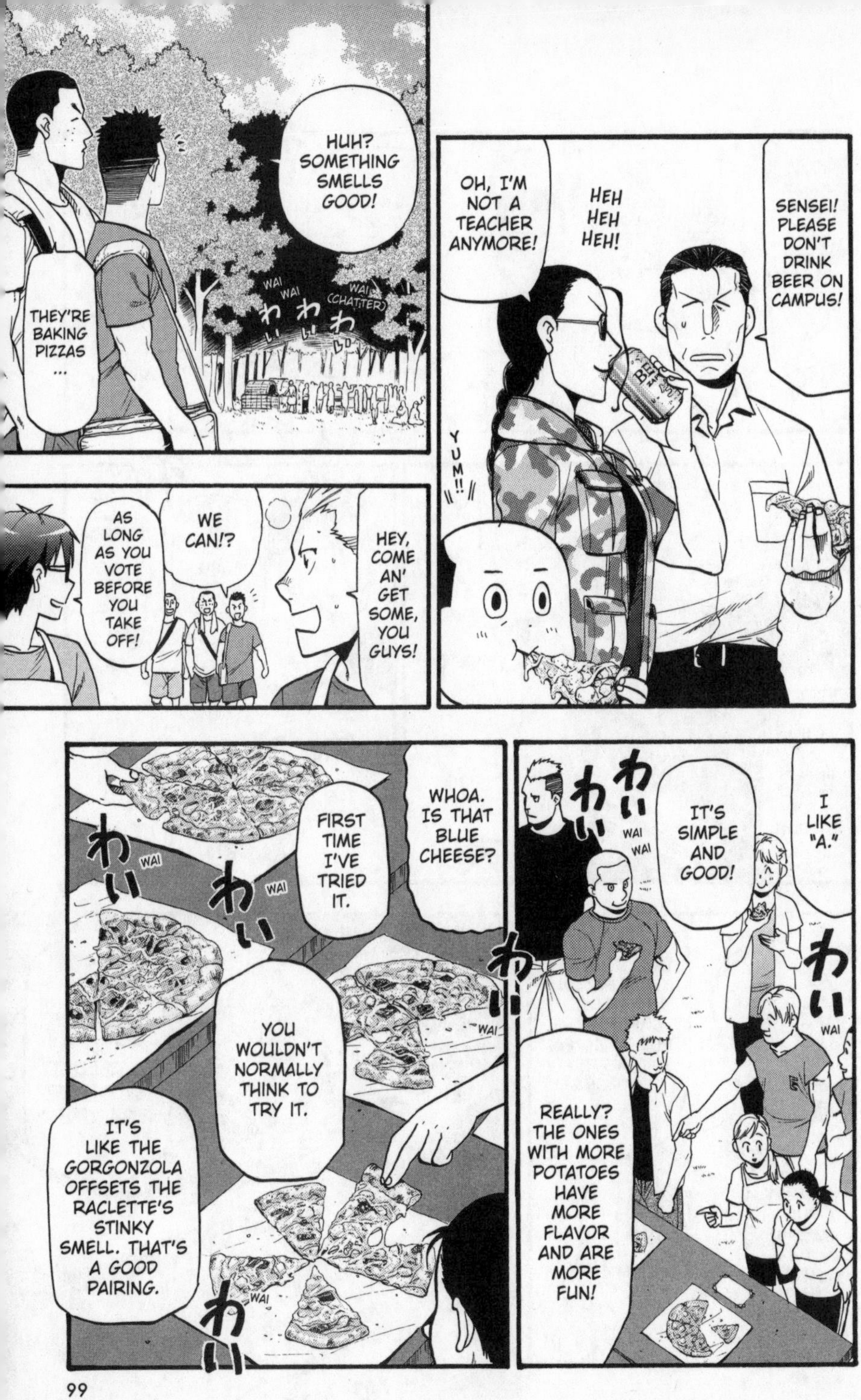

SENSEI! PLEASE DON'T DRINK BEER ON CAMPUS!
HEH HEH HEH!
OH, I'M NOT A TEACHER ANYMORE!
YUM!!
HUH? SOMETHING SMELLS GOOD!
WAI WAI WAI (CHATTER)
THEY'RE BAKING PIZZAS ...
HEY, COME AN' GET SOME, YOU GUYS!
WE CAN!?
AS LONG AS YOU VOTE BEFORE YOU TAKE OFF!
I LIKE "A."
IT'S SIMPLE AND GOOD!
WAI WAI
WAI
REALLY? THE ONES WITH MORE POTATOES HAVE MORE FLAVOR AND ARE MORE FUN!
WAI
WHOA. IS THAT BLUE CHEESE?
FIRST TIME I'VE TRIED IT.
WAI
WAI
YOU WOULDN'T NORMALLY THINK TO TRY IT.
IT'S LIKE THE GORGONZOLA OFFSETS THE RACLETTE'S STINKY SMELL. THAT'S A GOOD PAIRING.
WAI

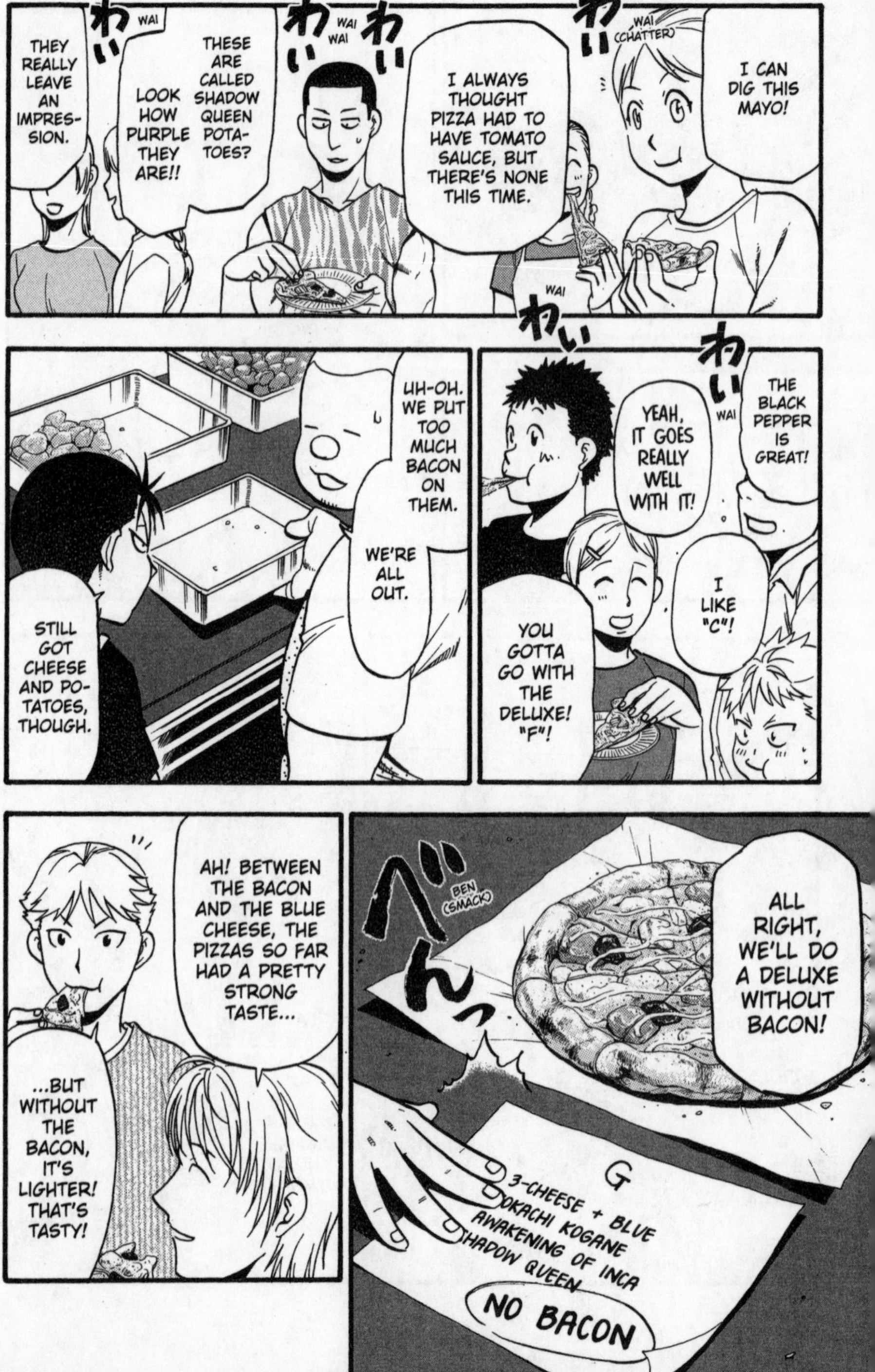

わい
WAI (CHATTER)
I CAN DIG THIS MAYO!
I ALWAYS THOUGHT PIZZA HAD TO HAVE TOMATO SAUCE, BUT THERE'S NONE THIS TIME.
わい
WAI WAI
わい
THESE ARE CALLED SHADOW QUEEN POTA-TOES?
LOOK HOW PURPLE THEY ARE!!
わい
WAI
THEY REALLY LEAVE AN IMPRES-SION.
わい
WAI
THE BLACK PEPPER IS GREAT!
YEAH, IT GOES REALLY WELL WITH IT!
WAI
わい
I LIKE "C"!
YOU GOTTA GO WITH THE DELUXE! "F"!
UH-OH. WE PUT TOO MUCH BACON ON THEM.
WE'RE ALL OUT.
STILL GOT CHEESE AND PO-TATOES, THOUGH.
べんっ
BEN (SMACK)
ALL RIGHT, WE'LL DO A DELUXE WITHOUT BACON!
G
3-CHEESE + BLUE
OKACHI KOGANE
AWAKENING OF INCA
HADOW QUEEN
NO BACON
AH! BETWEEN THE BACON AND THE BLUE CHEESE, THE PIZZAS SO FAR HAD A PRETTY STRONG TASTE...
...BUT WITHOUT THE BACON, IT'S LIGHTER! THAT'S TASTY!

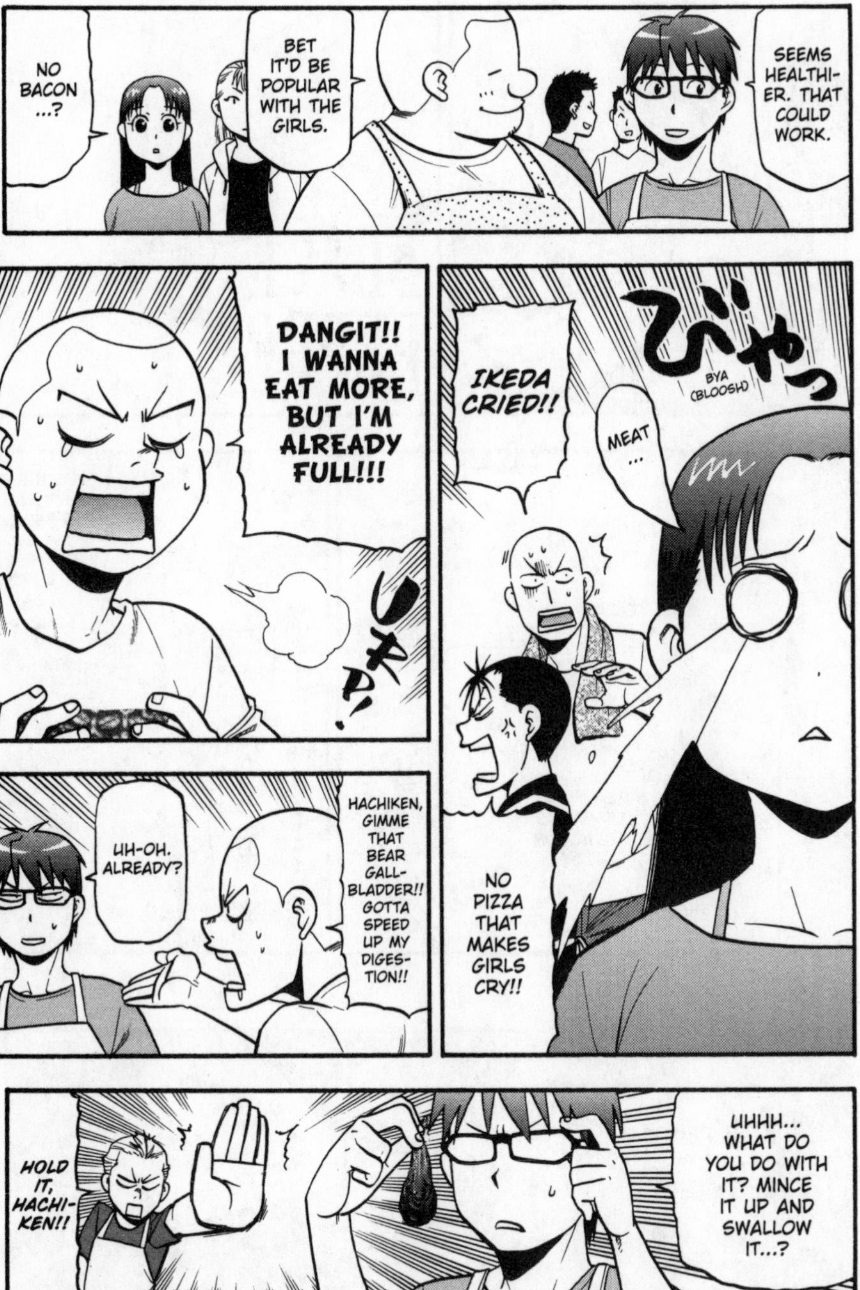

SEEMS HEALTHIER. THAT COULD WORK.
BET IT'D BE POPULAR WITH THE GIRLS.
NO BACON ...?
びゃっ
BYA (BLOOSH)
IKEDA CRIED!!
MEAT ...
NO PIZZA THAT MAKES GIRLS CRY!!
DANGIT!! I WANNA EAT MORE, BUT I'M ALREADY FULL!!!
HACHIKEN, GIMME THAT BEAR GALL-BLADDER!! GOTTA SPEED UP MY DIGES-TION!!
UH-OH. ALREADY?
UHHH... WHAT DO YOU DO WITH IT? MINCE IT UP AND SWALLOW IT...?
HOLD IT, HACHIKEN!!

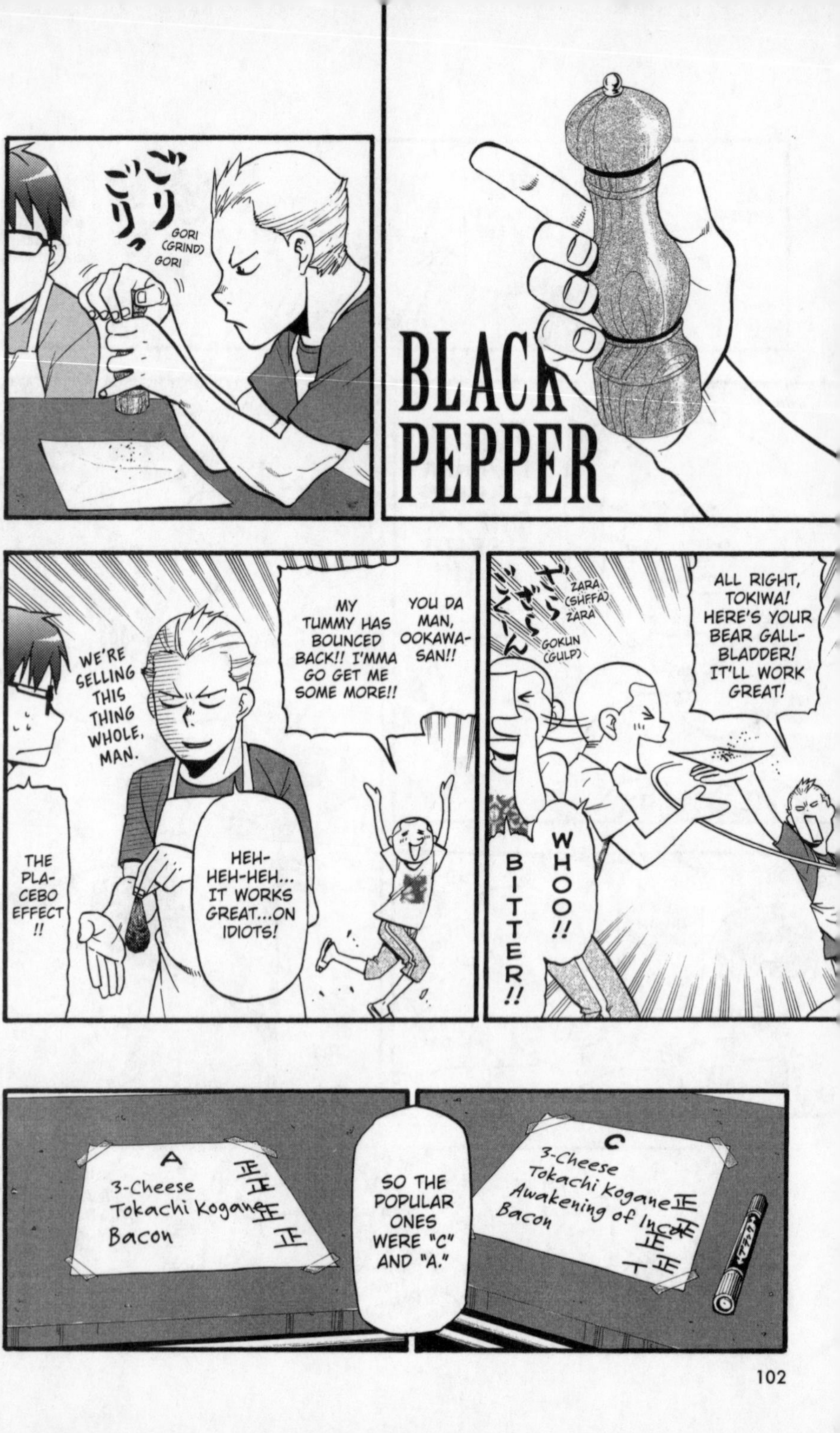
BLACK PEPPER
ゴリごりっ
GORI (GRIND) GORI
ざらざら
ZARA (SHFFA) ZARA
ごくーん
GOKUN (GULP)
ALL RIGHT, TOKIWA! HERE'S YOUR BEAR GALL-BLADDER! IT'LL WORK GREAT!
WHOO!!
BITTER!!
YOU DA MAN, OOKAWA-SAN!!
MY TUMMY HAS BOUNCED BACK!! I'MMA GO GET ME SOME MORE!!
WE'RE SELLING THIS THING WHOLE, MAN.
HEH-HEH-HEH... IT WORKS GREAT...ON IDIOTS!
THE PLA-CEBO EFFECT!!
C
3-Cheese Tokachi Kogane Awakening of Inca Bacon
SO THE POPULAR ONES WERE "C" AND "A."
A
3-Cheese Tokachi Kogane Bacon

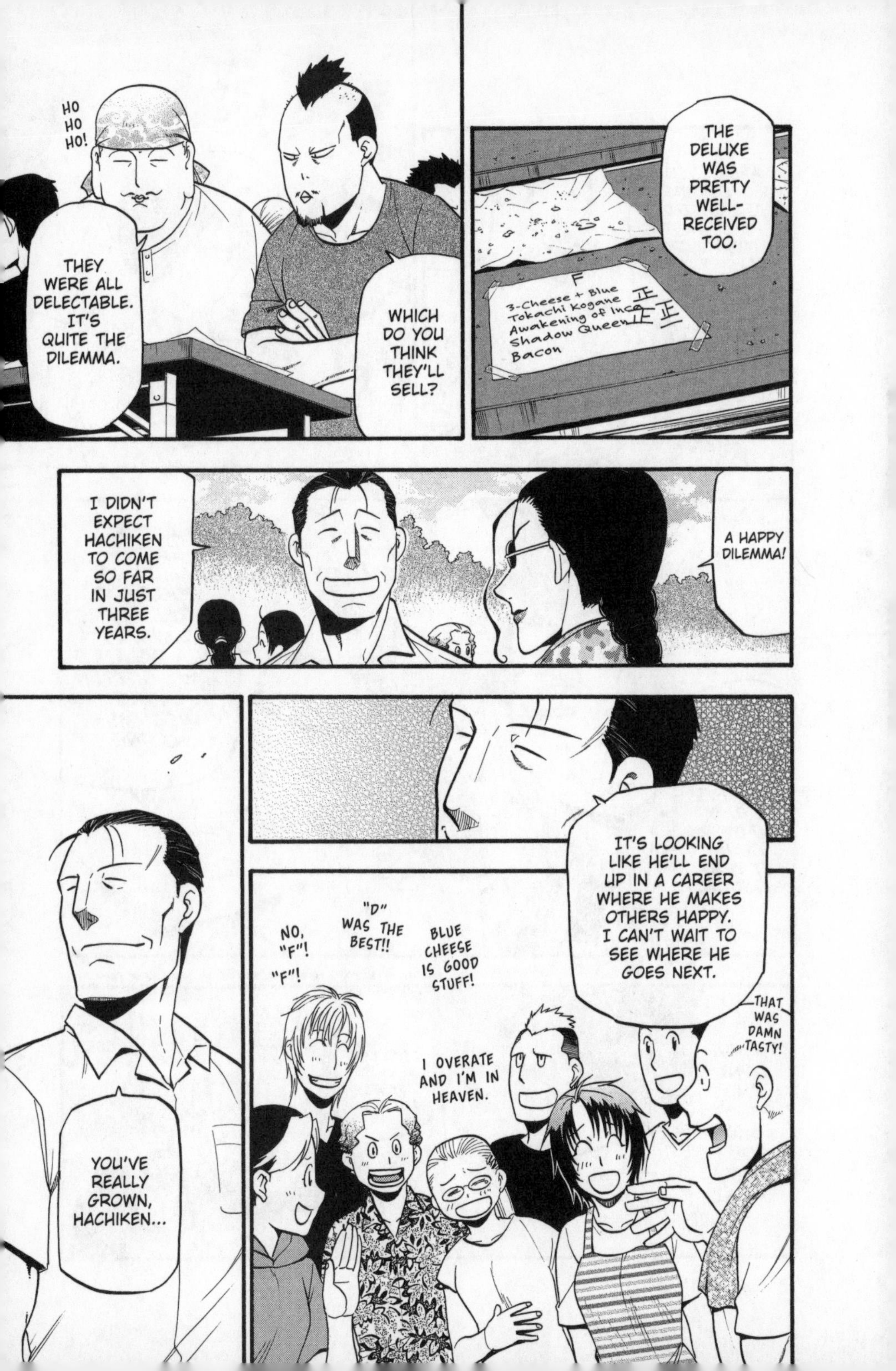
THE DELUXE WAS PRETTY WELL-RECEIVED TOO.
F
3-Cheese + Blue
Tokachi Kogane
Awakening of Inca
Shadow Queen
Bacon
WHICH DO YOU THINK THEY'LL SELL?
HO HO HO!
THEY WERE ALL DELECTABLE. IT'S QUITE THE DILEMMA.
A HAPPY DILEMMA!
I DIDN'T EXPECT HACHIKEN TO COME SO FAR IN JUST THREE YEARS.
IT'S LOOKING LIKE HE'LL END UP IN A CAREER WHERE HE MAKES OTHERS HAPPY. I CAN'T WAIT TO SEE WHERE HE GOES NEXT.
THAT WAS DAMN TASTY!
I OVERATE AND I'M IN HEAVEN.
BLUE CHEESE IS GOOD STUFF!
"D" WAS THE BEST!!
NO, "F"!
"F"!
YOU'VE REALLY GROWN, HACHIKEN...

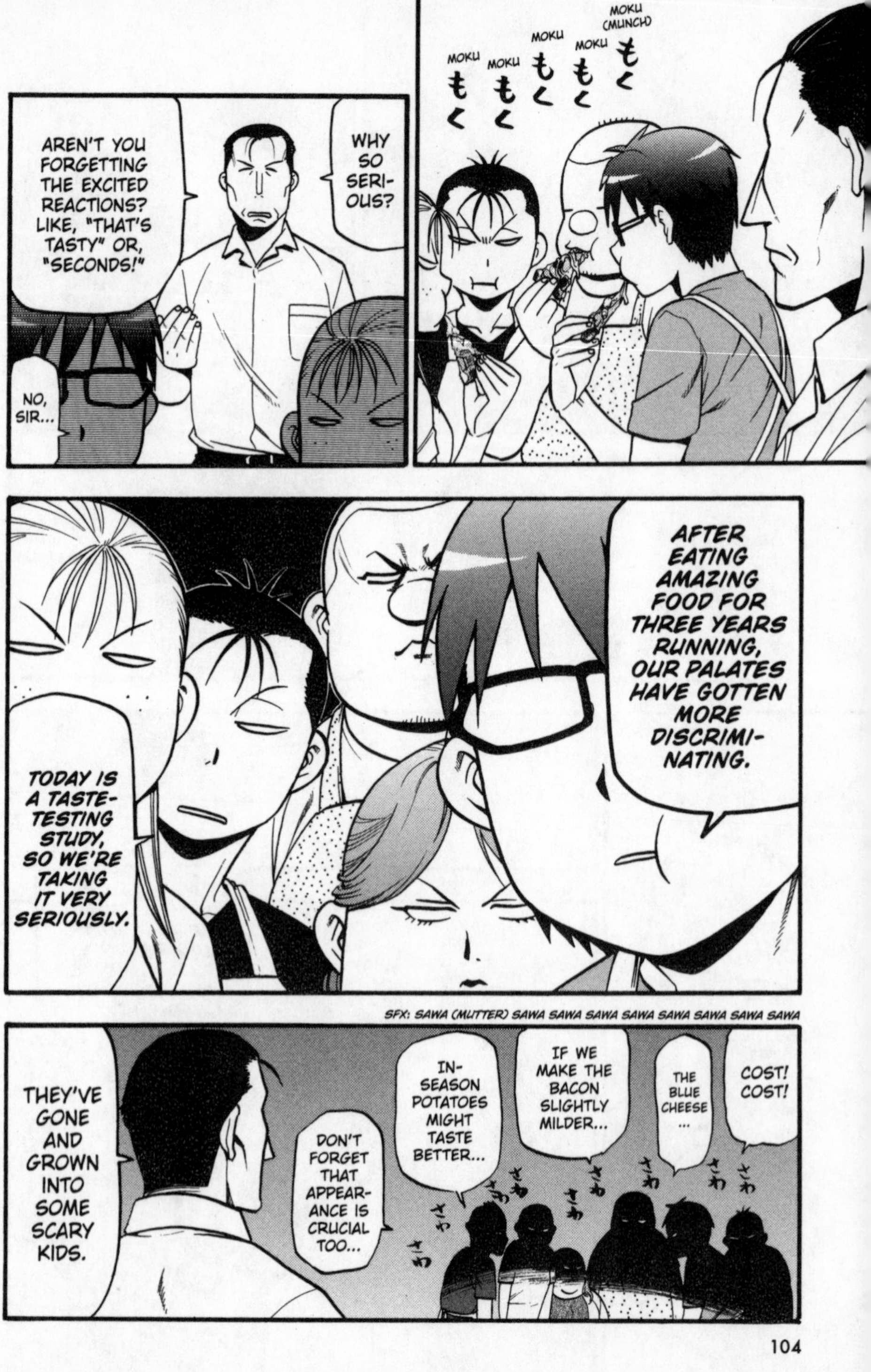
MOKU (MUNCH) もく
MOKU もく
MOKU もく
MOKU もく
MOKU もく
WHY SO SERI-OUS?
AREN'T YOU FORGETTING THE EXCITED REACTIONS? LIKE, "THAT'S TASTY" OR, "SECONDS!"
NO, SIR...
AFTER EATING AMAZING FOOD FOR THREE YEARS RUNNING, OUR PALATES HAVE GOTTEN MORE DISCRIMI-NATING.
TODAY IS A TASTE-TESTING STUDY, SO WE'RE TAKING IT VERY SERIOUSLY.
SFX: SAWA (MUTTER) SAWA SAWA SAWA SAWA SAWA SAWA SAWA SAWA
COST! COST!
THE BLUE CHEESE...
IF WE MAKE THE BACON SLIGHTLY MILDER...
IN-SEASON POTATOES MIGHT TASTE BETTER...
DON'T FORGET THAT APPEAR-ANCE IS CRUCIAL TOO...
THEY'VE GONE AND GROWN INTO SOME SCARY KIDS.

Silver Spoon

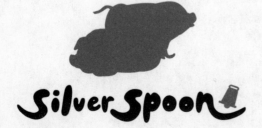

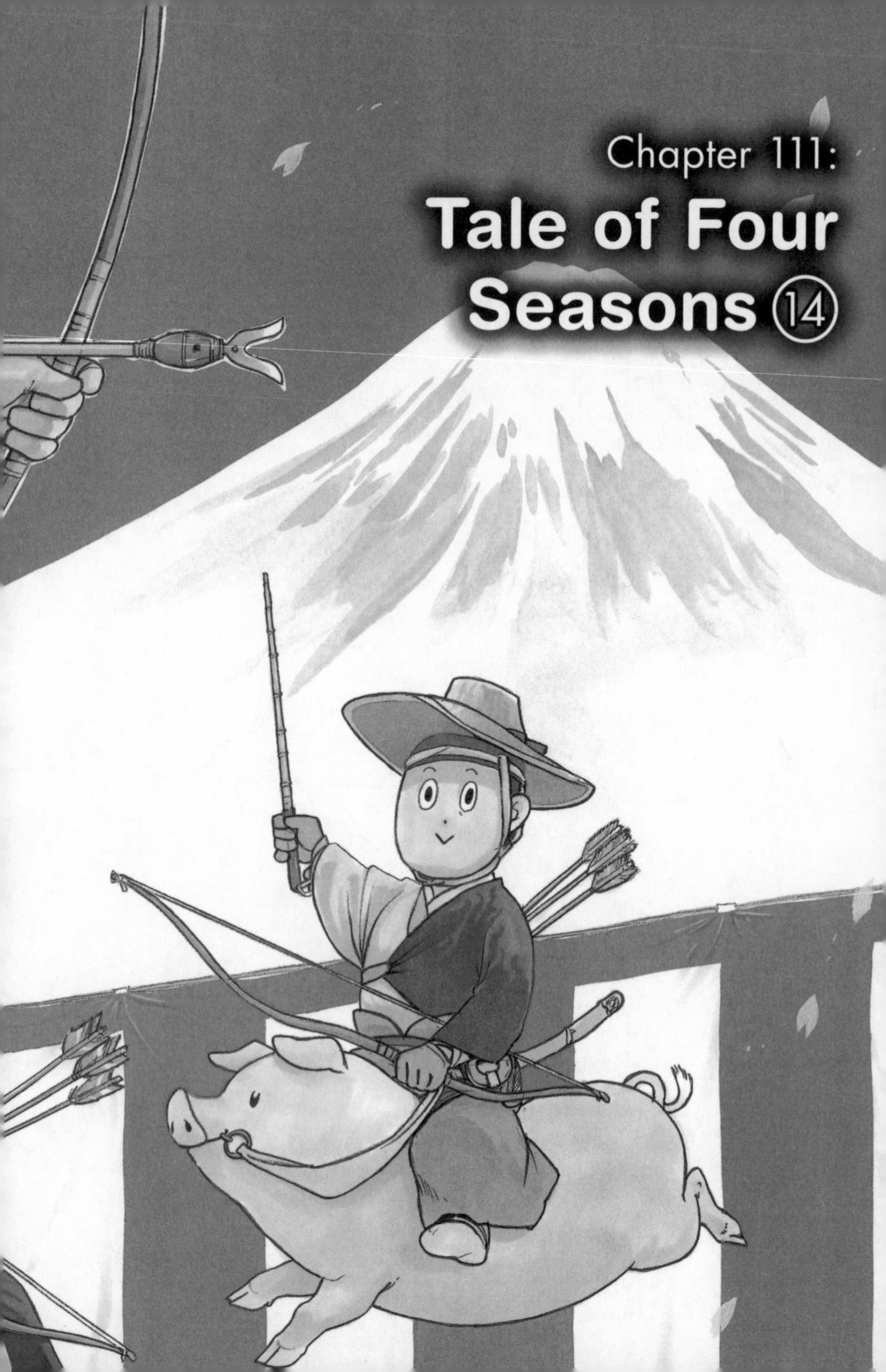
Chapter 111:
Tale of Four Seasons ⑭

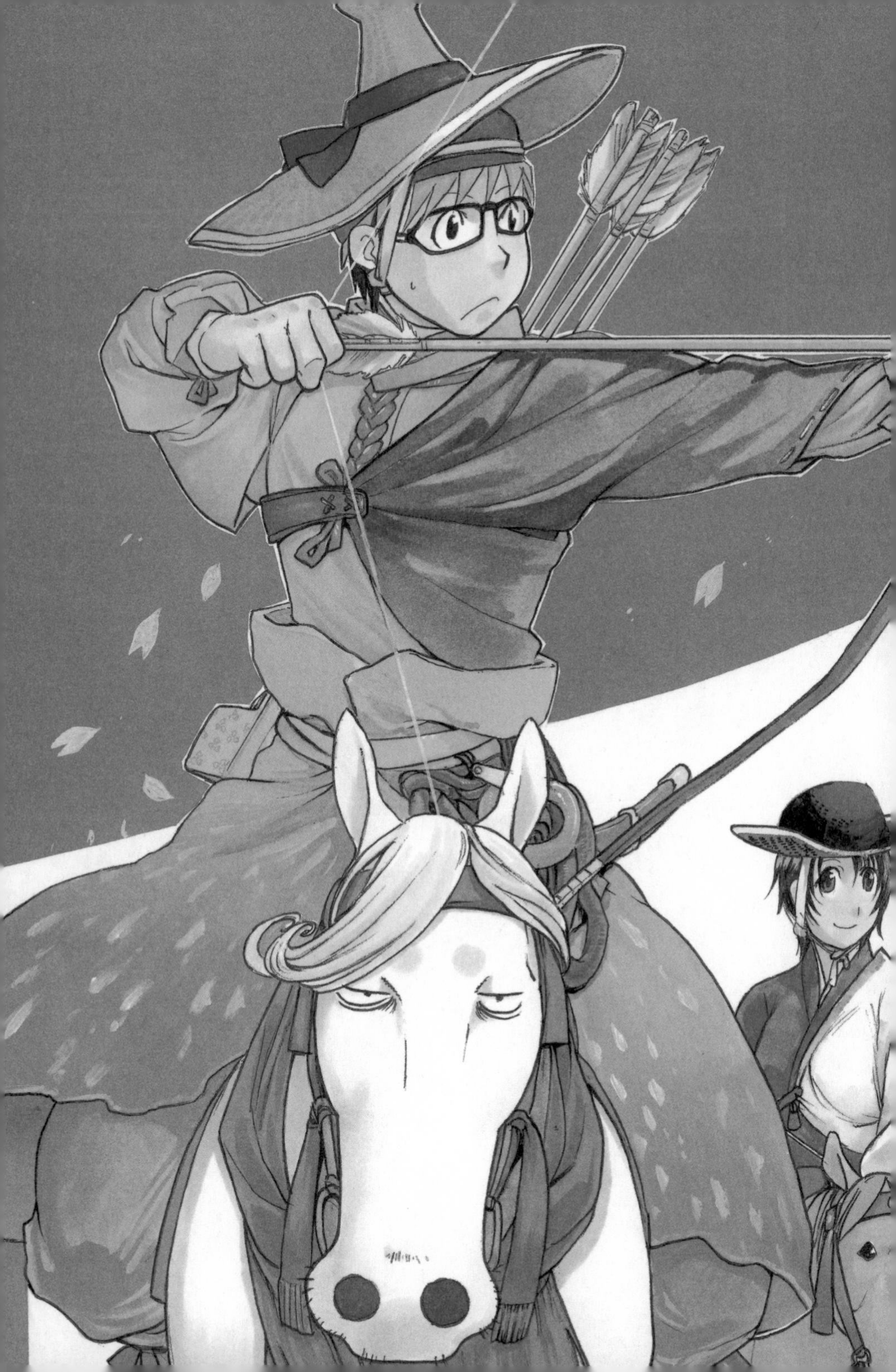

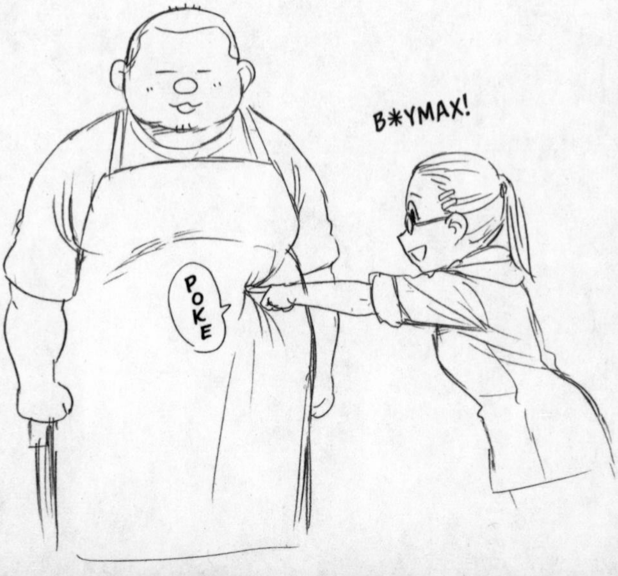
B*YMAX!
POKE

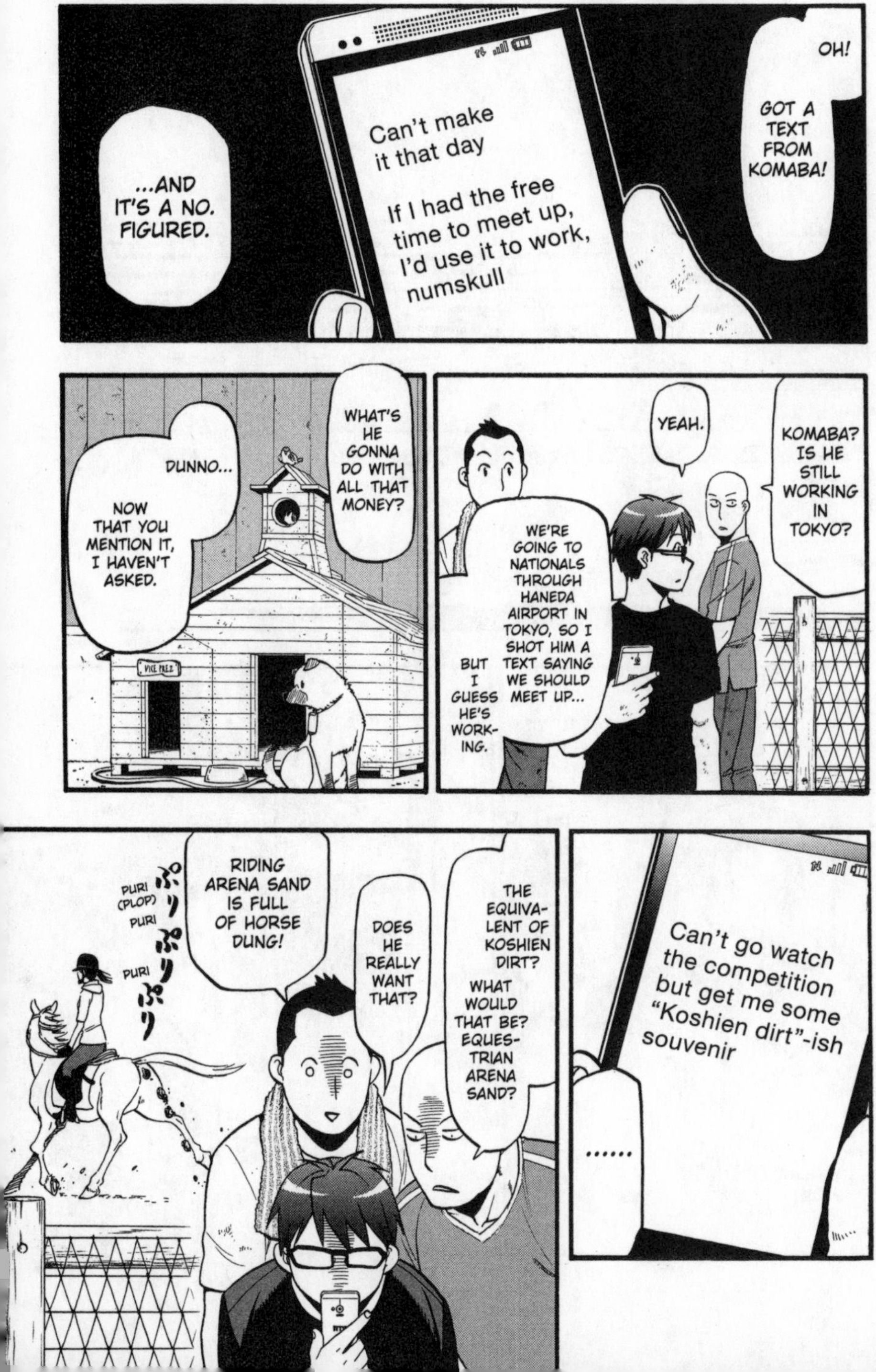
OH!
GOT A TEXT FROM KOMABA!
Can't make it that day
If I had the free time to meet up, I'd use it to work, numskull
...AND IT'S A NO. FIGURED.
KOMABA? IS HE STILL WORKING IN TOKYO?
YEAH.
WE'RE GOING TO NATIONALS THROUGH HANEDA AIRPORT IN TOKYO, SO I SHOT HIM A TEXT SAYING WE SHOULD MEET UP...
BUT I GUESS HE'S WORKING.
WHAT'S HE GONNA DO WITH ALL THAT MONEY?
DUNNO...
NOW THAT YOU MENTION IT, I HAVEN'T ASKED.
VICE PREZ
Can't go watch the competition but get me some "Koshien dirt"-ish souvenir
......
THE EQUIVALENT OF KOSHIEN DIRT?
WHAT WOULD THAT BE? EQUESTRIAN ARENA SAND?
DOES HE REALLY WANT THAT?
RIDING ARENA SAND IS FULL OF HORSE DUNG!
ぷりぷりぷり
PURI (PLOP) PURI
PURI

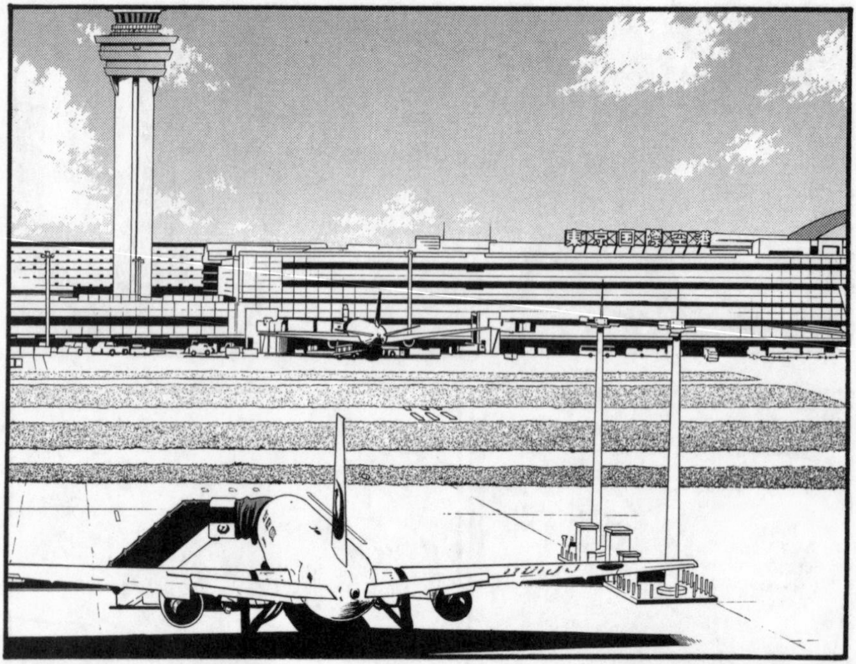

SIGN: TOKYO INTERNATIONAL AIRPORT

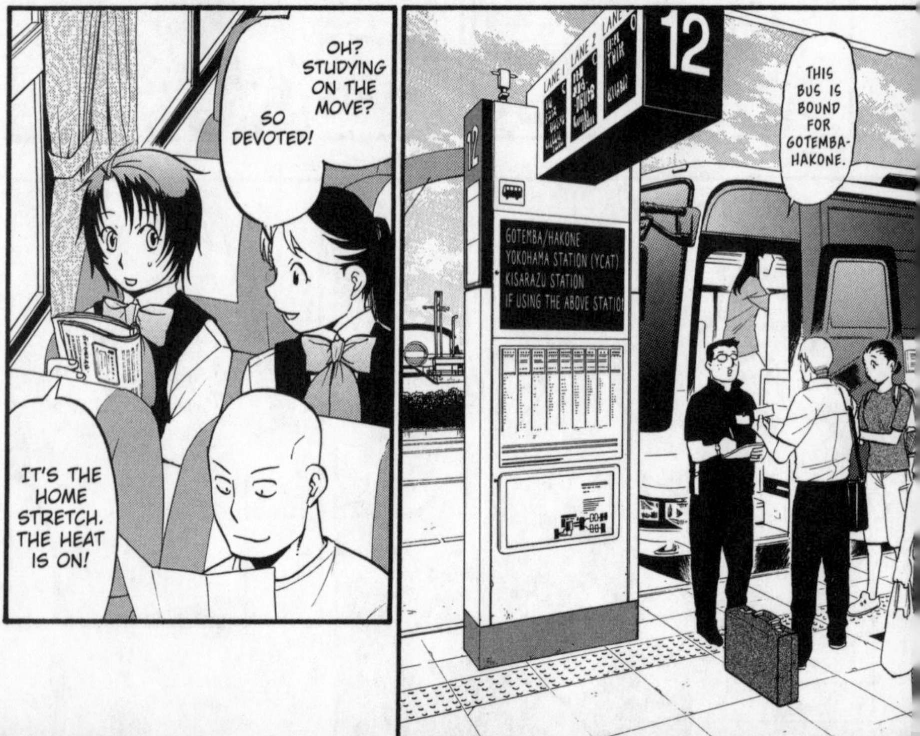
12
GOTEMBA/HAKONE
YOKOHAMA STATION (YCAT)
KISARAZU STATION
LANE 1
LANE 2
THIS BUS IS BOUND FOR GOTEMBA-HAKONE.
OH? STUDYING ON THE MOVE?
SO DEVOTED!
IT'S THE HOME STRETCH. THE HEAT IS ON!

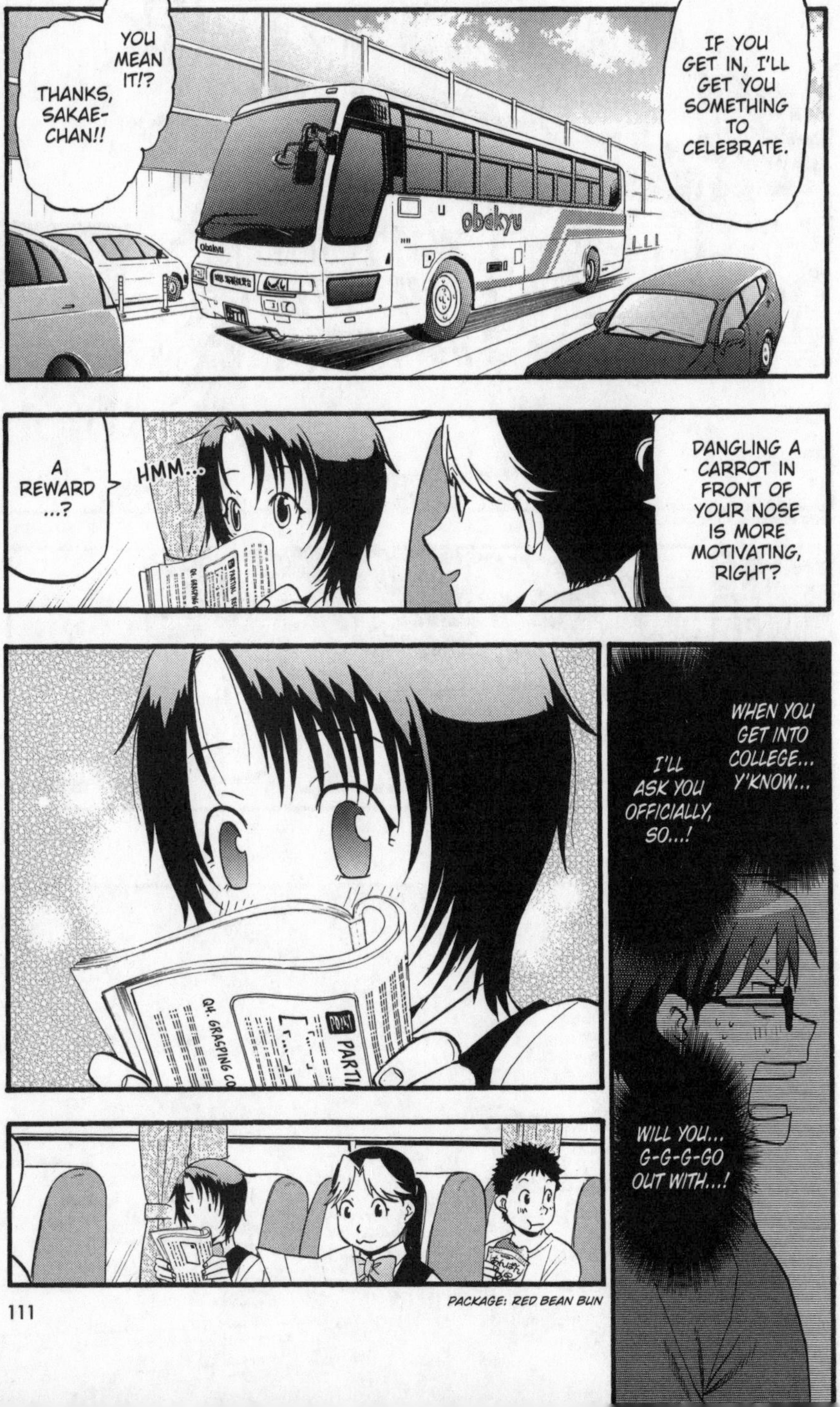
IF YOU GET IN, I'LL GET YOU SOMETHING TO CELEBRATE.
YOU MEAN IT!?
THANKS, SAKAE-CHAN!!
obakyu
DANGLING A CARROT IN FRONT OF YOUR NOSE IS MORE MOTIVATING, RIGHT?
HMM...
A REWARD ...?
WHEN YOU GET INTO COLLEGE... Y'KNOW...
I'LL ASK YOU OFFICIALLY, SO...!
WILL YOU... G-G-G-GO OUT WITH...!
PACKAGE: RED BEAN BUN

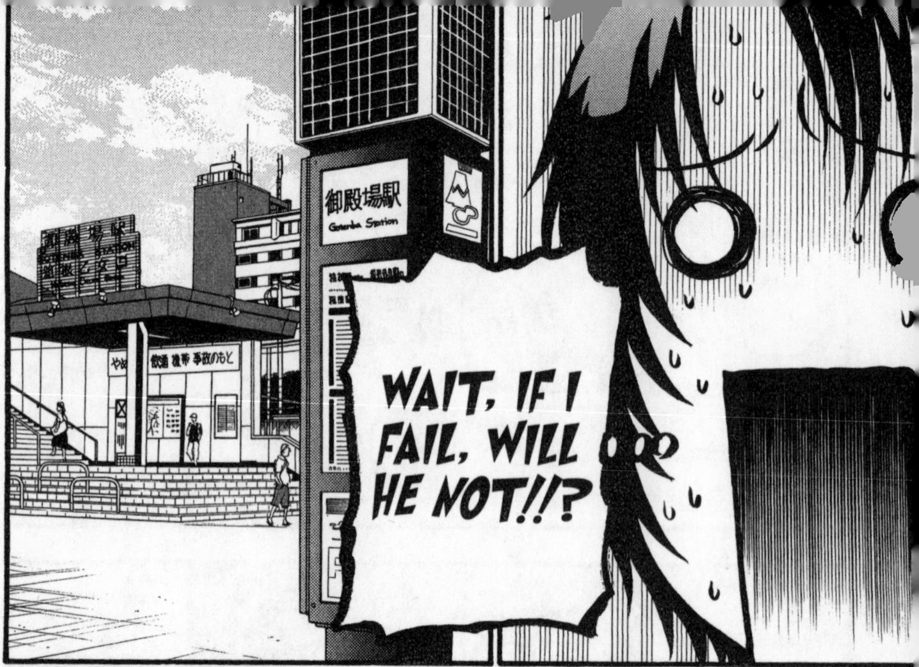
御殿場駅
Gotenba Station
WAIT, IF I FAIL, WILL HE NOT!!?
SIGN: DRINKING & PHONES CAUSE ACCIDENTS

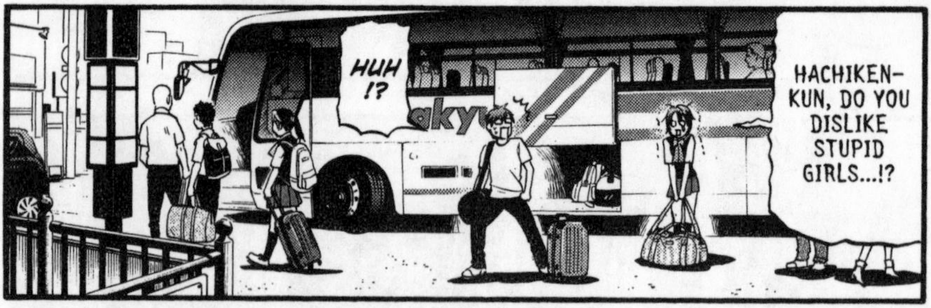
HACHIKEN-KUN, DO YOU DISLIKE STUPID GIRLS...!?
HUH!?

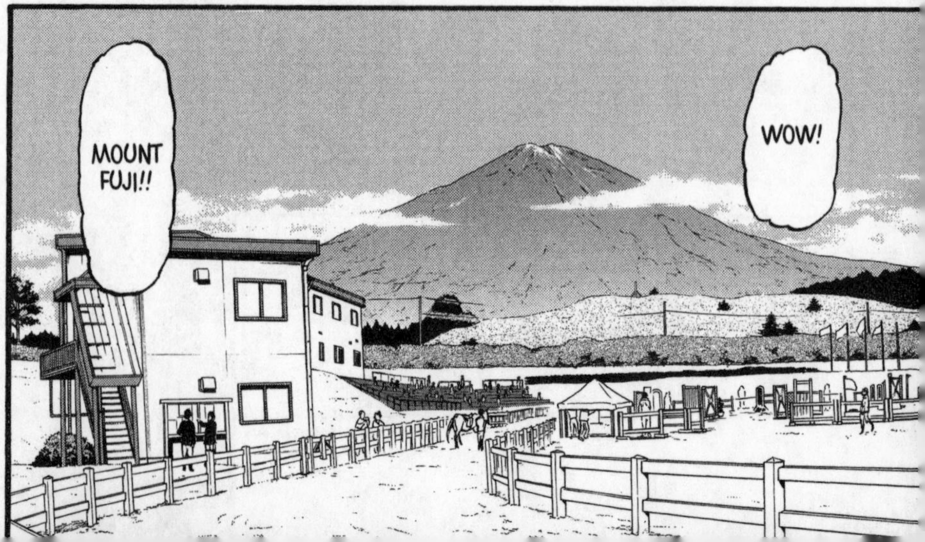
WOW!
MOUNT FUJI!!

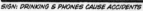

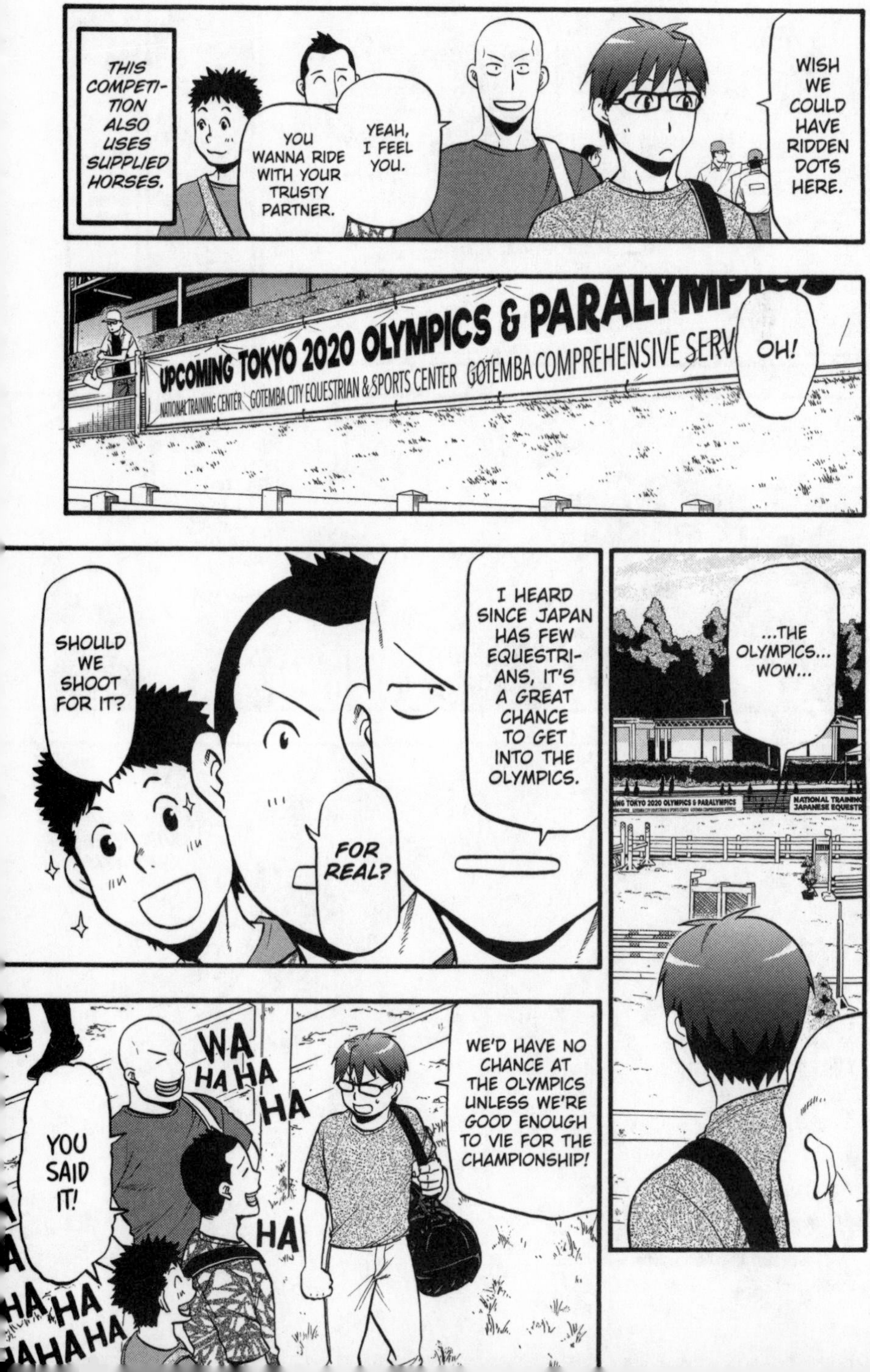
WISH WE COULD HAVE RIDDEN DOTS HERE.
YEAH, I FEEL YOU.
YOU WANNA RIDE WITH YOUR TRUSTY PARTNER.
THIS COMPETITION ALSO USES SUPPLIED HORSES.
OH!
UPCOMING TOKYO 2020 OLYMPICS & PARALYMPICS
NATIONAL TRAINING CENTER GOTEMBA CITY EQUESTRIAN & SPORTS CENTER GOTEMBA COMPREHENSIVE SERV
...THE OLYMPICS... WOW...
I HEARD SINCE JAPAN HAS FEW EQUESTRIANS, IT'S A GREAT CHANCE TO GET INTO THE OLYMPICS.
FOR REAL?
SHOULD WE SHOOT FOR IT?
WE'D HAVE NO CHANCE AT THE OLYMPICS UNLESS WE'RE GOOD ENOUGH TO VIE FOR THE CHAMPIONSHIP!
WA HA HA HA HA
YOU SAID IT!
HA
HA HA HAHA

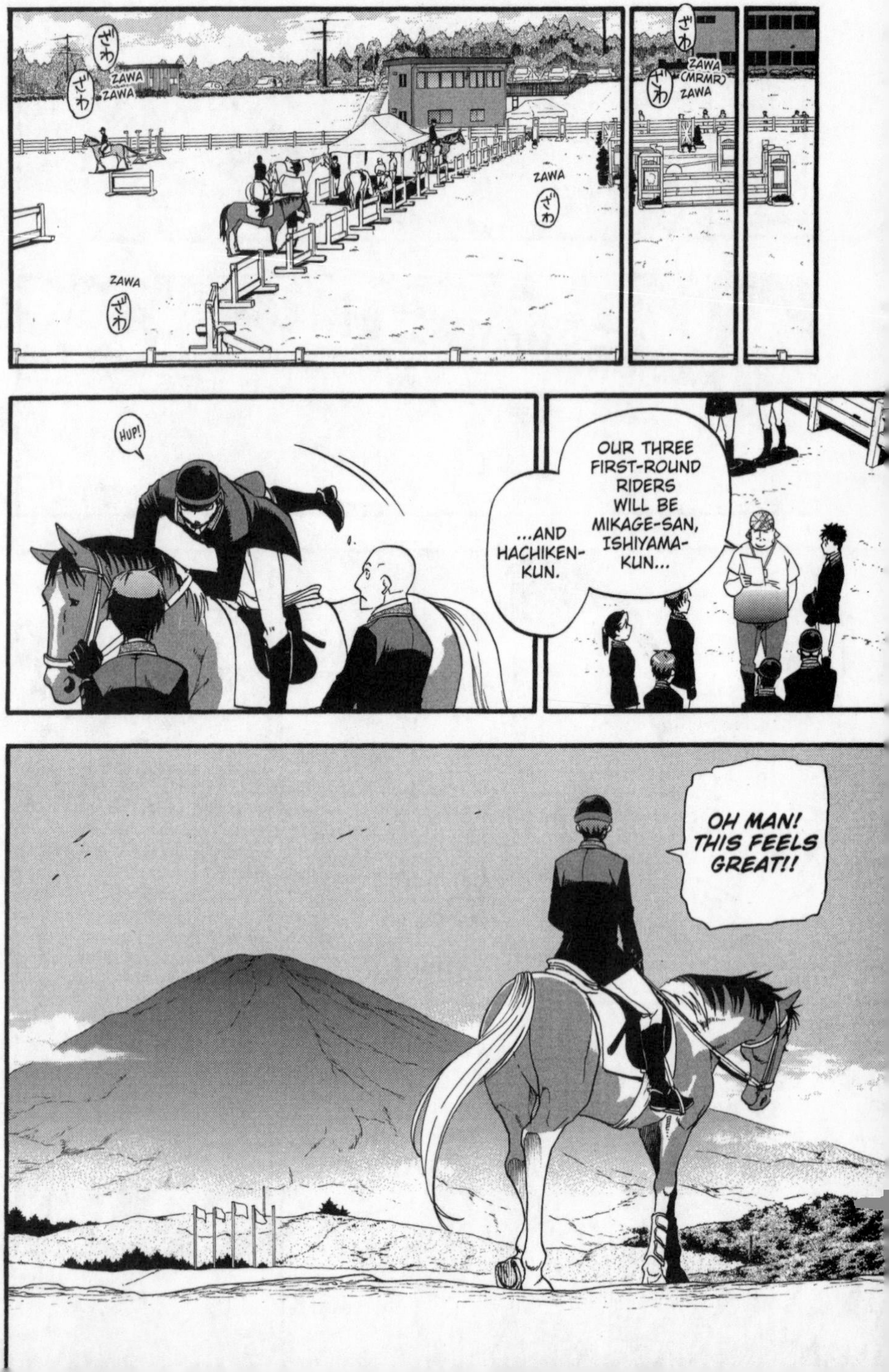
ざわ ZAWA (MRMR)
ざわ ZAWA
ざわ ZAWA
ざわ ZAWA
ZAWA ざわ
ZAWA ざわ
OUR THREE FIRST-ROUND RIDERS WILL BE MIKAGE-SAN, ISHIYAMA-KUN...
...AND HACHIKEN-KUN.
HUP!
OH MAN! THIS FEELS GREAT!!

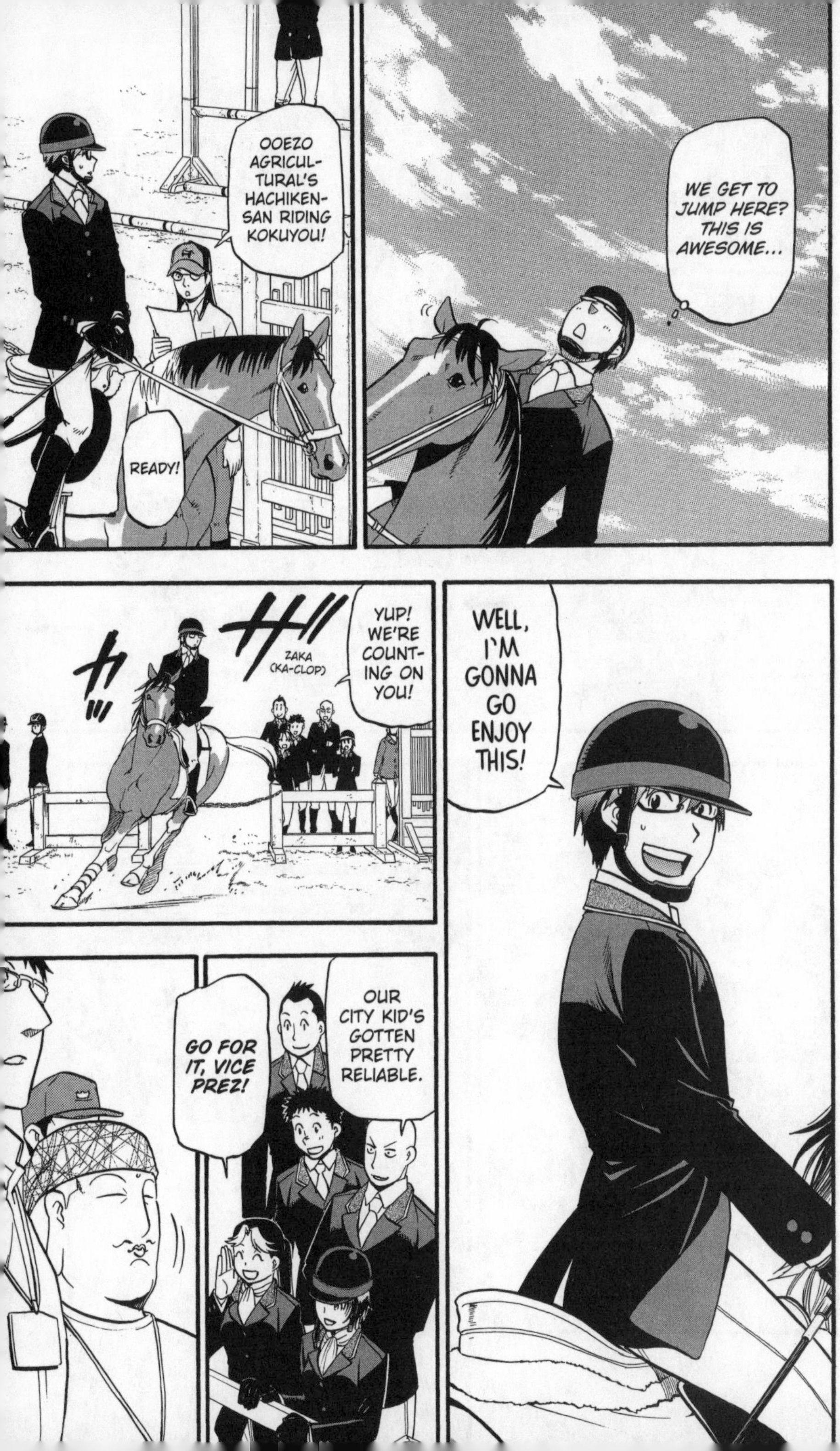
WE GET TO JUMP HERE? THIS IS AWESOME...
OOEZO AGRICULTURAL'S HACHIKEN-SAN RIDING KOKUYOU!
READY!
WELL, I'M GONNA GO ENJOY THIS!
YUP! WE'RE COUNTING ON YOU!
ZAKA (KA-CLOP)
OUR CITY KID'S GOTTEN PRETTY RELIABLE.
GO FOR IT, VICE PREZ!

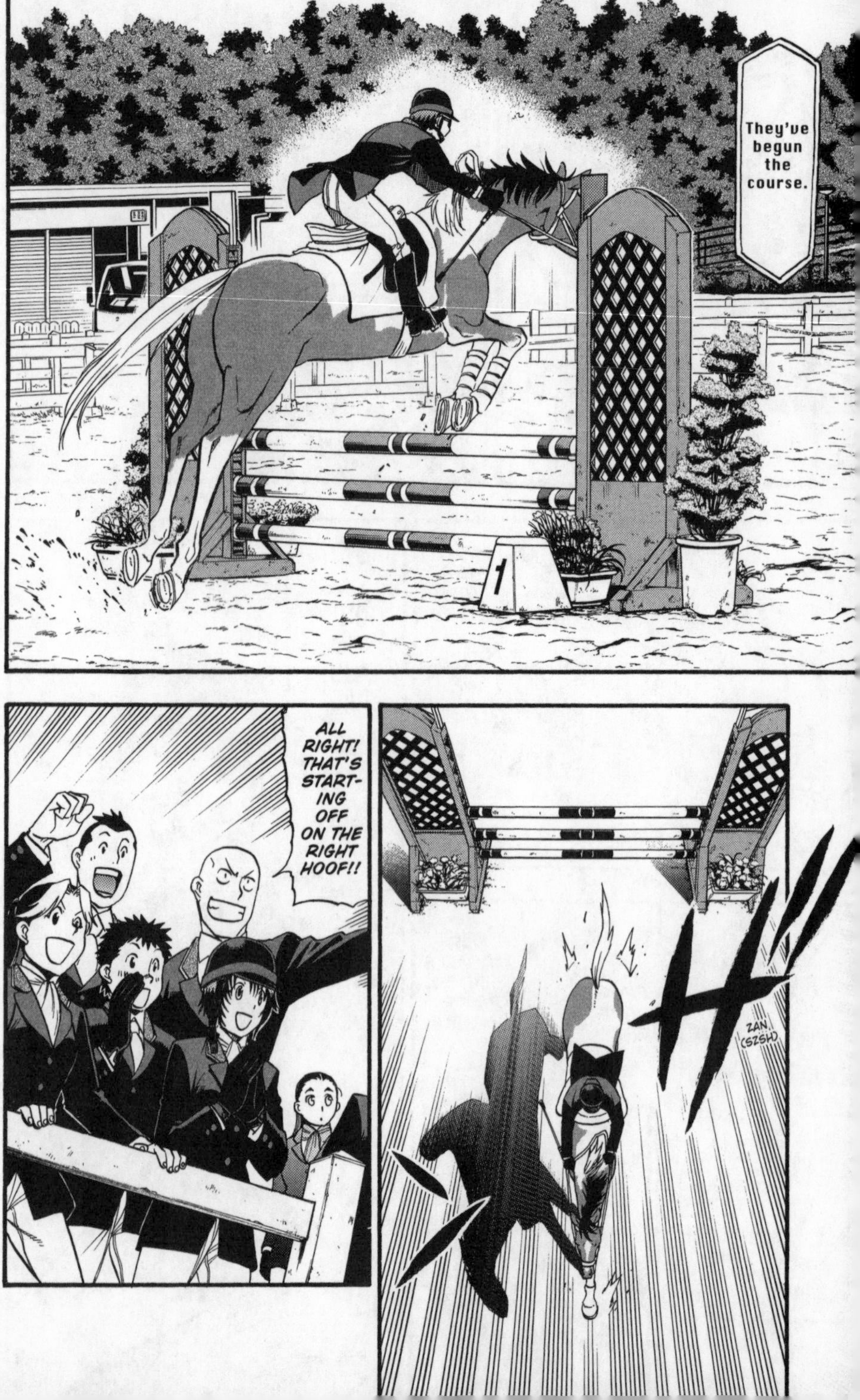
They've begun the course.
ZAN (SZSH)
ALL RIGHT! THAT'S STARTING OFF ON THE RIGHT HOOF!!

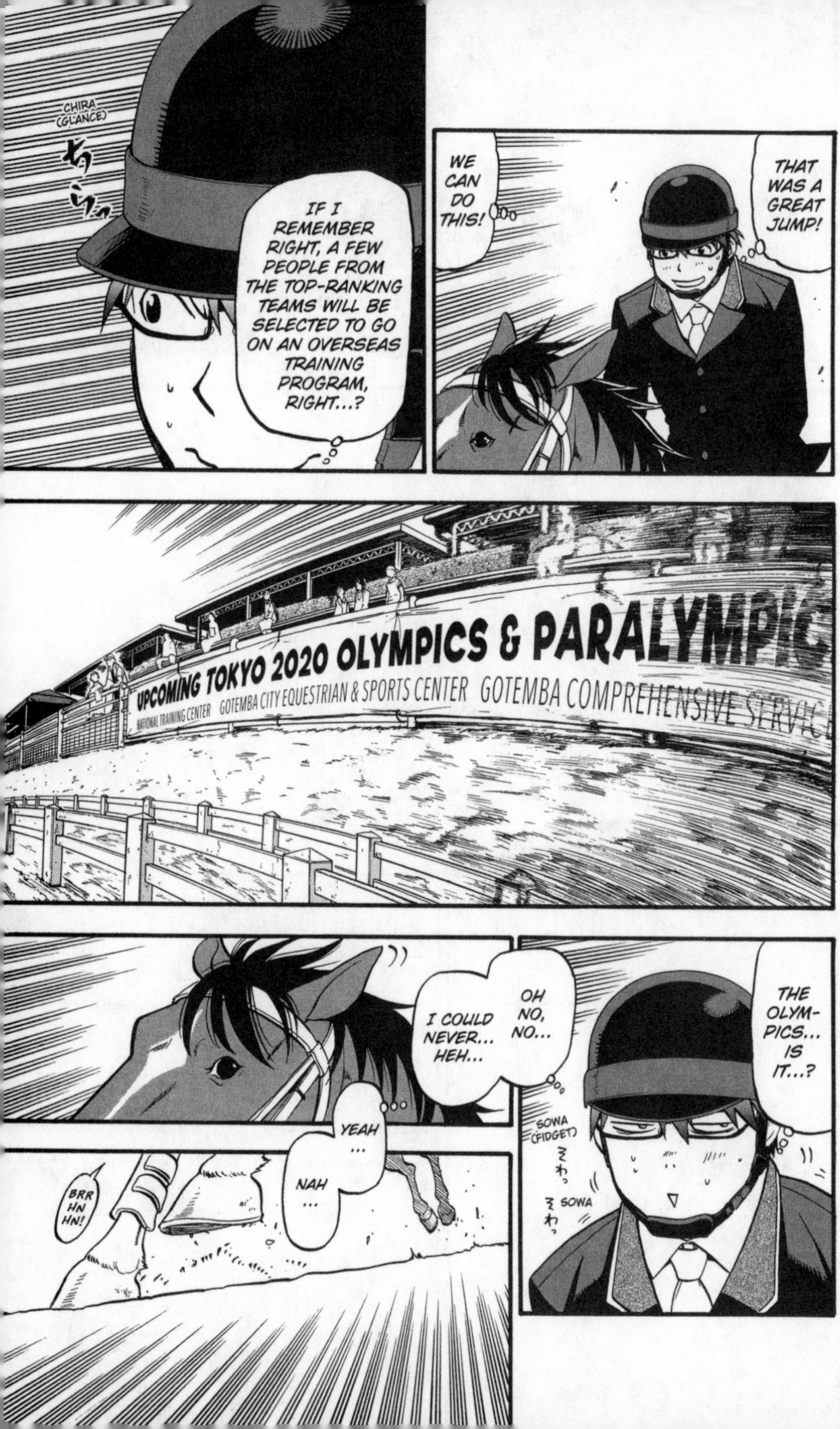

THAT WAS A GREAT JUMP!
WE CAN DO THIS!
IF I REMEMBER RIGHT, A FEW PEOPLE FROM THE TOP-RANKING TEAMS WILL BE SELECTED TO GO ON AN OVERSEAS TRAINING PROGRAM, RIGHT...?
CHIRA (GLANCE)
ちらっ
UPCOMING TOKYO 2020 OLYMPICS & PARALYMPIC
NATIONAL TRAINING CENTER
GOTEMBA CITY EQUESTRIAN & SPORTS CENTER
GOTEMBA COMPREHENSIVE SERVIC
THE OLYMPICS... IS IT...?
SOWA (FIDGET)
そわっ
SOWA
そわっ
OH NO, NO...
I COULD NEVER... HEH...
YEAH...
NAH...
BRRHNHN!

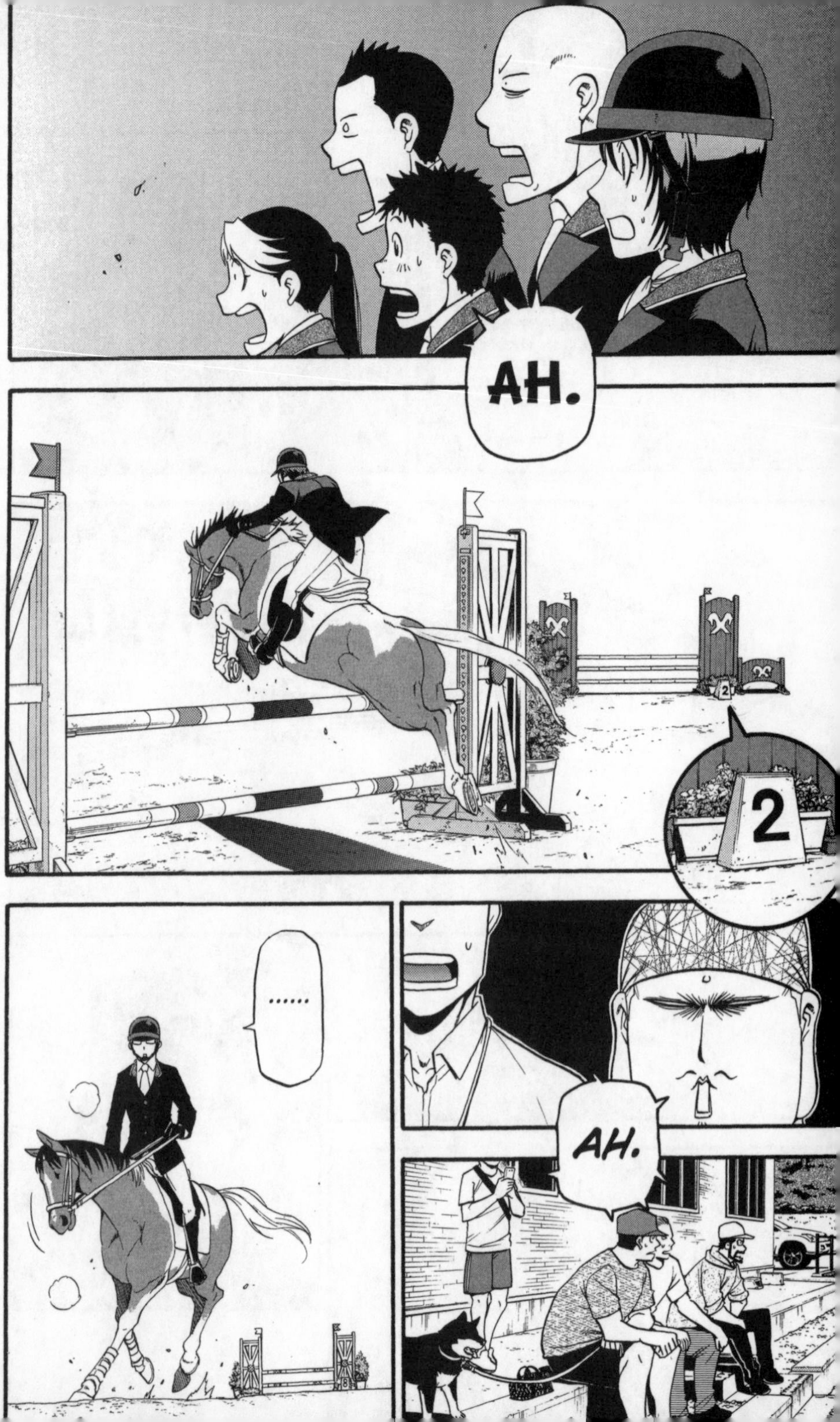
AH.
2
AH.
......

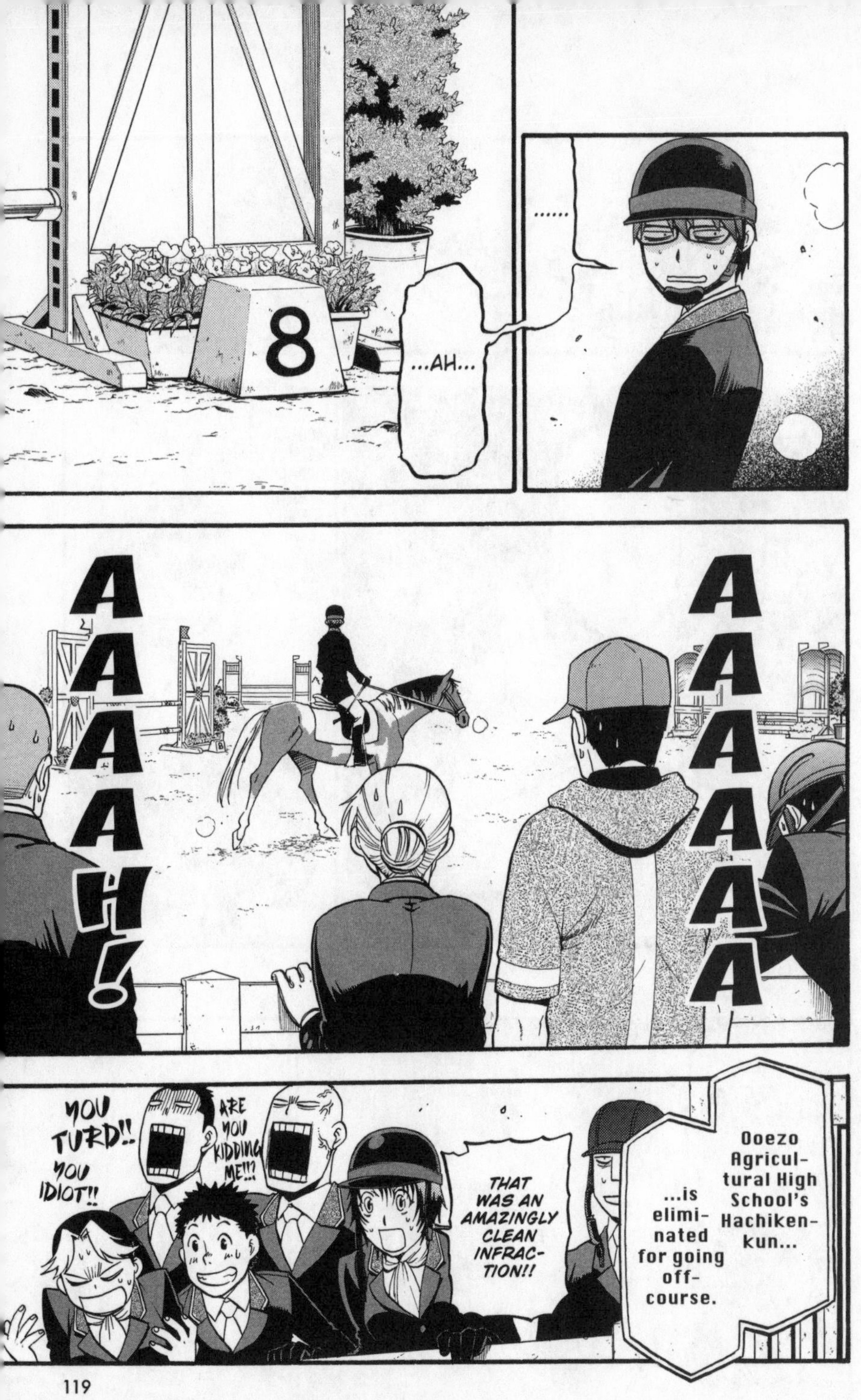
......
...AH...
AAAAAA
AAAAH!
Ooezo Agricultural High School's Hachiken-kun...
...is eliminated for going off-course.
THAT WAS AN AMAZINGLY CLEAN INFRACTION!!
ARE YOU KIDDING ME!!?
YOU TURD!!
YOU IDIOT!!

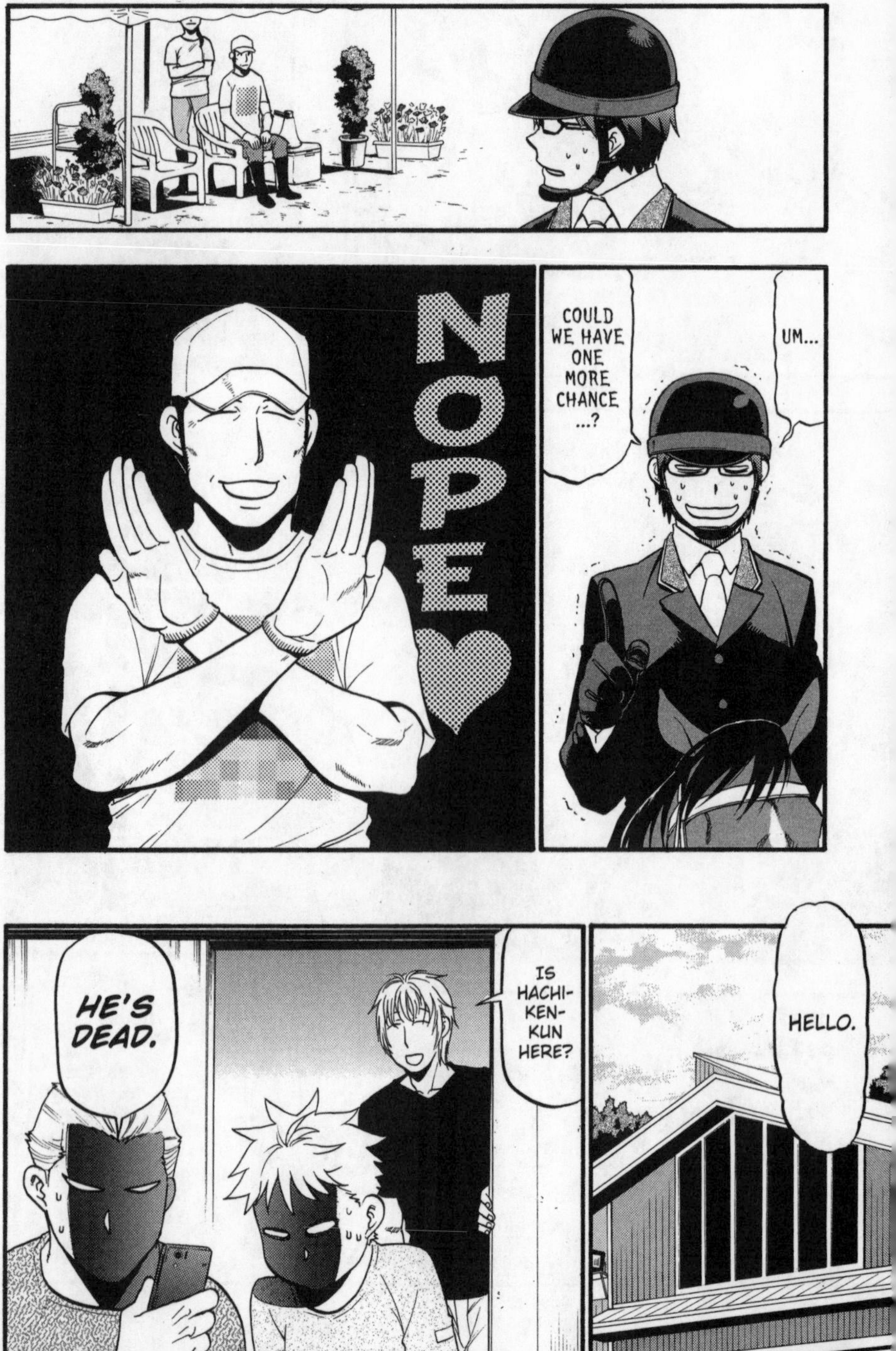
UM...
COULD WE HAVE ONE MORE CHANCE ...?
NOPE♥
HELLO.
IS HACHI-KEN-KUN HERE?
HE'S DEAD.

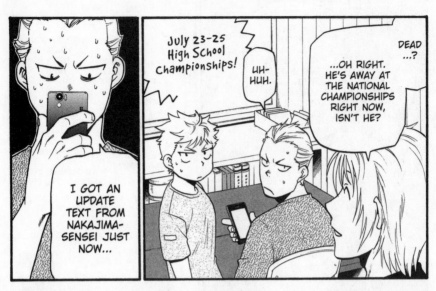

DEAD ...?
...OH RIGHT. HE'S AWAY AT THE NATIONAL CHAMPIONSHIPS RIGHT NOW, ISN'T HE?
UH-HUH.
July 23-25 High School Championships!
I GOT AN UPDATE TEXT FROM NAKAJIMA-SENSEI JUST NOW...
Two of our riders have gone. Hachiken-kun got a 255. Mikage-san got an 8.
255!
WHOA! THAT'S SUCH A HIGH SCORE!
...HUH? WAIT A SEC...
SHOW JUMPING IS SCORED USING A PENALTY POINT SYSTEM, RIGHT?
UH-HUH.
THE TEAM'S SCORE IS THE TOTAL OF ALL THREE COMPETITORS' PENALTY POINTS. SO EVEN IF YOU GET ELIMINATED AND CAN'T FINISH THE COURSE AS AN INDIVIDUAL, YOU STILL GET A SCORE.

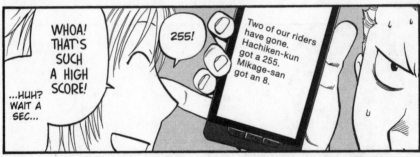

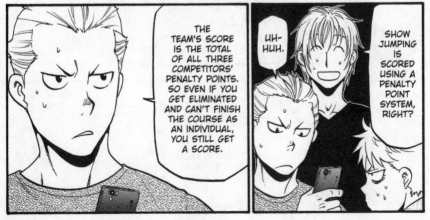

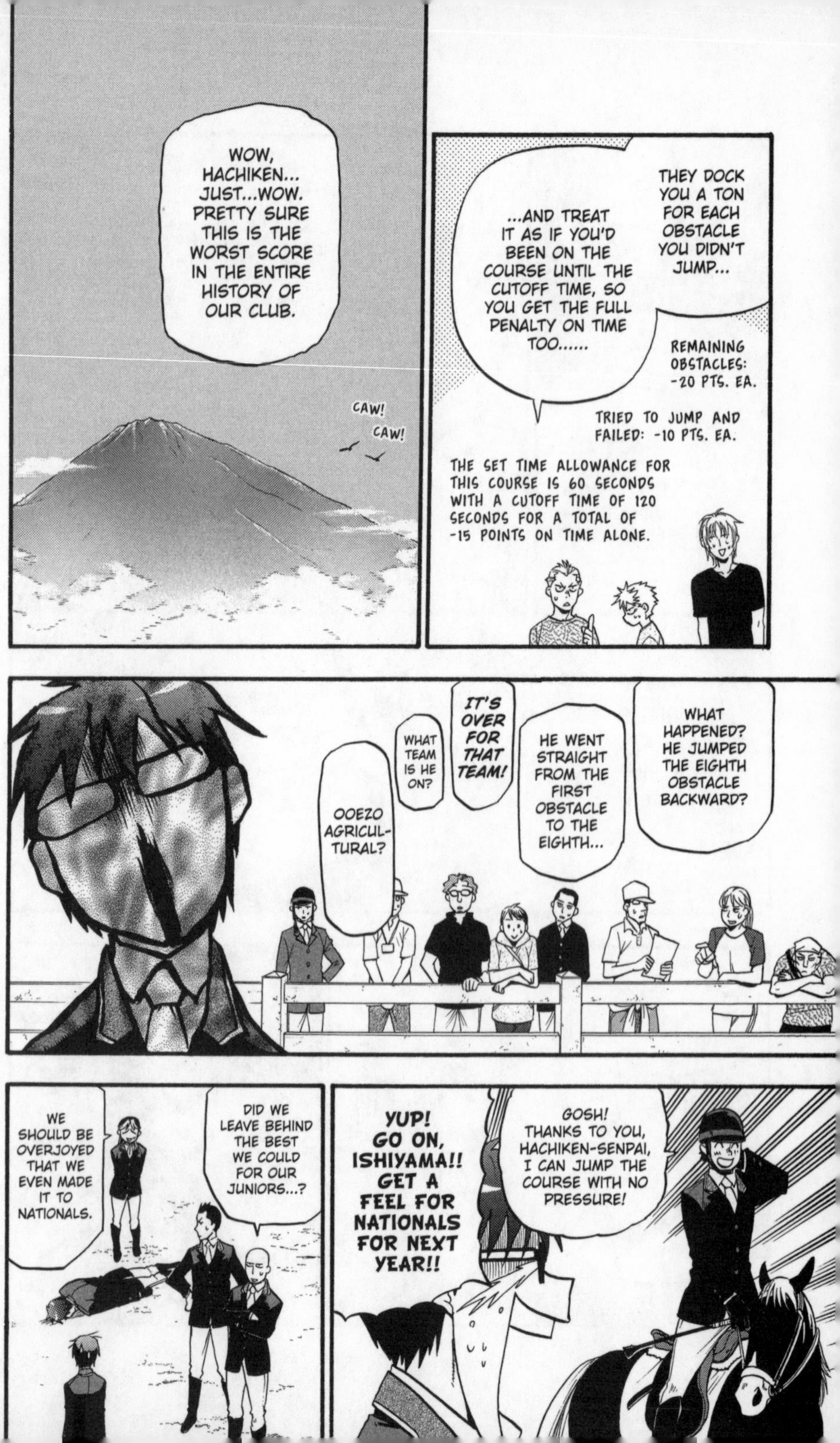
THEY DOCK YOU A TON FOR EACH OBSTACLE YOU DIDN'T JUMP...
...AND TREAT IT AS IF YOU'D BEEN ON THE COURSE UNTIL THE CUTOFF TIME, SO YOU GET THE FULL PENALTY ON TIME TOO......
REMAINING OBSTACLES: -20 PTS. EA.
TRIED TO JUMP AND FAILED: -10 PTS. EA.
THE SET TIME ALLOWANCE FOR THIS COURSE IS 60 SECONDS WITH A CUTOFF TIME OF 120 SECONDS FOR A TOTAL OF -15 POINTS ON TIME ALONE.
WOW, HACHIKEN... JUST...WOW. PRETTY SURE THIS IS THE WORST SCORE IN THE ENTIRE HISTORY OF OUR CLUB.
CAW!
CAW!
WHAT HAPPENED? HE JUMPED THE EIGHTH OBSTACLE BACKWARD?
HE WENT STRAIGHT FROM THE FIRST OBSTACLE TO THE EIGHTH...
IT'S OVER FOR THAT TEAM!
WHAT TEAM IS HE ON?
OOEZO AGRICUL-TURAL?
GOSH! THANKS TO YOU, HACHIKEN-SENPAI, I CAN JUMP THE COURSE WITH NO PRESSURE!
YUP! GO ON, ISHIYAMA!! GET A FEEL FOR NATIONALS FOR NEXT YEAR!!
DID WE LEAVE BEHIND THE BEST WE COULD FOR OUR JUNIORS...?
WE SHOULD BE OVERJOYED THAT WE EVEN MADE IT TO NATIONALS.

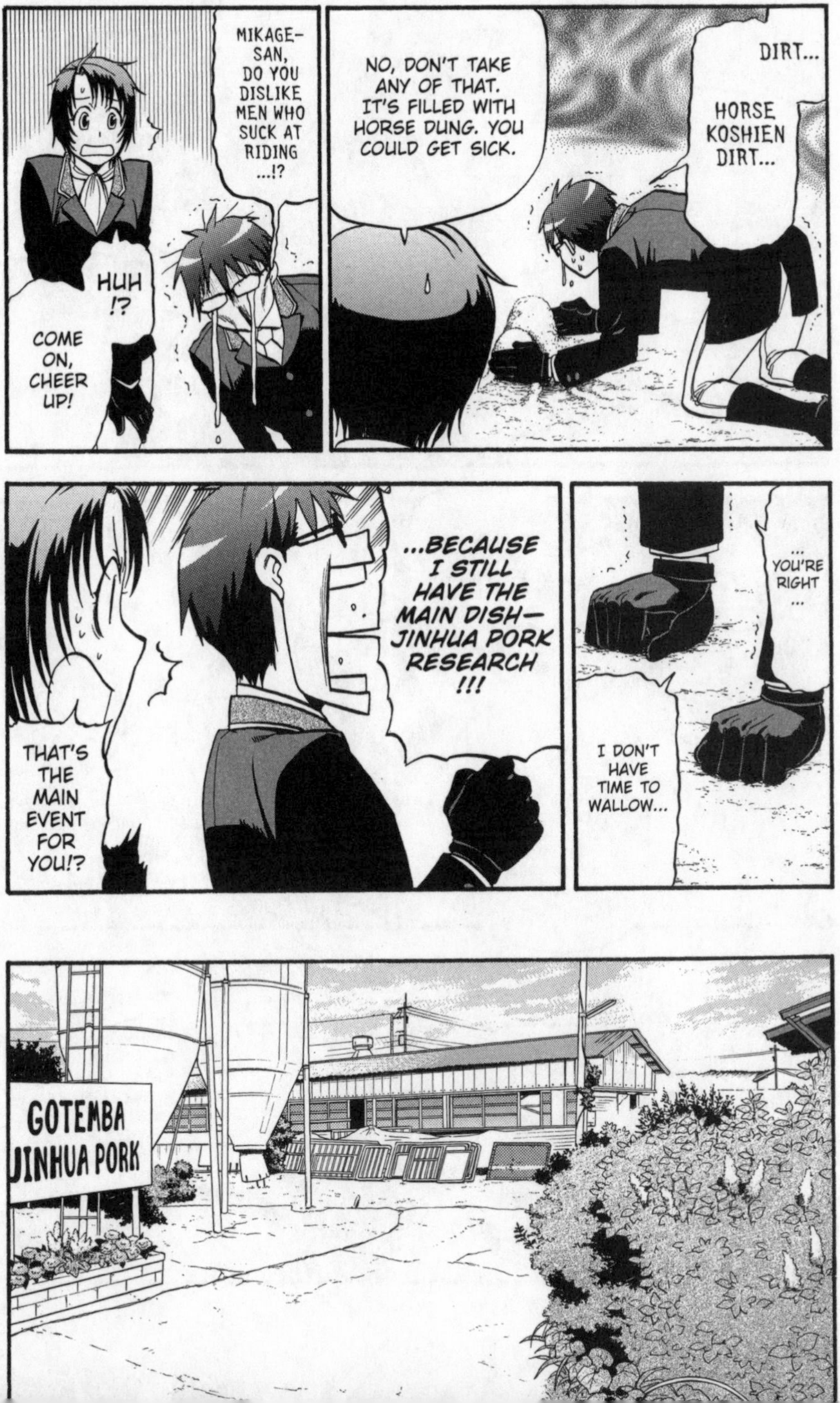
DIRT...
HORSE KOSHIEN DIRT...
NO, DON'T TAKE ANY OF THAT. IT'S FILLED WITH HORSE DUNG. YOU COULD GET SICK.
MIKAGE-SAN, DO YOU DISLIKE MEN WHO SUCK AT RIDING ...!?
HUH !?
COME ON, CHEER UP!
...YOU'RE RIGHT ...
I DON'T HAVE TIME TO WALLOW...
...BECAUSE I STILL HAVE THE MAIN DISH—JINHUA PORK RESEARCH !!!
THAT'S THE MAIN EVENT FOR YOU!?
GOTEMBA JINHUA PORK

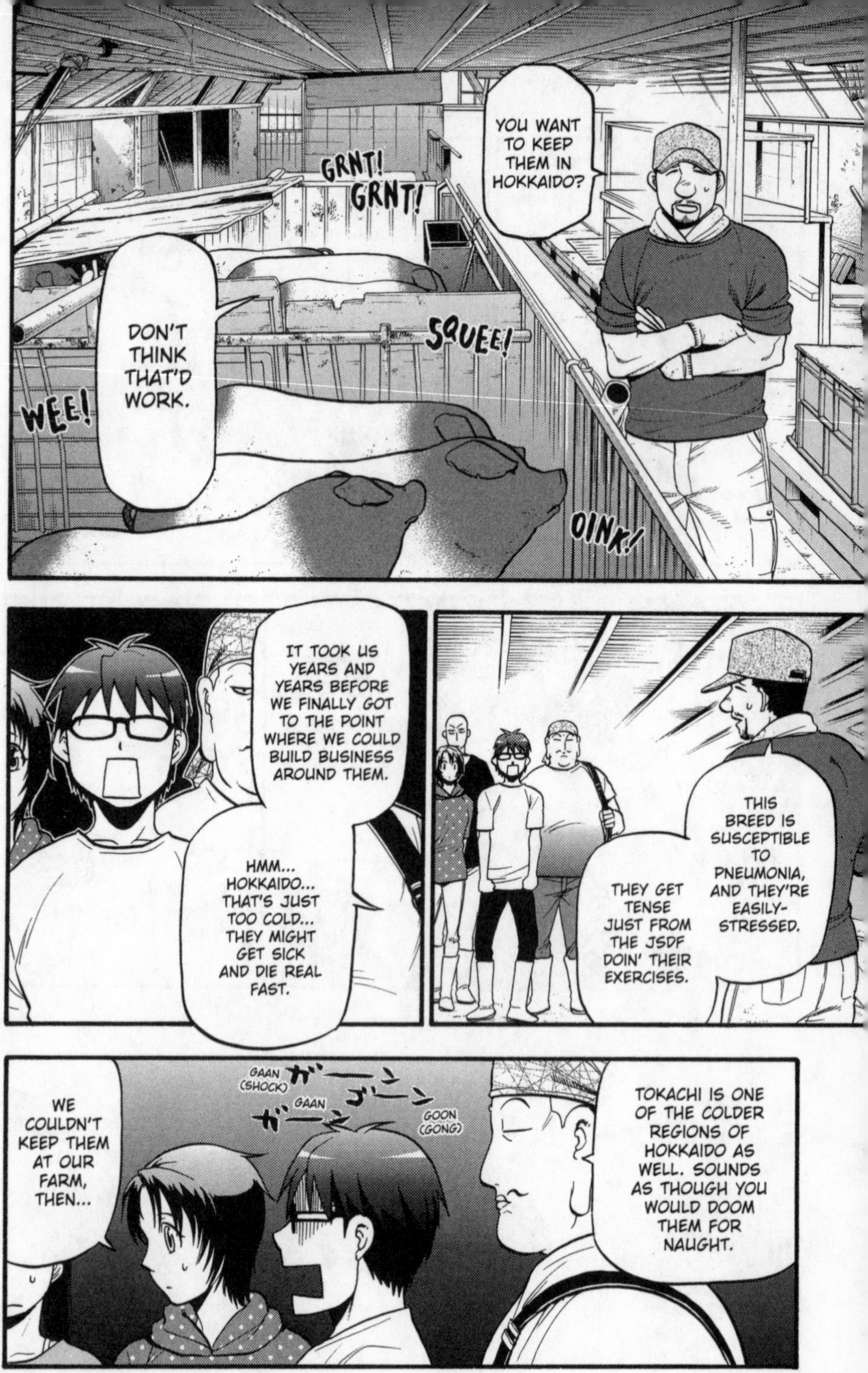
YOU WANT TO KEEP THEM IN HOKKAIDO?
GRNT! GRNT!
SQUEE!
DON'T THINK THAT'D WORK.
WEE!
OINK!
THIS BREED IS SUSCEPTIBLE TO PNEUMONIA, AND THEY'RE EASILY-STRESSED.
THEY GET TENSE JUST FROM THE JSDF DOIN' THEIR EXERCISES.
IT TOOK US YEARS AND YEARS BEFORE WE FINALLY GOT TO THE POINT WHERE WE COULD BUILD BUSINESS AROUND THEM.
HMM... HOKKAIDO... THAT'S JUST TOO COLD... THEY MIGHT GET SICK AND DIE REAL FAST.
TOKACHI IS ONE OF THE COLDER REGIONS OF HOKKAIDO AS WELL. SOUNDS AS THOUGH YOU WOULD DOOM THEM FOR NAUGHT.
GOON (GONG)
GAAN (SHOCK)
GAAN
WE COULDN'T KEEP THEM AT OUR FARM, THEN...

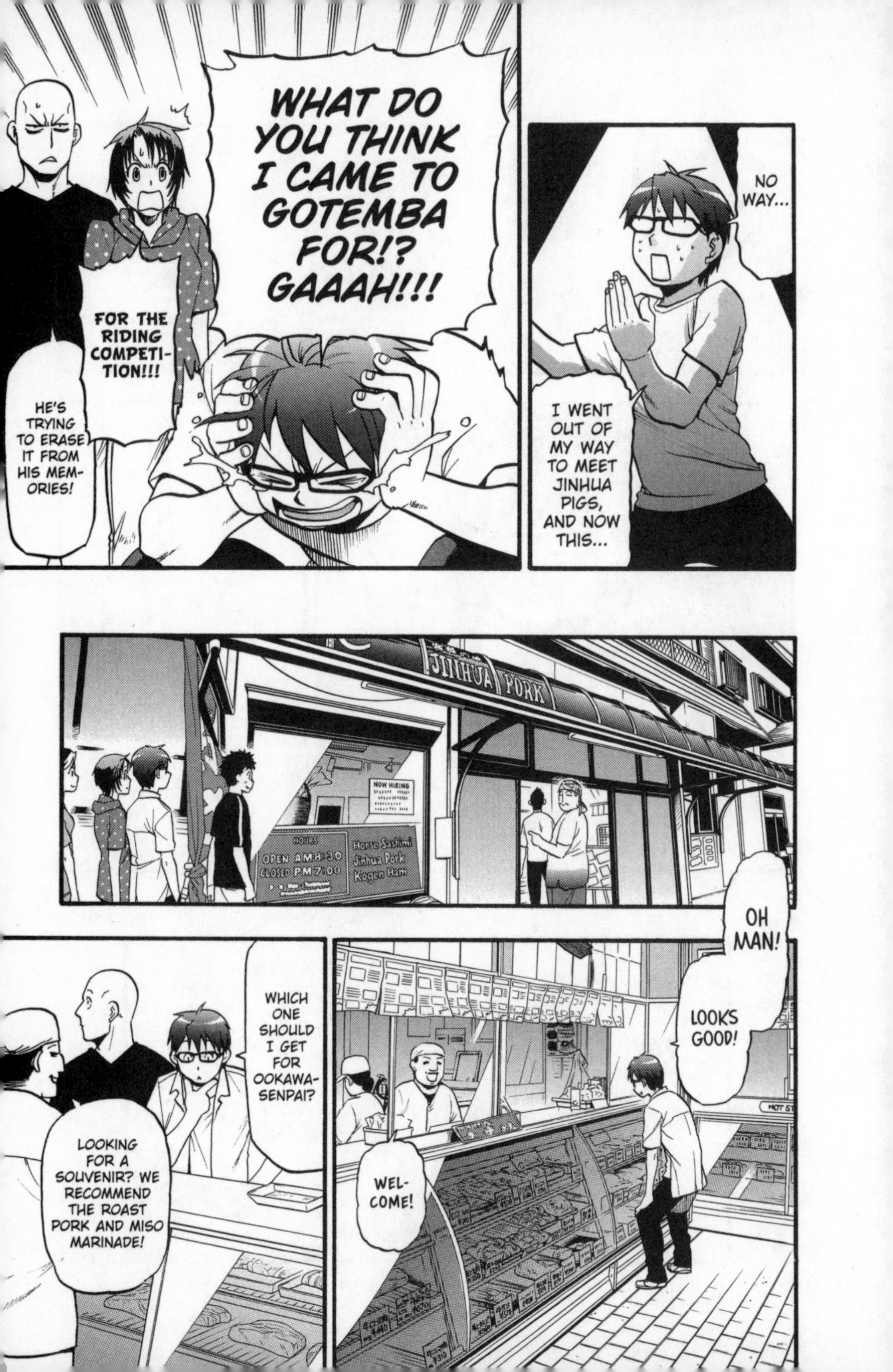
NO WAY...
I WENT OUT OF MY WAY TO MEET JINHUA PIGS, AND NOW THIS...
WHAT DO YOU THINK I CAME TO GOTEMBA FOR!? GAAAH!!!
FOR THE RIDING COMPETITION!!!
HE'S TRYING TO ERASE IT FROM HIS MEMORIES!
JINHUA PORK
NOW HIRING
HOURS
OPEN AM 8:30
CLOSED PM 7:00
Horse Sashimi
Jinhua Pork
Kogen Ham
OH MAN!
LOOKS GOOD!
WELCOME!
WHICH ONE SHOULD I GET FOR OOKAWA-SENPAI?
LOOKING FOR A SOUVENIR? WE RECOMMEND THE ROAST PORK AND MISO MARINADE!

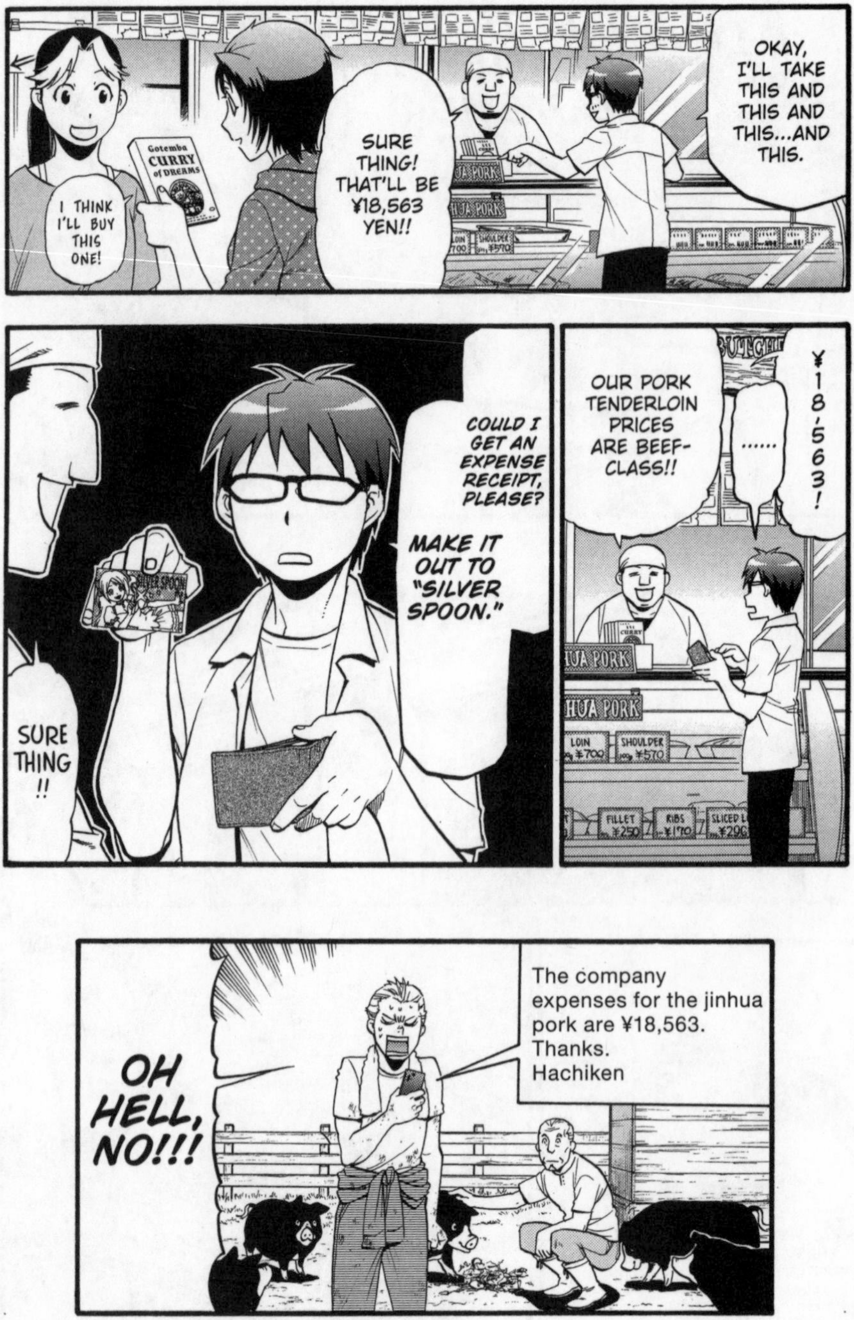
OKAY, I'LL TAKE THIS AND THIS AND THIS...AND THIS.
SURE THING! THAT'LL BE ¥18,563 YEN!!
Gotemba CURRY of DREAMS
I THINK I'LL BUY THIS ONE!
¥18,563!
......
OUR PORK TENDERLOIN PRICES ARE BEEF-CLASS!!
LOIN ¥700
SHOULDER ¥570
FILLET ¥250
RIBS ¥170
COULD I GET AN EXPENSE RECEIPT, PLEASE?
MAKE IT OUT TO "SILVER SPOON."
SILVER SPOON
SURE THING!!
The company expenses for the jinhua pork are ¥18,563. Thanks. Hachiken
OH HELL, NO!!!

Silver Spoon

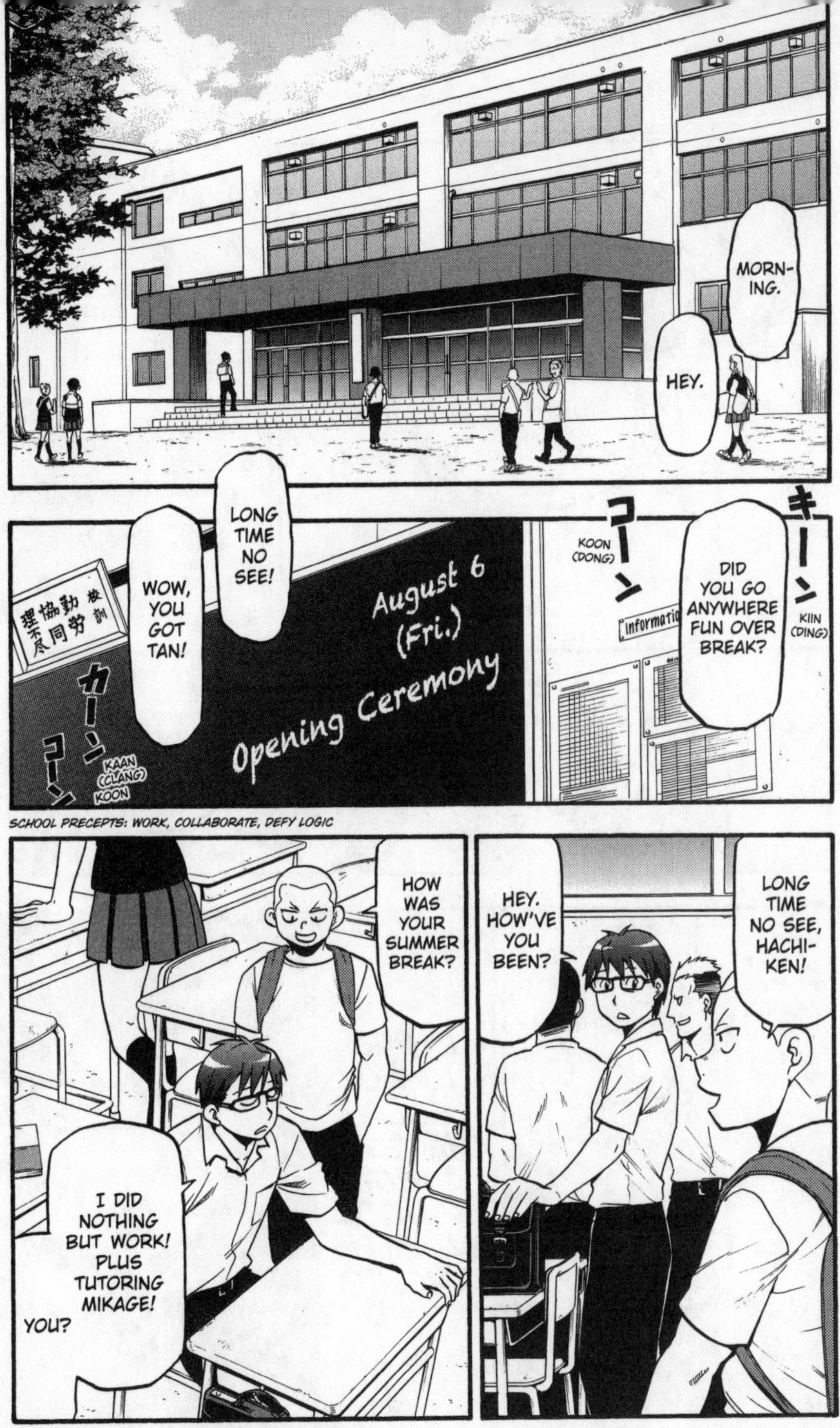
MORNING.
HEY.
KIIN (DING)
KOON (DONG)
DID YOU GO ANYWHERE FUN OVER BREAK?
August 6 (Fri.) Opening Ceremony
LONG TIME NO SEE!
WOW, YOU GOT TAN!
KAAN (CLANG) KOON
SCHOOL PRECEPTS: WORK, COLLABORATE, DEFY LOGIC
LONG TIME NO SEE, HACHIKEN!
HEY. HOW'VE YOU BEEN?
HOW WAS YOUR SUMMER BREAK?
I DID NOTHING BUT WORK! PLUS TUTORING MIKAGE!
YOU?

Chapter 112:

Tale of Four Seasons⑮

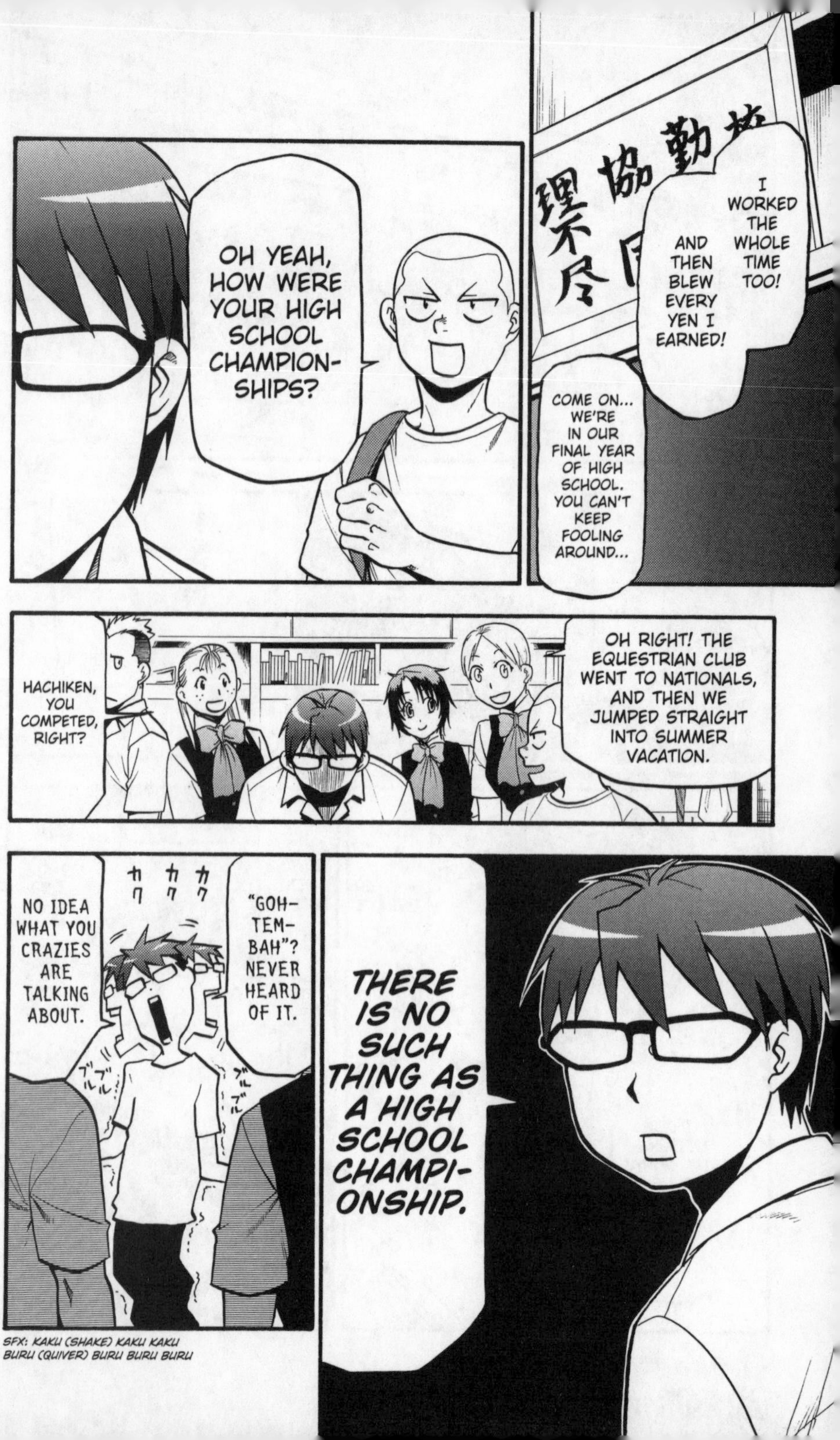
I WORKED THE WHOLE TIME TOO!
AND THEN BLEW EVERY YEN I EARNED!
COME ON... WE'RE IN OUR FINAL YEAR OF HIGH SCHOOL. YOU CAN'T KEEP FOOLING AROUND...
OH YEAH, HOW WERE YOUR HIGH SCHOOL CHAMPIONSHIPS?
OH RIGHT! THE EQUESTRIAN CLUB WENT TO NATIONALS, AND THEN WE JUMPED STRAIGHT INTO SUMMER VACATION.
HACHIKEN, YOU COMPETED, RIGHT?
THERE IS NO SUCH THING AS A HIGH SCHOOL CHAMPIONSHIP.
"GOH-TEM-BAH"? NEVER HEARD OF IT.
NO IDEA WHAT YOU CRAZIES ARE TALKING ABOUT.
カク カク カク
ブルブル
ブルブル
SFX: KAKU (SHAKE) KAKU KAKU
BURU (QUIVER) BURU BURU BURU

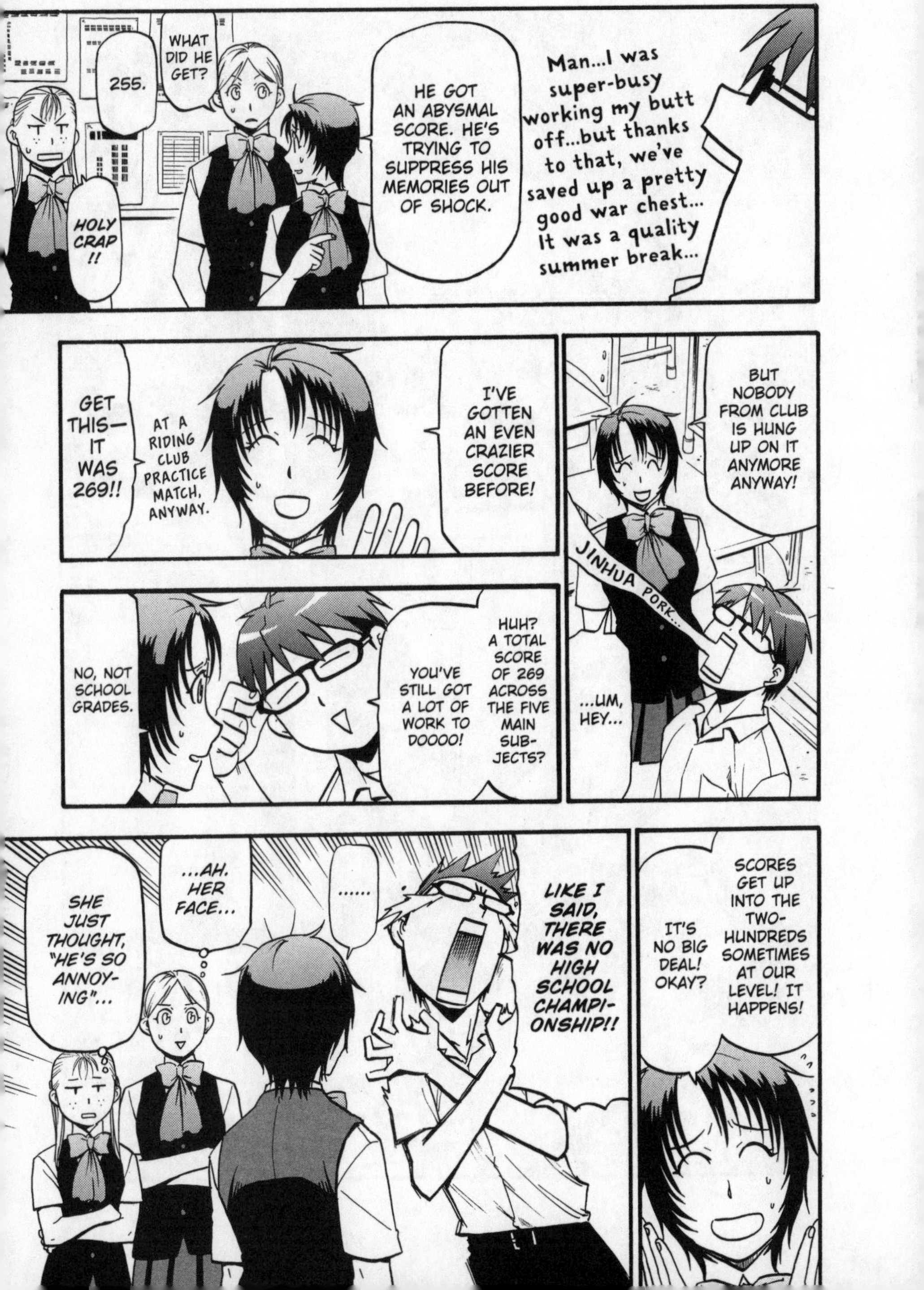

Man...I was super-busy working my butt off...but thanks to that, we've saved up a pretty good war chest... It was a quality summer break...
HE GOT AN ABYSMAL SCORE. HE'S TRYING TO SUPPRESS HIS MEMORIES OUT OF SHOCK.
WHAT DID HE GET?
255.
HOLY CRAP!!
BUT NOBODY FROM CLUB IS HUNG UP ON IT ANYMORE ANYWAY!
JINHUA PORK...
...UM, HEY...
I'VE GOTTEN AN EVEN CRAZIER SCORE BEFORE!
GET THIS—IT WAS 269!!
AT A RIDING CLUB PRACTICE MATCH, ANYWAY.
HUH? A TOTAL SCORE OF 269 ACROSS THE FIVE MAIN SUB-JECTS?
YOU'VE STILL GOT A LOT OF WORK TO DOOOO!
NO, NOT SCHOOL GRADES.
SCORES GET UP INTO THE TWO-HUNDREDS SOMETIMES AT OUR LEVEL! IT HAPPENS!
IT'S NO BIG DEAL! OKAY?
LIKE I SAID, THERE WAS NO HIGH SCHOOL CHAMPI-ONSHIP!!
......
...AH. HER FACE...
SHE JUST THOUGHT, "HE'S SO ANNOY-ING"...

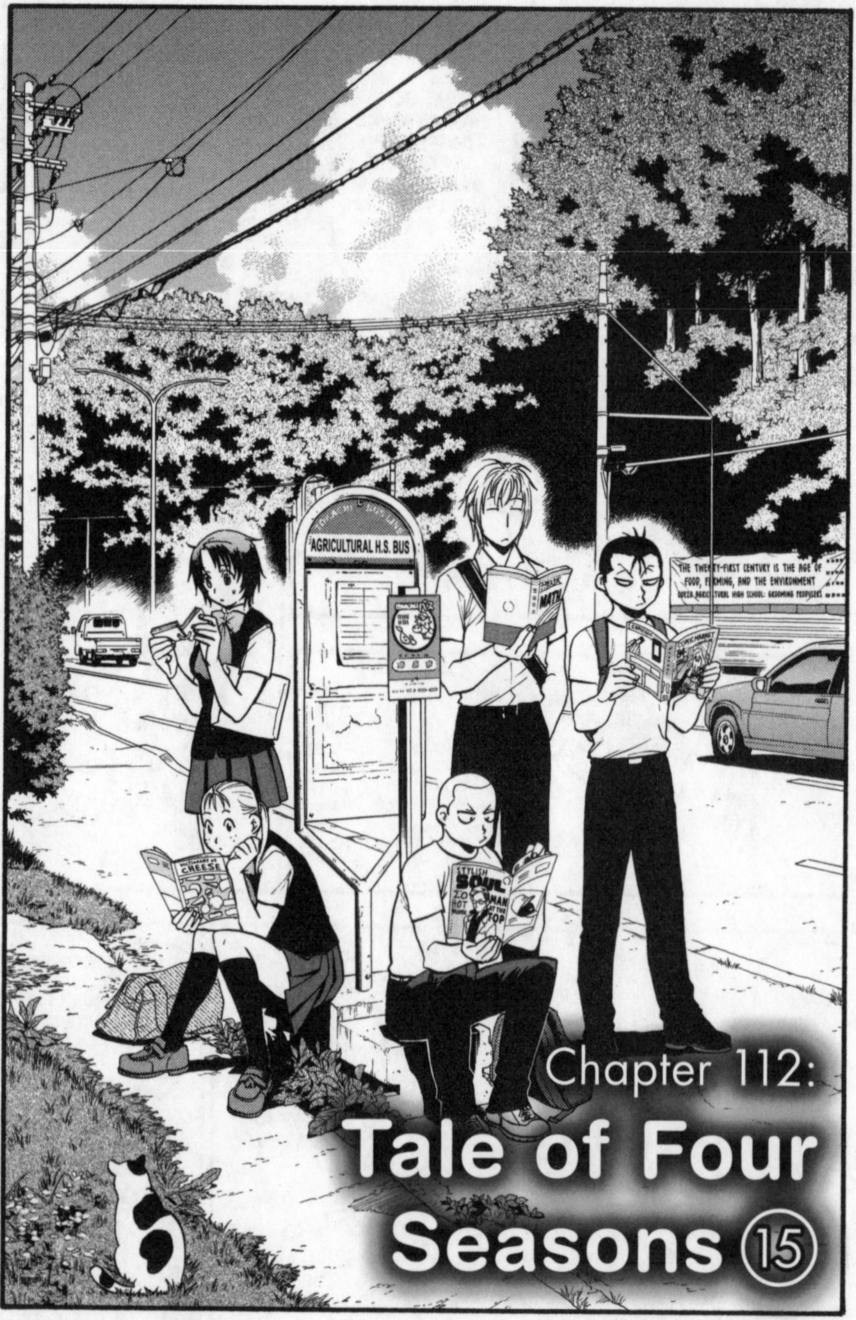
AGRICULTURAL H.S. BUS
THE TWENTY-FIRST CENTURY IS THE AGE OF
FOOD, FARMING, AND THE ENVIRONMENT
AGRICULTURAL HIGH SCHOOL: GROOMING PRODUCERS
MATH
CHEESE
STYLISH SOUL
MAN AT THE TOP
Chapter 112:
Tale of Four Seasons ⑮

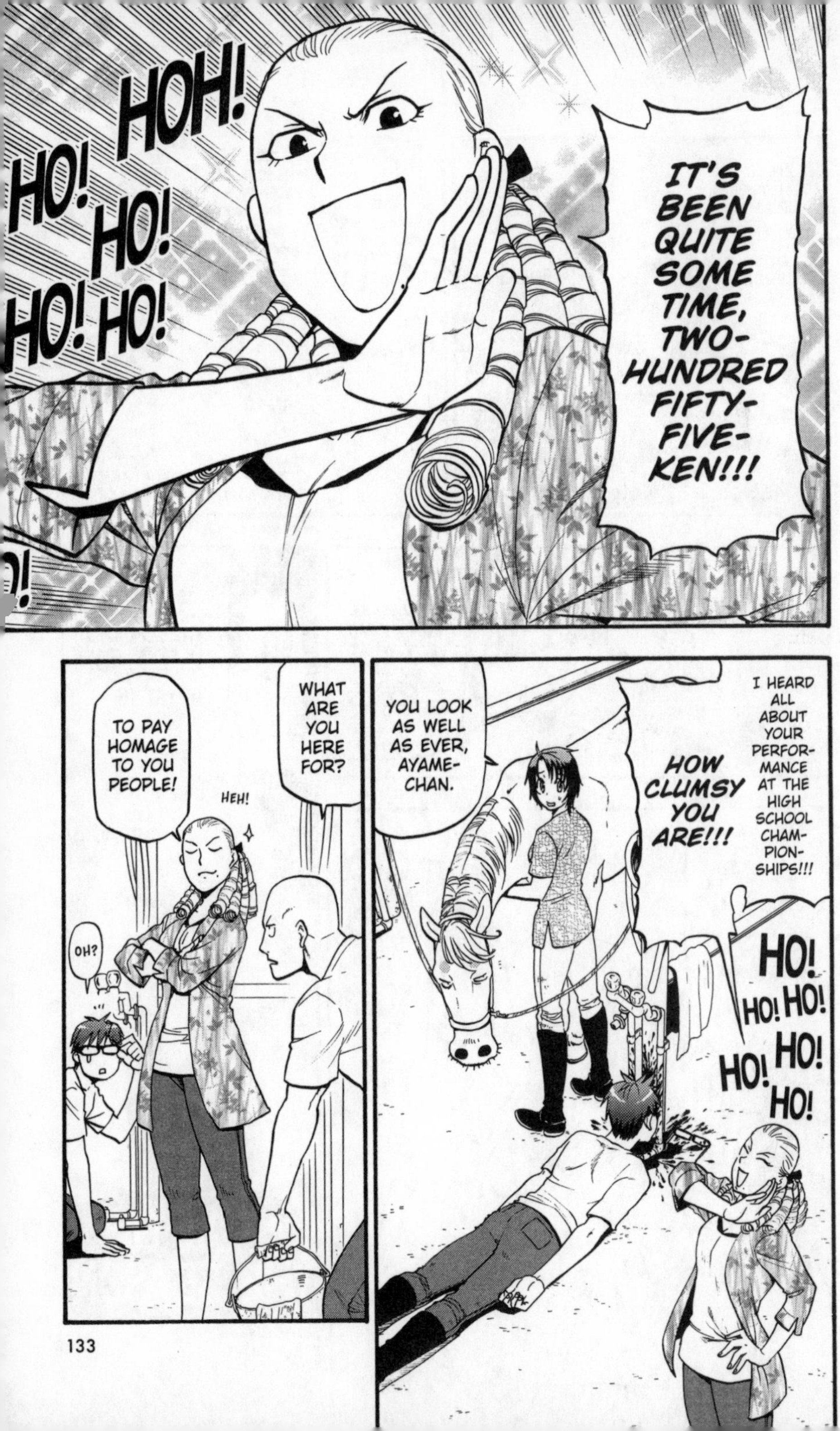
IT'S BEEN QUITE SOME TIME, TWO-HUNDRED FIFTY-FIVE-KEN!!!
HOH! HO! HO! HO! HO!
I HEARD ALL ABOUT YOUR PERFORMANCE AT THE HIGH SCHOOL CHAMPIONSHIPS!!!
HOW CLUMSY YOU ARE!!!
HO! HO! HO! HO! HO! HO!
YOU LOOK AS WELL AS EVER, AYAME-CHAN.
WHAT ARE YOU HERE FOR?
TO PAY HOMAGE TO YOU PEOPLE!
HEH!
OH?

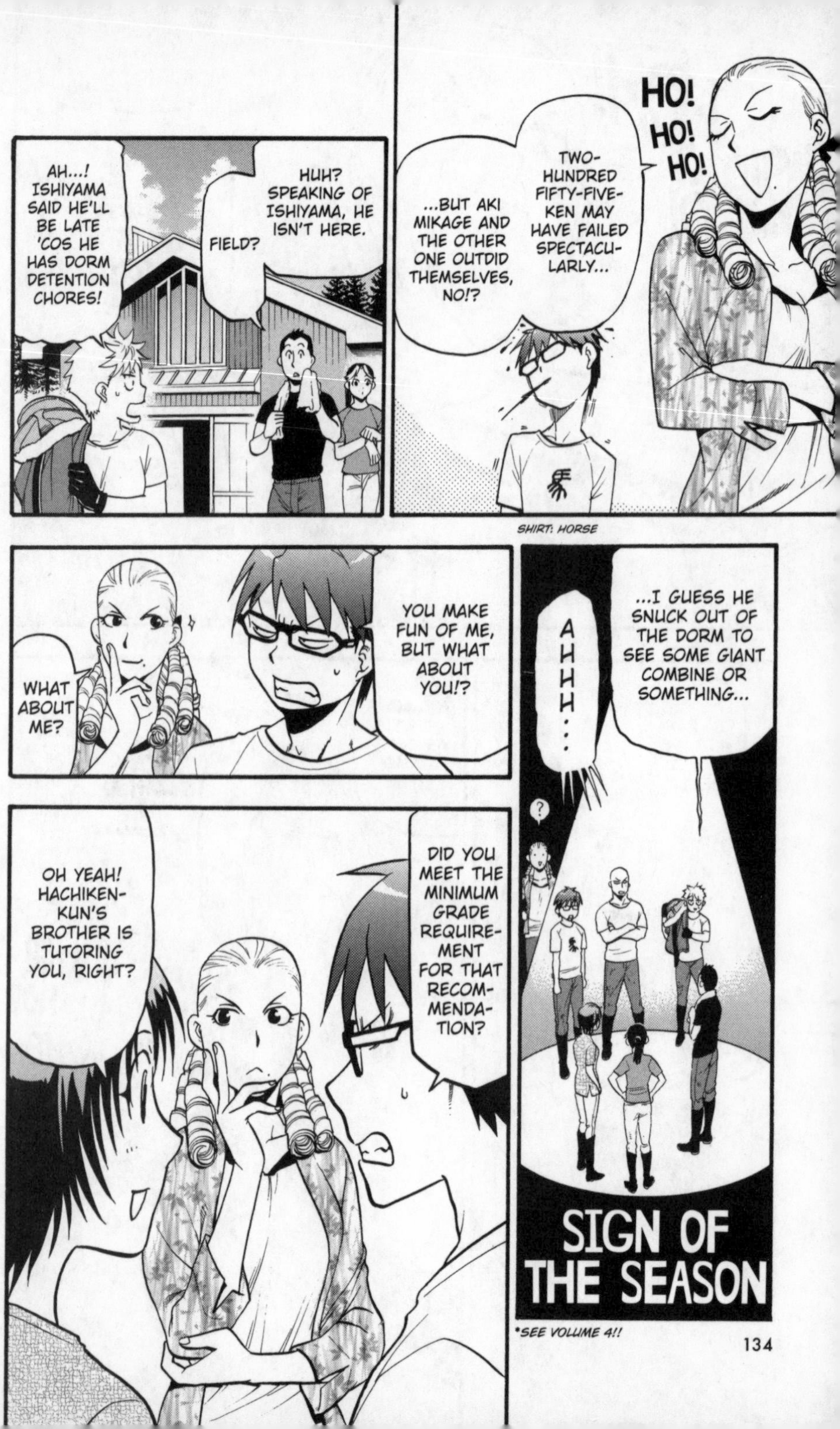
HO! HO! HO!
TWO-HUNDRED FIFTY-FIVE-KEN MAY HAVE FAILED SPECTACULARLY...
...BUT AKI MIKAGE AND THE OTHER ONE OUTDID THEMSELVES, NO!?
SHIRT: HORSE
HUH? SPEAKING OF ISHIYAMA, HE ISN'T HERE.
FIELD?
AH...! ISHIYAMA SAID HE'LL BE LATE 'COS HE HAS DORM DETENTION CHORES!
...I GUESS HE SNUCK OUT OF THE DORM TO SEE SOME GIANT COMBINE OR SOMETHING...
AHHH...
?
SIGN OF THE SEASON
*SEE VOLUME 4!!
YOU MAKE FUN OF ME, BUT WHAT ABOUT YOU!?
WHAT ABOUT ME?
DID YOU MEET THE MINIMUM GRADE REQUIREMENT FOR THAT RECOMMENDATION?
OH YEAH! HACHIKEN-KUN'S BROTHER IS TUTORING YOU, RIGHT?

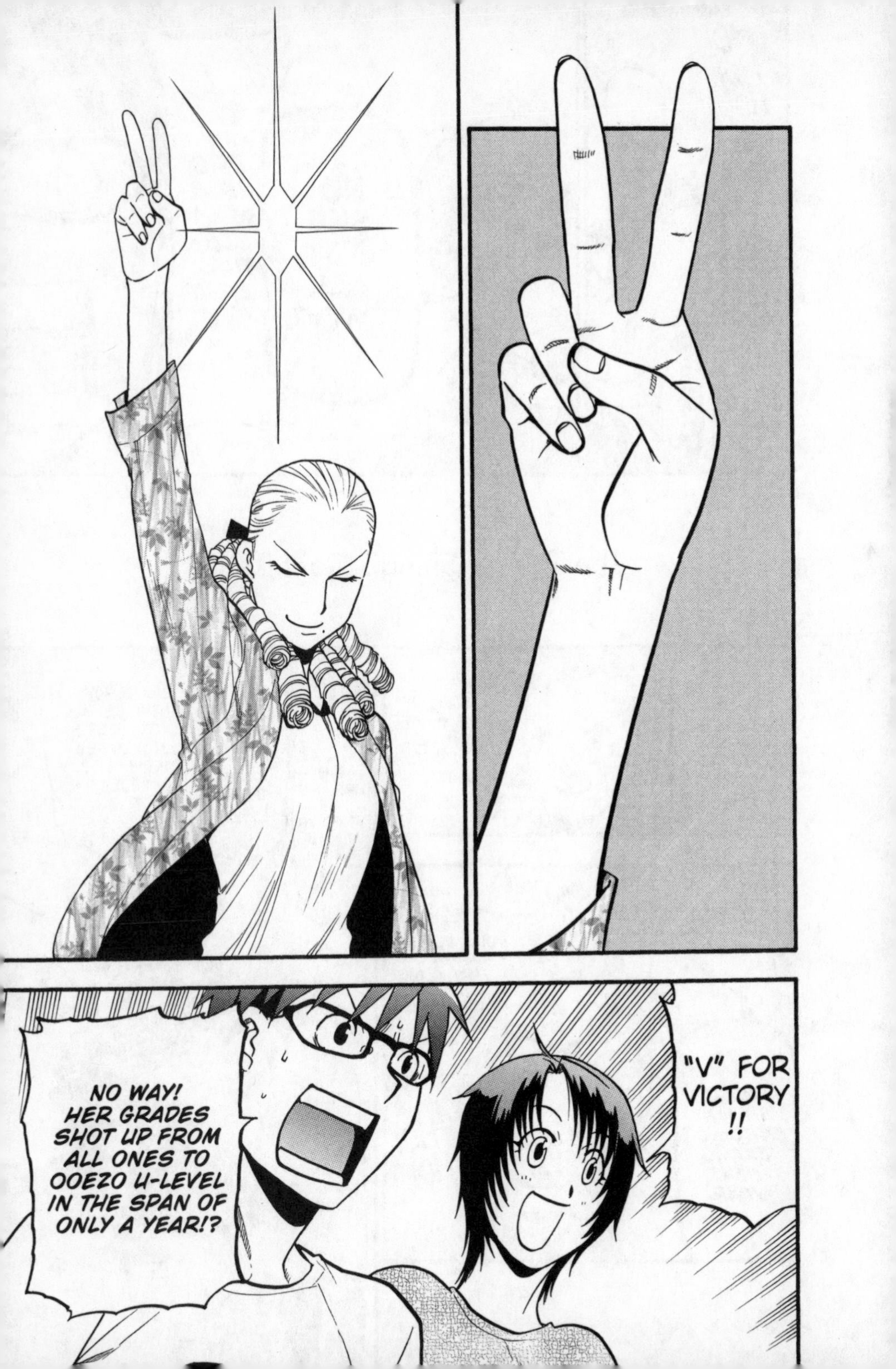
"V" FOR VICTORY !!
NO WAY! HER GRADES SHOT UP FROM ALL ONES TO OOEZO U-LEVEL IN THE SPAN OF ONLY A YEAR!?

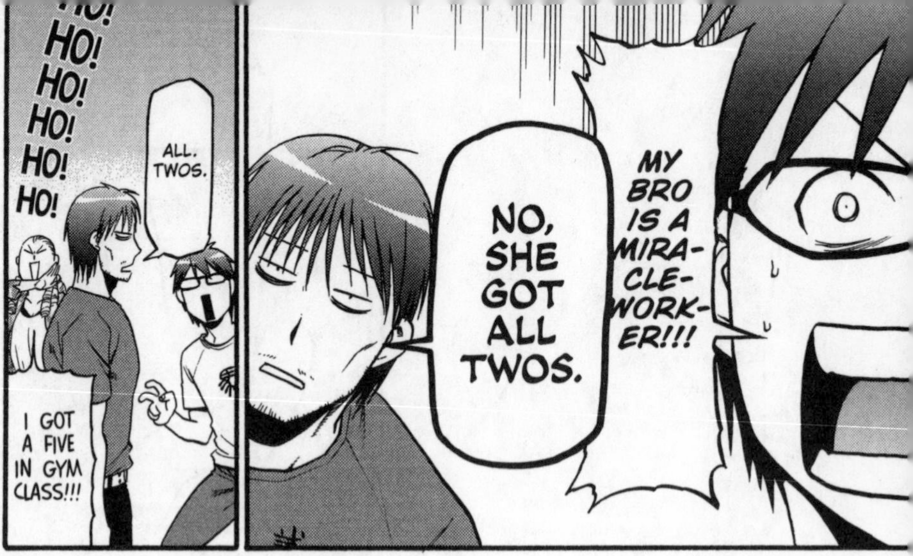

MY BRO IS A MIRA-CLE-WORKER!!!
NO, SHE GOT ALL TWOS.
ALL. TWOS.
HO! HO! HO! HO! HO!
I GOT A FIVE IN GYM CLASS!!!

The Tale of Shingo Hachiken

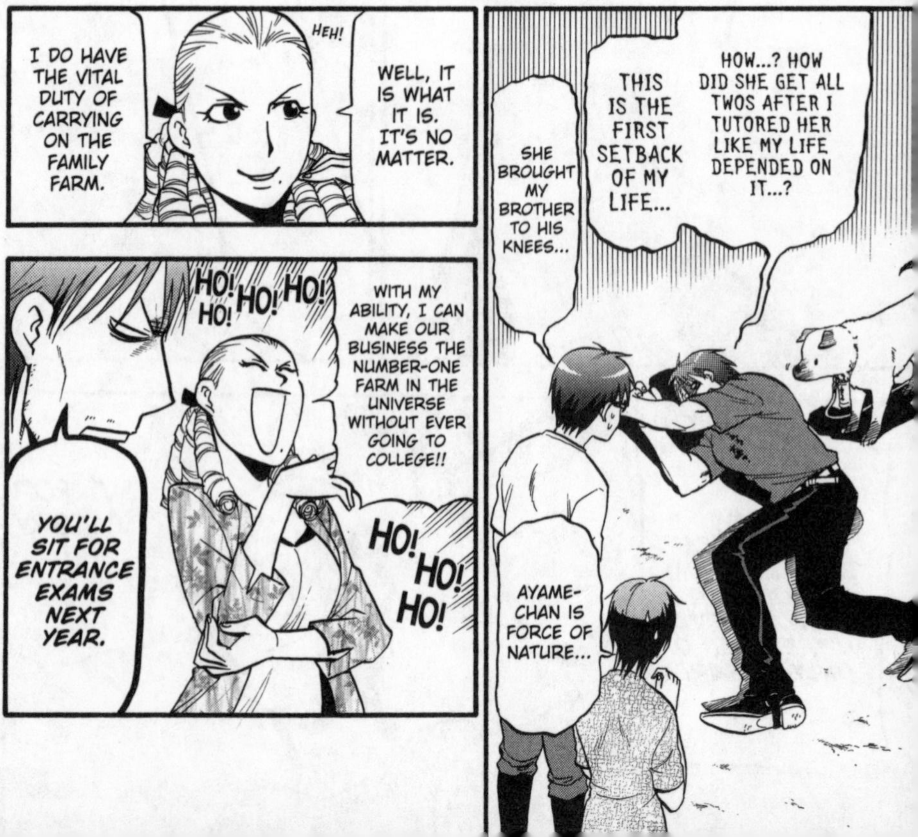

HOW...? HOW DID SHE GET ALL TWOS AFTER I TUTORED HER LIKE MY LIFE DEPENDED ON IT...?
THIS IS THE FIRST SETBACK OF MY LIFE...
SHE BROUGHT MY BROTHER TO HIS KNEES...
AYAME-CHAN IS FORCE OF NATURE...
HEH!
WELL, IT IS WHAT IT IS. IT'S NO MATTER.
I DO HAVE THE VITAL DUTY OF CARRYING ON THE FAMILY FARM.
HO! HO! HO! HO!
WITH MY ABILITY, I CAN MAKE OUR BUSINESS THE NUMBER-ONE FARM IN THE UNIVERSE WITHOUT EVER GOING TO COLLEGE!!
HO! HO! HO!
YOU'LL SIT FOR ENTRANCE EXAMS NEXT YEAR.

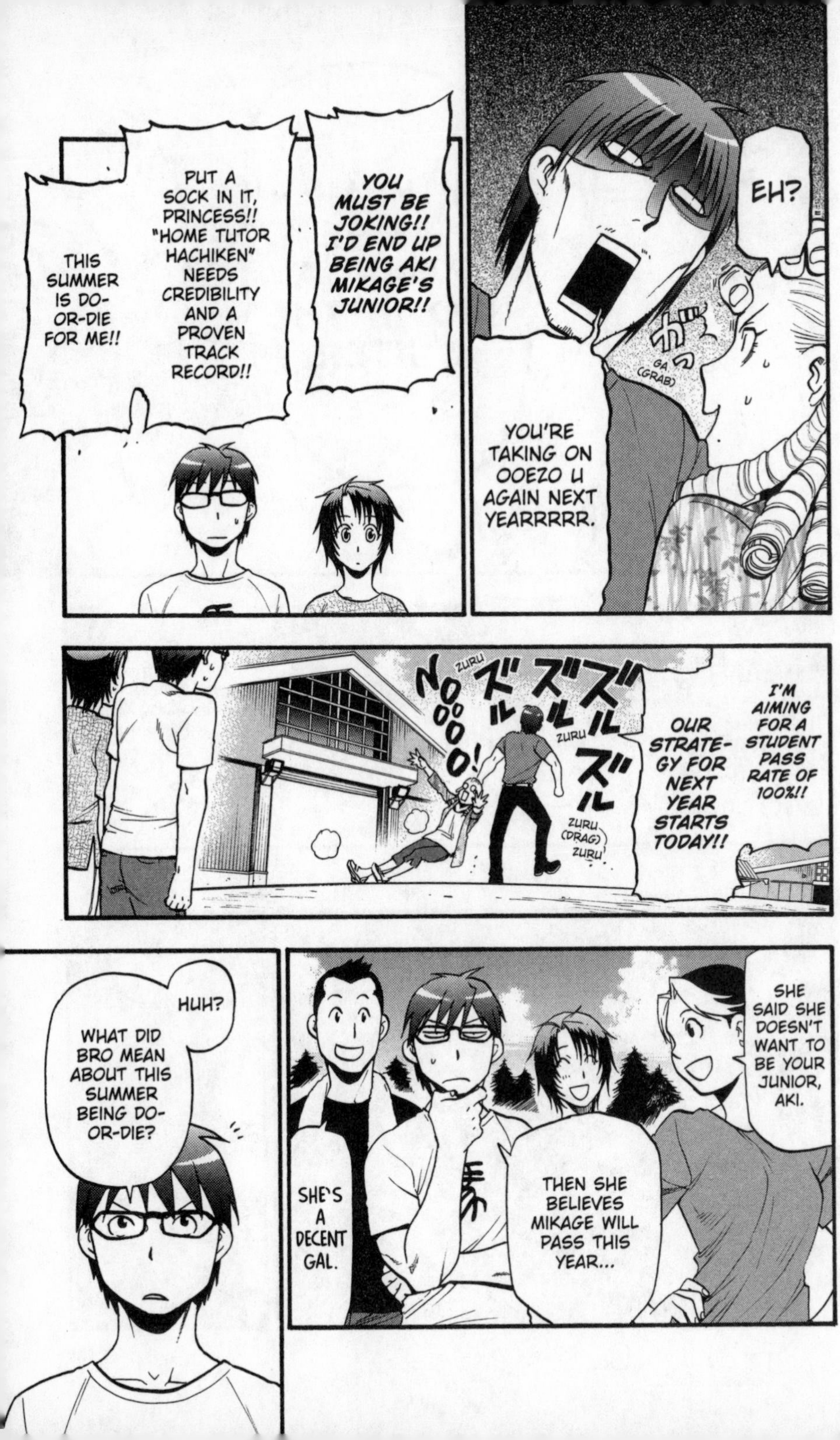
EH?
ガッ
GA (GRAB)
YOU'RE TAKING ON OOEZO U AGAIN NEXT YEARRRRR.
YOU MUST BE JOKING!! I'D END UP BEING AKI MIKAGE'S JUNIOR!!
PUT A SOCK IN IT, PRINCESS!! "HOME TUTOR HACHIKEN" NEEDS CREDIBILITY AND A PROVEN TRACK RECORD!!
THIS SUMMER IS DO-OR-DIE FOR ME!!
I'M AIMING FOR A STUDENT PASS RATE OF 100%!!
OUR STRATEGY FOR NEXT YEAR STARTS TODAY!!
ズルズルズル
ZURU ZURU ZURU (DRAG) ZURU
NOOOOO!
SHE SAID SHE DOESN'T WANT TO BE YOUR JUNIOR, AKI.
THEN SHE BELIEVES MIKAGE WILL PASS THIS YEAR...
SHE'S A DECENT GAL.
HUH?
WHAT DID BRO MEAN ABOUT THIS SUMMER BEING DO-OR-DIE?

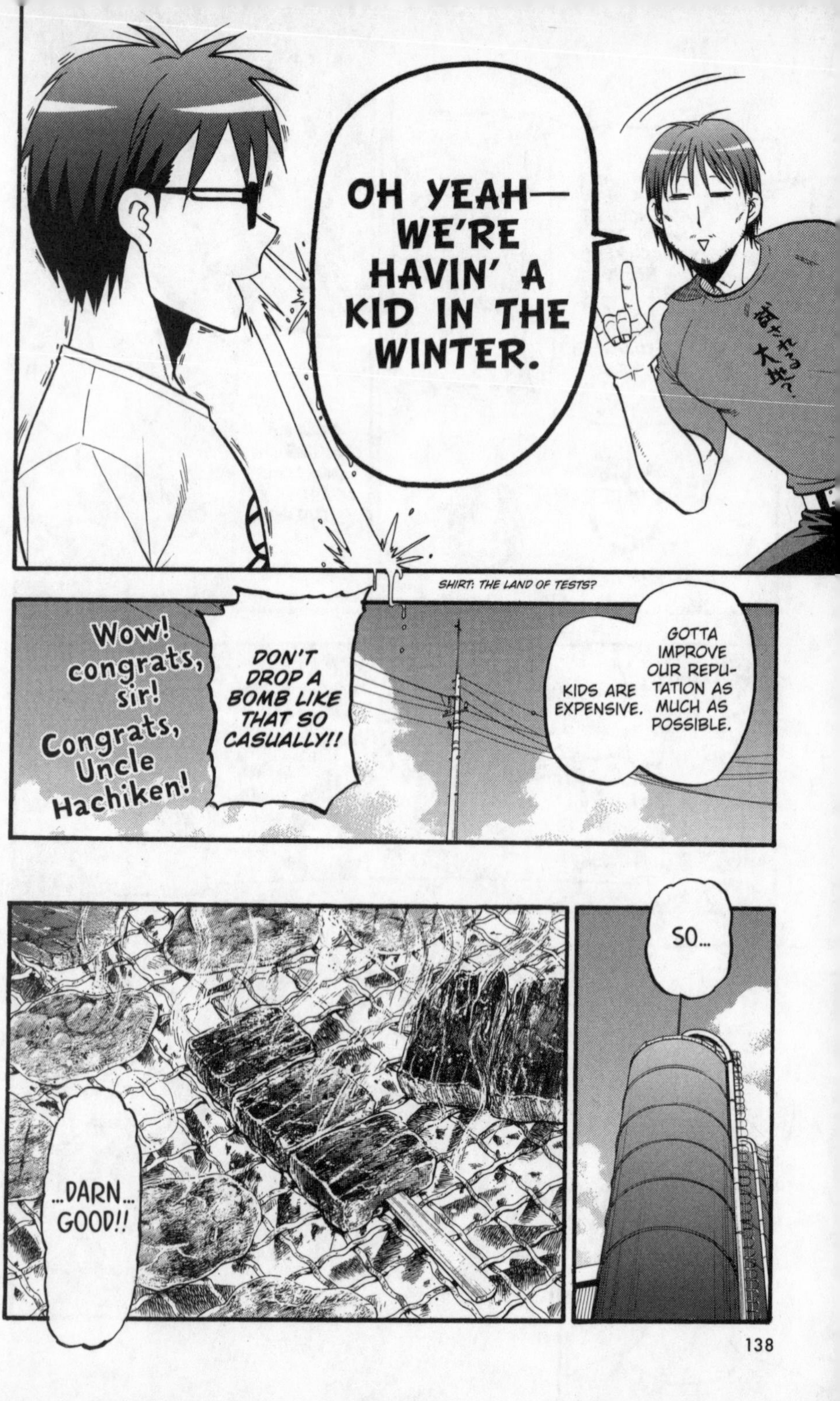
OH YEAH— WE'RE HAVIN' A KID IN THE WINTER.
SHIRT: THE LAND OF TESTS?
KIDS ARE EXPENSIVE. GOTTA IMPROVE OUR REPUTATION AS MUCH AS POSSIBLE.
DON'T DROP A BOMB LIKE THAT SO CASUALLY!!
Wow! congrats, sir! Congrats, Uncle Hachiken!
SO...
...DARN... GOOD!!

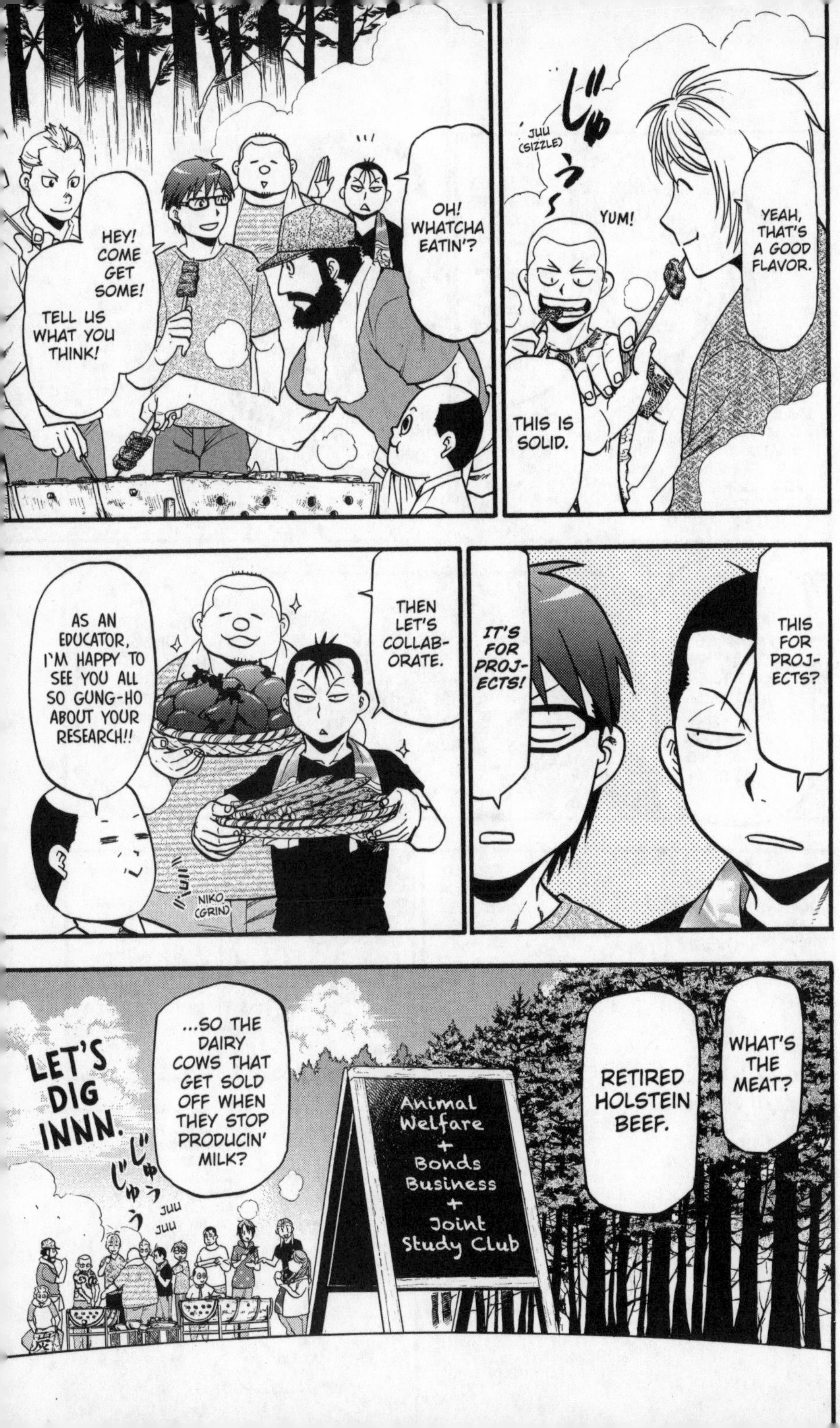
じゅう
JUU (SIZZLE)
YEAH, THAT'S A GOOD FLAVOR.
YUM!
THIS IS SOLID.
OH! WHATCHA EATIN'?
HEY! COME GET SOME!
TELL US WHAT YOU THINK!
THIS FOR PROJ-ECTS?
IT'S FOR PROJ-ECTS!
THEN LET'S COLLAB-ORATE.
AS AN EDUCATOR, I'M HAPPY TO SEE YOU ALL SO GUNG-HO ABOUT YOUR RESEARCH!!
NIKO (GRIND)
WHAT'S THE MEAT?
RETIRED HOLSTEIN BEEF.
...SO THE DAIRY COWS THAT GET SOLD OFF WHEN THEY STOP PRODUCIN' MILK?
Animal Welfare + Bonds Business + Joint Study Club
LET'S DIG INNN.
じゅう じゅう
JUU JUU

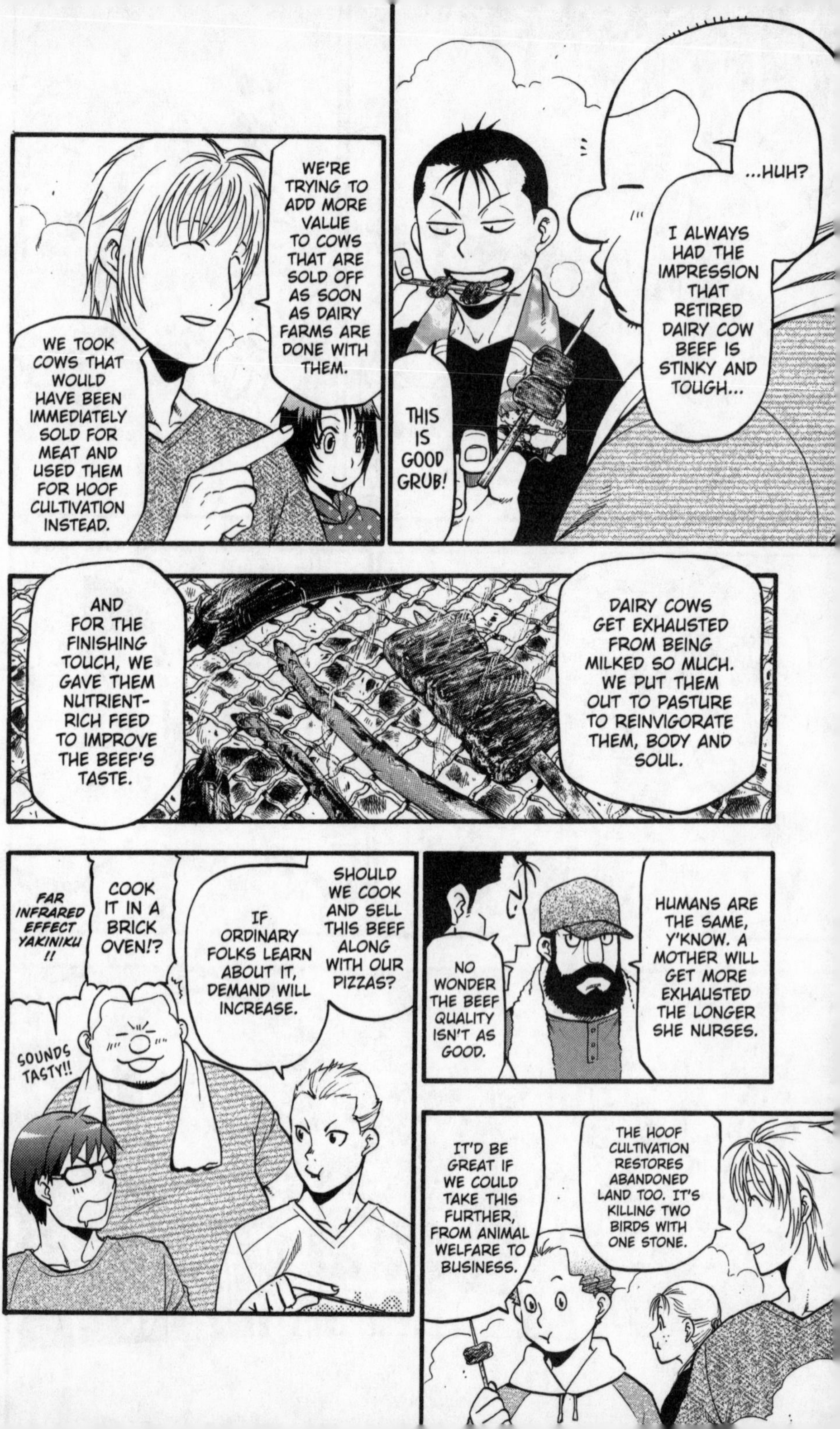
...HUH?
I ALWAYS HAD THE IMPRESSION THAT RETIRED DAIRY COW BEEF IS STINKY AND TOUGH...
THIS IS GOOD GRUB!
WE'RE TRYING TO ADD MORE VALUE TO COWS THAT ARE SOLD OFF AS SOON AS DAIRY FARMS ARE DONE WITH THEM.
WE TOOK COWS THAT WOULD HAVE BEEN IMMEDIATELY SOLD FOR MEAT AND USED THEM FOR HOOF CULTIVATION INSTEAD.
DAIRY COWS GET EXHAUSTED FROM BEING MILKED SO MUCH. WE PUT THEM OUT TO PASTURE TO REINVIGORATE THEM, BODY AND SOUL.
AND FOR THE FINISHING TOUCH, WE GAVE THEM NUTRIENT-RICH FEED TO IMPROVE THE BEEF'S TASTE.
HUMANS ARE THE SAME, Y'KNOW. A MOTHER WILL GET MORE EXHAUSTED THE LONGER SHE NURSES.
NO WONDER THE BEEF QUALITY ISN'T AS GOOD.
THE HOOF CULTIVATION RESTORES ABANDONED LAND TOO. IT'S KILLING TWO BIRDS WITH ONE STONE.
IT'D BE GREAT IF WE COULD TAKE THIS FURTHER, FROM ANIMAL WELFARE TO BUSINESS.
SHOULD WE COOK AND SELL THIS BEEF ALONG WITH OUR PIZZAS?
IF ORDINARY FOLKS LEARN ABOUT IT, DEMAND WILL INCREASE.
COOK IT IN A BRICK OVEN!?
FAR INFRARED EFFECT YAKINIKU!!
SOUNDS TASTY!!

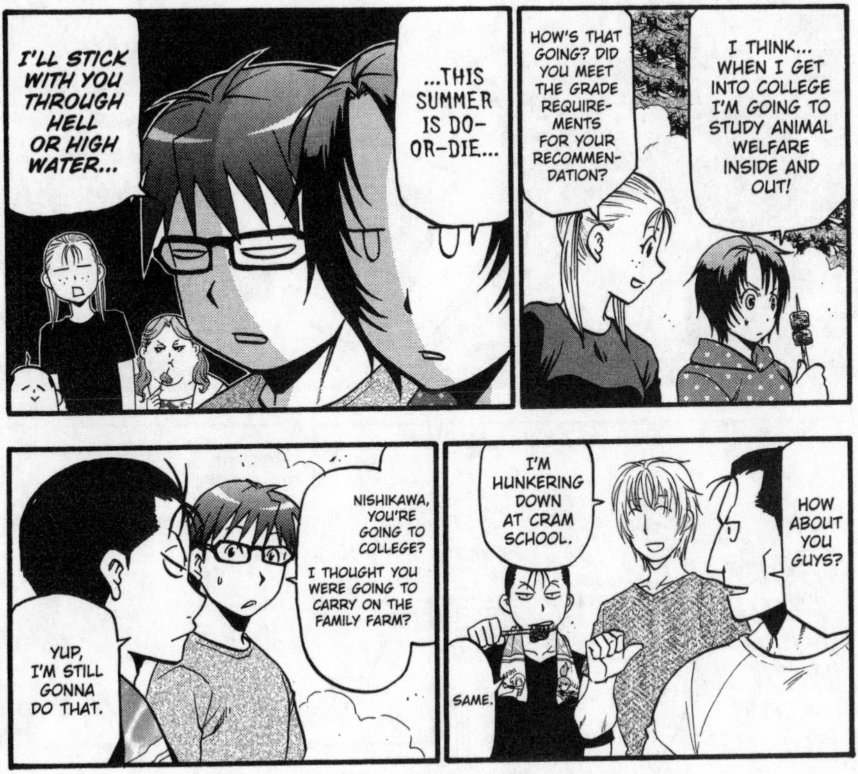
I THINK... WHEN I GET INTO COLLEGE I'M GOING TO STUDY ANIMAL WELFARE INSIDE AND OUT!
HOW'S THAT GOING? DID YOU MEET THE GRADE REQUIREMENTS FOR YOUR RECOMMENDATION?
...THIS SUMMER IS DO-OR-DIE...
I'LL STICK WITH YOU THROUGH HELL OR HIGH WATER...
HOW ABOUT YOU GUYS?
I'M HUNKERING DOWN AT CRAM SCHOOL.
SAME.
NISHIKAWA, YOU'RE GOING TO COLLEGE? I THOUGHT YOU WERE GOING TO CARRY ON THE FAMILY FARM?
YUP, I'M STILL GONNA DO THAT.

The Tale of Hajime Nishikawa

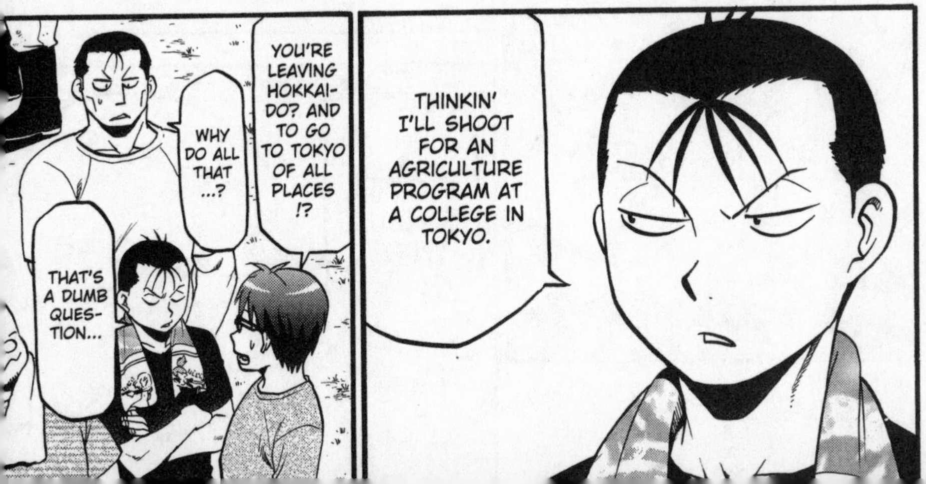
THINKIN' I'LL SHOOT FOR AN AGRICULTURE PROGRAM AT A COLLEGE IN TOKYO.
YOU'RE LEAVING HOKKAIDO? AND TO GO TO TOKYO OF ALL PLACES!?
WHY DO ALL THAT...?
THAT'S A DUMB QUESTION...

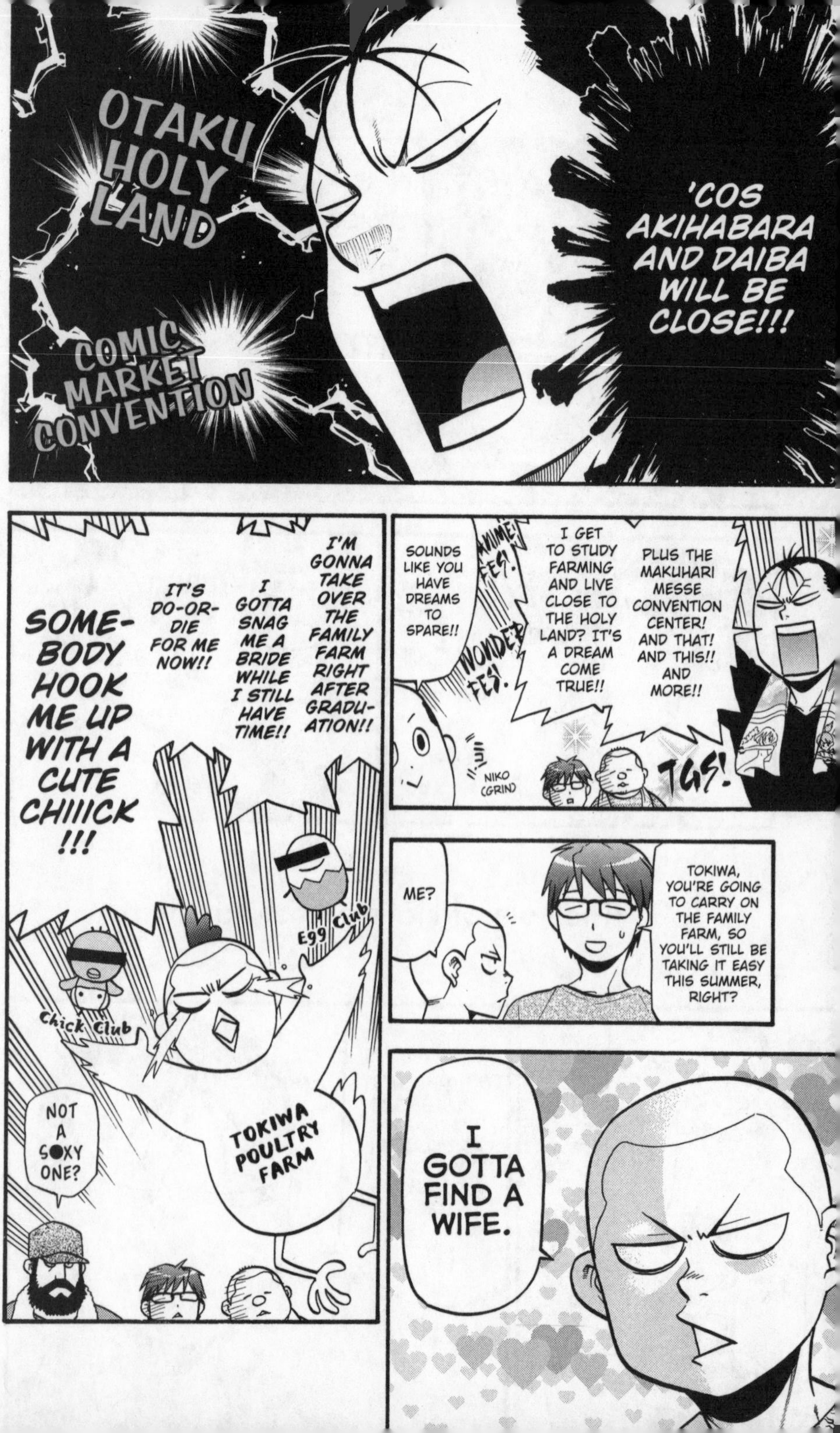
'COS AKIHABARA AND DAIBA WILL BE CLOSE!!!
OTAKU HOLY LAND
COMIC MARKET CONVENTION
PLUS THE MAKUHARI MESSE CONVENTION CENTER! AND THAT! AND THIS!! AND MORE!!
TGS!
I GET TO STUDY FARMING AND LIVE CLOSE TO THE HOLY LAND? IT'S A DREAM COME TRUE!!
ANIME! FES!
WONDER FES!
SOUNDS LIKE YOU HAVE DREAMS TO SPARE!!
NIKO (GRIND)
TOKIWA, YOU'RE GOING TO CARRY ON THE FAMILY FARM, SO YOU'LL STILL BE TAKING IT EASY THIS SUMMER, RIGHT?
ME?
I GOTTA FIND A WIFE.
I'M GONNA TAKE OVER THE FAMILY FARM RIGHT AFTER GRADUATION!!
I GOTTA SNAG ME A BRIDE WHILE I STILL HAVE TIME!!
IT'S DO-OR-DIE FOR ME NOW!!
SOMEBODY HOOK ME UP WITH A CUTE CHIIICK!!!
Egg Club
Chick Club
TOKIWA POULTRY FARM
NOT A S●XY ONE?

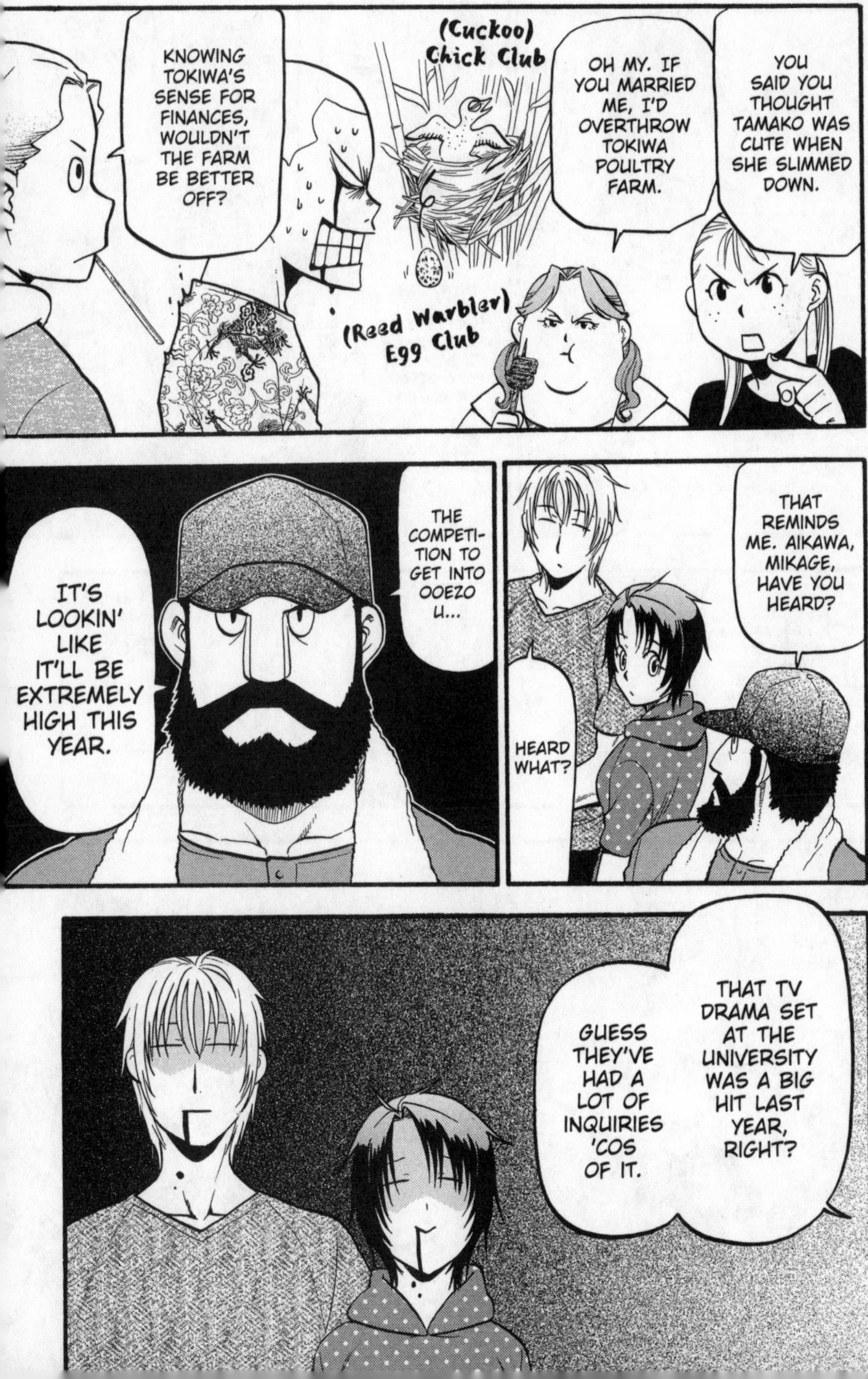
YOU SAID YOU THOUGHT TAMAKO WAS CUTE WHEN SHE SLIMMED DOWN.
OH MY. IF YOU MARRIED ME, I'D OVERTHROW TOKIWA POULTRY FARM.
(Cuckoo) Chick Club
(Reed Warbler) Egg Club
KNOWING TOKIWA'S SENSE FOR FINANCES, WOULDN'T THE FARM BE BETTER OFF?
THAT REMINDS ME. AIKAWA, MIKAGE, HAVE YOU HEARD?
HEARD WHAT?
THE COMPETI-TION TO GET INTO OOEZO U...
IT'S LOOKIN' LIKE IT'LL BE EXTREMELY HIGH THIS YEAR.
THAT TV DRAMA SET AT THE UNIVERSITY WAS A BIG HIT LAST YEAR, RIGHT?
GUESS THEY'VE HAD A LOT OF INQUIRIES 'COS OF IT.

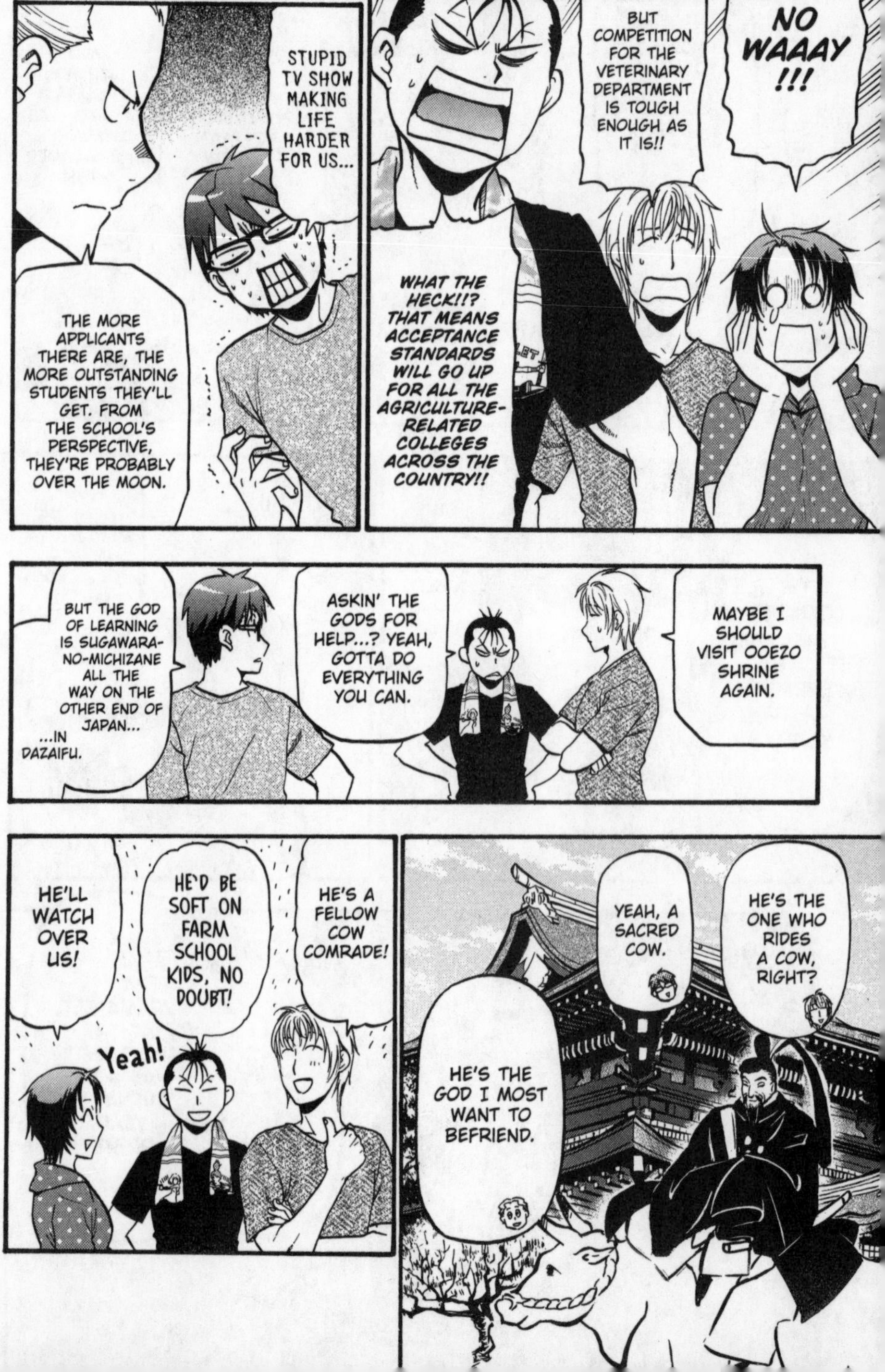
NO WAAAY!!!
BUT COMPETITION FOR THE VETERINARY DEPARTMENT IS TOUGH ENOUGH AS IT IS!!
WHAT THE HECK!!? THAT MEANS ACCEPTANCE STANDARDS WILL GO UP FOR ALL THE AGRICULTURE-RELATED COLLEGES ACROSS THE COUNTRY!!
STUPID TV SHOW MAKING LIFE HARDER FOR US...
THE MORE APPLICANTS THERE ARE, THE MORE OUTSTANDING STUDENTS THEY'LL GET. FROM THE SCHOOL'S PERSPECTIVE, THEY'RE PROBABLY OVER THE MOON.
MAYBE I SHOULD VISIT OOEZO SHRINE AGAIN.
ASKIN' THE GODS FOR HELP...? YEAH, GOTTA DO EVERYTHING YOU CAN.
BUT THE GOD OF LEARNING IS SUGAWARA-NO-MICHIZANE ALL THE WAY ON THE OTHER END OF JAPAN...
...IN DAZAIFU.
HE'S THE ONE WHO RIDES A COW, RIGHT?
YEAH, A SACRED COW.
HE'S THE GOD I MOST WANT TO BEFRIEND.
HE'S A FELLOW COW COMRADE!
HE'D BE SOFT ON FARM SCHOOL KIDS, NO DOUBT!
HE'LL WATCH OVER US!
Yeah!

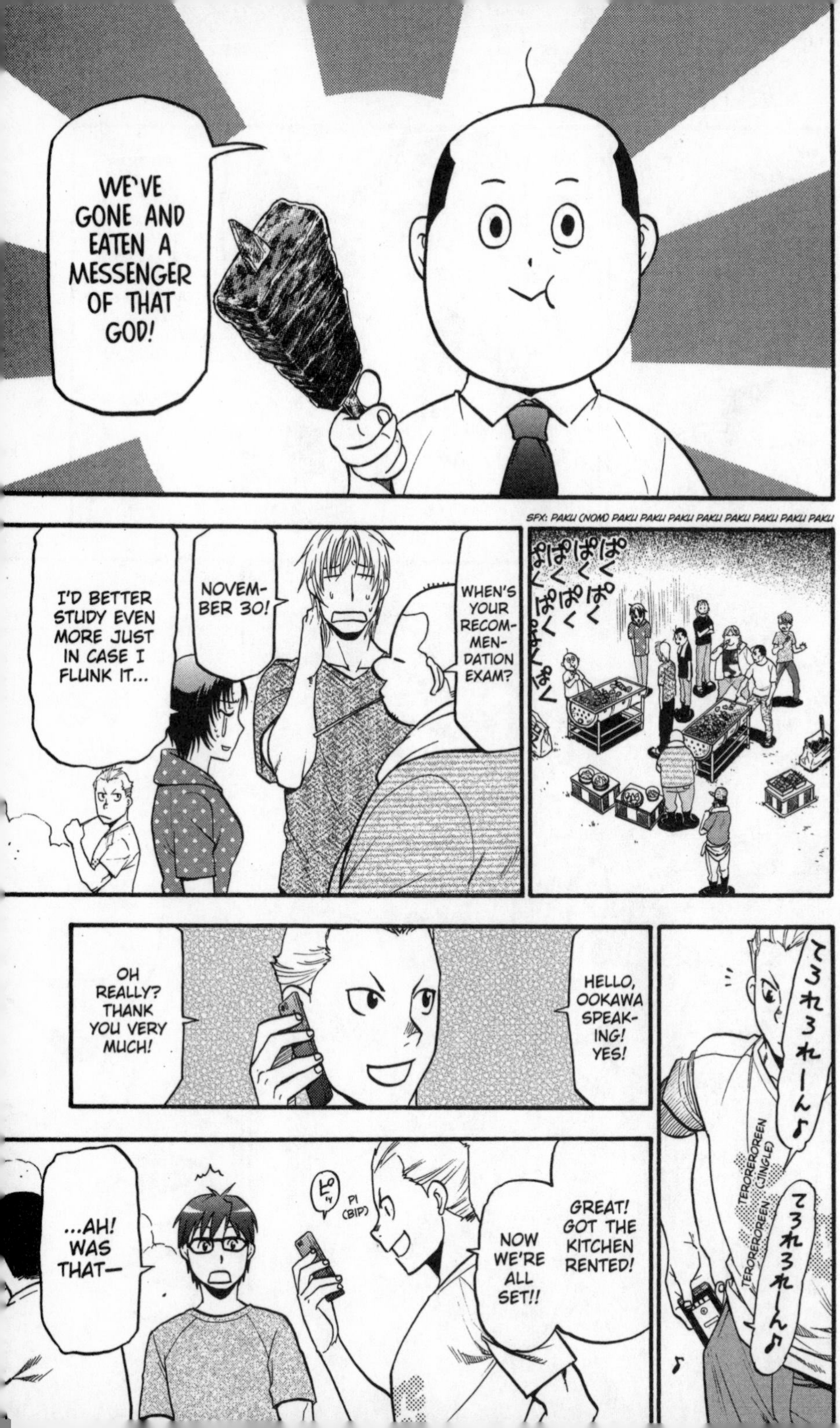
WE'VE GONE AND EATEN A MESSENGER OF THAT GOD!
SFX: PAKU (NOM) PAKU PAKU PAKU PAKU PAKU PAKU PAKU PAKU
ぱくぱくぱくぱくぱくぱくぱくぱくぱく
WHEN'S YOUR RECOMMENDATION EXAM?
NOVEMBER 30!
I'D BETTER STUDY EVEN MORE JUST IN CASE I FLUNK IT...
てろれろれーん♪
TERORERORREN (JINGLE)
てろれろれーん♪
TERORERORREN
HELLO, OOKAWA SPEAKING! YES!
OH REALLY? THANK YOU VERY MUCH!
GREAT! GOT THE KITCHEN RENTED!
NOW WE'RE ALL SET!!
ピ
PI (BIP)
...AH! WAS THAT—

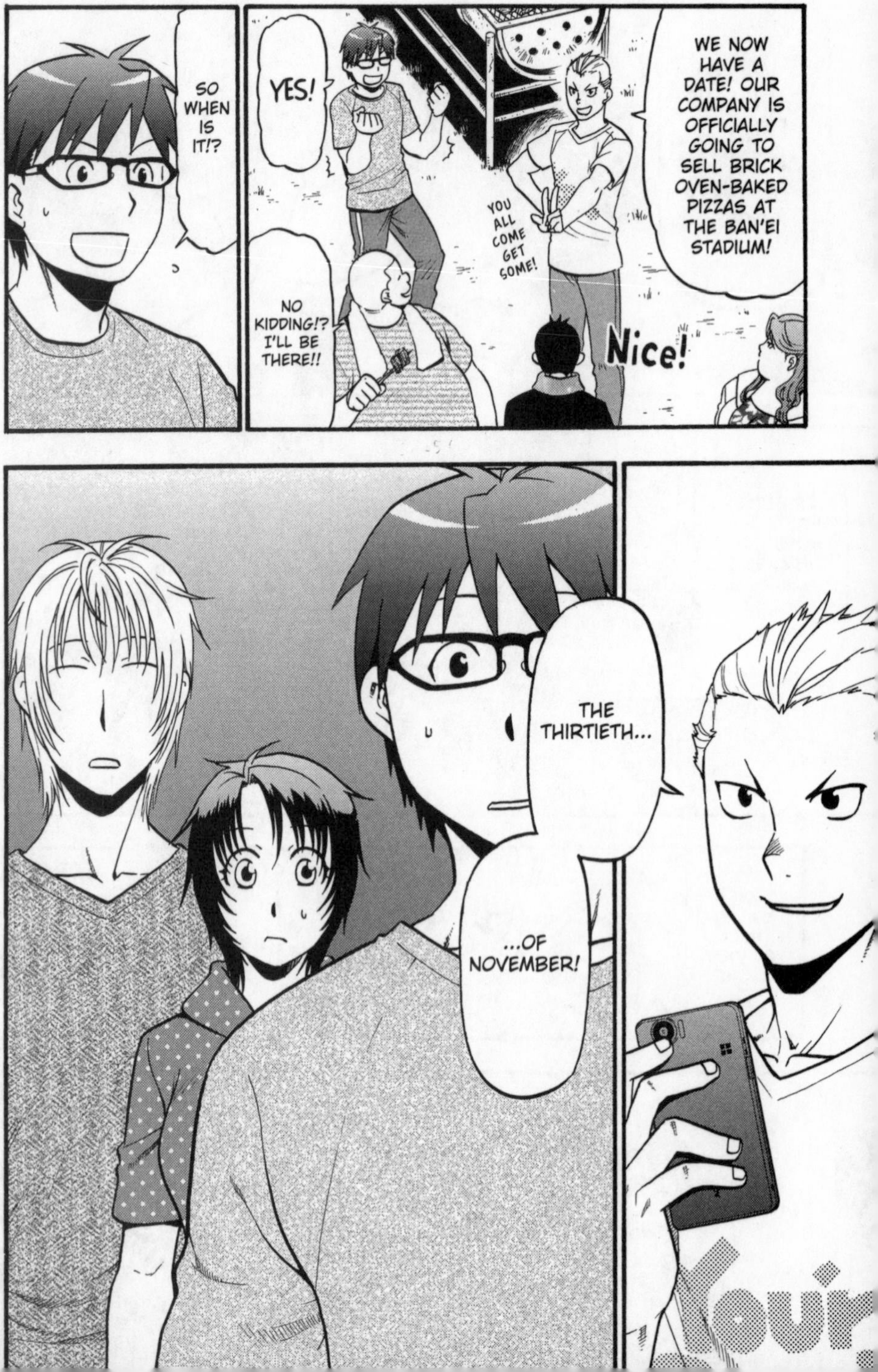
WE NOW HAVE A DATE! OUR COMPANY IS OFFICIALLY GOING TO SELL BRICK OVEN-BAKED PIZZAS AT THE BAN'EI STADIUM!
YOU ALL COME GET SOME!
Nice!
YES!
NO KIDDING!? I'LL BE THERE!!
SO WHEN IS IT!?
THE THIRTIETH...
...OF NOVEMBER!

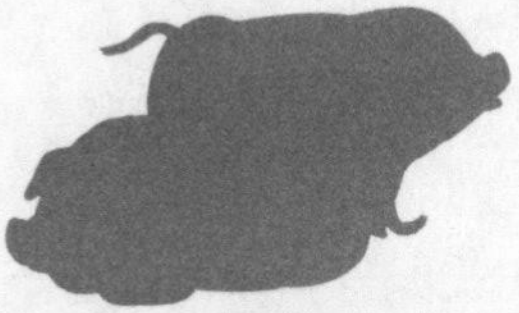

Silver Spoon

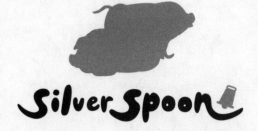

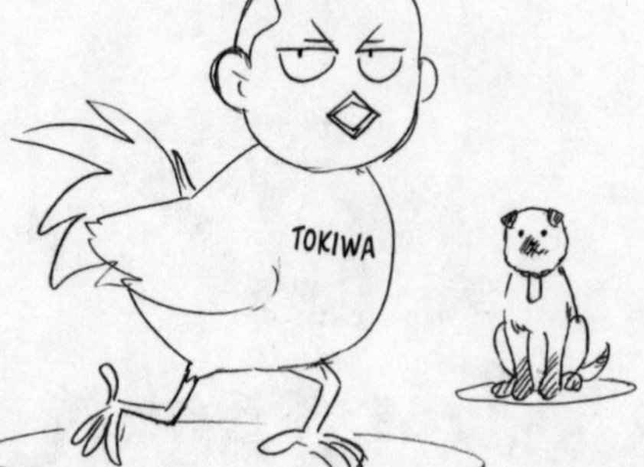
TOKIWA

Chapter 113:
Tale of Four Seasons⑯

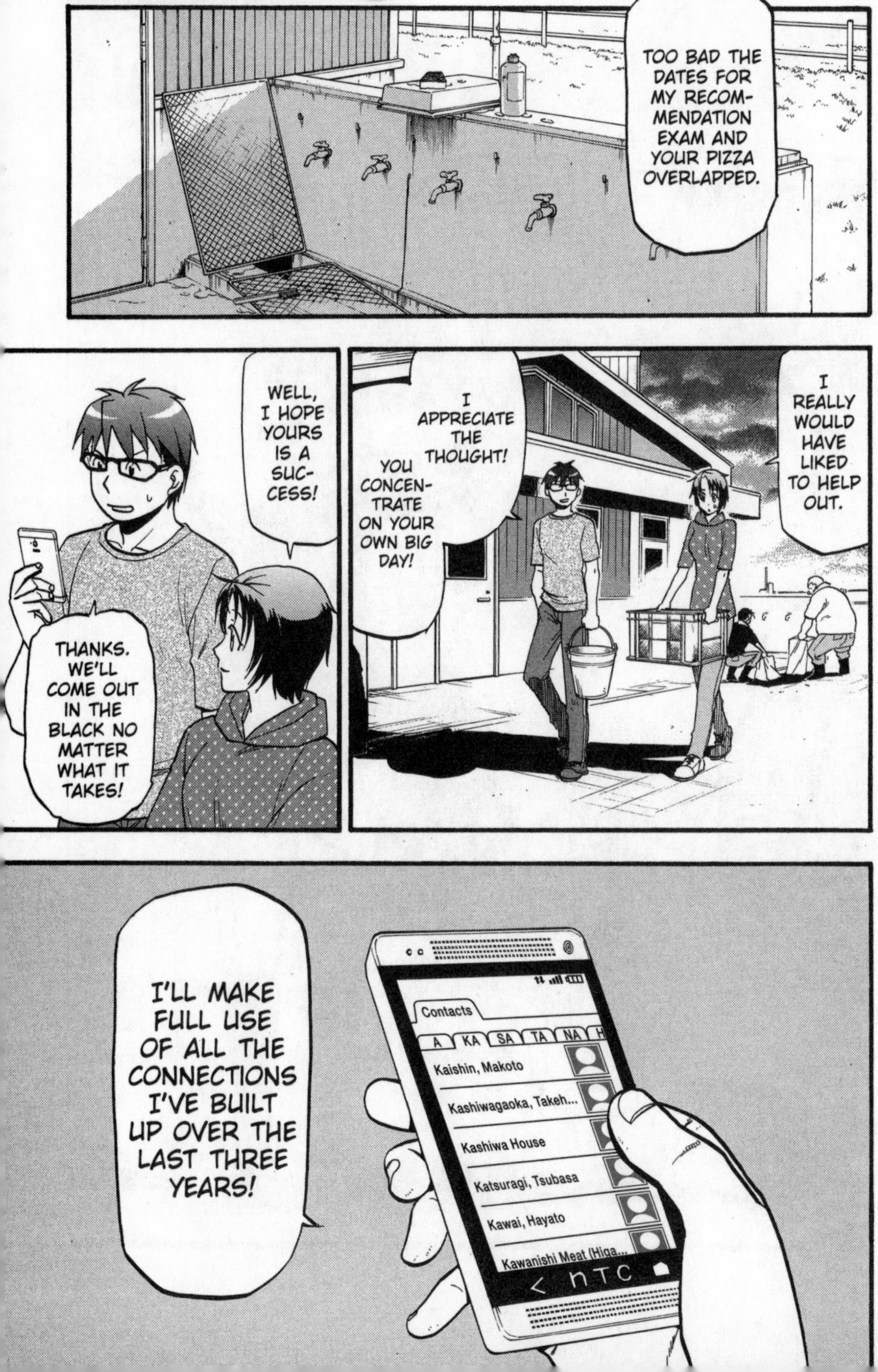
TOO BAD THE DATES FOR MY RECOMMENDATION EXAM AND YOUR PIZZA OVERLAPPED.
I REALLY WOULD HAVE LIKED TO HELP OUT.
I APPRECIATE THE THOUGHT!
YOU CONCENTRATE ON YOUR OWN BIG DAY!
WELL, I HOPE YOURS IS A SUCCESS!
THANKS. WE'LL COME OUT IN THE BLACK NO MATTER WHAT IT TAKES!
I'LL MAKE FULL USE OF ALL THE CONNECTIONS I'VE BUILT UP OVER THE LAST THREE YEARS!
Contacts
A KA SA TA NA
Kaishin, Makoto
Kashiwagaoka, Takeh...
Kashiwa House
Katsuragi, Tsubasa
Kawai, Hayato
Kawanishi Meat (Higa...
hTC

Chapter 113: Tale of Four Seasons ⑯

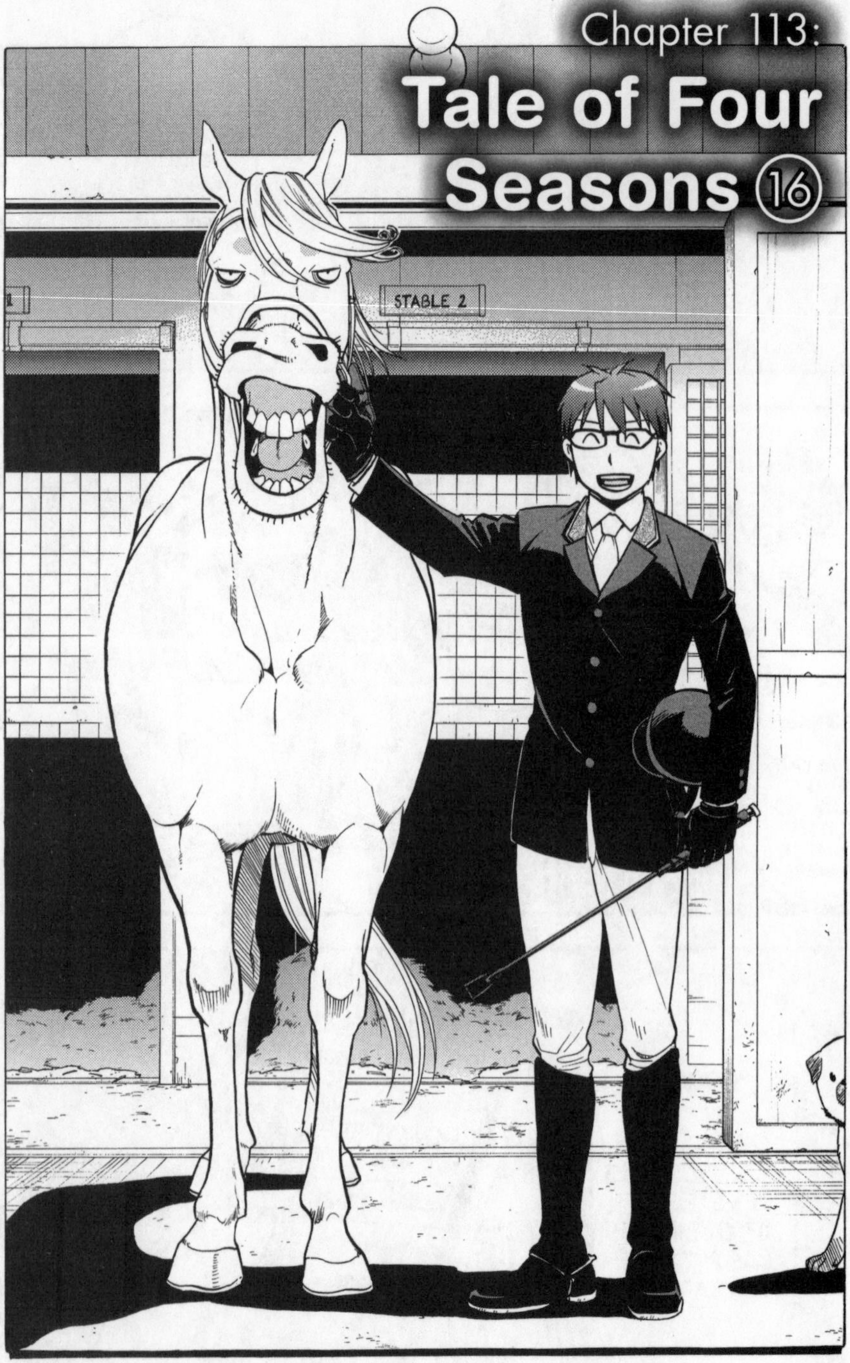
STABLE 2

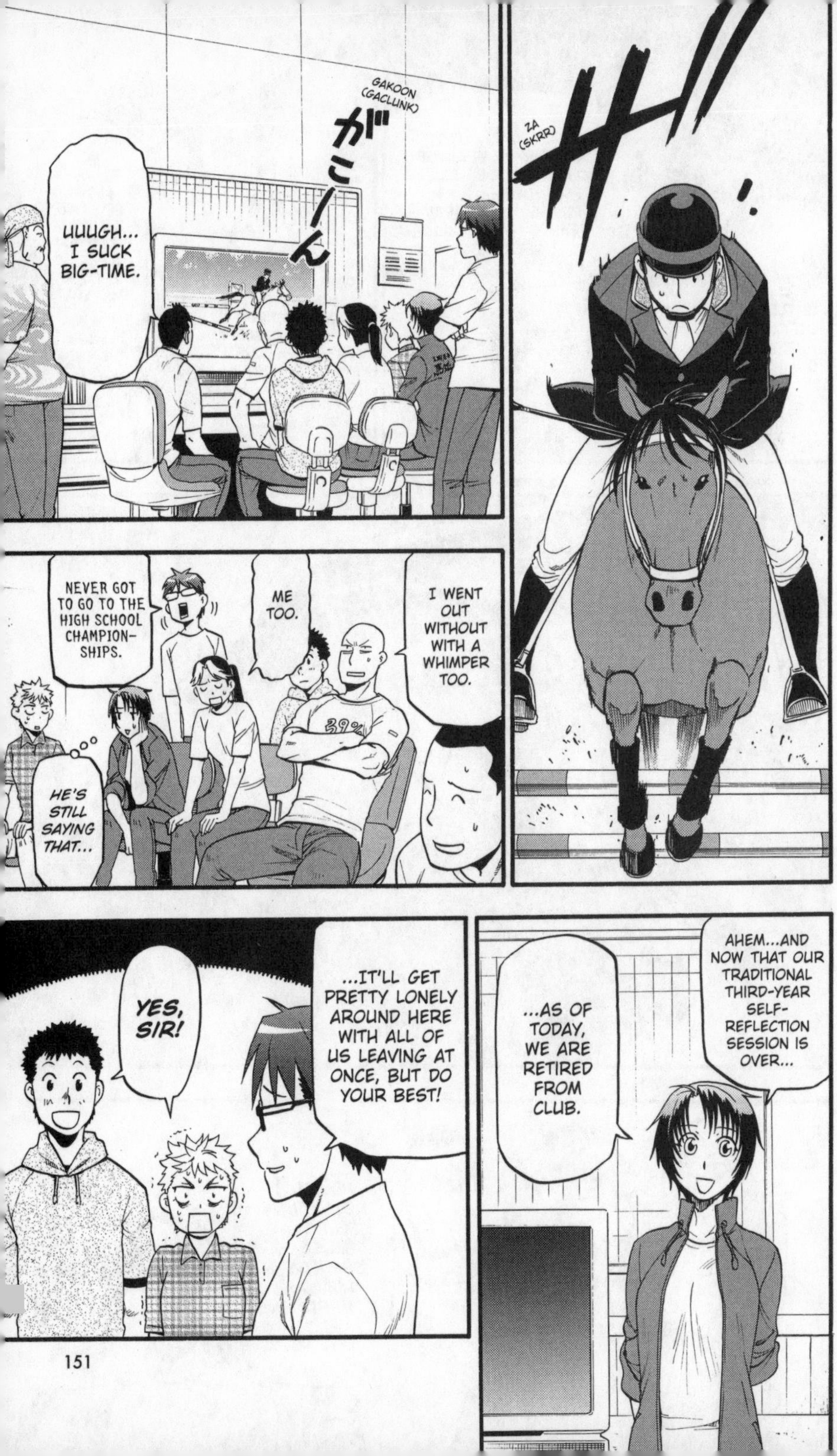
ZA (SKRR)
ザッ
GAKOON (GACLUNK)
がこーん
UUUGH... I SUCK BIG-TIME.
I WENT OUT WITHOUT WITH A WHIMPER TOO.
ME TOO.
NEVER GOT TO GO TO THE HIGH SCHOOL CHAMPION-SHIPS.
HE'S STILL SAYING THAT...
AHEM...AND NOW THAT OUR TRADITIONAL THIRD-YEAR SELF-REFLECTION SESSION IS OVER...
...AS OF TODAY, WE ARE RETIRED FROM CLUB.
...IT'LL GET PRETTY LONELY AROUND HERE WITH ALL OF US LEAVING AT ONCE, BUT DO YOUR BEST!
YES, SIR!

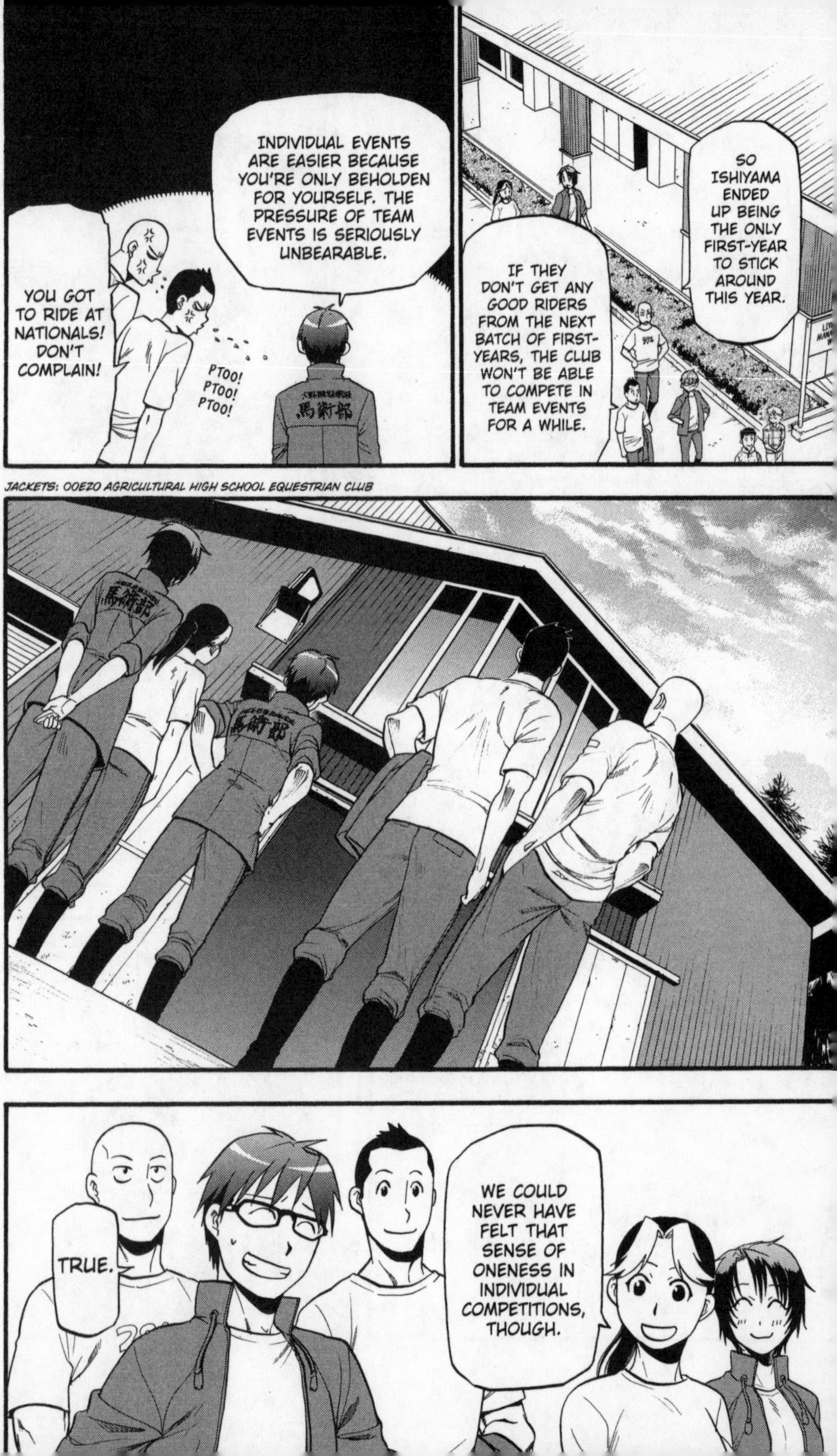
SO ISHIYAMA ENDED UP BEING THE ONLY FIRST-YEAR TO STICK AROUND THIS YEAR.
IF THEY DON'T GET ANY GOOD RIDERS FROM THE NEXT BATCH OF FIRST-YEARS, THE CLUB WON'T BE ABLE TO COMPETE IN TEAM EVENTS FOR A WHILE.
INDIVIDUAL EVENTS ARE EASIER BECAUSE YOU'RE ONLY BEHOLDEN FOR YOURSELF. THE PRESSURE OF TEAM EVENTS IS SERIOUSLY UNBEARABLE.
YOU GOT TO RIDE AT NATIONALS! DON'T COMPLAIN!
PTOO! PTOO! PTOO!
JACKETS: OOEZO AGRICULTURAL HIGH SCHOOL EQUESTRIAN CLUB
WE COULD NEVER HAVE FELT THAT SENSE OF ONENESS IN INDIVIDUAL COMPETITIONS, THOUGH.
TRUE.

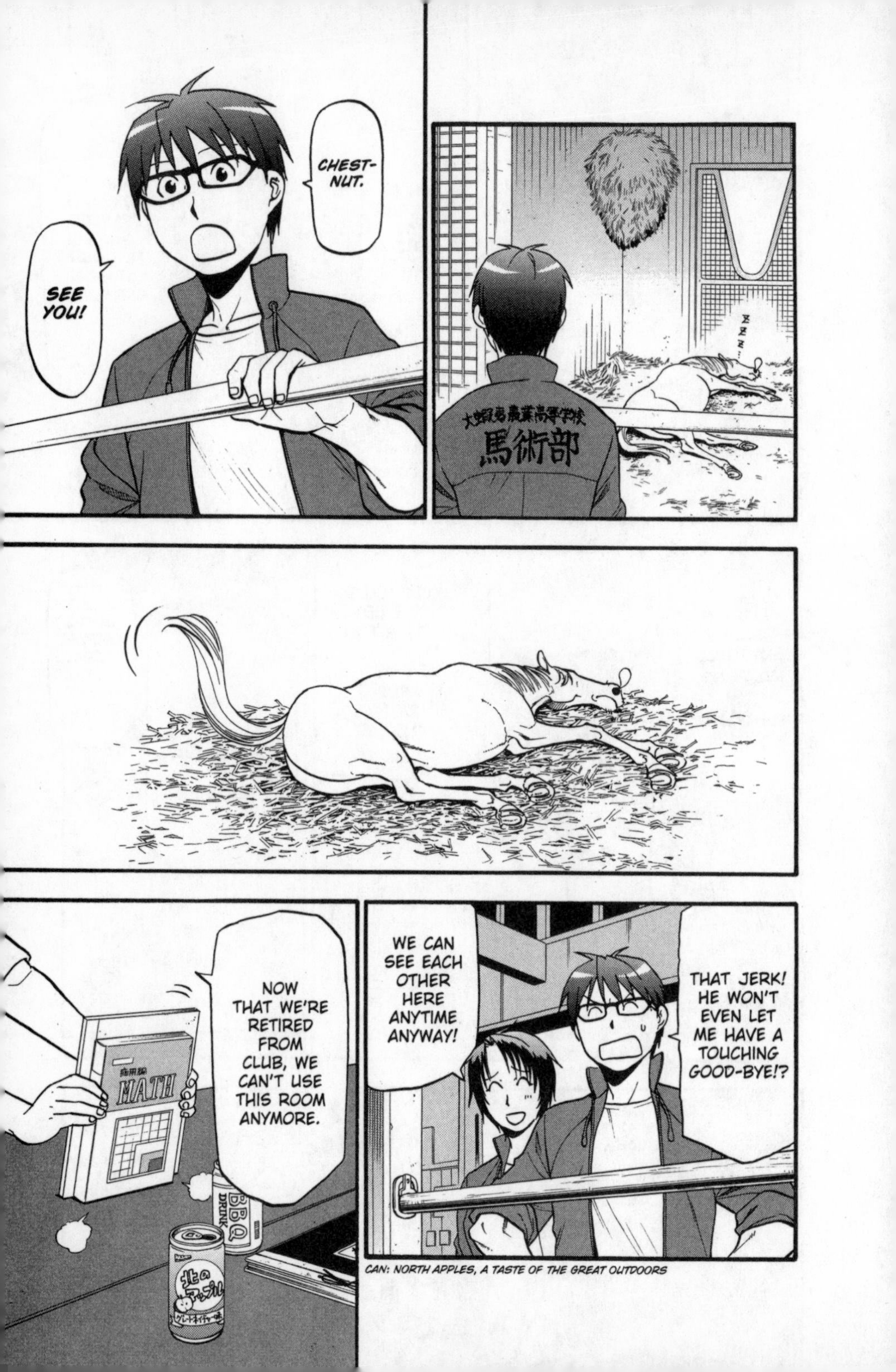

大蝦夷農業高等学校
馬術部
Z Z Z...
CHEST-NUT.
SEE YOU!
THAT JERK! HE WON'T EVEN LET ME HAVE A TOUCHING GOOD-BYE!?
WE CAN SEE EACH OTHER HERE ANYTIME ANYWAY!
NOW THAT WE'RE RETIRED FROM CLUB, WE CAN'T USE THIS ROOM ANYMORE.
MATH
BBQ DRINK
北のアップル

CAN: NORTH APPLES, A TASTE OF THE GREAT OUTDOORS

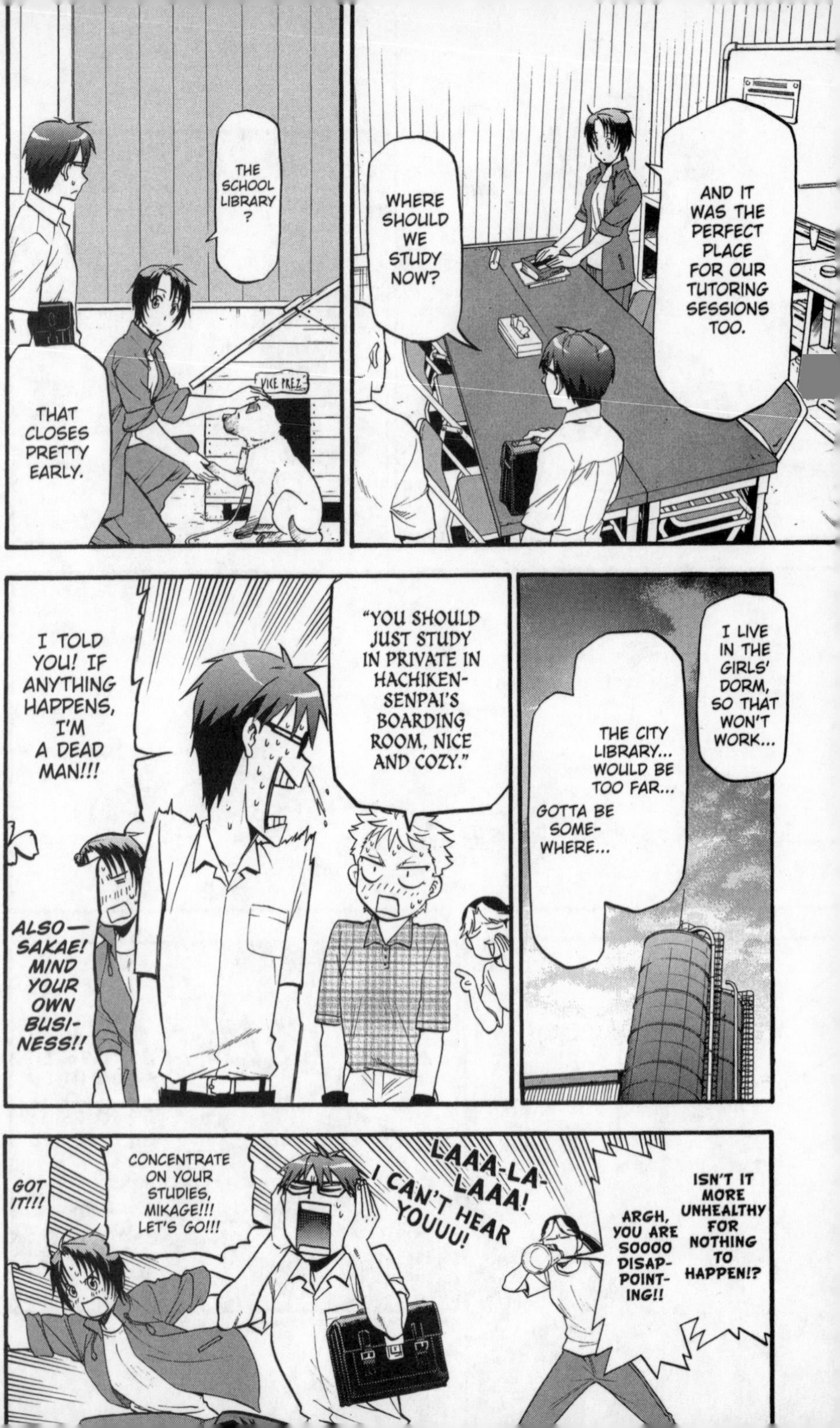
AND IT WAS THE PERFECT PLACE FOR OUR TUTORING SESSIONS TOO.
WHERE SHOULD WE STUDY NOW?
THE SCHOOL LIBRARY?
THAT CLOSES PRETTY EARLY.
I LIVE IN THE GIRLS' DORM, SO THAT WON'T WORK...
THE CITY LIBRARY... WOULD BE TOO FAR...
GOTTA BE SOME-WHERE...
"YOU SHOULD JUST STUDY IN PRIVATE IN HACHIKEN-SENPAI'S BOARDING ROOM, NICE AND COZY."
I TOLD YOU! IF ANYTHING HAPPENS, I'M A DEAD MAN!!!
ALSO— SAKAE! MIND YOUR OWN BUSI-NESS!!
ISN'T IT MORE UNHEALTHY FOR NOTHING TO HAPPEN!?
ARGH, YOU ARE SOOOO DISAP-POINT-ING!!
LAAA-LA-LAAA! I CAN'T HEAR YOUUU!
CONCENTRATE ON YOUR STUDIES, MIKAGE!!! LET'S GO!!!
GOT IT!!!

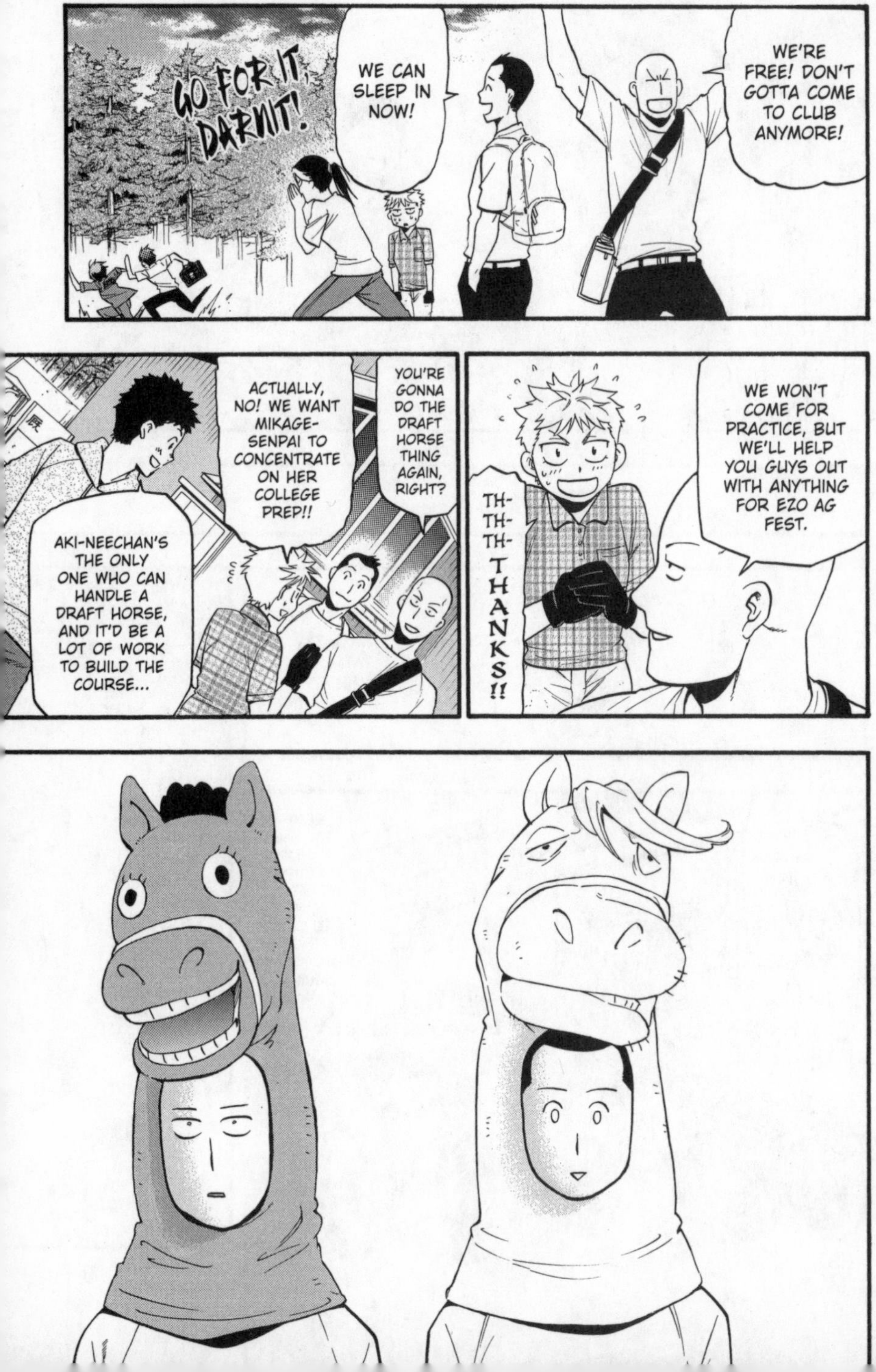
WE'RE FREE! DON'T GOTTA COME TO CLUB ANYMORE!
WE CAN SLEEP IN NOW!
GO FOR IT, DARNIT!
WE WON'T COME FOR PRACTICE, BUT WE'LL HELP YOU GUYS OUT WITH ANYTHING FOR EZO AG FEST.
TH-TH-TH-THANKS!!
YOU'RE GONNA DO THE DRAFT HORSE THING AGAIN, RIGHT?
ACTUALLY, NO! WE WANT MIKAGE-SENPAI TO CONCENTRATE ON HER COLLEGE PREP!!
AKI-NEECHAN'S THE ONLY ONE WHO CAN HANDLE A DRAFT HORSE, AND IT'D BE A LOT OF WORK TO BUILD THE COURSE...

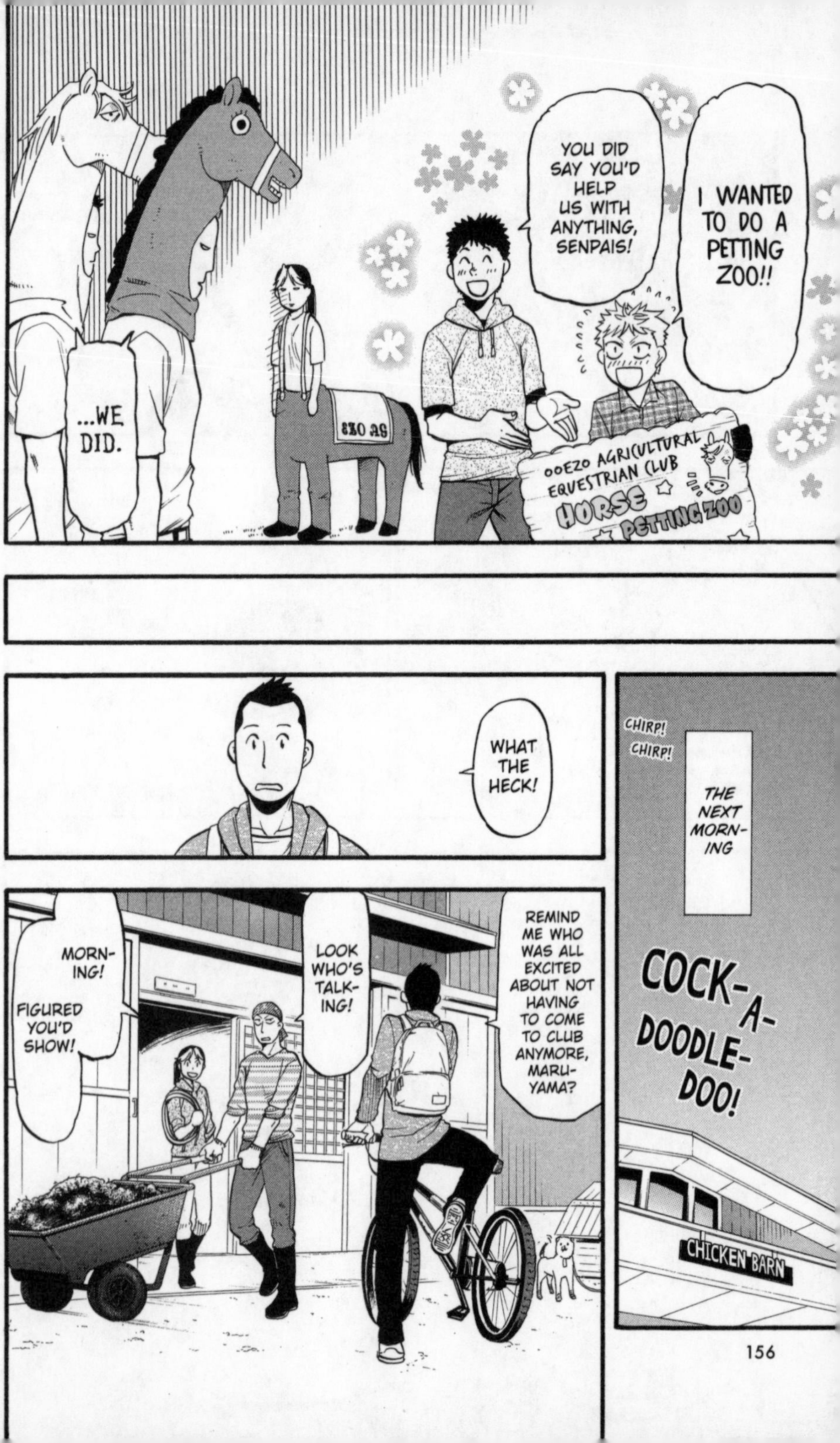
I WANTED TO DO A PETTING ZOO!!
YOU DID SAY YOU'D HELP US WITH ANYTHING, SENPAIS!
OOEZO AGRICULTURAL EQUESTRIAN CLUB
HORSE PETTING ZOO
...WE DID.
CHIRP! CHIRP!
THE NEXT MORNING
COCK-A-DOODLE-DOO!
CHICKEN BARN
WHAT THE HECK!
REMIND ME WHO WAS ALL EXCITED ABOUT NOT HAVING TO COME TO CLUB ANYMORE, MARUYAMA?
LOOK WHO'S TALKING!
MORNING! FIGURED YOU'D SHOW!

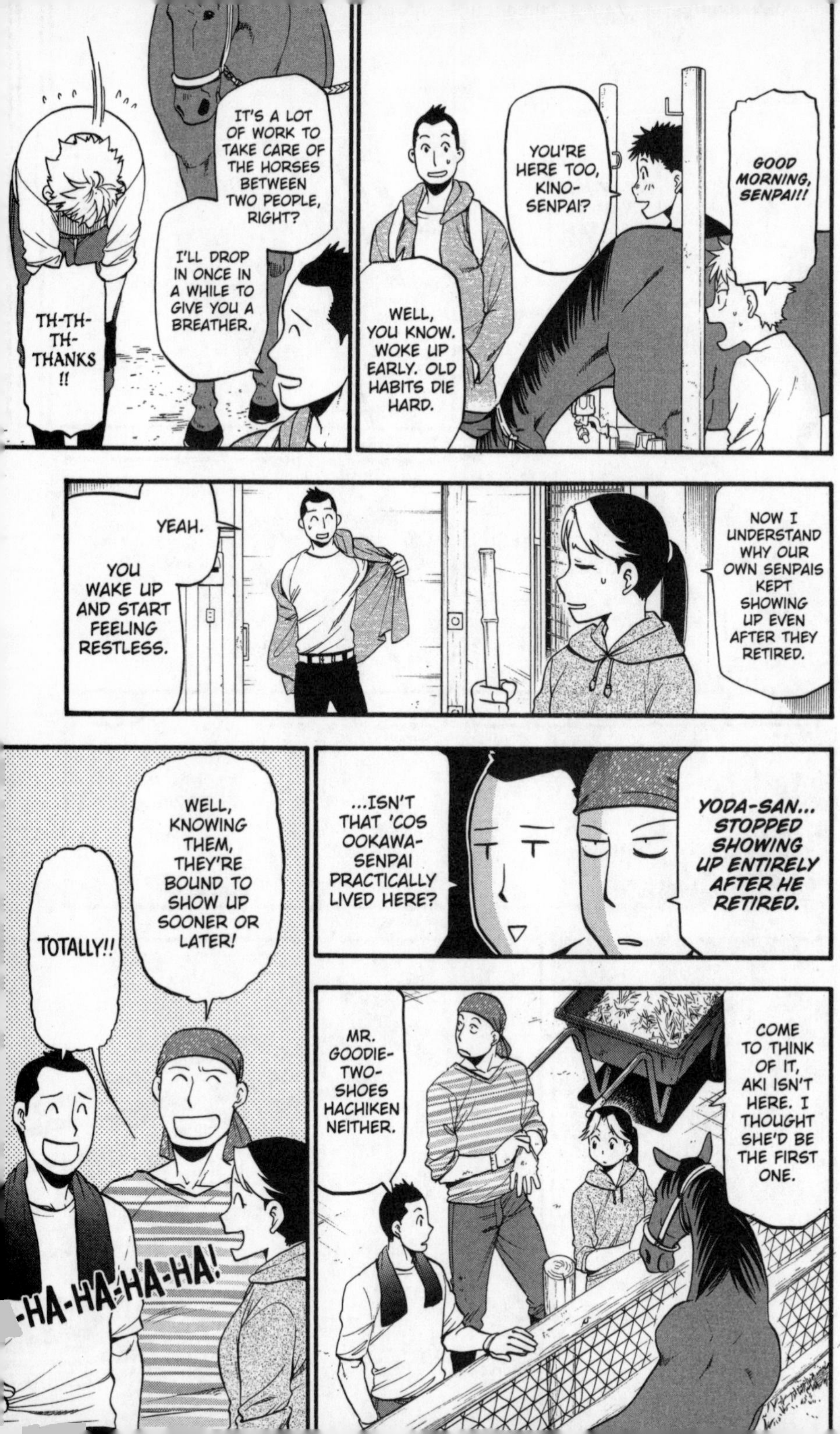
GOOD MORNING, SENPAI!!
YOU'RE HERE TOO, KINO-SENPAI?
WELL, YOU KNOW. WOKE UP EARLY. OLD HABITS DIE HARD.
IT'S A LOT OF WORK TO TAKE CARE OF THE HORSES BETWEEN TWO PEOPLE, RIGHT?
I'LL DROP IN ONCE IN A WHILE TO GIVE YOU A BREATHER.
TH-TH-TH-THANKS!!
NOW I UNDERSTAND WHY OUR OWN SENPAIS KEPT SHOWING UP EVEN AFTER THEY RETIRED.
YEAH.
YOU WAKE UP AND START FEELING RESTLESS.
YODA-SAN... STOPPED SHOWING UP ENTIRELY AFTER HE RETIRED.
...ISN'T THAT 'COS OOKAWA-SENPAI PRACTICALLY LIVED HERE?
COME TO THINK OF IT, AKI ISN'T HERE. I THOUGHT SHE'D BE THE FIRST ONE.
MR. GOODIE-TWO-SHOES HACHIKEN NEITHER.
WELL, KNOWING THEM, THEY'RE BOUND TO SHOW UP SOONER OR LATER!
TOTALLY!!
-HA-HA-HA-HA-HA!

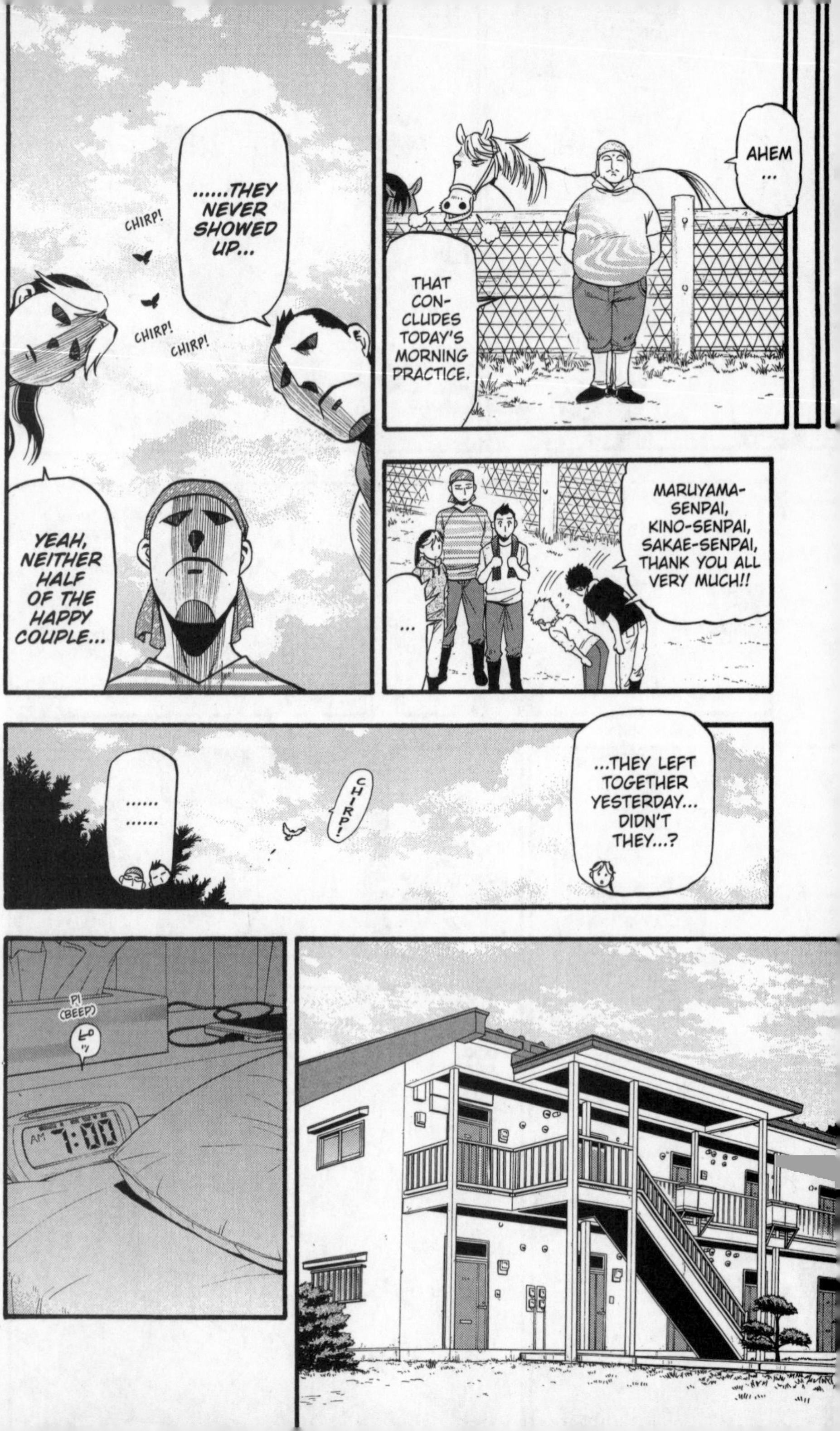
AHEM ...
THAT CON-CLUDES TODAY'S MORNING PRACTICE.
MARUYAMA-SENPAI, KINO-SENPAI, SAKAE-SENPAI, THANK YOU ALL VERY MUCH!!
...
......THEY NEVER SHOWED UP...
CHIRP!
CHIRP!
CHIRP!
YEAH, NEITHER HALF OF THE HAPPY COUPLE...
...THEY LEFT TOGETHER YESTERDAY... DIDN'T THEY...?
CHIRP!
......
......
PI (BEEP)
ピッ
AM 7:00

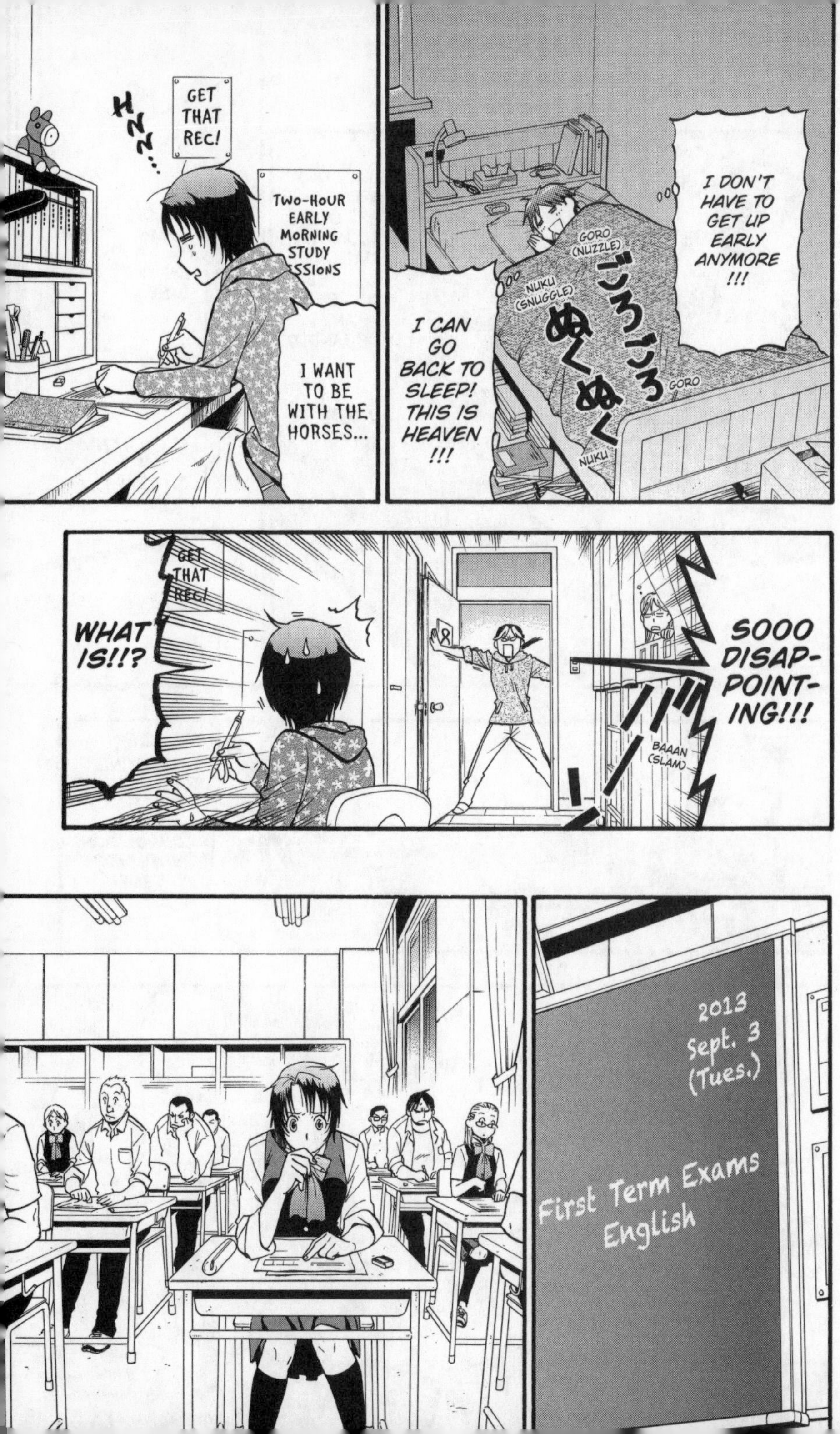

I DON'T HAVE TO GET UP EARLY ANYMORE !!!
GORO (NUZZLE)
ごろごろ
NUKU (SNUGGLE)
ぬくぬく
GORO
NUKU
I CAN GO BACK TO SLEEP! THIS IS HEAVEN !!!
GET THAT REC!
HNN...
TWO-HOUR EARLY MORNING STUDY SSIONS
I WANT TO BE WITH THE HORSES...
SOOO DISAP-POINTING!!!
BAAAN (SLAM)
GET THAT REC!
WHAT IS!!?
2013 Sept. 3 (Tues.)
First Term Exams English

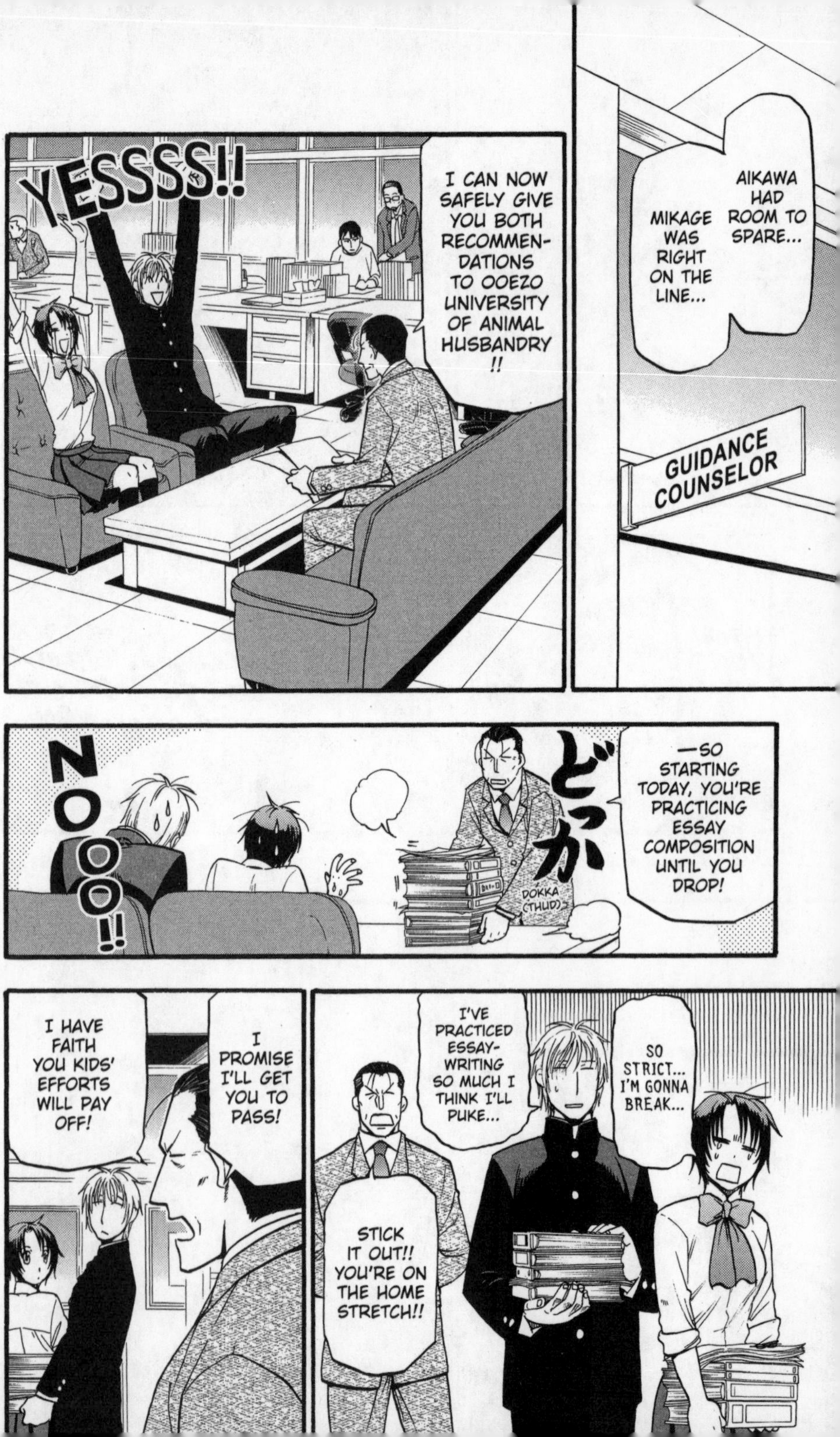
AIKAWA HAD ROOM TO SPARE...
MIKAGE WAS RIGHT ON THE LINE...
GUIDANCE COUNSELOR
I CAN NOW SAFELY GIVE YOU BOTH RECOMMEN-DATIONS TO OOEZO UNIVERSITY OF ANIMAL HUSBANDRY!!
YESSSS!!
—SO STARTING TODAY, YOU'RE PRACTICING ESSAY COMPOSITION UNTIL YOU DROP!
どっか
DOKKA (THUD)
NOOOO!!
SO STRICT... I'M GONNA BREAK...
I'VE PRACTICED ESSAY-WRITING SO MUCH I THINK I'LL PUKE...
STICK IT OUT!! YOU'RE ON THE HOME STRETCH!!
I PROMISE I'LL GET YOU TO PASS!
I HAVE FAITH YOU KIDS' EFFORTS WILL PAY OFF!

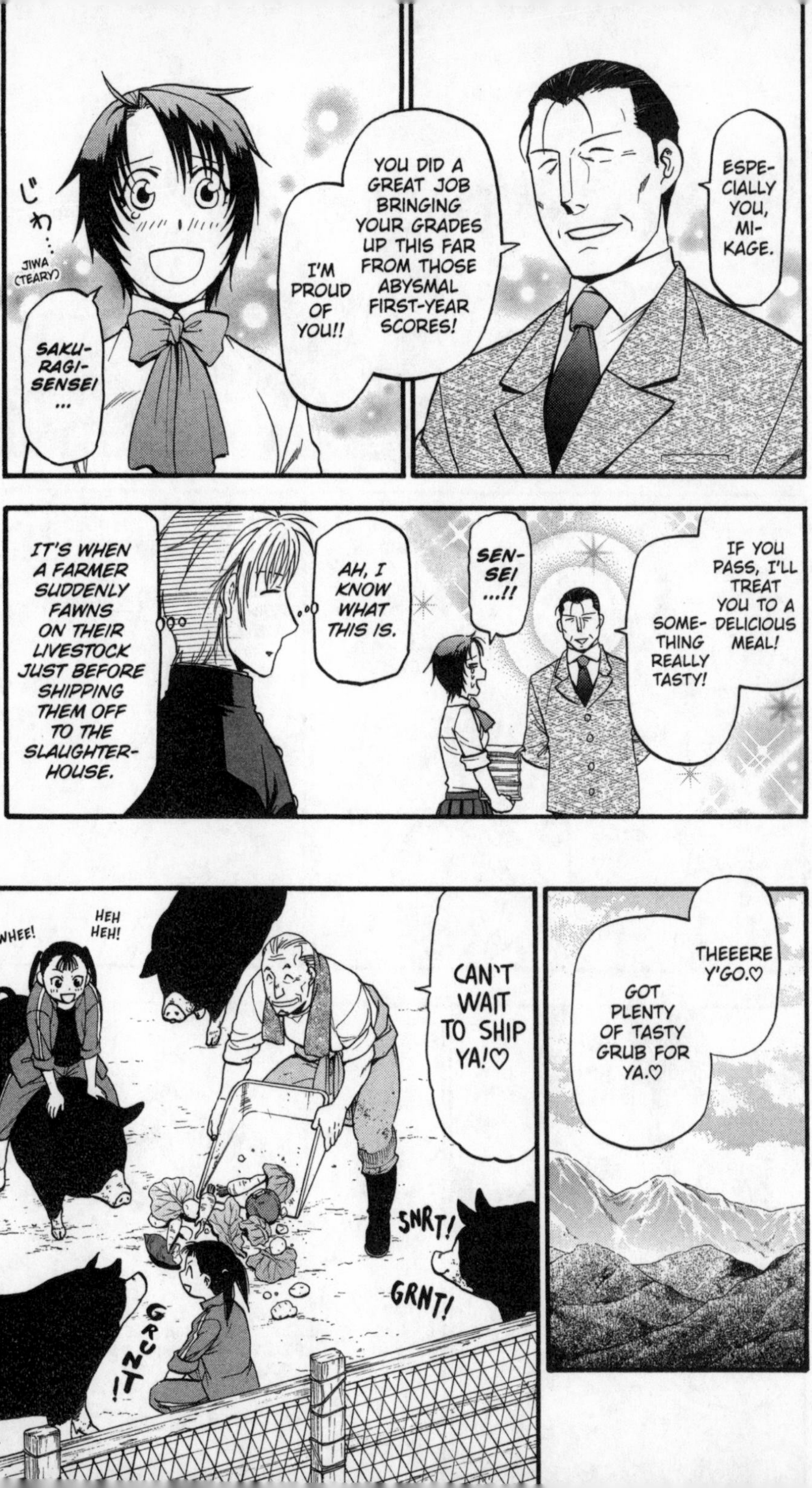
ESPECIALLY YOU, MIKAGE.
YOU DID A GREAT JOB BRINGING YOUR GRADES UP THIS FAR FROM THOSE ABYSMAL FIRST-YEAR SCORES!
I'M PROUD OF YOU!!
じわ…
JIWA (TEARY)
SAKURAGI-SENSEI...
IF YOU PASS, I'LL TREAT YOU TO A DELICIOUS MEAL!
SOMETHING REALLY TASTY!
SENSEI...!!
AH, I KNOW WHAT THIS IS.
IT'S WHEN A FARMER SUDDENLY FAWNS ON THEIR LIVESTOCK JUST BEFORE SHIPPING THEM OFF TO THE SLAUGHTERHOUSE.
THEEERE Y'GO.♡
GOT PLENTY OF TASTY GRUB FOR YA.♡
CAN'T WAIT TO SHIP YA!♡
HEH HEH!
WHEE!
SNRT!
GRNT!
GRUNT!

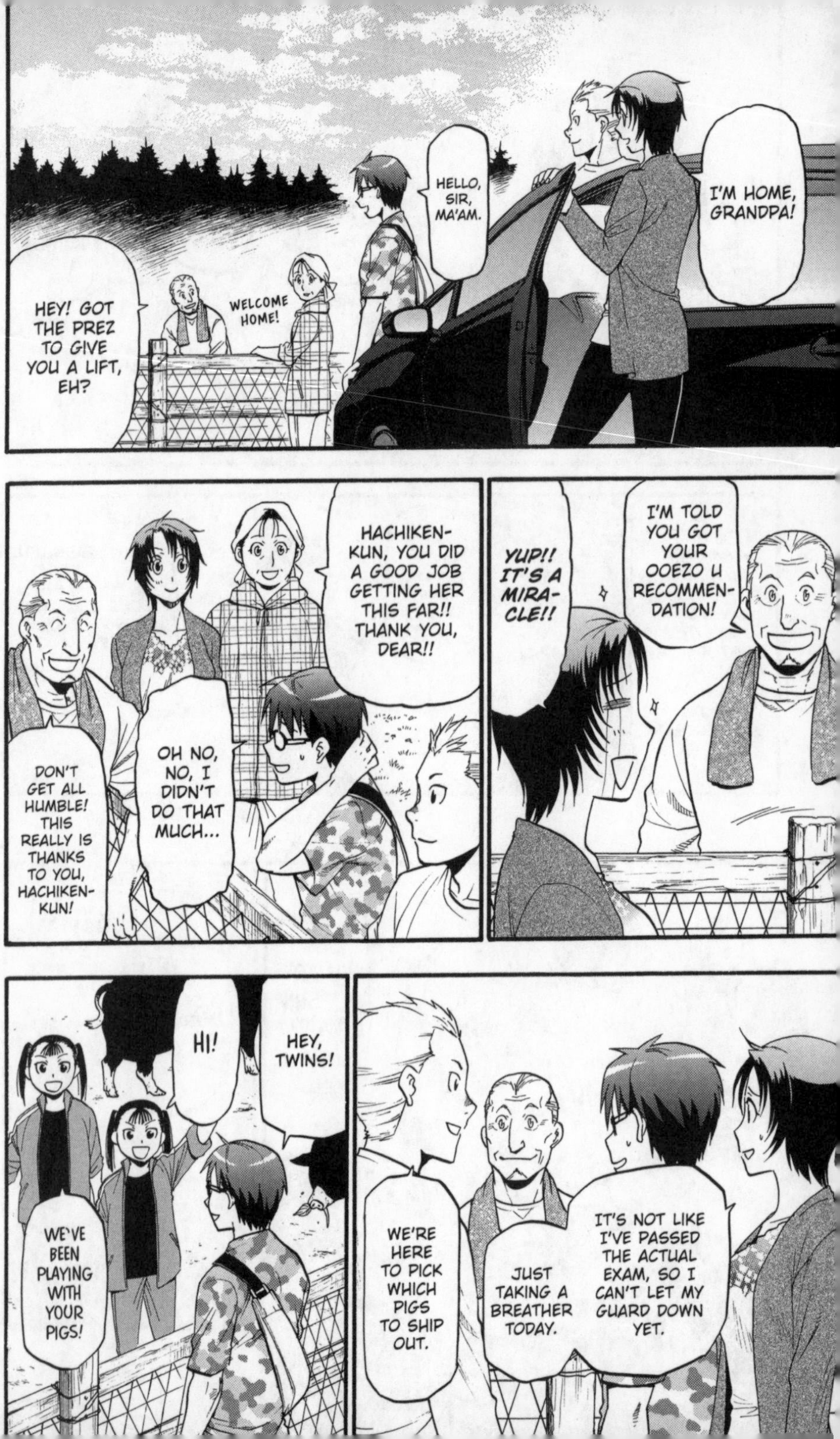
I'M HOME, GRANDPA!
HELLO, SIR, MA'AM.
WELCOME HOME!
HEY! GOT THE PREZ TO GIVE YOU A LIFT, EH?
I'M TOLD YOU GOT YOUR OOEZO U RECOMMEN-DATION!
YUP!! IT'S A MIRA-CLE!!
HACHIKEN-KUN, YOU DID A GOOD JOB GETTING HER THIS FAR!! THANK YOU, DEAR!!
OH NO, NO, I DIDN'T DO THAT MUCH...
DON'T GET ALL HUMBLE! THIS REALLY IS THANKS TO YOU, HACHIKEN-KUN!
IT'S NOT LIKE I'VE PASSED THE ACTUAL EXAM, SO I CAN'T LET MY GUARD DOWN YET.
JUST TAKING A BREATHER TODAY.
WE'RE HERE TO PICK WHICH PIGS TO SHIP OUT.
HEY, TWINS!
HI!
WE'VE BEEN PLAYING WITH YOUR PIGS!

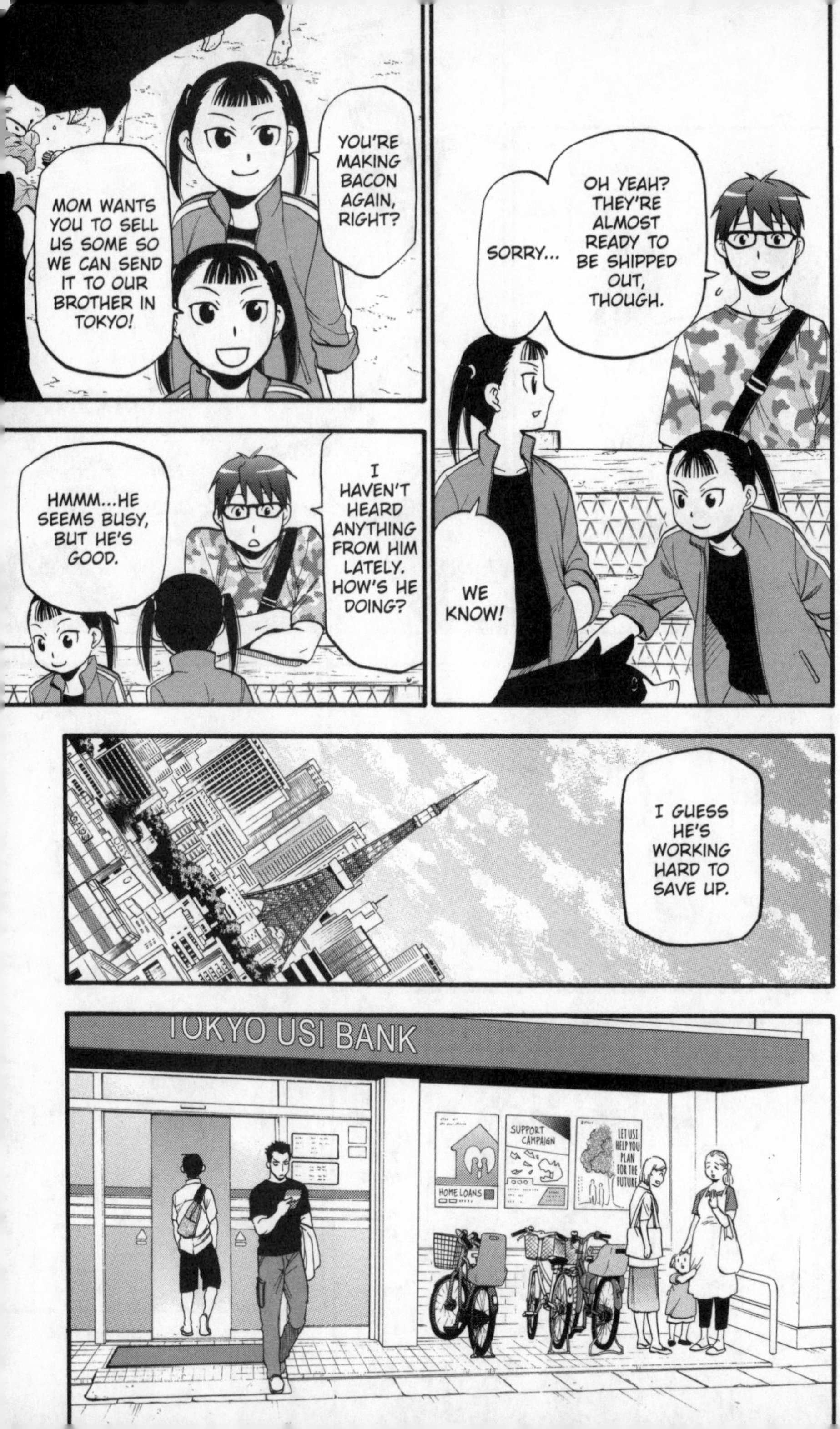
OH YEAH? THEY'RE ALMOST READY TO BE SHIPPED OUT, THOUGH.
SORRY...
WE KNOW!
YOU'RE MAKING BACON AGAIN, RIGHT?
MOM WANTS YOU TO SELL US SOME SO WE CAN SEND IT TO OUR BROTHER IN TOKYO!
I HAVEN'T HEARD ANYTHING FROM HIM LATELY. HOW'S HE DOING?
HMMM...HE SEEMS BUSY, BUT HE'S GOOD.
I GUESS HE'S WORKING HARD TO SAVE UP.
TOKYO USI BANK
SUPPORT CAMPAIGN
HOME LOANS
LET USI HELP YOU PLAN FOR THE FUTURE

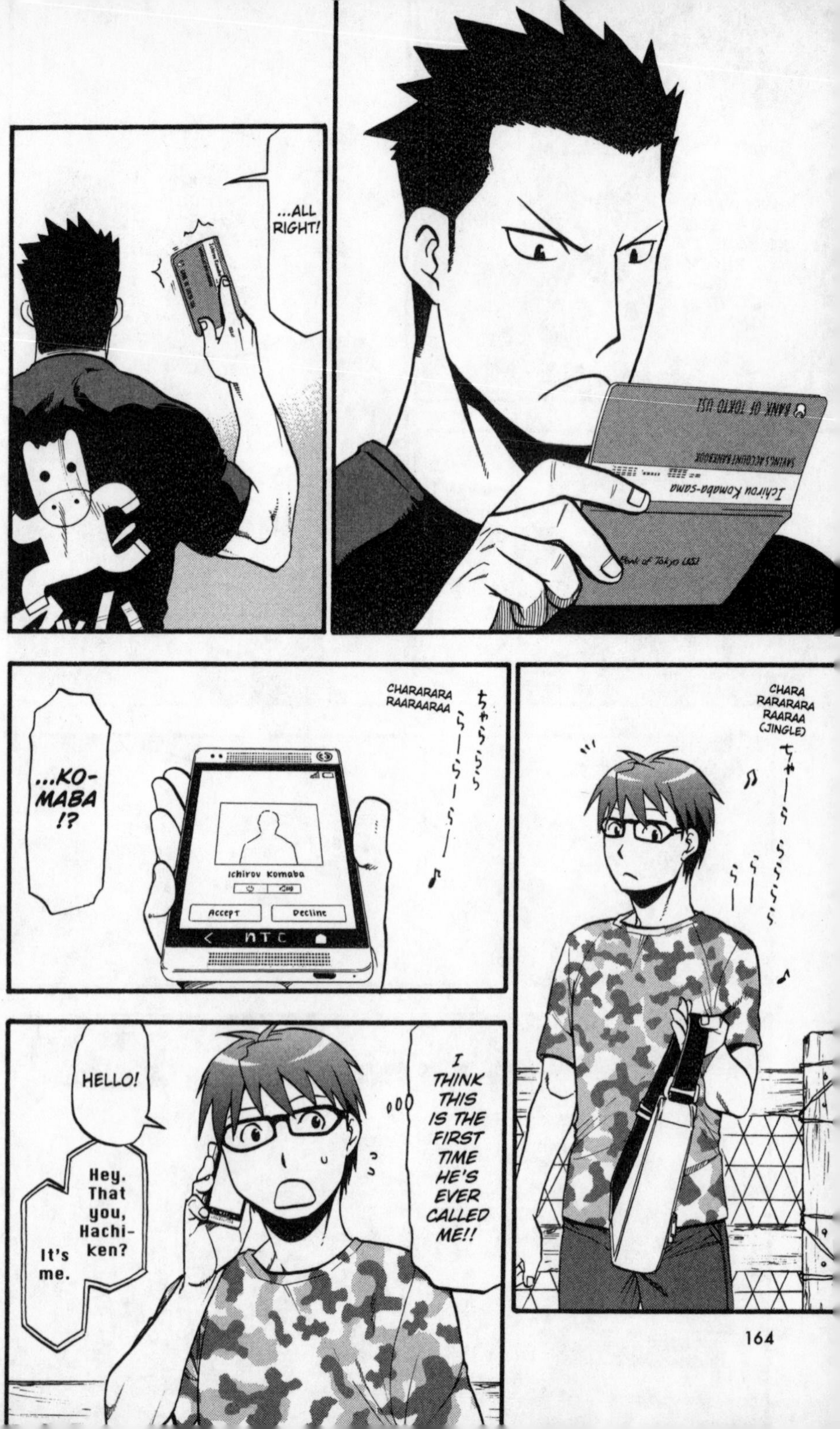
BANK OF TOKYO USJ
SAVINGS ACCOUNT BANKBOOK
Ichirou Komaba-sama
Bank of Tokyo USJ
...ALL RIGHT!
CHARA RARARARA RARAA (JINGLE)
ちゃーらららら らー らー
CHARARARA RAARAARAA
ちゃららら らーらーらー
...KO-MABA!?
Ichirou Komaba
Accept
Decline
HTC
I THINK THIS IS THE FIRST TIME HE'S EVER CALLED ME!!
HELLO!
Hey. That you, Hachi-ken? It's me.

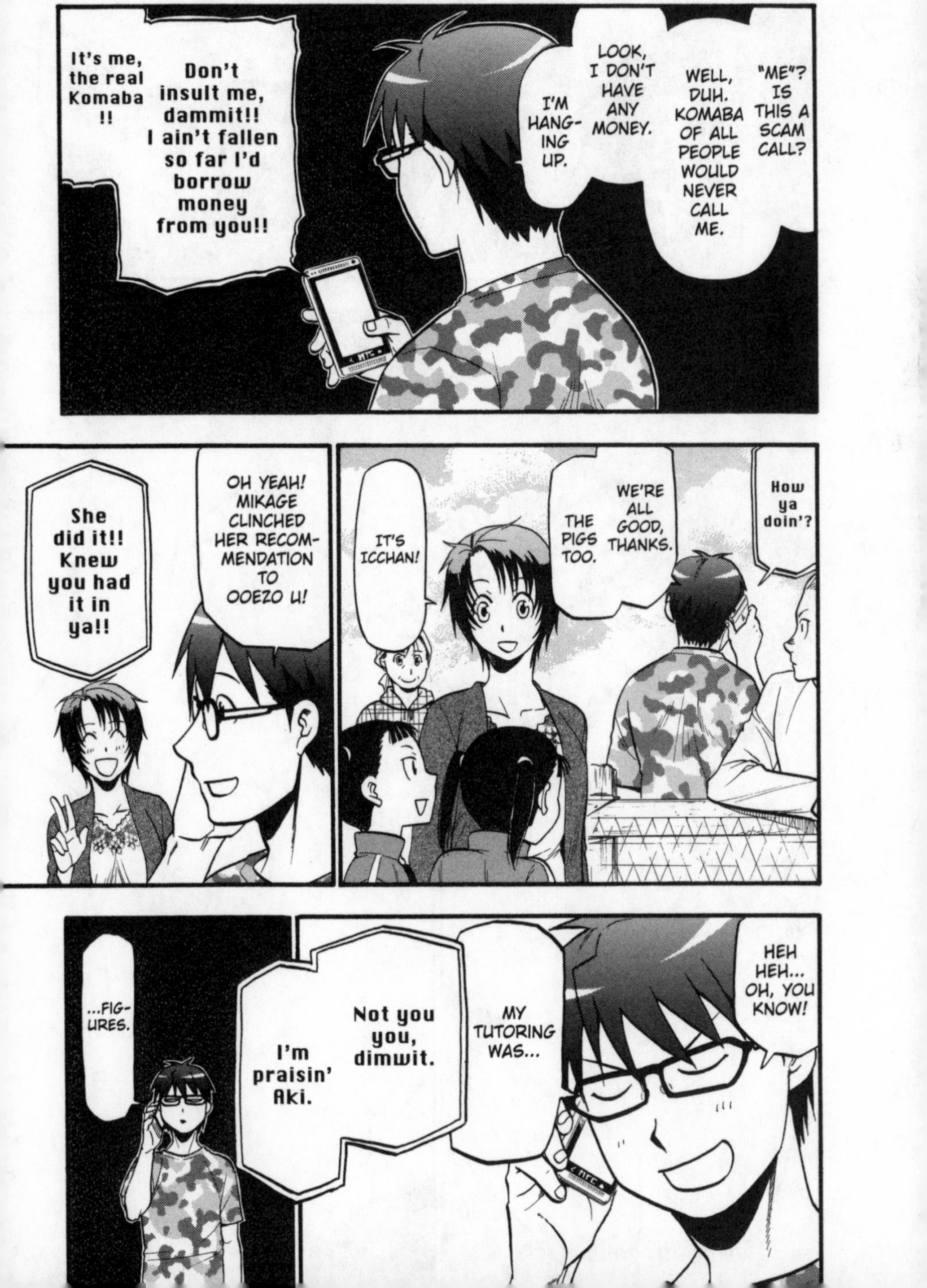
"ME"? IS THIS A SCAM CALL?
WELL, DUH. KOMABA OF ALL PEOPLE WOULD NEVER CALL ME.
LOOK, I DON'T HAVE ANY MONEY.
I'M HANG-ING UP.
Don't insult me, dammit!! I ain't fallen so far I'd borrow money from you!!
It's me, the real Komaba!!
How ya doin'?
WE'RE ALL GOOD, THANKS.
THE PIGS TOO.
IT'S ICCHAN!
OH YEAH! MIKAGE CLINCHED HER RECOM-MENDATION TO OOEZO U!
She did it!! Knew you had it in ya!!
HEH HEH... OH, YOU KNOW!
MY TUTORING WAS...
Not you you, dimwit.
I'm praisin' Aki.
...FIG-URES.

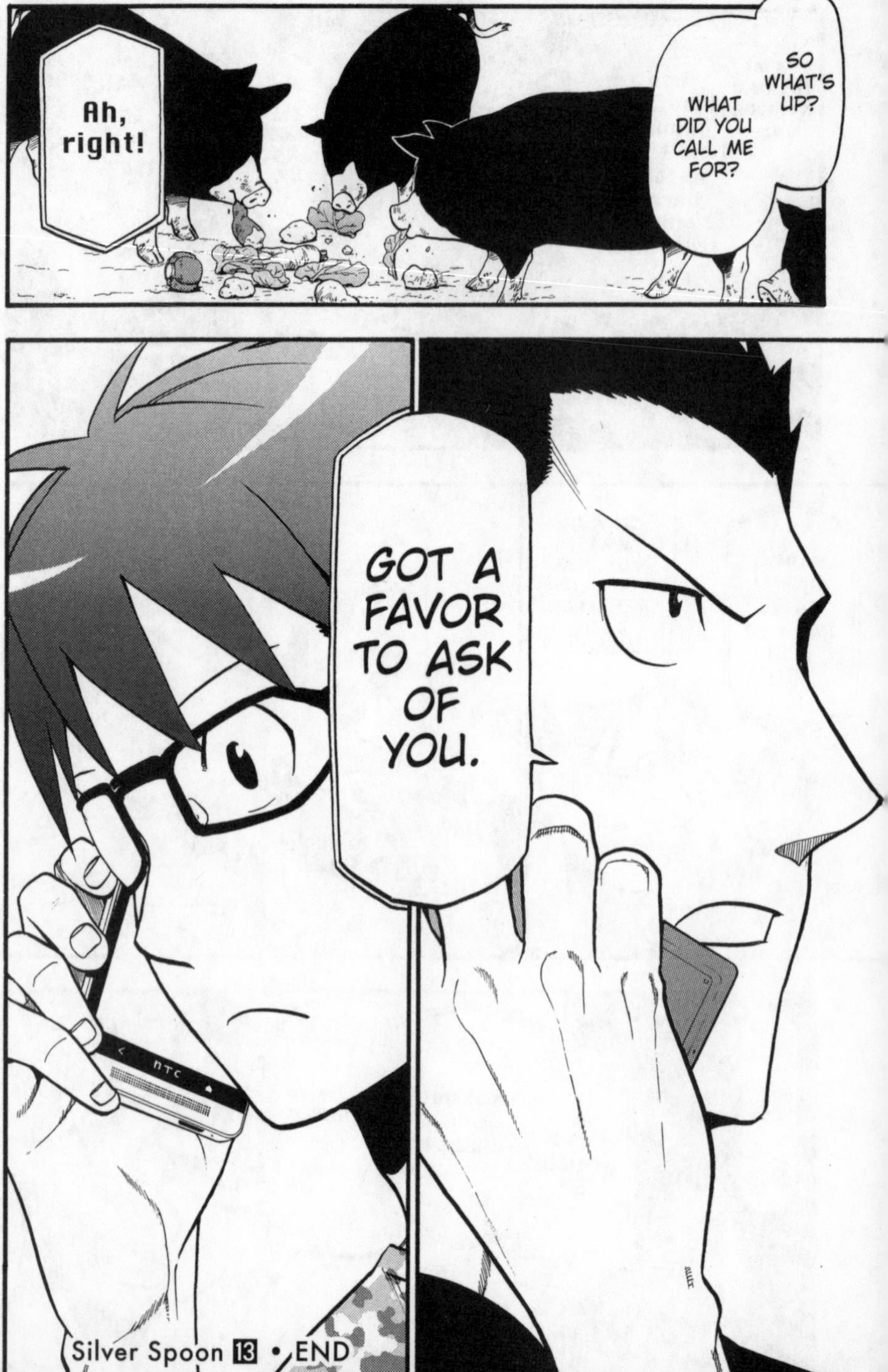
SO WHAT'S UP? WHAT DID YOU CALL ME FOR?
Ah, right!
GOT A FAVOR TO ASK OF YOU.
Silver Spoon 13 • END

Silver Spoon

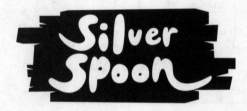

Eating Greens

ISN'T A PIZZA WITH JUST MEAT, POTATOES, AND CHEESE PRETTY NUTRITIONALLY-UNBALANCED?
YEAH. NEEDS SOME GREEN.
BUT ADDING GREEN VEGE-TABLES WILL ADD TO OUR COST...
HMMM...
I KNOW JUST THE THING!!
ARTI-FICIAL GAR-NISH.
THE PLASTIC STUFF YOU SEE IN CATERING AND STUFF.
GO (POW)

Eating Greens 2

I'LL ADD EUGLENA.
GREEN!
EUGLENA? THE GREEN BUGS!?
PEOPLE CALL THEM THAT, BUT THEY'RE ACTUALLY A COUSIN OF ALGAE.
THEY'RE GETTIN' A LOT OF ATTENTION RIGHT NOW AS A FOOD OF THE FUTURE.
OH YEAH, I THINK WE DID TOUCH ON THEM IN CLASS...
THEY'RE ECO-FRIENDLY AND FULL OF VITAMINS.
NOT ONLY THAT, THE NUTRIENTS IN 'EM ARE EASY FOR THE BODY TO ABSORB.
SOME PEOPLE SAY THEY'LL BE A GOOD DIET FOOD.
WOW... PUTTIN' THEM ON PIZZA COULD ACTUALLY BE A GOOD IDEA...
ALSO, YOU CAN USE 'EM TO MAKE JET FUEL.
DOU (BOOM)
FLYING PIZZA!!?

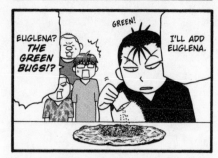

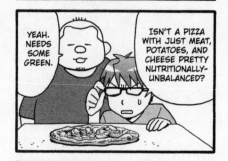

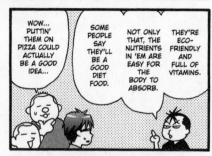

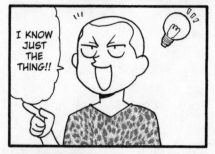

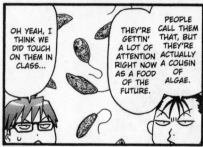

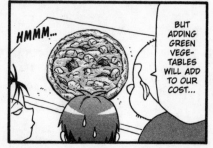

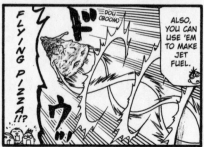

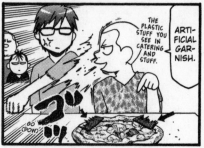

Cow Shed Diaries: "Totally Tournament Things" Chapter

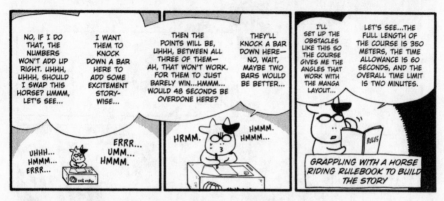

LET'S SEE...THE FULL LENGTH OF THE COURSE IS 350 METERS, THE TIME ALLOWANCE IS 60 SECONDS, AND THE OVERALL TIME LIMIT IS TWO MINUTES.
I'LL SET UP THE OBSTACLES LIKE THIS SO THE COURSE GIVES ME THE ANGLES THAT WORK WITH THE MANGA LAYOUT...
RULES
GRAPPLING WITH A HORSE RIDING RULEBOOK TO BUILD THE STORY
THEY'LL KNOCK A BAR DOWN HERE—NO, WAIT, MAYBE TWO BARS WOULD BE BETTER...
THEN THE POINTS WILL BE, UHHH, BETWEEN ALL THREE OF THEM—AH, THAT WON'T WORK. FOR THEM TO JUST BARELY WIN...HMMM... WOULD 48 SECONDS BE OVERDONE HERE?
HMMM. HMMM...
HRMM.
I WANT THEM TO KNOCK DOWN A BAR HERE TO ADD SOME EXCITEMENT STORY-WISE...
NO, IF I DO THAT, THE NUMBERS WON'T ADD UP RIGHT. UHHH, UHHH, SHOULD I SWAP THIS HORSE? UMMM, LET'S SEE...
ERRR... UMM... HMMM.
UHHH... HMMM... ERRR...
I DID IT!
I GOT THE SCORES AND THE COURSE TO FIT THE NEEDS OF THE STORY!!
HUH? LOCAL RULES?
THESE RULES WOULDN'T APPLY TO THAT TOURNAMENT?
EZO
ROUGH DRAFT
DO-OVER.

Silver Spoon 13!
My local supermarket started stocking Jinhua pork. Uh-oh...
I'm gonna eat a ton...

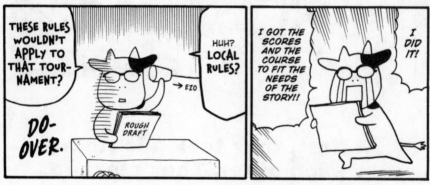

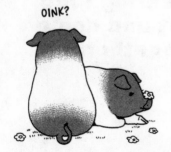

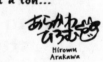

あらかわひろむ
Hiromu Arakawa

OINK?

~ Special Thanks ~
Everyone who helped with collecting material, interviews, and consulting,
All of my assistants,
My editor, Mr. Tsubouchi,

AND YOU!!

NEXT......

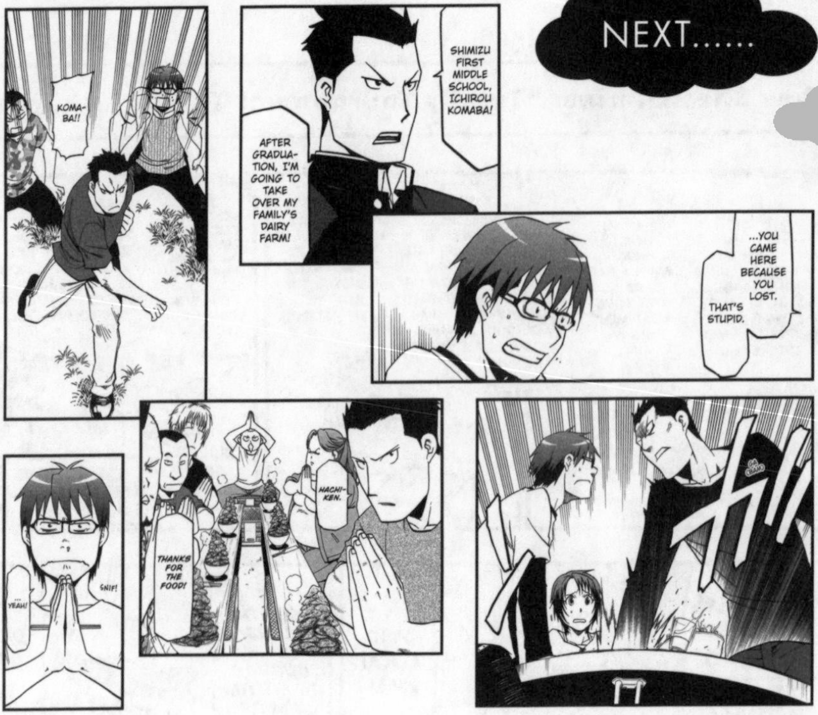
SHIMIZU FIRST MIDDLE SCHOOL, ICHIROU KOMABA!
AFTER GRADUATION, I'M GOING TO TAKE OVER MY FAMILY'S DAIRY FARM!
...YOU CAME HERE BECAUSE YOU LOST.
THAT'S STUPID.
KOMA-BA!!
HACHI-KEN.
THANKS FOR THE FOOD!
SNIF!
...YEAH!

At first, they took a loathing to each other. They clashed and didn't see eye-to-eye. But as they lived alongside each other at Ezo Ag, eating food from the same pot and doing stupid things together...

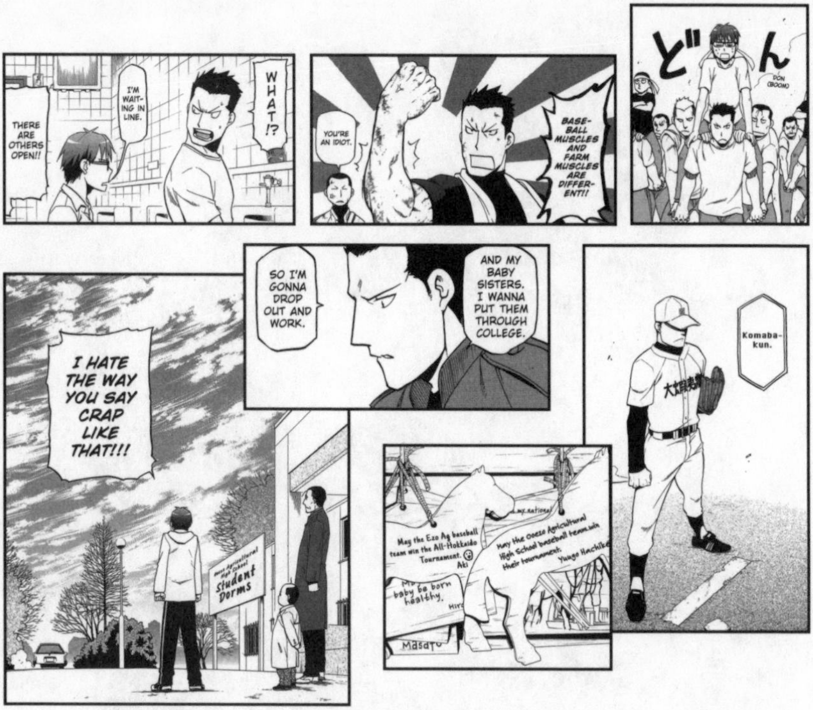
どん
DON (BOOM)
BASE-BALL MUSCLES AND FARM MUSCLES ARE DIFFER-ENT!!
YOU'RE AN IDIOT.
WHAT!?
I'M WAIT-ING IN LINE.
THERE ARE OTHERS OPEN!!
Komaba-kun.
AND MY BABY SISTERS. I WANNA PUT THEM THROUGH COLLEGE.
SO I'M GONNA DROP OUT AND WORK.
May the Ooezo Agricultural High School baseball team win their tournament.
Yugo Hachiken
May the Ezo Ag baseball team win the All-Hokkaido Tournament.
Aki
Student Dorms
I HATE THE WAY YOU SAY CRAP LIKE THAT!!!

...at some point, they became faithful friends. This bond forged by absurdity is on another level! *Silver Spoon* 14, coming soon!! The end is in sight!!

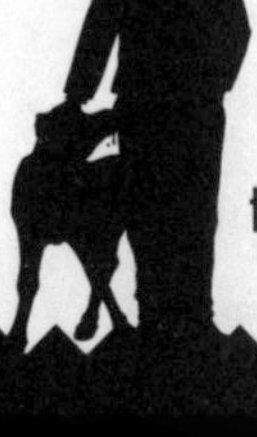

to be continued......

Silver Spoon

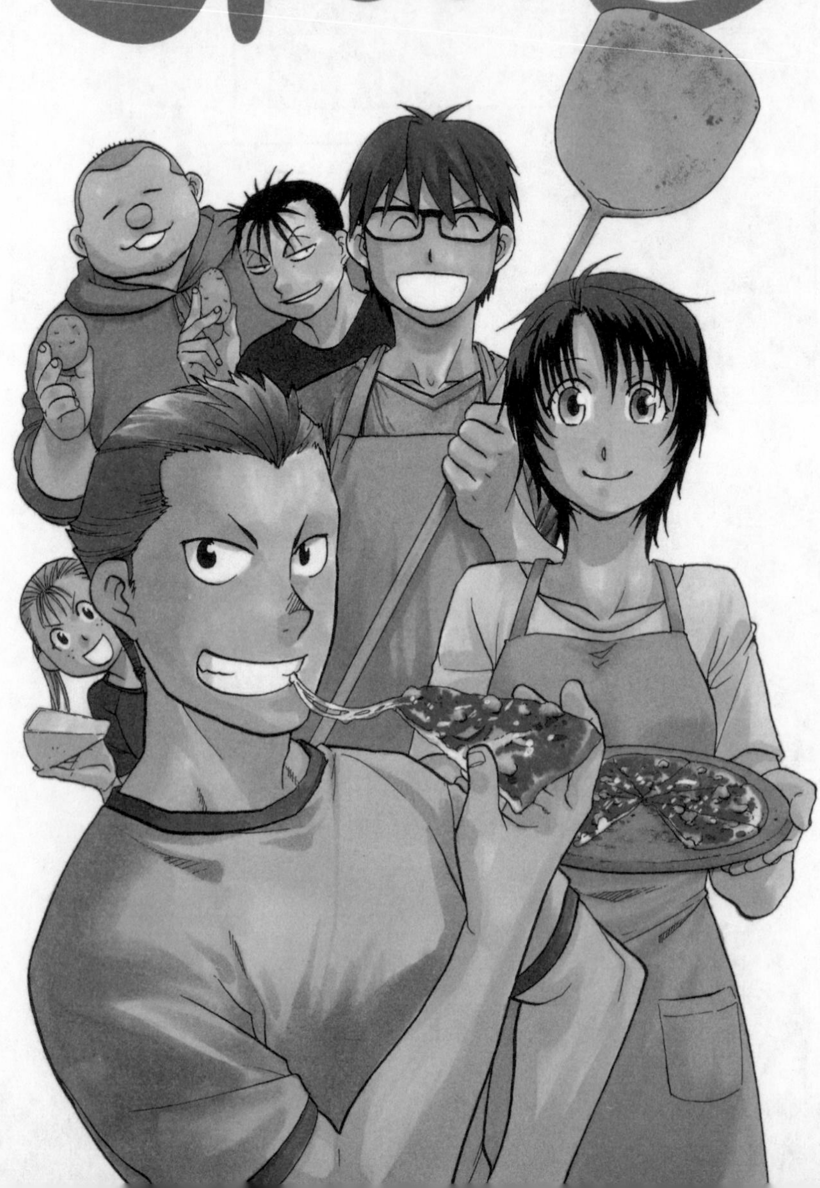

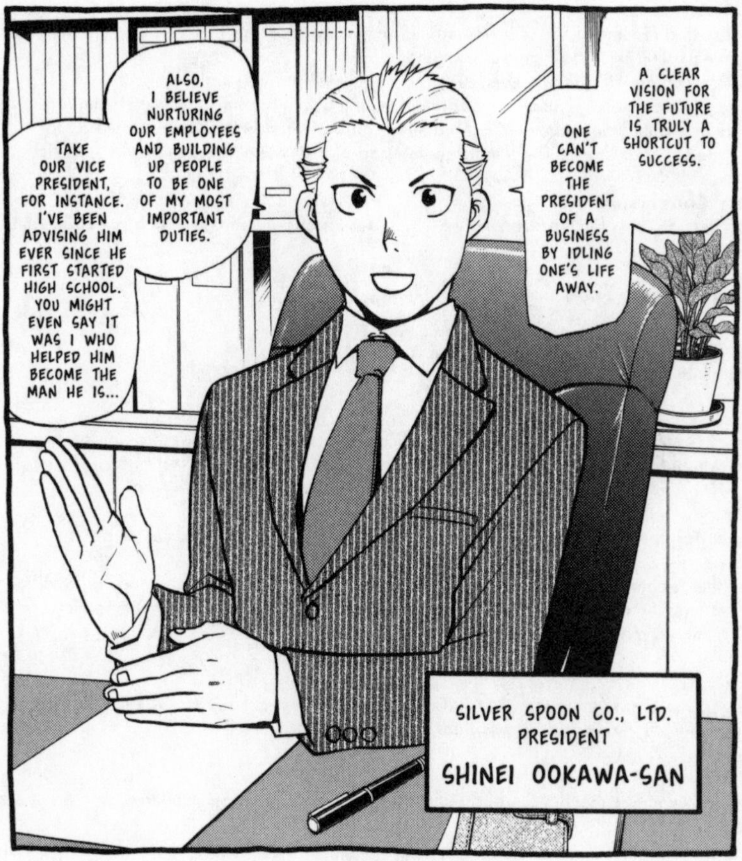
A CLEAR VISION FOR THE FUTURE IS TRULY A SHORTCUT TO SUCCESS.
ONE CAN'T BECOME THE PRESIDENT OF A BUSINESS BY IDLING ONE'S LIFE AWAY.
ALSO, I BELIEVE NURTURING OUR EMPLOYEES AND BUILDING UP PEOPLE TO BE ONE OF MY MOST IMPORTANT DUTIES.
TAKE OUR VICE PRESIDENT, FOR INSTANCE. I'VE BEEN ADVISING HIM EVER SINCE HE FIRST STARTED HIGH SCHOOL. YOU MIGHT EVEN SAY IT WAS I WHO HELPED HIM BECOME THE MAN HE IS...
SILVER SPOON CO., LTD. PRESIDENT
SHINEI OOKAWA-SAN

Translation Notes

Common Honorifics

no honorific: Indicates familiarity or closeness; if used without permission or reason, addressing someone in this manner would constitute an insult.

-san: The Japanese equivalent of Mr./Mrs./Miss. If a situation calls for politeness, this is the fail-safe honorific.

-sama: Conveys great respect; may also indicate the social status of the speaker is lower than that of the addressee.

-kun: Used most often when referring to boys, this honorific indicates affection or familiarity. Occasionally used by older men among their peers, but it may also be used by anyone referring to a person of lower standing.

-chan, -tan: An affectionate honorific indicating familiarity used mostly in reference to girls; also used in reference to cute persons or animals of either gender.

-sensei: A respectful term for teachers, artists, or high-level professionals.

-niisan, nii-san, aniki, etc.: A term of endearment meaning "big brother" that may be more widely used to address any young man who is like a brother, regardless of whether he is related or not.

-neesan, nee-san, aneki, etc.: The female counterpart of the above, *nee-san* means "big sister."

Currency Conversion

While conversion rates fluctuate, an easy estimate for Japanese yen conversion is ¥100 to 1 USD.

Page 61
Higashimurayama is a city within the Tokyo Metropolis.

Page 66
In Japanese, tarsiers are called *meganezaru*—literally, "glasses monkey."

Page 91
The bean dish Mayumi is referring to is *natto*, sticky fermented soybeans with a powerful smell, taste, and texture that are often eaten on rice.

Page 109
Haneda Airport (or Tokyo International Airport) is a major airport located in Tokyo.

Koshien (the Japan high school baseball championships) is a massively popular and idealized tournament, and the dirt from the stadium is often taken home as a memento by the athletes who have the opportunity to play there.

Page 129
In Japan, spring break is the vacation between school years, not summer break. Hachiken and his peers are now well into their third and final year of high school.

Page 135
Once again, Ayame is making fun of the number in Hachiken's name...this time, with his score from the championships.

Page 138
The slogan on Shingo's shirt was a Hokkaido PR slogan.

Page 142
Akihabara is considered a mecca for otaku for its special-interest shopping. Daiba is where the Comic Market popularly known as Comiket is held. The event is a huge market for independent or amateur artists to sell their own self-published books (*doujinshi*). Makuhari Messe is a convention center outside Tokyo that hosts the annual video game exhibition Tokyo Game Show, the toys and figure exhibition Wonder Festival, and more.

Page 142
Egg Club and *Chick Club* are maternity/childcare magazines.

Page 144
Sugawara-no-Michizane (845–903) was a scholar, poet, and politician who has been deified as a god of learning. The city of Dazaifu is in Fukuoka Prefecture on Kyushu Island, the southernmost of Japan's main islands.

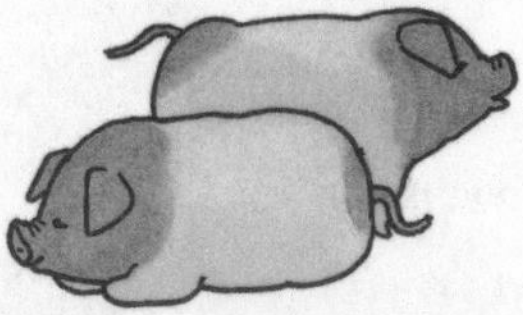

Silver Spoon

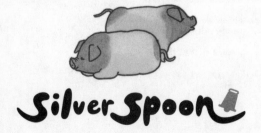

Silver Spoon 13

HIROMU ARAKAWA

Translation: **Amanda Haley** Lettering: **Abigail Blackman**

This book is a work of fiction. Names, characters, places, and incidents are the product of the author's imagination or are used fictitiously. Any resemblance to actual events, locales, or persons, living or dead, is coincidental.

GIN NO SAJI SILVER SPOON Vol. 13
by Hiromu ARAKAWA
© 2011 Hiromu ARAKAWA
All rights reserved.
Original Japanese edition published by SHOGAKUKAN.
English translation rights in the United States of America, Canada, the United Kingdom, Ireland, Australia and New Zealand arranged with SHOGAKUKAN through Tuttle-Mori Agency, Inc.

English translation © 2020 by Yen Press, LLC

Yen Press, LLC supports the right to free expression and the value of copyright. The purpose of copyright is to encourage writers and artists to produce the creative works that enrich our culture.

The scanning, uploading, and distribution of this book without permission is a theft of the author's intellectual property. If you would like permission to use material from the book (other than for review purposes), please contact the publisher. Thank you for your support of the author's rights.

Yen Press
150 West 30th Street, 19th Floor
New York, NY 10001

Visit us at yenpress.com
facebook.com/yenpress
twitter.com/yenpress
yenpress.tumblr.com
instagram.com/yenpress

First Yen Press Edition: February 2020

Yen Press is an imprint of Yen Press, LLC.
The Yen Press name and logo are trademarks of Yen Press, LLC.

The publisher is not responsible for websites (or their content) that are not owned by the publisher.

Library of Congress Control Number: 2017959207

ISBNs: 978-1-9753-5314-8 (paperback)
978-1-9753-1222-0 (ebook)

10 9 8 7 6 5 4 3 2

WOR

Printed in the United States of America